The Watchman's Daughter

D1428721

Also by Alexandra Connor

The Witchmark
Thomas
The Hour Of The Angel
The Mask Of Fortune
The Well Of Dreams
The Green Bay Tree
Winter Women; Midsummer Men
The Moon Is My Witness
Midnight's Smiling
Green Baize Road
An Angel Passing Over
Hunter's Moon
The Sixpenny Winner
The Face In The Locket
The Turn Of The Tide
The Tailor's Wife
The Lydgate Widow

The Watchman's Daughter

ALEXANDRA CONNOR

headline

Copyright © 2007 Alexandra Connor

The right of Alexandra Connor to be identified as the Author of the Work has been asserted by her in accordance with the Copyright, Designs and Patents Act 1988.

First published in 2007
by HEADLINE PUBLISHING GROUP

First published in paperback in 2008
by HEADLINE PUBLISHING GROUP

3

Apart from any use permitted under UK copyright law, this publication may only be reproduced, stored, or transmitted, in any form, or by any means, with prior permission in writing of the publishers or, in the case of reprographic production, in accordance with the terms of licences issued by the Copyright Licensing Agency.

All characters in this publication are fictitious and any resemblance to real persons, living or dead, is purely coincidental.

Cataloguing in Publicaton Data is available from the British Library

ISBN 978 0 7553 2376 0

Typeset in Sabon by Avon DataSet Ltd,
Bidford-on-Avon, Warwickshire

Printed and bound in Great Britain by
Mackays of Chatham plc, Chatham, Kent

Headline's policy is to use papers that are natural, renewable and recyclable products and made from wood grown in sustainable forests. The logging and manufacturing processes are expected to conform to the environmental regulations of the country of origin.

HEADLINE PUBLISHING GROUP
An Hachette Livre UK Company
338 Euston Road
London NW1 3BH

www.headline.co.uk

For my mother, Ella Crossley – a class act.

Research is vital when writing a book, and any help
in that area is invaluable. So I want to give a
verbal bouquet to the following:
Rita Whitlock, Preston Tourist Office; Laura Waterhouse,
Preston Library; and Cathy Bath, Preston Museum Shop.
Special thanks also to Susan Winder at
W. H. Smith, Preston.

Ladies, you were great.

No one taught us sign language; we taught ourselves. A necessary way of communication between my brother and myself. Because Micky was dumb. Or should I say mute? That's the right term. He certainly wasn't stupid, he just couldn't speak. My parents were anxious and a little nervous around him, I think, and not well educated enough – or rich enough – to get him specialised tutoring. So we did it ourselves, Micky and me, our secret signing making an intense and unbreakable bond between us.

Our father was the nightwatchman on the Albert Edward Dock. I remember when he got the job, how he swaggered around in his greatcoat and showed us how he lit the cumbersome iron lamp. 'Do it outside!' my grandmother snapped, but my mother winked at him, smiling her encouragement. Later I heard my parents laughing in the yard and looked out to see them sitting on the back step, the watchman's lamp lighting the underside of their faces.

I suppose that when we are very young, life seems simple. There was a safety to our days then, a reassuring routine that kept the reality of poverty, the rent man and unemployment at bay. In our house on Amber Street, we lived to the accompaniment of the mill siren, the rag-and-bone man calling for trade and, far off, the hooters of the ships, coming in to unload their cargo on a late tide. I was proud of my father being the nightwatchman. I walked around the docks with him and listened to his tales, looking up into the skeletal rigging, the water darkly green below. When Micky was old enough, he joined us. But the place never held the same fascination for my brother. He only came to be with me, because we were so close, but he always seemed uneasy around the Albert Edward. Years later, I wondered if he had had some kind of precognition about the place.

But I loved the docks. Mesmerised, I tagged along with my father when I could and grew used to being teased by the sailors, the burly Russians coming in with their loads of Siberian timber. I was happy to be my father's child. I was happy under the blank grey skies, scratched with rigging, the dull boom and scrape of the boats' underbellies echoing godlessly on the late tide. I was known, recognised, as Jim Shaw's girl.

In those far-off, uncomplicated days, I didn't realise that I had inherited a title I would one day make infamous – The Watchman's Daughter.

PART ONE

Better to light a candle than to curse the darkness.

Proverb

ONE

Preston, 1922

Of course no one knew they were there, hidden, listening and watching through a crack in the door. It was past ten at night then, and no one in the pub would have expected two children at the back entrance, the girl no more than ten, the boy around eight. Holding each other's hands tightly, they looked in. Their father was sitting in the back snug, a glossy younger man beside him, and a horse-faced man with a lantern jaw facing them both. Impressed, the girl studied her attractive uncle, leaning over to talk to his brother, the lanky man – their half-brother – chewing tobacco as he stared at the cards in his hand.

'Get on with it!' he muttered.

Their father, Jim, exchanged a knowing look with Silky, his brother, then glanced back to the heavy-jawed man.

'Ah, come on, Ivan, have another drink first.'

'I don't hold with drinking,' Ivan replied sanctimoniously. He was the puritan of the family, the one who thought it his duty to be the moral arbitrator – a trait he had inherited from his grandfather, a man always fiercely judgemental of everyone – including himself. Ivan had few passions in life, except religion and cards. He was good at cards, well known for it, in fact. If he stayed sober. Which he did with everyone but his brothers. With every other man in Preston Ivan never touched a drop, but with Jim and Silky he sometimes relented. And they waited for it avidly.

Slowly Jim slid the beer closer.

'I've told yer,' Ivan repeated, 'I don't hold with drinking.'

'You don't have to hold with it; you swallow it,' Silky replied, the fug of cigarette smoke circling around his dark hair and shadowing his slow-blinking eyes. 'Come on, relax.'

'I'm a God-fearing man,' Ivan replied, his hands shuffling the cards deftly. He could be a right pain, could Ivan, but he was good at the core. 'A bit of cards is all right, but drinking and smoking's something else.'

'Yeah, it's drinking and smoking,' Jim replied.

Kat smiled at her father's wry retort. He might not have Silky's charm or sensual good looks, but he had a shiny, good-tempered face, to match the good-tempered man he was. Now he leaned over and filled all three of their glasses, the froth of the beer slopping over on to the cards. Murmuring under his breath, Ivan wiped them on his sleeve and resumed his shuffling. From the front of the pub Kat could hear the sound of the other drinkers and the harsh shouts of the landlord throwing out a rowdy customer. But the landlord never threw the Shaw brothers out on a Tuesday night. Not when he got a cut for the use of the back room.

'Look,' Kat whispered to her brother. 'Look, Micky, watch this.'

Straining forward, both of them watched Ivan deal out the cards with a professional's skill, his hand movements so fast they were almost a blur. Then slowly and purposefully he leaned back, holding his own cards close to his chest. At the same time, Jim pushed the beer even further towards him, while Silky took a long, even swallow of his own drink.

'I can see yer've a good hand.'

'*I never!*' Ivan snorted. His half-brothers exchanged a glance and watched as Ivan reached for his drink. It was the giveaway sign, the one they waited for. The movement that said, *I've got the winning hand*. Together they watched Ivan drink. Outside the door the two kids watched. They all watched, holding their breath.

'Your call,' Silky said, as Jim finished off his pint and lit another cigarette. Clenching it between his lips, he closed one eye against the rising smoke and jiggled his foot impatiently. The atmosphere in the cramped back room was becoming thick with smoke and the smell of beer, the landlord's shabby fire in the grate peering blearily through the smog.

'Watch this, Micky,' Kat said again, nudging her brother.

Ivan was trying so hard to cover his excitement that his mouth dried and he took another drink. And everyone knew that Ivan couldn't drink . . . His long, bony-jawed face flushed with the hit of the alcohol, his mouth working overtime as he talked to himself in a muted whisper.

'Make yer move,' Jim said, hustling him.

'Come on, Ivan,' Silky joined in, knowing that the only way they would get so much as a farthing from their parsimonious brother was to get him pissed first. 'Make your play.'

The tension made Kat take in a breath as she watched her father and uncles. The whole scenario – the pub's back room, the cigarette smoke, the beer, the well-handled pack of cards – enthralled her. She was suddenly propelled from the humdrum life of school, poor food, bad weather and no money, and transported into this glamorous, exciting little cocoon. She knew the familiar sights and sounds of the pub – they lived next door, after all – but that evening everything seemed changed. Her father and uncles weren't working-class Preston men in a back street drinking hole; they were worldly figures from a story. Mississippi gamblers like she had heard about in school. They weren't in a grim pub; they were on the river, with the sound of cicadas and water lapping in the slushy night . . . Mesmerised, Kat cast Silky in the role of handsome hero, her uncle's flashy suit from the market turned into a silk dinner jacket. Even Ivan became another man: cunning as an alligator, a man no one would mess with.

And of course her father had the starring role, the good-natured, prosperous bar owner, riding the waves of booze and money and good humour.

Peering through the gap in the door, Kat watched them, laughing silently with them when Ivan began to sing off key, Jim refilling his glass and Silky taking an obvious, over-dramatic look at his cards. They were all tipsy, giddy with smoke and beer, in good spirits, Ivan finally slamming down his cards and Silky scooping up the few shillings on the table with triumphant ease.

Aware that they could be discovered at any moment, Kat hurried Micky home. Creeping through the back door, they made their way upstairs, Micky slipping into the room he shared with his older brother, Billy. Back in her own room, cold and shivering, Kat huddled under the bedclothes. Sighing, she closed her eyes, remembering what she had seen and recalling everything, detail by detail. Her father and her uncles playing cards. Three brothers who had survived the Great War, done their fighting and wanted to relish the peace. Three brothers getting smoky lungs and drunker by the hour.

It was a memory she would never forget. Long after the family was ripped apart, long after booze became something she feared, long after the back room of the pub was closed. In her mind she held the image of the three men laughing – and the sound ghosted down the years like a friend.

TWO

Six years later

Tripping over a piece of planking, Jim Shaw cursed and then righted himself, reaching for the lamp he had dropped.

'Bugger,' he said, shaking it vigorously.

It stayed out. He shook it again, watching as a weak beam gradually illuminated the uneven ground in front of him. Satisfied, Jim moved ahead, holding the light at shoulder height. He knew this patch of the Albert Edward Dock as well as he knew his own living room, but it paid to be able to see where you were going. There were too many bloody shadows and too many flaming surprises to be caught out.

Pausing, Jim listened to the slow lap of the tide, only a couple of yards away from his feet in the dock below. He liked water, thought there was something poetic about it. Even *this* water, slimy in summer and freckled with dock rats the size of Jack Russells. You could get some space in your head when you were near water, Jim thought, remembering Missie Shepherd again.

It had been his daughter's fifteenth birthday. Katherine – Kat to everyone – had walked with him to the bottom of their street, and then waited until her father had disappeared out of sight before going home. Jim knew only too well that if you worked as a nightwatchman on the Preston docks, you had to make time for your family. Make sure you saw some of their growing up or before you knew it they were older and tougher and had no time for *you* . . . She'd made such a fuss of him that day, getting all excited about a little trinket box he'd bought off the market.

'Oh Dad, I love it!' she had said, throwing her arms around him, all ivory prettiness. 'It's just what I wanted!'

If she had known it was cheap, she hadn't said. Not that she would have done, not Kat. Too careful of people's feelings, especially his. Delighted that he had pleased her so much, Jim had gone on to work. And if he had stopped off on the way at The Dutchman's Arms, who cared? It had been a bloody cold night; surely no one could have blamed a man for getting the blood moving around his veins? You needed something to keep out the winter chill when you had to walk round the freezing docks until six the next morning. And if the pint had been followed by a couple more, so what? It had hardly made a dent on his thirst, let alone clouded his judgement.

So with the pints inside him and buoyed up with Kat's delight at his gift, Jim had moved from The Dutchman's Arms to the docks. His round had begun as it always did, in the gloomy little office by the first warehouse. *Office*, Jim thought bitterly. What bloody wag had christened it that? It was little more than a rat hole, with its dank fire, mean little window covered with a damp spotted blind, and one third-hand chair, the horsehair stuffing of which poked into your arse. Anyway, that night – like every night – Jim had signed himself in and checked the rota. His job was simple, if long-winded. He would begin at the bank of massive warehouses, walking round and checking each door was locked, no windows broken, nor any other signs of damage. Particularly the kind of damage the down-and-outs did when they broke in, looking for something to steal, or a bed for the night. When he had finished, he would make his mark on each door jamb with chalk. That way his boss knew that all the warehouses had been checked. Then he would progress further into the docks and on to the quayside. Here he was looking for drunks – whom he then moved on. Sailors too pissed to find their way back to their ships on their own, or men who had got into fights and were stumbling around trying to get their bearings. Although not a big man, Jim was tough and took no nonsense. Occasionally, though, even he was unnerved.

Like the time he had checked Quay 14 and found a man hanging from a wire noose over the side of a docked ship. The vessel had been Norwegian, the captain assuring everyone that the man had committed suicide – but Jim was never convinced. He had heard a commotion in the minutes before he found the body, panicked cries silenced suddenly in the dark. When the light from his lamp had struck the body, it was still swinging eerily in the winter night. And besides the crimes, there were the accidents. It wasn't uncommon for bodies to be washed up in the dock. Men and women on their uppers, poor, sick, or too drunk to fight the tide after a fall. Then there were the deliberate suicides, people who had *chosen* to drown – probably somewhere a long way from Preston. For weeks, sometimes months, their bodies had ridden the tides, and finally came to rest at the Albert Edward. Jim had seen them washed up on the silt. Often they were too decomposed for him to tell if they were male or female; frequently they were naked, the water having stripped them with its relentless ebb and flow.

Purposefully Jim walked on, putting the thought out of his mind. He would check the quaysides, make his mark on the anchor hold, then return to the hut and tick off the warehouses and quays in the ledger. The whole process would then be repeated at three in the morning and again at six, just before he finished his shift and Stanley Cunliffe came on for the day watch. Jim thought about the sweaty, thick-necked Stanley and what a bastard he was; always taking backhanders, creeping around the ships' captains for favours and bullying everyone else. Like Missie Shepherd. Not much older than Jim's own daughter, Missie had been whoring on the docks for over a year. Jim always turned a blind eye. Not like Stanley, who moved her on with a quick slap, or a jab in the ribs if she was sleeping it off. Jim hated cruelty, and tried to compensate. Couple of times he had even given Missie Shepherd a bob or two, told her to get herself a proper job. But a week later she would be back.

In the daytime the Albert Edward was a rough place, but at night, the dark, dangerous docks were no place for a woman – even a working whore. Jim had lost count of the times he had tried to tell Missie to stay away.

'But there's always good trade 'ere,' she'd tell him.

'There's a lot of villains too. Stay off the docks, luv. Some bad types here.'

'Yer not bad.'

Only a few days ago he had caught her leaning against one of the warehouse walls pulling down her skirt as a docker ran off, doing up his trousers. More concerned for the girl than embarrassed, Jim had walked over to her.

'Jesus, luv, I saw yer hours ago. Have yer been here all night?'

Resigned, she had shrugged. 'I got thrown out of me lodgings yesterday. If I don't want to sleep rough, I've got to get the money fer rent.'

Sighing, Jim had studied her. God, if it been his daughter, his Kat, lifting her skirts to keep a roof over her head . . .

'What about family, Missie? Have yer got no one?'

'Nah, no one . . . Me mam's dead, but she never said much about me father. Only some rubbish 'bout him being a big shot.' Missie had paused, her head turning in the direction of one of the dockside pubs. It had been closing time; soon the sailors would be weaving their way back to their ships. Rich pickings for a working girl. 'Got to go now,' she said hurriedly, then added, 'Thanks, Mr Shaw. Yer've always treated me right. I'm obliged to yer fer that.'

His thoughts returning to the present, Jim started as one of the great hulking ships at the dockside creaked mournfully in the wind, the anchor chain knocking against the stone siding. But from inside there came no sound. The crew were off for the night; those who remained on board were sleeping. In the morning they would unload the vast stacks of timber on to the quayside, to be transported to the Preston factories or further inland for building work – but in those silent night hours the crew slept on, rocked on the lapping water of the northern dock.

Weaving momentarily on his feet, Jim realised that the cold air mixed with the beer was making him slightly light-headed. Whistling, and trying to kid himself that he was sober as a Cheshire magistrate, he moved on. But rounding the furthest end of Warehouse 17, he nearly tripped over a hump of discarded rags. Muttering, he held the torch towards the bundle. Missie Shepherd was sleeping rough. Obviously she hadn't made enough money for the rent that night.

'Hey now, Missie, come on, luv. Yer've got to move.' Jim leaned down and touched her shoulder. 'Come on, luv, wake up.'

She didn't respond. Obviously the worse for wear, Jim thought sympathetically, his own head beginning to thump. But when he touched her shoulder for the second time, Missie suddenly rolled over on to her back, landing with a muffled thud. Surprised, Jim held the light higher. Her throat was cut, severed from ear to ear. Missie Shepherd would never work the docks again.

And neither would he, Jim had realised in that instant. If he called for help, people would smell the beer on his breath and that would be the end of the watchman's job. The end of security, end of regular money. Jesus, he had thought, wiping his mouth with the back of his hand. What the hell was he going to do? After another moment's hesitation, he reached down and felt for a pulse. Instinct told him that Missie Shepherd was dead, but he was hoping that she wasn't. That by some miracle he could help her to her feet and see her off and no one would be any the wiser.

Her wrist was hardly more than a winter twig in his hand. His lamplight fell on the pool of blood around her body and seeping into his boots. Breathing heavily, he tried to calm himself.

'Steady, lad, steady now.' He had shone the lamp around, searching the shadows, then looking back to Missie. 'Aye, luv, yer were warned often enough. The docks are no place fer a girl. No place at all.'

And then he had thought of *his* girl, his Kat. Around the same age. God Almighty, what if it had been her? Another thought followed on immediately. *Was the killer still out there?* Relax, Jim urged himself, no one was after him. It had probably been some customer Missie had short-changed. A madman with a knife was the least of Jim's worries. Stepping back, he fought a different kind of panic. Should he pretend he hadn't found her? After all, poor Missie was beyond help, and if he didn't report it he wouldn't be involved. Wouldn't risk being found out drinking on the job. A hard but decent job. He thought of Anna, his wife, and of his mother, Ma Shaw. Jesus, he couldn't bugger up now, not with a family to support. Jim sighed desperately. He had lost too many jobs because of drink. Damn near lost the roof over his family's head a couple of times. But that was in the past. Well, nearly . . . His conscience pricked him. If he was honest, sobriety had been temporary. For a year he'd stayed off the booze, but eight weeks earlier he had stopped by The Dutchman's Arms to give a message to Captain Taylor. The Captain, a fair sort of a bloke, had offered Jim a drink, not taking no for an answer . . . That drink had tasted so good, bringing with it as it did a rush of confidence, a swift pushing away of problems. With each mouthful Jim shrugged off Amber Street and the burden of rent; his elder son's contempt; Anna's worrying health and his mother's insidious nagging. By the time he was two thirds down the glass, Jim was happy and at peace with the world.

It wasn't going to last.

Blinking, he stared at Missie Shepherd again. He would move the body. No, he thought, he couldn't do that. Then what *should* he do? Wiping the back of his hand across his mouth, he fumbled for a solution. He would do his round of the warehouses and dockside, then come back and pretend he had just found Missie. Yes, he thought eagerly, that would work. The cold air would have sobered him up good and proper. By the time he went to report the murder, no one would be able to tell that Jim Shaw had been drinking on duty.

Casting one last look at Missie, Jim hesitated. He couldn't in all honesty leave her exposed like that, not for the dock rats to find. Tenderly he took off her shawl and laid it over her face. She wasn't much more than a kid. What a hell of a way – and place – to end up . . . A sudden noise made Jim flinch. Automatically he turned out the lamp and shrank back into the shadows. Was there someone still out there? The same man who had butchered Missie Shepherd? His heartrate accelerated, his mouth drying. Slow footsteps were approaching Warehouse 17. Jim moved backwards hurriedly. He had the advantage of knowing the docks and could move quickly, even in the darkness, skirting Warehouse 17 and making for the office. Inside he would be safe. From any danger – or any questions.

Closing the office door behind him, Jim peeked through the window. In the distance he could see a man walking around the side of Warehouse 17 – and coming straight for him. His mouth dried. The figure keeping walking. He could feel his body begin to shake, and then realised – with queasy relief – that he knew the man.

'Yer bloody fool!' Jim hissed to himself, going to the door and beckoning for his brother to come in. 'What yer doing, Ivan, creeping around out there without a light?

'What were *you* doing? Running off like a bleeding criminal?' Ivan replied.

Striking a match, Jim relit the lamp, then studied his

visitor. Ma Shaw had been married twice: first to Jim's father, then to Nobby Lomax, a club-footed hobgoblin of a man from over Huddersfield way. No one knew why she had chosen such a weird consort. No one dared ask; and when he died soon after Ivan was born, he was forgotten within months. But if Ma Shaw had expected his son to be like his father, she – and everyone else in Preston – had been in for a shock. Ivan had taken after his grandfather. A big child, broody, with a sanctimonious streak. By the time he had reached fifteen and begun working on the docks, he had honed his curtness to perfection. He had a good heart, but – God only knew why – he couldn't show it, his concern always coming over as criticism.

'Yer've been drinking!' he snapped suddenly at Jim. 'Yer going to be sacked fer that. Then think where yer'll be. Yer've got to be more responsible, Jim. Or, like Ma says, drink will be the end of yer. Yer'll be out on the bloody street, that's where yer'll end up. Yer family desperate, no money, no roof over their heads. And all because yer can't stop drinking. The boss will have yer fer this . . .'

'Not if yer keep it quiet,' Jim said hurriedly, appealing to his half-brother's better nature. 'Ah, come on, Ivan . . .'

'I don't hold with drinking,' Ivan replied. He had been a member of the Temperance League since his teens. 'Yer should have more willpower.'

'Ah, piss off,' Jim replied, out of patience, as he filled the kettle and put it on to boil. 'Yer a stuffed shirt, Ivan, and no mistake.'

'I know my duty. And I know yer. Just like Ma does. She knows yer fer what yer are, and always has done.'

Tensing, Jim waited to see what his half-brother would say next. Ivan was looking smug that he had something over Jim. Something he could harangue him with. And when he'd finished predicting doom for Jim's family, then what? Would he report him? Jesus, wouldn't that be just like Ivan? Reckoning that he was doing Jim a favour, saving his bleeding soul.

No wonder Ivan had never married or had kids, Jim thought ruefully. What woman would want him?

'By rights I should tell Mr Fleetwood,' Ivan went on. After all, it would be the responsible thing to do. And the right thing for his brother. Maybe not a decision that would make him popular, but life was hard, and if Jim was going to get back on the straight and narrow, maybe it was worth putting a fright on him now.

'Hey now, Ivan, let's not be hasty!' Jim replied hurriedly. 'I need this job.'

'But not enough to stay sober.'

'I found a body,' Jim said suddenly, watching with satisfaction as Ivan's face grew waxy.

'A *what*?'

'Missie Shepherd. Round the back of Warehouse 17.'

'She's a prossie!'

'She *was* a prossie, poor soul,' Jim said, feeling no compunction about lying. 'That's why I had a drink, Ivan, I had to steady my nerves. Finding her like that, with her throat cut. And God knows if the murderer's still out there.'

Ivan looked queasy. 'Yer think he might be?'

'Why don't yer have a look?'

'Nah,' Ivan said, white as hill snow. 'He'll be gone by now.'

'Yer right, and besides, he were after the girl.'

'On the game, what did she expect?' Ivan went on, shaking his head. 'No whore can expect to die safe in her bed.'

Seeing how shocked Ivan was, Jim pressed his advantage.

'That's why I had to have a drink, to steady myself. Yer understand that, Ivan? I mean, even you can see that finding a dead body would shake up a man good.' He hurried on, despising himself for having to kow-tow to his half-brother. But if Ivan told the boss, Jim would be fired. Then he would have to go home, tell Anna – and his mother. Jesus, Jim thought, he would lie until his tongue was on fire to avoid that. 'Yer see how my hands are still shaking? I were in shock.'

'When did it happen?'

'Only minutes ago.'

'Yer should have told Mr Fleetwood,' Ivan replied. 'I'll go and tell him if yer like.'

Jim's eyes narrowed as he watched his half-brother walk to the door.

'But yer'll stay nothing about my having a drink?'

'I should fer yer own sake . . .'

'But?'

'I won't this time,' Ivan replied, adding pompously, 'But if I ever catch yer drinking on duty again, Jim, I'll report yer. Family or no family.'

'Thanks, Ivan, I won't forget yer kindness.'

THREE

Preston Docks had originally been opened in June 1892 by the Duke of Edinburgh, and was then the biggest single dock in the country. So big that the Albert Edward Dock water area covered forty acres, was 3,200 feet long and 600 feet wide. Built to handle cargo ranging from oil to cattle, it accommodated ships from as near as Belfast and London and from as far as Hamburg and Norway. But it hadn't always been so impressive. For centuries, the River Ribble had been busy with small craft, but traffic had been limited due to the shifting unmarked channel passage to the docks. Finally, in an attempt to expand the waterway's possibilities, intensive dredging had deepened the navigable depth from sixteen feet to over twenty-two. From then on the big ships came. One of the loads most commonly brought into the dock was timber, much of it from Russia and the Baltic, the amount tripling as the house-building boom developed in the early 1920s.

Oddly enough, people from outside Preston seldom connected the place with seafaring, the dock being sixteen miles inland from the open sea. But for the dockers it provided steady paid work; hard, but out in the open air. Men who didn't fancy factory work in the mill, or in engineering, went on the docks. Beside, you didn't need education to be a docker, and most of the men who worked there had left school at twelve or thirteen, following their fathers on to the dockside. And so, around the Albert Edward, a small community built up, with its own shops and pubs. And whores. At night, the dockers went inland; home to the cluttered terraces around Kirkham Street and Fylde Road, where the handloom weavers' houses stood. Originally workshops, these buildings were later sublet as cellar dwellings and soon became notorious.

From the first, Ma Shaw had been determined that none of her three sons would go into the factory trade – or face the hardship of the living and working conditions. As the cotton trade had thrived, more workers were employed and more and more cheap housing had been thrown up. Housing that was shoddy and insanitary. In fact, at one time, the child mortality rate in Preston was the highest in the country. So bad were the conditions that the average age of death was around eighteen years, with people squeezed like rats into a labyrinth of back streets. The entrances to these euphemistically named 'courts' were the sordid alleyways off the main streets. And the worst housing had been around Lower Friargate, along Church Street and the notorious Glovers Court. If you ended up there, you had nothing much – and nothing left to lose.

By comparison, the Shaws weren't too badly off. They struggled and fretted about the bills, but they had escaped the bull pits of the slums, just edging on to one of the poor but respectable areas. Not in the cauldron, but within reaching – or falling – distance. And the memory of what was only streets away had kept Ma Shaw on her toes throughout her life. Equally perspicacious, Silky ran a tattoo parlour but had always turned away the worst drunks and the dirtiest whores. 'Get sober and come back,' he would say to the drunks. And to the roughest whores: 'Just get out.' As for Ivan, he was too fastidious to let himself slide into the rapacious viciousness of slum life.

Jim, however, was another matter. His mother's dread of the slums didn't extend to him. Blithely believing that he and his family would never end up there, Jim took chances a wiser man might have avoided. For periods conscientious, he would then be suddenly reckless and go back on the booze. And after the first drink, he couldn't stop. If Anna had been a less forgiving wife, she could have put her foot down, but she believed in her husband, believed that he would never let her down. Even when he did, she gave him another chance. After all, without him, where would she have ended up? In fact, although Anna should have worried more about her husband, she was only really concerned about Billy, nicknamed Billy Fists around Preston because of his boxing ambitions.

The amateur pugilist was at that moment avoiding Ivan's dour gaze as he pushed a cartload of timber over to the warehouse on the dockside. Billy couldn't stand his uncle and made it obvious; Ivan was making it equally obvious that he thought Billy was a rough-head. Unloading some of the Russian timber, Billy wiped the sweat off his forehead and looked upwards. Later he would work off his extra energy at the gym, the owner even suggesting that he might make a professional boxer one day. Billy sighed. On either side of him were banked the bales of wood, a crane moving overhead as it swung another load on to the dockside. The early sun was shining mercilessly, throwing hot shimmers off the water and flattering the Albert Edward into some mockery of a northern Venice.

Leaning against the nearest wall, Billy rolled a cigarette. He was thinking about the unnatural heat and getting uncomfortable as sweat pooled under his arms. Then he thought about Jane Rimmer and felt his temperature rise even further. God, she was a looker all right, and she knew it. Billy smiled to himself. He had quite a girl, quite a girl. One most men would like to see on their arm. Mind you, Jane was a handful; she liked the good things and didn't pull her punches.

'If yer want to keep me interested, Billy Shaw, yer need to spoil me,' she had said only the previous night.

'I do spoil yer! I took yer to the pictures on Friday.'

She had squeezed the well-developed muscles in his left arm. 'Took me to see a cartoon! Not that Popeye's got anything on yer, Billy. Yer the best-built man in Preston,' she had teased him, winking, the sexual innuendo just under the surface. 'In fact, there's not another man with what yer've got.'

Grabbing hold of her, Billy had kissed her, Jane pulling away, pretending annoyance. 'Aye now! Yer can't take liberties.'

'I thought yer liked me taking liberties.'

'I like yer taking me out as well,' she had replied crisply. 'But yer mean, right mean, Billy Shaw. Surely yer don't have to give *all* yer wages to yer mam, do yer?'

He had felt the implied sneer and flushed. 'Cut it out, Jane! Families round here pools their wages, yer know that.'

'I were just teasing. Just having a bit of fun . . .'

Like hell, Billy thought, taking a drag on his cigarette. Jane liked to push him as far as she could. Liked to torment him. And it suited him – for a while. He had never been short of female attention, his obvious masculinity and hint of a future boxing career turning certain girls' heads. They liked the toughness of Billy Shaw – and he played on that.

Suddenly spotting his uncle across the dock, Billy watched Ivan Lomax critically. Now what did *that* bastard spend his money on? No wife, no family, just himself to keep and the rent to pay on his poky rooms. Didn't even drink – and unless Billy missed his guess, his unprepossessing uncle was still a virgin. A well-off virgin . . . What a luxury to have all your wages to yourself, Billy thought. To be able to feel your pockets jangle with change long after Friday. No such luck for him; his wage made it from the dock to his mother's apron in double-quick time. Not that that was unusual. He was only seventeen and living at home; like every other lad he had to donate his wages, especially now, after he had lost his last job for fighting.

The worst thing about having to tell his mother had been the look on her face. No shouting, no nastiness, just crushing disappointment. That had been the hardest part to bear, because Billy Shaw loved his mother and would have defended her with his life. As he would his sister. Or his little brother . . . Taking a long drag on his cigarette, Billy sighed. Poor bloody Micky, poor dumb Micky. Wasn't it enough that he couldn't talk? But no, he was tiny too. Only the size of a thru'penny bit, a magnet for bullies. Of course when Billy was around, no one messed with Micky. But Billy couldn't *always* be around.

His mind went back to a drizzling afternoon earlier that spring, to a patch of rough ground behind the UCP tripe shop.

'Put up yer hands!' Billy had said, trying to encourage his younger brother.

Micky stood, weedy in his vest and shorts, his hambone fists raised aimlessly. Micky Shaw, thirteen years old, hardly any flesh on him, eyes huge and poignant; the butt of the neighbourhood jokes, the first to be singled out, and the last in every queue. The scrap of a lad everyone picked on – because he was small, thin, nervy. And mute. Micky Shaw, who had never said one word in his life.

For months Billy had been watching Micky, and had finally decided that he needed toughening up. And the only way Billy had known to do that was to teach him to fight. Only trouble was, Micky wasn't a natural athlete.

'Keep yer hands up!'

Micky's expression had been weary, then irritated. He *was* holding up his bloody hands! It was all right for Billy; he was a hard man, big in the bone and the fist. But Micky was a weakling, and all his brother's tireless encouragement wasn't going to change that.

'Come fer me!'

Micky had stared at him, horrified.

'Come on, try and hit me!'

Micky, who had seen what had happened to men who had taken on his brother, hesitated.

'Make a lunge fer me!' Billy ordered. 'LUNGE!'

Shaken, Micky had lunged, then lost his footing and fallen over. Smiling forced encouragement, Billy had hauled his little brother to his feet.

'Yer just need practice,' he had said, although by the time another hour had passed, it was obvious that pugilism would never be the answer to Micky's bullying. Shrugging resignedly, Billy finally stopped, looping a big arm around Micky's shoulder and giving him a hurried, but affectionate, squeeze.

'Maybe I were wrong. I just thought I could teach yer to defend yerself like. Yer know, take on them bullies. Anyway, strikes me that boxing's not yer game, Micky,' he had gone on tactfully, then added, 'Tell yer what, though, I could teach yer to sprint – that way at least yer'd outrun the buggers.'

His thoughts returning to the present, Billy realised guiltily that being part of a family was tiring. And tying. All his life he had been looking out for someone else, and he was getting resentful. If it wasn't Micky, it was his father, Ma Shaw going on and on about how the Shaw men were all bloody rabble. OK, so it had been unlucky that he and Jim had been sacked in the same week, but Christ, she had laboured the point . . . Billy kept watching Ivan across the dockside, imagining a life without responsibility. A life with privacy. A room of his own where he could take Jane and lark about. A place he could get some peace in, some bloody quiet.

'Oi, Shaw! Yer bleeding hypnotised, or wot?'

Surprised, Billy jerked off the wall. Hands on hips, the foreman, Mr Fleetwood, was staring at him impatiently.

'I want that timber unloading before dinner, yer got it?'

Billy nodded, managing to make the gesture somehow rebellious. 'Yes, sir.'

'Don't bloody "yes, sir" me, yer bugger! Get back to work – there's plenty of men looking fer a job if yer don't want it.'

FOUR

Restless, Kat turned over in bed, then got up. It was no good, she could never sleep if she knew her father wasn't home. And why was that? she wondered. He was always back by six in the morning, coming in as the rest of the family rose, and Kat got Micky ready for school. It was not that she always saw him – sometimes he would have gone upstairs to bed by the time she came down but if he wasn't home, she always knew. And this morning he wasn't home.

She waited, hearing her younger brother's fitful snoring coming from the room he shared with Billy. The room next to her parents' bedroom. On paper, the house would have sounded spacious – three bedrooms – but in reality it was cramped, the rooms partitioned off into separate areas, her own 'bedroom' tiny, hardly more than a big cupboard. But it had a window, Kat reminded herself, and if she stood on her bed she could look out over the rooftops towards Avenham Park, where the really grand houses were. Where people had proper bedrooms and a toilet indoors.

Suddenly she heard the key turn in the front door and smiled – her father was home. Tense, she waited for him to call for his wife. But for once, the call didn't come . . . Surprised, she listened, hearing her mother yawning as she made her way down the steep, narrow stairs, followed by the sound of her parents' muffled speech. *Something was wrong.* Her curiosity roused, Kat moved out on to the cramped landing, pulling her nightdress around her knees to warm her legs.

'. . . she were dead . . .'

'Dead!' Anna replied, her quiet voice unusually raised. 'Oh my God.'

'Poor lass . . . throat cut . . .'

Wide-eyed, Kat leaned forward to listen. Who had had their throat cut? God, this was exciting.

'. . . I were just coming round the side of Warehouse 17 and there she were. Her head half off.'

Scurrying into her brothers' bedroom, Kat paused for an instant to let her eyes adjust to the half-light. Then, touching Micky's shoulder, she gestured for him to follow her. At the top of the stairs, she looked at him. Her adored little brother, the silent, gentle, loving Micky. Kat's favourite.

'There's been a murder,' she whispered, watching his eyes widen. 'A girl, down at the docks.' Jerking her head downwards, she gestured for him to listen.

'. . . it were a terrible sight,' Jim went on, his voice snaking up the stairwell. 'I never saw anything like that even when I were fighting in the bloody war . . .'

'Don't swear, luv,' their mother replied, tenderly chastising. 'You'll feel better when you've got some breakfast inside you.'

'I don't think I could eat.'

The children exchanged a glance. Now this *was* serious.

'Flaming Ivan was there. Poking his nose in where it didn't belong. He reported it to Mr Fleetwood, all puffed up with importance.'

'Why didn't *you* report it, luv?'

Both children could hear the sudden hesitation in their father's voice. 'Oh, let him have his moment of glory, Anna. Yer know what he's like.'

Leaning back, Kat thought of her uncle and winced. Why should Ivan get the credit? He was always 'doing the right thing'. Thank God he didn't live with them, or their lives would be a misery. She thought of her other uncle then, Silky Shaw, as charming as Ivan was dour; as handsome as Ivan was lumbering; as amusing as Ivan was pedantic. Everyone – particularly women – loved Silky. She frowned for a moment, wondering what her uncle's real name was, then realised that she didn't know. To her – as to everyone – he was Silky Shaw. Silky by name, and by nature. It pleased her that her father and Silky were full brothers. Kat could just about bear the idea of Ivan being one of the family – but only as a half-brother to Jim.

From below there was silence, only the sound of their mother putting a pan on to the range to heat. There was never much money; breakfast would be a pint pot of strong tea and some bread and dripping. They only had jam on a Sunday, and then it was spread so thin, it was little more than a stain.

'She's going to make him breakfast after all,' Kat commented.

Micky nodded.

'He can't be that bad, then.'

Again Micky nodded. He was devoted to his sister, and accepted everything she said as gospel. After all, who defended him against all comers? Who had endless patience and kindness? Who spent hours with him? Oh, his mother was loving, Micky thought, but she was so often ill, so often weak herself that she had little time for him. But Kat – she was *always* there.

'Throat cut . . .' their father repeated from below.

Kat and Micky exchanged a glance.

'. . . from ear to ear . . .'

'Come on, luv,' their mother interrupted him. 'You eat your breakfast and you'll feel better. Don't brood on it.'

Kat, however, *was* brooding. She was already imagining the horror of being killed on the dockside, discarded like a lump of worthless Siberian timber left over from an incoming load. Since her earliest years, she had visited the docks with her father. She had fallen in love with the swampy green summer water and the freezing, echoing winter fogs. Her childhood dreams had been populated by the giant steel cranes, the thudding of the loads, the sullen murmur of the water. The docksides and warehouses had captured her imagination, and by the time she was seven she knew the loading bays, the times of the tides and the water markers as well as she knew her sums at school. Nothing girly for Kat Shaw; she was from a dock-working family, and there was talk of Micky joining them at the Albert Edward one day . . . She didn't like *that* idea, though. Didn't think a nervous mute boy would fare well amongst the rough men on the dockside – even with his family around.

Micky stood by his sister's side, as ever impressed by her good looks, the slightly hooded green eyes giving her an exotic appearance. Exotic for Preston, anyway, where the girls were either dough-faced and heavy, or wiry and narrow-featured. In amongst them his sister glowed, smooth and blonde, like an opal on a coal heap. But there was a lot more to Kat than her looks, as Micky knew only too well. Hadn't she, from their earliest years, been the only one who could communicate with him? He couldn't remember how it had started, only that his sister had taught him how to sign. Not like deaf people, just their own private language, so he could tell her what he was thinking, even joke with her. They had made it up as they went along, Kat being the guiding light and moving Micky's child's fingers into ever-changing, ever-articulate shapes. By the time he was five, he could tell Kat a whole story with his small, clever hands. Her patience had been constant, impressive. And he had worked hard to please her, because she was the only one who wouldn't accept that he was useless, handicapped, second rate. Micky Shaw might not be able to speak with his mouth, but his sister had taught him to talk with his hands and opened up the world for him.

Other members of the family tried to learn their language, but Micky was reluctant to share the secret. He communicated with Kat, no one else. And by doing so, he developed a bond with his sister nothing could break or impinge upon. Only one thing worried Micky: he could see that his sister was growing up. And he knew – because he could *hear* perfectly well – how the boys admired her. But they were also in awe of Kat Shaw. Some might watch her – and in the last year, when she had grown up so suddenly, hang around Amber Street corner – but they didn't approach. Kat might have no prospects and no dowry, but she carried herself like an empress.

'Come on,' she said quietly, 'we have to get you ready for school.'

He nodded reluctantly. If he was lucky today, he wouldn't be bullied, but he would be mocked. He always was. And at breaktime he would stand alone, propping up the school railings, watching the other kids hopscotching or skipping, before sidling back into the classroom and waiting silently for the next lesson to begin. At the end of the day, when the school bell rang, he would make for the school gates and wait for Kat.

He loved those minutes when he had her full attention. The attention many others would have longed for. But they didn't walk with Kat, they didn't listen to her stories, they didn't feel her hand squeeze theirs suddenly. For a few public minutes every day, Micky Shaw was the most envied boy in the county. All the good-looking boys, the tough lads, the smart kids couldn't hold a candle to him.

He might be mute, he might be puny, he might be the runt of the Shaw litter, but he was Kat's favourite. And that made him richer than a duke.

FIVE

'*I said a fucking ship!*' the docker hollered.

Silky hurried out from the back room of the tattoo parlour. In a glance he took in the scene: a burly man towering over the apprentice tattoo artist, the latter standing rigid as a corpse with the tattoo needle in his trembling right hand.

'*What kind of fucking ship is* this *supposed to be?*'

Smiling, Silky moved between the two men. He wasn't tall, but he didn't lack guts, and for all his greased good looks, he had never been known to back down from a fight.

'What's the problem here?'

'WHAT'S THE FUCKING PROBLEM?' the docker shouted, jabbing at his left bicep. 'I asked for a ship, not a bloody canoe. What is this guy? Some kind of bleeding poof?'

Silky put his head on one side, regarding the tattoo. It was crude, the edges blurred – the apprentice's hand had obviously been shaking uncontrollably. And it was big, too big to try and refashion into a ship. Unless it was the size of the *Titanic*. That was the trouble with apprentices, Silky thought, surveying the damage incredulously, they thought they were all Rembrandts. But drawing on paper wasn't the same as tattooing the arm of a pissed docker, and the kind of men who came in for tattoos weren't usually artistically inclined. When they asked for a ship, they wanted a ship. Usually with a skull and crossbones on the flag.

'It's very creative . . .'

'*It's bloody shit!*' the docker roared.

Silky hadn't earned his sobriquet for nothing. Keeping his tone even, he studied the tattoo carefully, resisting the impulse to knock the apprentice's teeth down his throat.

'I think the gentleman,' he began, taking the needle from the apprentice, 'needs something more dramatic . . .'

'*I want a fucking ship!*'

'. . . and impressive,' he carried on smoothly, leading the docker to a seat. Reluctantly, the man sat down, breathing heavily. By the door, the apprentice looked as though he was about to wet himself. 'Something powerful, in keeping with your build.'

'Aye?'

Silky had never seen a pig talk before and was fascinated. 'You need something extraordinary . . .'

'I need a fucking—'

'. . . something no other dock worker has.'

The docker stopped raging, looking at Silky intently. 'Oh aye? Like what?'

'A devil.'

'A what!'

'A devil,' Silky said, thinking on his feet. It would need to be a big black image to cover up the mess underneath. 'Anyone can have a ship, they're two a penny – but a *devil*. Just think what it would do for your reputation as a hard man. You'd have the Devil on your arm.' He paused, nodding encouragingly. 'People would talk about it all over the docks, and beyond. Your tattoo would be famous.'

The docker's eyes flickered. Maybe the idea of a devil *was* a good one. It would scare people off, for sure.

'With horns?'

Silky blinked. 'What?'

'I want horns on it. Big fucking horns.'

'Then horns,' Silky replied deftly, 'you shall have.'

* * *

Glancing in at the window of the tattoo parlour later that day, Ma Shaw spotted her son and paused. Silky was busy making a design on some ape's arm, his head bent, his long dark eyelashes almost girlish. Not that anyone could accuse Silky of being effeminate. God knows he had been chasing girls since he was old enough to walk. Studying her youngest son, she wondered when – or if – he would get married. After all, of her three offspring, only Jim had a family. And *what* a family. Ma Shaw had to admit that Anna was a pretty woman, but she was too frail, too damn sickly to bring up a batch of kids. If Jim had had any sense, he would have limited their offspring – for the sake of his wife's health, their cramped living quarters, and his own limited earning power.

Ma Shaw reached into her voluminous bag and drew out a peppermint. There was nothing she liked better than a good mint; kept you sharp. And she was sharp, all right. Not that Jim was, but his *daughter* . . . now there was another matter. Ma smiled to herself. Of course they should have kept to her full name, Katherine, but Jim insisted on shortening it, and Ma had to admit, reluctantly, that it suited her. There *was* something cat-like – quick, intelligent and fascinating – about Kat. It was a shame that her schooling was about to be cut short, but that was the way life went when you were poor. Everyone had to earn a living as soon as they could to bring in a wage. Besides, Kat liked her Saturday stint at Underwood's chemist. Admittedly, she did little but run around after Mrs Underwood – who could never get over her good fortune at having married a chemist – and she wasn't paid much. But it beat working at the mill any day, and it brought in some extra cash.

Catching her son's eye, Ma nodded briefly to Silky. *I'll pop back later*, she mouthed through the window. *With a bit of fish fer yer supper . . .*

Thanks, he mouthed back, watching his mother move off.

Of all her children, Ma loved Silky the most. If it had been possible, she would have sworn that Ivan wasn't hers, only everyone knew he was. Ma thought of his father, Nobby, and smiled. Poor bugger, ugly as a bat, hobbling around on his club foot like a grisly little gnome. Only Ma knew his one great talent: he was cracking in bed. She walked down Grimley Street, deep in memories. People had thought she was mad when she married Nobby – after all, she'd been quite handsome in her day – but she'd had no complaints. Many a night they had spent in the big double bed, giggling under the covers like kids, Ma discovering something she had never experienced before – passion. So when Nobby died she didn't miss his looks, or his small wage packet; she missed the one thing she could never talk about – his skill in the sack.

Wasn't that just like life? Ma thought bitterly, walking into Dover Street, her thoughts returning to her granddaughter. If Kat was careful and didn't rush into anything, she could find herself a decent match. Someone keen, with a regular job and the kind of attitude to keep it. A white-collar worker would be something, Ma thought. A man who served in a shop, perhaps, maybe even a clerk. After all, Kat was a fine girl with a good reputation. But . . . She paused, remembering that Jim and Ivan worked on the docks, and that Silky had a tattoo parlour. Now that *was* a sticking point, even Ma had to admit. There were jobs and jobs, but a tattoo parlour wasn't the epitome of respectability. In fact, she reasoned, if she herself had come across the shop unexpectedly, she would have been shocked. But it had been a part of her life so long, she didn't see it as others did.

Her grandfather, Norman Clegg, had won the place in a card game. His wife had been so enraged that she'd left him; upped and gone off with some other man she'd been seeing for years on the sly. Relieved of his snobbish wife, and the proud owner of a tattoo parlour, Norman had taken lessons from some old geezer over in Church Street. His hand shaking like an aspen leaf, the old man had demonstrated on Norman's own arm, his age and bad eyesight making a cod out of the immortal words ENGLAND THE BRAVE. For the rest of his life, Norman's arm sported the motto ENGLAND THE GRAVE. Not that he minded; he had a good sense of humour, and over the years grew very fat, so that the tattoo stretched and stretched . . . In the end, he was left with an abridged version of the original: GLAND HE RAVE.

'Hello! Wait for me!'

Ma turned at the sound of her granddaughter's voice. 'Shouldn't you be in school?'

Unfazed by the lack of welcome, Kat shrugged. 'It's four o'clock. Where are you going?'

'Not that it's yer business, but I'm off to get some fish for yer uncle Silky.'

Kat nodded, falling into step with her grandmother. She knew only too well that Ma Shaw terrified most people. Even her elder brother, Billy, was in awe of her, and Micky would run if he caught sight of her. But Kat liked her grandmother, understood how much she helped when her own mother was ill. How she kept the Shaw family together when her father was being silly.

Silly . . . Kat wondered why she couldn't say stupid, or drunk, or lazy. But she knew that whatever her father did, she would never be the one to criticise him. Others did that only too eagerly.

'How's yer dad?'

Kat winced. Ma Shaw could pick out her thoughts like a needle picked out pomegranate seeds. 'He's fine.'

'I heard he found a dead body.'

'Yeah, some woman on the docks.'

'That's what happens when yer let men have their way with yer,' Ma said sagely. 'She were a prossie. Yer know what that is, don't yer?'

'She sold her body,' Kat replied, surprising Ma, who had hoped to go into a long explanation about sex. 'Dad said she was a nice girl, though.'

'Well now, isn't that like yer father? Nice girl! I ask yer, how can a girl be nice when she's letting men have everything they want?'

'She wasn't letting them *have* it, she was charging them for it.'

Ma stopped dead, looking at her granddaughter in disbelief. 'Yer want to watch yer mouth, young lady! There's being clever, and being too damn clever fer yer own good.'

They walked on in silence for a while. Ma was the first to speak. 'Has yer mother talked to yer about things? Men, babies, the like?'

Kat didn't know about 'the like', but she was sure she didn't want Ma Shaw to explain it to her, so she nodded wisely.

'Oh yeah, everything.'

'*Everything?*'

She nodded again. 'Everything.'

'Well, I'm surprised, but I'm glad. A girl should know how to keep herself out of trouble, and yer growing up fast.' She looked Kat up and down, seeing how quickly she was developing. 'Yer'll be going to work soon, I suppose?'

'Dad said he'd heard about some job going in a grocer's shop on Friargate.'

'What would yer father know about groceries!' Ma snapped, although she was secretly pleased that Jim was trying to keep Kat out of the grinding work of the mills. 'Is he still liking his job as a watchman?'

'Apart from the dead bodies, yes.'

Ma stole a quick glance at her granddaughter, but Kat wasn't being smart-mouthed, just honest.

'And he's keeping the hours? No late starts? Early leavings?'

Kat rose to her father's defence at once. 'Dad's always on time!'

'It's nice yer stick up fer him, luv, but yer should keep an eye on him. He's always been a bit unreliable. And Billy can be the same.

'Yer old enough to hear this,' Ma Shaw said patiently.

'Women rule men, yer understand? It's a fact of life, perhaps not one yer mother told yer, but it's true never the less. We don't let men know it, but we're the boss of them. When times are hard, it's the women who have to hold the family together. And yer know what I mean well enough. Yer remember last year?'

Kat hung her head, thinking back to the terrible time when her father had been drinking and Billy had been fired for fighting. No money coming in, only Ma Shaw keeping them going with donations from her savings, and Silky's generous offerings. No help from Ivan, though.

'I remember.'

'Yer dad's a good man, but he's not got much willpower – and yer brother's got a right temper on him. Some hothead he is. I'd throw a bucket of cold water over Billy now and then, that would keep him cooled down.' Ma Shaw touched Kat's shoulder briefly, then her voice hardened again. 'Yer right to feel the way yer do. Love them all yer want, but remember this – in this life yer have to know yer can depend on yerself. Not on a mother, a father, or a husband. In the end there's one person and one person only who'll be the making or the death of yer, and that's yerself.'

'Dad doesn't mean to let us down! He promised he would never drink again. Said he'd keep this job until he died.' Kat looked at her grandmother fiercely. 'And I believe him!'

'It's to yer credit that yer do, luv,' Ma Shaw replied softly.

'You worry too much, Ma, honest you do,' Kat said lightly. 'I have to go now, see you later.'

Smiling wryly, Ma accepted Kat's kiss on her cheek and then watched as her granddaughter walked off.

I'd like to believe yer father too, she thought to herself, I really would. But hadn't she smelt beer on her son's breath only the other day? All drunks were liars, she knew that, but for once she wanted to put aside her reservations and believe that her son was going to be responsible. That the watchman would *keep* his watch – and his word.

SIX

Sighing, Anna sat down by the kitchen table, her hands clasped on her knee. It was so quiet, so warm – and she was happy. Maybe she shouldn't be, maybe she should be worried, but she wasn't. The thought glowed inside her, fizzed with pleasure. *She was happy . . .* And why not? Hadn't Jim settled into his watchman's job and stayed off the beer? Wasn't Billy working on the docks? Kat growing up pretty? Even Micky seemed less nervous. And now this. This wonderful news . . .

Outside the window, Amber Street was soaking in sunshine. It made the grim terrace look unexpectedly pretty, the roofs gilded, a pot of geraniums shimmering on the pub windowsill next door. Of course that was why Jim had taken the house in the first place: because the rent was low, being next to The Horse and Cart pub. They were newly married then, and he'd told Anna – with complete conviction – that it was only going to be temporary.

'A few months, maybe a year,' he had said. 'And it's not a bad place, luv, not too much noise to bother us. They told me it's not a rough house.'

Well, that was true most of the time, but as the years passed, The Horse and Cart changed hands many times, and by the time Billy was born, the peaceful corner pub had become a temporary boxing ring. More fights broke out there than at the docks. Then the landlord was knifed. Mr

Parker, the next landlord, was a big-nosed gossiping liar with sticky fingers. On the very day Kat came into the world, he left The Horse and Cart with a week's takings.

For a while the pub stood empty, and then a rotund, good-natured bald man arrived, wearing a pork-pie hat and an expression of hope: Mr Horace Armitage, newly widowed, with a belly like a whale's forehead. He cleaned up the pub within the month. Out went the fights, the whores and the deadbeats. Under new management, The Horse and Cart became respectable. And quiet. Until Horace bought a piano . . . Like Jim said at the time, nothing was perfect.

The music had never bothered Anna, and she never mentioned moving either. At the beginning of her married life she might have believed in Jim's plans, but as time went on she realised they weren't leaving Amber Street. Despite giving birth to Billy when she was little more than a child herself – and facing Ma Shaw's wrath – Anna was contented. She had no family of her own, and no money; she was little more than a foundling really, one of many poor girls who considered herself lucky to have found a man and married him. Then to have had two healthy children, Billy and Kat.

Ma Shaw always said that it was Jim's drinking that was the cause of Micky's problem. That somehow the trauma of Jim going off on one of his binges affected Anna so much that the baby was born with a defect. Terrified by Ma Shaw, Anna nevertheless defended her husband, knowing how much Jim blamed himself, believed himself responsible for his handicapped child. The baby being born dumb was just one of those things, Anna told Ma Shaw. It was down to God, not Jim.

Besides, Anna thought to herself, Jim stayed sober for a long time after Micky was born. Swore he was off the booze for good, that he would get a job and hold it down and save some money. He loved her, Anna thought, he always had. He wasn't thoughtless or unkind, just weak. And maybe a little stupid, risking his wife's fragile health. But then again, she could have aborted any of her babies. God knew how many other women did. She could have said nothing, just got rid of them . . . Anna shivered at the thought. What would her life have been without them? They were everything to her, and the public expression of her love for her husband. Whatever the cost to her health, Anna relished her pregnancies, flying in the face of the midwife's advice. Not that Mrs Soley was *really* a midwife; she was just a local woman who had been delivering the children of poor families for three decades. If you couldn't afford the doctor – and who could in Amber Street? – you called in Mrs Soley.

'Yer mad,' she had told Anna in the past. 'Yer not fit fer more babies.'

'I'll be OK,' Anna had reassured her. 'Nothing will happen to me.'

'Yer might be right. After all, God looks after drunks and fools. Just make sure that this one's yer last,' Mrs Soley had told her after Micky. 'Or yer'll be *really* pushing yer luck, girl.'

Anna smiled at the memory. It had all been worth it. No mother loved her children more, and Jim idolised his kids. It was the least she could do in repayment for his rescuing her. For marrying her and taking her on, some poor scrap with nothing to her name. Besides, it wasn't so bad to have a handicapped child. Micky could hear, even if he couldn't speak. And if he *was* little and puny, he would grow. He was only thirteen; everyone knew that lads had growing spurts. Oh yes, Anna told herself, people would be surprised by Micky one day. He was bright, unusual; one look in those fathomless eyes told anyone that. In time her frail, pitied little lad would prove himself. But not yet . . .

From next door, Anna could hear the piano start up in The Horse and Cart and drummed her fingers in time to the music. Then, humming, she got to her feet and began to peel some potatoes, the sun circling in through the window and lighting the first round curve of her pregnant form.

SEVEN

Straightening her dress for the third time in a minute, Kat waited patiently for Mr Unwin to acknowledge her. Her thoughts went back to the previous night, and she flushed at the recall. God, she had acted like a right idiot . . . At Anna's request, she had been sent to wait on the corner of Amber Street, the week's rent in her pocket. For the first time she had been charged with paying Old Man Pitt, their landlord, and had been relishing the responsibility. Billy had been doing extra shift time and her father had been called in to work early, and Kat had suddenly felt like a grown-up, a woman with money.

Eyeing the street, she had waited for the old man's car to draw up, her foot tapping the pavement impatiently. A couple of old school friends passed and Kat waved, but no landlord appeared. In the distance she could hear the chime of the town hall clock; then she felt a light tap on her shoulder.

'Are you waiting for me?' an attractive young man asked. 'Mr Armitage said you were paying the rent today.'

'What?' Kat stammered, fascinated by the well-dressed dark-haired god on Amber Street.

'I'm Mr Pitt's son, Andrew.'

'*Andrew* . . .' Kat replied, as though hypnotised.

'I'm collecting the rents this week,' he explained, smiling and putting out his hand.

Kat just stood there.

'Your rent? For your house?' he went on, mystified but kindly. 'You have it ready for me?'

Flustered, Kat had pulled the money out of her pocket – along with the rent book – and promptly dropped them both into the gutter. Bending down, she retrieved them and, blushing, handed them to Andrew Pitt. Light-headed, she felt as though she was watching herself – and thinking what an ass she was – for standing next to the landlord's son she had been stricken with an intense and immediate infatuation.

Andrew had pocketed the money and then made an entry in the Shaws' rent book, passing it back to Kat with another smile before, baffled by her strange expression, walking off. Transfixed, Kat watched him round the corner, then, still in an emotional fog, turned – and walked straight into the door jamb of her own house.

Flushing with the memory, Kat straightened her hair and continued to wait at the grocer's shop just off Friargate. Her grey coat, darned at the elbow and cuff, had been pressed into service, and she had borrowed Anna's best dress. But nothing could disguise the cheap black stockings and the hand-knitted beret . . . Her job at Underwood's chemist had come to a sudden, shabby end; Mr Underwood had run off with a woman from Hanky Park. Not only that, but he had stolen all the drugs as well and left his stunned wife with debts up to her ears. And no money to pay for an assistant, even a cheap one like Kat . . .

Around her, Kat could see the tins of cocoa powder, dried eggs, salt and bags of sugar stacked up. A fly buzzed nonchalantly against the outside window pane as she waited for the owner, Mr Gregory Unwin, to finish serving a customer. Across the street she could make out the factory chimneys looming over the tops of the shop roofs, and she made herself a promise – no working in the mills. She couldn't even bear to think about it, being cooped up in amongst so many people with so much noise. Of course, if she had been able to choose her job, she would have gone to work on the docks with her father. She smiled to herself, imagining the uproar that would provoke. *No decent woman works on the Albert Edward . . .* And that was true. The only women who *did* work there were a couple of hard-faced pub landladies, and the working girls. No respectable females. And who could blame them? The place was dangerous, sailors coming in all the time on foreign ships. Strange men with strange accents, on land for a few days or sometimes only a night. Transients, her father told her. Drunks looking for whores, or a fight.

Of course, many of the sailors were respectable, hardworking grafters. But those weren't the ones Jim worried about. He feared the desperate men who had fled their homelands, working their passages to England and then disappearing as soon as they docked. The men with nothing to lose . . . Kat knew only too well that her father suspected one of these men of the murder of Missie Shepherd. Some stranger who had come without a name, in darkness, and then disappeared. How could you find a man like that? Jim would ask his daughter. A person with no identity, no home, just someone who could do whatever they liked, then slip away without ever being caught . . .

'But then again,' he had gone on, 'it might be the bloke on the next street. Someone yer see every day and never think twice about. But whoever it is, he'll be a rough bastard and he'll mix with a rough crowd.'

The thought made Kat shiver as she continued to wait. Maybe it wouldn't be bad working at the grocer's, she thought, glancing over to Mr Unwin, who was chatting on relentlessly. Her mind turned to the morose Ivan, the tough Billy . . . even though her father was a friendly man, he didn't talk like this one did. Sighing, she waited. Another customer arrived and the whole process began again, the news dissected along with some other woman's reputation.

Finally the shop emptied, and Mr Unwin turned to her and looked her up and down. His smooth skin, soft as a child's, puckered into a smile, one supple hand tapping her quickly on the shoulder.

'Oh, you *are* a pretty girl,' he crooned. 'Quite an ornament. Can you count?'

'Pardon?'

'Pardon!' Mr Unwin repeated, the word making him ecstatic. 'How delightful you are! I asked if you could work out the money for people?'

'Oh yes, I was good at arithmetic in school.'

He sighed. 'And very clean.'

'What is?'

'*You* are very clean.'

Kat had never been complimented on her hygiene before, and she flushed. She caught sight of Micky out of the corner of her eye. He was waiting for her across the road, kicking at the kerbside impatiently

'You must be polite. Always very polite,' Mr Unwin went on, his tone light. 'But you mustn't talk to people unless they talk to you.' He paused, smoothing his fine blond hair. 'All the ladies talk to me, of course. I'm *known*.'

Kat knew only too well what Mr Unwin was known for.

'He's a bleeding poof!' Billy had said the previous night. Anna tried to silence him, but Billy wasn't having it. 'Everyone knows Gregory Unwin; they talk about him down the Roxy, about how he's got a boyfriend over Wigan way—'

'Billy!' Anna said, her tone uncharacteristically sharp. 'Not in front of your sister.'

'But if Kat's going to work there, she should know.'

'Mr Unwin's got a boyfriend?' Kat said, suddenly realising what Billy had said. '*But he's a man!*'

Anna rolled her eyes. 'Now see what you've done?'

'He's one of them.'

Kat frowned at her brother. 'One of them? Who?'

'Them,' Billy replied, putting one hand on his hip and lisping: 'Oh, Mr Unwin, yer lemons are *gorgeous*.'

Flicking the tea towel at him with irritation, Anna turned back to her daughter. 'Don't listen to Billy. Mr Unwin's a very kind man, with a nice shop. If yer got the job there yer'd be happy, I know yer would. It's one up from the mill or the factory, Kat. It's clean, in a nice street. Yer'll meet nice people.' Her voice dropped, her embarrassment palpable. 'But yer'll have to make allowances for Mr Unwin, luv. People live their lives in different ways. Not that it makes them wrong, just different.'

'Oh, he's *different* all right,' Billy had replied, laughing.

'Kat . . .' Anna had gone on, ignoring her son and looking into her daughter's face earnestly. 'Don't judge Mr Unwin, luv. He's not bad, just not like most other folk. Don't hold it against him.'

Remembering her mother's words, Kat looked up into the expectant face of Gregory Unwin. She thought for a moment that it was funny that a man had a boyfriend, and wanted to laugh – but then she saw something else in his face. Something she hadn't expected. A sadness, a look Kat recognised and knew only too well. The expression of the victim, the outcast. The same expression Micky had.

'I'd really like to work here, Mr Unwin,' she said, smiling genuinely. 'I think you've got a lovely shop.'

No one bothered with an autopsy for Missie Shepherd. The cause of death was obvious: a cut throat, a murder. What wasn't obvious was who was responsible. Almost a month had passed since Jim had found the body, and yet the police were no nearer to catching the killer. The murder of a prostitute was not considered as important as the killing of a respectable woman. The fact that Missie Shepherd had been put out to work by her mother at the age of ten wasn't considered. Neither was anyone concerned about the years Missie had plied her trade in Hanky Park, or around some of the worst doss houses in Moss Side. All anyone remembered was that she was a whore. After all, hadn't she been asking for it? What respectable woman would be down the docks at night?

It was typical, Jim told Anna later that night. No one cared about some poor prostitute.

'Missie wasn't a bad sort,' he said, taking off his jacket and fanning himself in the heat. Evening, but no let-up in the warmth. 'Just a silly girl . . .'

'Jim—'

'. . . hardly any older than Kat,' Jim continued. 'My God, what a way to end up.'

'Jim—'

'I'm so glad Kat got that job with Mr Unwin.'

Laughing, Anna slid into his lap. Jim was surprised.

'Well hello there! What's this in aid of?'

'I've something to tell yer.'

'Oh yeah?'

'Something important,' she went on, smiling broadly. 'I'm pregnant.'

To her horror, Jim's face set. Taking her hands, he sighed and then shook his head slowly. 'Oh, luv . . .'

'It's good news!'

'No it's not,' he said, his tone shaken. 'Yer know what the doctor said after Micky were born. Yer not to have more children.'

'I'll be fine!' Anna said, suddenly close to tears. 'Don't go putting ideas in my head, Jim Shaw. I'm not to be upset.'

'Anna, I'm not trying to upset yer, luv, I'm just worried.'

'You don't want the baby!'

'I don't want anything to happen to yer!' he said sharply, genuinely worried. 'Anna, yer my life.'

'And you're mine,' she responded tenderly. 'It'll be wonderful to have a new baby around.'

He wasn't convinced, but what choice was there? Abortion? Not likely; neither he nor Anna would condone that. But she wasn't strong, and then there was the question of money. God, it was a good thing he hadn't been caught out drinking on the job. To lose a wage now didn't bear thinking about. He would have to watch himself: no slip-ups, no letting his wife down. His mind turned to his mother and he winced inwardly. Ma Shaw wouldn't like this. She would have plenty to say: how could yer let poor Anna have another baby? And what are yer going to feed it on? Yer a bloody fool, Jim Shaw, a bloody fool.

Already stinging from the criticism he knew would come, Jim thought of his younger son, Micky. What if – oh God – what if the new baby was handicapped? Mute, or deaf? Or blind? Nah, he thought, dismissing the idea, Micky had been a one-off, the doctor had said, a million-to-one chance.

'What yer thinking?' Anna asked softly, laying her head on his shoulder.

'I was thinking about the baby,' he lied.

'I want another girl.'

'A girl would be nice,' Jim agreed, still thinking about Micky and that million-to-one chance.

'A sister for Kat.'

'Yeah.'

'All girls should have a sister. And the little one would have someone to look up to.'

He nuzzled his wife's hair tenderly. 'I bet yer Kat will take over the baby if yer don't watch out. She's a strong mothering streak, that girl. Always looking out for Micky.'

'No.'

He leaned back, looking into his wife's face. 'No what?'

'It won't happen again, Jim. This baby will be perfect.' Anna paused, smiling serenely. 'This child will be just perfect.'

Micky was counting. He liked to count, it passed the time in the break when he was standing on his own against the playground wall. No one wanted to play with the dumb kid, as he was called. But to be honest, Micky wasn't bothered. He didn't want to play with the others; he liked to be on his own, thinking. OK, so maybe not all the time, but it wasn't so bad really. Micky shifted his feet. His shoes – secondhand from the Baker kids on the next street – were way too big. But he'd grow into them, or so his mother told him. Just like she told him he would grow into the jumper he had inherited from Billy. Only a year later it was *still* too big, the sleeves rolled up almost ten inches, the hem coming halfway down his thighs. Pretty funny, if you weren't wearing it. Of course some of the bully boys had taunted Micky about it, then stopped short when Billy called by at the school. Micky hadn't told his brother; Billy had just stopped on the off chance, but no one believed that. In their eyes. Micky had told on them, and so he became worse than dumb. He was a dumb coward.

Reaching into his pocket, Micky fingered the blue oil crayon. He was ashamed, bitterly ashamed of stealing it – but he wasn't going to give it back. Instead he was going to use it . . . He thought of the pieces of paper he had hidden behind the cheap wardrobe in the bedroom he shared with Billy. No one had taught him how to draw, but one day he had done a quick sketch of their street and been stupefied. It was good. Crikey, he had thought, not bad for a dumb kid. Maybe good enough to keep him off the docks? Away from the dreaded Albert Edward? Micky smiled to himself bleakly. Of course drawing wouldn't keep him off the docks. But one day it might get him *out*. One day it might, please God, be his escape.

Over the next few weeks he had drawn a horse and cart, a barrow, and kids playing. Which was easy, because most of the time no one paid much attention to him. Then he had drawn the pub next door, and even done a quick outline of Horace Armitage, an outline that was more of a caricature. Even Micky himself had been stunned at the likeness – the red-veined cheeks, the long, pendulous nose like a turkey's wattle, the short bandy legs – and then he had realised that it was *too* good and that Mr Armitage probably wouldn't see the funny side. So he had hidden it, along with the caricatures he had done of his teacher and Uncle Ivan.

It gave him a feeling of power to know that he could, in a dozen or so lines, capture a person in all their faults and failings. As someone who had been bullied for the thirteen years he had been alive, it was sweet revenge. With a pencil he could reduce even his most terrifying tormentors to jokes. Defusing their power by making them ridiculous . . . His hand closed over the oil crayon protectively. He knew that stealing was wrong – his mother would be mortified if she found out – but he had wanted that crayon so much and knew they couldn't afford to buy any. After all, since when were crayons necessities? His conscience pricked him. He had stolen two crayons now, both from the art class, when Mr Pickles had been hopelessly trying to instil some love of painting into a class of rough-heads. What good was drawing? they said. What good was drawing bloody fruit? Yer didn't see pictures in the mills or down the docks.

Micky had watched Mr Pickles struggle manfully, knowing that the teacher would have encouraged him if he had just plucked up the courage to ask for help. But why give his classmates more to rag him about? he thought desperately. Art was for sissies; everyone knew that. So he had stolen the crayons furtively, and hidden the drawings behind the wardrobe, not even showing Kat, because suddenly his sister was preoccupied with the new baby. *New baby*, Micky thought with envy. Everyone would forget about him when the new baby came. He would become even more invisible, even more overlooked.

His momentary self-pity lifted as quickly as it had come. Maybe it would be *good* for him if everyone's attention was elsewhere. It would give him more time to himself to make pictures – and some sort of sense of his world. Then one day he would surprise everyone, he thought, hugging his dream to himself. He would show them his drawings, make stacks of money, and then be able to buy the best paints in England.

Micky clutched the oil crayon in his pocket tightly. He might not be able to speak, but he was beginning to find his own voice, and talk in his own way. He was just doing it on paper, that was all.

EIGHT

Winter came in sharp. The wind bowled down Friargate, tossing leaves aside like ninepins, and making the flag on the town hall flap like a bookie's arm. Head down, Ma Shaw scurried along, muttering to herself. What a flaming idiot Jim was! Another baby on the way, and hardly enough money coming in to keep the rent paid as it was. She thought suddenly of Micky. Poor lad, he would have to get out and earn his keep now. No more schooling for him. He might be only thirteen, but that was old enough for dock or mill work. Coughing hoarsely, Ma shuffled across the road, her shawl pulled over her head to cut out the worst of the November cold. Of course Jim had only told her about the baby when it was too late for anyone to do anything about it. Five and a half months gone – and no option but to have the child now. Not that Anna would have considered aborting it anyway. Oh no, Ma Shaw thought with impatience, she would rather risk her health, or even her life. And for what? After all, Micky had been born with a handicap; why risk another mishap?

Ma thought about her son and glowered. It was true she hadn't caught even the slightest whiff of beer on Jim's breath for months, but there was always that queasy sensation that he could fall from grace at any time. And if he faltered now, it would mean disaster. He would lose his job for sure, and then where would they be? She thought back to the previous hard times and winced.

'Ma!'

She turned to see Silky running up to her, flushed and slightly out of breath, his voice hoarse. 'I've been calling you for two streets . . .'

'I was thinking.'

'You don't think with your ears,' Silky responded deftly, falling into step with his mother. 'Did you hear about Robin Wells?'

She stopped short. Robin Wells had the worst reputation in the worst part of town, a reputation he had worked hard to earn. Having been born into a respectable family, he had stolen from his father and left home at the age of sixteen, making for London. Thirty years later he had returned with a sleek car, a wad of money in his pocket, a whore of a girlfriend on his arm – and a reputation for violence matched only by the likes of Pa Gallager in Hanky Park. His appetite for corruption was formidable, and yet he also had a magnetism about him, a sexual aura that was as unsettling as his vicious reputation. Six feet in height, stocky in build, Robin Wells had the smile of a baby and the eyes of a corpse. There were no weak points in his character, no softness to exploit. He was – and he relished it – feral, conniving, and feared.

'I heard he was back again. Can't keep away from Preston for long,' she said, giving her son a slow look. It was common knowledge that Silky had had a run-in with Robin Wells many years earlier. They had fought over a girl, Silky triumphing, even though the romance hadn't lasted. Stung and humiliated, Wells had responded in typical fashion.

'You watch your back, Shaw,' he had threatened, the hard eyes unreadable. 'One day – when you least expect it – I'll pay you back, you can be sure of that. I'll get you for this.'

With another man, the threat would have been forgotten. Just hot air. But not Robin Wells. When he threatened someone, they stayed threatened – until he made his move.

'Yer worried?' Ma Shaw asked her son, the cold wind making conversation difficult as they walked on.

'He might have forgotten our run-in.'

'You haven't.'

Smiling, Silky reassured his mother. 'I don't think Wells is back in Preston just to settle an old score.'

'So why *is* he back?' Ma asked, unnerved. 'Exactly what has this town got for the likes of Robin Wells?'

Silky wasn't the only one thinking about Robin Wells. In the grimy little office on the dock side, Ivan was brooding over a mug of bitter tea, remembering how Wells had made him look a right fool once. And it had all been Silky's fault . . . Ivan thought of his half-brother and burned. Everyone loved Silky, handsome, charming Silky. If he pulled a gun on a person they would say it was a joke. Bloody Silky could do no wrong . . . Ivan glowered into the mean little fire in the stove, his bony hands wrapped tightly around the tin mug . . . And he was mad about the women, as crazy for them as they were for him. So crazy that he had taken up with Robin Wells's girl.

Flinching, Ivan remembered the furore when the affair became public.

'Are you bleeding mad?' Jim had asked his brother. 'Wells won't let you get away with this.'

Silky was blithely unconcerned. 'She chose me. It's not my fault.'

'Try telling Robin Wells that!' Jim had replied, knowing the man's reputation and genuinely terrified for his brother. 'God, Silky, have you no sense?'

Apparently not, Ivan thought, remembering the events that had followed. Silky had asked his half-brother to mind the tattoo parlour whilst he took the girl out for the day, Ivan only agreeing after Silky had slipped him a few bob. Ivan had immediately shut up shop, turning the sign to CLOSED and settling down with the paper. Before long, he had dozed off, only to be woken a short while later by the banging of a fist on the door.

'COME OUT, YOU BASTARD!' roared a voice. Ivan had jerked to his feet as he realised it was Robin Wells. 'OPEN UP!'

Terrified, Ivan had frantically looked for a place to hide as Wells kept banging. Finally, desperate to escape, he had made for the back door – only to find one of Wells's dead-eyed cohorts waiting to shove him back inside. Wells had then come into the tattoo parlour and stood over the cowering Ivan.

'So, where's your brother?'

'He's out.'

'I can see that, I'm not a fucking idiot,' Wells had replied, picking up the tattoo needle and pressing the floor pedal down with the toe of his shoe. The instrument had whirled into life, and Wells had motioned for Ivan to be put in the chair. Panicked, Ivan had begun to beg, his voice incoherent, urine snaking down the inside of his left leg as he was held down.

'If there's one thing I hate above a man stealing another man's woman . . .' Wells had said, his tone unreadable, 'it's a coward. Now, I want you to give your brother a message—'

'Half-brother,' Ivan had stammered out.

Wells had raised his eyebrows and paused for an instant, then, without warning, he had plunged the tattoo needle into Ivan's forearm. Screaming, Ivan had tried to drag his arm away, but he was held down as Wells pressed the needle down further. The smell of burning flesh had become pungent in the room, Ivan about to faint, Wells's face impassive. Finally he had stepped back, his head on one side as he regarded the crude image he had scratched out on the sobbing man's arm: a matchstick man hanging from a gallows.

'Nice . . .' he had said, as Ivan looked blindly at the blood pouring from the tattoo. 'I never knew I was so gifted.' Then he had leaned down to Ivan: 'Now, when you see your brother, you tell him that Robin Wells can predict the future – then you show him that.'

Trying to shake off the memory, Ivan pulled his sleeve down over his arm. He had shown Silky the tattoo and they – and the rest of the town – had waited for Wells to make his move. But he never did. Instead, Silky had continued to go out with Wells's woman – hard-faced, red-haired, cold-eyed and sexy – until their affair petered out and she left Preston. And *still* Wells hadn't made his move. No one could ever figure out why. Because Silky had been so bold? So unrepentant? Perhaps Robin Wells had even admired him for not running scared? Whatever it was, Ivan had long brooded over the fact that it was he, and not Silky, who bore Wells's mark. And all because of a woman.

Always nervous around women, from that day onwards Ivan had feared them. Couldn't really see why God in all His wisdom had made them. Of course there was the question of children, but if He had thought the matter out more carefully, He could have organised the whole thing without involving females. Taking another sip of his tea, Ivan's thoughts turned to Jim. Immoral, it was, having *another* kid! But how typical of his brother, Ivan decided critically. Everyone knew Jim was on and off the booze all the time. Oh, he was holding down the watchman's job at the moment, but how long would that last? How long before something happened and he was back drinking? And relying on Ma Shaw to dig him out when he got into difficulties? Ivan had never needed digging out; he had looked after himself, even taken the brunt for Silky – and where had it got him?

Still staring into the fire, Ivan frowned. He was lonely, without a woman or kids. Without friends. *And he was the clean-living one!* It was so unfair, he thought, baffled. Why didn't anyone like him? And then he realised why. How could *anyone* love him when he couldn't stand himself? Another thought followed on quickly: one day he would prove himself. He would show the world that there was something special about him. He might be the odd one out now, might be unappealing and diffident, awkward and unwanted. But one day he would have his chance – and he would grab it. *He would be a hero . . .*

Ivan felt a glow inside. It was an old fantasy, but it comforted him. And more importantly, he believed it.

NINE

Wincing, Anna straightened up, then poked the kitchen fire. She wasn't going to let on, but the pregnancy was taking its toll on her. Perhaps she *had* been a little optimistic; after all, Mrs Soley had admonished her in no uncertain terms, while for years, Jim and Ma Shaw had been reminding her of her heart condition, fussing around her as though she was an invalid. But she was stronger than they thought, if perhaps not *that* strong. Lowering herself into a kitchen chair, she decided that she would start to peel the vegetables later, when she had had a little rest.

Slowly she breathed in, then looked around her. The rental on the Amber Street house had risen over the years, God only knew why. Certainly there were no extras to show for it, no running water or one of the indoor toilets she had read about in magazines. In fact she couldn't imagine having anything so luxurious. A mangle was the highlight of her domestic help. Above her on the overhead rack hung Billy's overalls and Jim's shirts. Kat did her own washing now, and as for Micky, he was no trouble, almost embarrassed about having his mother wash his underwear. Anna thought of her younger son and felt guilty. Perhaps she was looking forward to the new baby a little *too* much, but Micky wasn't close to her. He was – to all intents and purposes – more Kat's child than hers.

Suddenly feeling the baby kick inside her, Anna moved her hand over her belly protectively, listening for Kat's footsteps.

Anna might not be able to show her tiredness with anyone else, but with her daughter she could relax. In fact, Kat had automatically taken as much off her mother's shoulders as possible as the pregnancy had continued, and was obviously looking forward to the new baby. Jim might fret and Ma Shaw might glower like a hot coal, but Kat was ecstatic, already knitting jumpers and tiny woollen caps and urging Micky to help repaint the old crib. With perilously little money available, the layette was a poor one, but that didn't matter to Anna. What mattered to her was that her two youngest children were making the baby welcome even before it was born.

Billy was another matter. He had been annoyed from the first, openly challenging his father about the pregnancy, and Jim reacting violently. Ever protective, Billy then asked his mother whether she didn't think she was too old to have another child. Cheek of it! Anna thought, vaguely amused. Too old – at thirty-four? Mind you, it did seem odd to be having a new baby when her eldest son was seventeen, nearly eighteen, and a full-grown man.

A sudden pain made Anna wince, her hands moving over her stomach again. She would have to be careful, but she knew that the baby would be all right. That this child would be perfect, and that against the odds they would both survive. Her certainty was unshakeable. People might think she was fragile, but Anna was a survivor. She had come through a gruelling childhood to become a wife and mother. Her children loved her and her husband loved her. And she also knew that Jim wanted this baby. How did she know? Because he'd been off the drink since the day she told him she was pregnant.

'So go on, guess!' Billy said, his hand raised high above his head, Micky trying to jump up and catch it. 'Guess!'

'I'm not guessing,' Kat replied, teasing him, 'and I'm not jumping up and down like a monkey in the street.'

Billy pulled a wry face. 'You don't want what I've got, then?'

'Not if I have to leap up and down for it.'

'Yer've got all grown-up all of a sudden,' Billy replied, tucking his parcel into his pocket and looping one arm around his sister and the other round Micky. 'Maybe my little sister isn't so little any more.'

Kat raised her eyebrows loftily. 'I'm a young woman now.'

'Yer a moron!' Billy said, squeezing her tightly. 'Are you in love or something?'

She jabbed him in the ribs. 'NO!'

'But yer blushing!' Billy replied, laughing and facing her. 'So who's the lucky man? Do Ma and Pa know that there's going to be a wedding in the family, as well as a new baby?'

'Oh shut up, Billy!' she snapped, walking off.

Winking at Micky, Billy ran after her, taking the package out of his pocket and waving it under her nose. 'Go on, guess what it is.'

'A camel.'

'Yer not trying,' he teased her, pulling off the wrapping and opening the lid of a small container. At once Micky leaned forward to sniff the contents, and Kat pulled a face.

'God, what is that!'

'Caviar,' Billy said, looking smug. 'I got it off one of the ships. A sailor gave it to me, said it were right expensive. Only the richest people in the world can afford it.'

'What do you do with it?'

'Black-lead the grate,' Billy replied smartly. 'Yer *eat* it, stupid, it's a . . . delicacy.'

Unimpressed, Micky pulled a face at his sister, then both of them looked at Billy as Kat said blithely, 'OK, if you eat it, *you* try it first.'

'Nah, you can go first,' he said magnanimously, not fancying the pungently salty fish roe. 'Seeing as how yer a young lady.'

She pushed his hand away. 'Oh no, you must have the first

go, Billy! It's only fair, you got it. Micky and I will try it after you.'

Kat and Micky stood watching, arms folded, as their brother stuck his forefinger into the caviar, took a lump out and then put it very slowly in his mouth. His eyes widened, his tongue rolling the caviar around his mouth.

'So?' Kat asked. 'Is it wonderful?'

He was thinking he might be sick, but he wasn't going to admit it and swallowed noisily instead. 'Great . . . you try it now, Micky.'

Happily Micky took some and put it in his mouth, his expression altering from hope to horror.

'Now you,' Billy said, offering the tin to Kat.

Defiantly she took some, her eyes watering at the taste. Billy laughed as Micky spat his caviar into the drain, but Kat swallowed manfully, facing up to her brother. She wasn't going to give Billy the satisfaction.

'Delicious . . .' she stammered at last, the taste clinging to her lips and throat and making her queasy.

His expression was glassy. '*You like it?*'

'I LOVE it!' she said, with real feeling. 'I could eat the whole lot. In fact, I could eat it every day, all day, for the rest of my life.'

'Shit,' Billy replied, disappointed, handing her the tin and walking off, Micky trailing behind him.

Kat was just wondering what to do with the noisome article when she rounded the corner into Amber Street and saw Horace Armitage.

'Hey, Mr Armitage,' she called out. 'What are you doing?'

Outside The Horse and Cart, the landlord was painting the pub door red, panting heavily in the cold sunshine as he paused and turned to Kat. He was – like others recently – surprised by the change in her. No longer a little girl, she had grown several inches in height and rustled up some impressive curves. In fact, even to an elderly widower like Horace Armitage, Kat was stunning.

'I thought I'd paint the door for Christmas. Make it festive like.'

'Will it dry in all this cold?'

'I never thought of that,' Horace replied, looking back at his handiwork. 'I just thought it would be cheery. I'm having a bit of a singalong on Friday; you fancy coming, Kat? There'll be lots of other ladies there.'

Kat would have jumped at the chance, but knew her mother wouldn't approve. Even though The Horse and Cart was next door, it was still a pub, and respectable girls didn't go into public houses alone. Besides, any reminder of drink might send Jim back on the bottle, and that would be nothing short of disastrous. But the idea of a singalong appealed to Kat. She had found working for the effeminate Mr Unwin no hard task, provided she listened to his gossip and was nice to the customers, but she was bored. Even the impending birth of the baby was getting problematic, her mother relying on her more every day. And then there was Micky, suddenly holding back from her . . . Kat frowned, staring hard at Horace Armitage's door. She and Micky had never had any secrets before, but for the last couple of weeks her brother had been remote, almost distant. She had questioned him, of course. Was he being bullied at school? Was he ill? But all her queries had been shrugged off. And then she had wondered if Micky was jealous about the baby . . .

Her gaze travelled up and down the newly painted door. It would never dry in the cold, she thought, wondering how she could manage to get to the singalong on Friday. Maybe she could ask Billy to go with her. Of course he wasn't legally old enough to drink, but he could pass for twenty anywhere – and besides, no one would argue with him.

'Well, can you come, luv, or not?'

'I don't think so, Mr Armitage,' Kat replied, suddenly pausing as a tall young man came into view. He was walking as though he was in a great hurry, his thick dark hair blowing in the wind, his head slightly bowed.

'Damn that,' Horace, said, flicking off some particles that had blown up and stuck to the new paint. Then he glanced down the street. 'It's the landlord's son come early. He's here for the rent.'

'I thought *you* were the landlord of The Horse and Cart?'

'Nay, luv,' Horace replied, shaking his head. 'I couldn't afford to own this place, I've just got the licence. The Pitts own the pub, this street and the three around it. Surely you know about old Mr Pitt?'

Kat nodded. 'Yeah.' She knew about his son too.

Flushing, she glanced down as Andrew approached them, smiling. Smoothing back his thick hair with his hands, he glanced at the red door and made a face.

'That's bright, Mr Armitage. Did my father approve the change?'

Wrong-footed, the publican stammered, 'I didn't think . . . I mean . . .'

'It's only paint,' Kat said, her natural protective instincts roused. 'Surely no one could object to that? Not at Christmas?'

Andrew Pitt was amused. At first he had been dreading taking over his father's rounds, but the old man had been bad with his chest since October and was in no mood to walk the streets, even his *own* streets. So he had dispatched his son and heir to patrol the Pitt kingdom. Gather the rents, check the premises, see if there'd been any damage, fighting or fires. Then come back and tell him all about it. *And any scandal you overhear. I like the scandal best . . .* Longing for the warmth of the office, Andrew had, nevertheless, set about the task. There had been no damage, fires or fights to report. Nothing interesting at all – except for the blazing red pub door he was now looking at. And the girl standing beside it. The one he had spoken to before, the strange girl with the interesting face.

'I didn't say my father *wouldn't* approve . . .'

'I think it cheers up the street,' Kat went on gamely.

Andrew smiled. 'I like it too.'

'This is Katherine Shaw,' Horace said, interrupting them politely. 'She lives next door.'

'I know. I know all the Shaws,' Andrew said, not quite managing to cover the fact that he knew their whole history. 'I heard your mother was having another child?'

Kat nodded, then suddenly went on the defensive. 'My father's got a good job now. He's nightwatchman down at the docks. He's very well thought of.'

She realised then that she was making a fool of herself, her fifteen-year-old confidence fading in the presence of this rich young man. Because he obviously *was* rich; he had the buffed leather shoes, the well-cut suit, the overcoat that fitted like a second skin. He might not be handsome, as Silky was, but Andrew Pitt had what Kat knew the Shaws would never possess – old money. And the poise that went with it.

Unaware of Kat's turmoil, Horace Armitage was wondering if Andrew Pitt would report the painting of the pub door to Old Man Pitt – and what it would mean if he did. Suddenly his innocent attempt at the festive spirit looked like downright stupidity. Pitt wasn't a hard man; perhaps his age had slowed him down a little, made him a tad more tolerant. But could the same be said for his son? He would be keen, eager to make an impression – perhaps eager to make an example of something like a badly painted door?

'I could change it, Mr Pitt . . .'

'But that would be a shame,' Kate said, turning to Horace and then looking back to Andrew. 'Who cares about the colour of a door?'

She sounded light-hearted, but Kat knew how life could turn on such trifles. A stern landlord could evict a family on a whim, knowing full well they had no redress. There had been a time when the notorious Robin Wells had owned some flats and terrorised his tenants. When you were poor, with no chance of legal appeal, and no influence, landlords had total power over you.

Kat knew all this only too well, but wouldn't be cowed. She might be fascinated by him, but who was this Andrew Pitt? Just some lucky man born into money. What right had he – with his wavy hair and expensive clothes – to stand in judgement?

'It doesn't matter, Kat,' Horace Armitage said hurriedly. 'It would be no problem to change it.'

Imploringly, Kat turned back to Andrew. 'Don't make him do it, please.'

Amused, Andrew studied the girl in front of him. She was very young, but interesting. Someone he would definitely tell his father about. To think of such a treasure in dingy Amber Street . . . By nature kind, he was more than willing to back down – but something stopped him. He liked the girl's nerve, and wanted to play her along for a while.

'My father would make Mr Armitage repaint the door.'

'But you're not your father,' Kat replied, her tone even.

'No, but I might be like him.'

'I don't think so,' Kat said, taking in a breath and trying to keep her nerve. 'I think you're a nicer man.'

Surprised, Andrew was momentarily taken aback. Something in her manner was so open, it touched him. Another woman would have used her charm to flirt her way out of trouble, but this girl used her honesty. He admired that.

'All right, keep it red.' He smiled at Kat and then turned back to Mr Armitage. 'But repaint it after Christmas, you hear? I don't want anyone thinking I'm a soft touch.'

The incident stayed with Andrew for a long time afterwards. Suddenly the drudgery of the streets didn't seem quite so tedious, or depressing. Of course he wasn't interested in Kat Shaw romantically; she was probably no more than sixteen and he was twenty-three and in love with someone else – but he liked her guts.

It was almost an hour later that he arrived home. Throwing down his coat and rent books, Andrew walked into the study, skirting his father, who was asleep in the armchair. As the only son, he knew that in time he would inherit the property and commercial offices, and that he was being groomed for his eventual inheritance on the streets. Learning the hard way, Old Man Pitt would have said . . . There had been no featherbedding for Andrew. His father and mother might be devoted to him, but they both knew how much character meant in life – and how a lack of it could lead to disaster.

Which made Andrew think suddenly of Joan Fairchild, the woman he was in love with. The woman he intended to marry. Only he hadn't got around to proposing, too scared she would turn him down. Because Andrew Pitt, for all his background and composure, was besotted with Joan and clumsily in love. The daughter of the owner of Fairchild Engineering Ltd, Joan had the clothes to make her pretty, the money to make her sweet and the parents to spoil her. Vivacious and amusing, she was popular for her looks and for her father's fortune. Everyone wanted Joan around because she was good company and rich. Because of that, the choices in her life were endless. There were no restrictions on anything. What she wanted, she got. Her future was organised to perfection by meticulous, indulgent parents. Joan would marry Andrew Pitt, and the two families – with the two thriving family businesses – would be united. Miss Joan Fairchild would become Mrs Andrew Pitt. There was just one problem – Joan didn't love him.

And the more she didn't give a damn, the more Andrew cared. He wondered fleetingly how it was that his friends could have easy, happy, reciprocal romances, but not him. Not that he suspected Joan of having given her affections elsewhere. Or of fooling around; she wasn't that type of girl and certainly not stupid enough to ruin her chances. She just wasn't in love with him. Damn it, he thought helplessly, why couldn't he make her love him? Why couldn't that flaming giddiness he felt infect her? Why was it that he was clumsy, tongue-tied and gauche when she was around – and she was as cool as lemonade? Not unkind, just sisterly.

He winced at the thought. Was there anything more mortifying for a man to have a woman think of him as a *brother*? Wasn't that the most crucifying, belittling impression to make? That he had absolutely no physical appeal whatsoever?

'What *are* you doing, standing there like a lost sheep?'

Andrew turned to his mother, shrugging. 'I was thinking about Joan.'

Ivy Pitt sighed, impatient and sympathetic at the same time, her well-corseted body unbending in its pastel dress. Andrew could never remember seeing his mother without her hair done and her figure controlled, drawn in, and up, by corsetieres and dressmakers. Even her kindly maternal caresses in his youth had had the embrace of steel about them.

'Have you asked her to marry you?'

'Do I look like I have?' he replied. 'No, not yet . . . Anyway, what if she says no?'

'What if she says yes?' Ivy replied, taking a seat and studying her son.

She had to admit that she had played a blinder with Andrew. Looks had never really been her strong suit, and as for Duncan, even in his youth her husband had had a limited appeal. But Andrew was different; really rather engaging in a refreshing, self-deprecating way. His cocky friends might brag about their conquests, but Andrew was always discreet. He did, however, lack one vital thing – swagger. Now Ivy had been alive long enough to know that that was what women liked. They might marry money or stability; they might choose steady men as husbands. But the ones who made a woman lie awake at night were always the men with nerve. Did arrogance give a man sexual allure? Ivy wondered, knowing she could never ask Duncan for his opinion; her husband probably thought that allure was something you caught badgers with.

'Perhaps I should wait a bit longer,' Andrew said, cutting into his mother's thoughts. 'Joan's not in love with me. You know that, and so do I.'

'I blame her mother.'

Andrew knew all too well where the conversation was going. Joan's mother, Gwen, had been best friends with Ivy many years earlier. They had been inseparable and later they had dated two friends – Duncan Pitt and Gareth Fairchild – and enjoyed many mutual evenings out. Romance had turned to love for both of them, both girls nabbing eligible men, the playing field even. Until the day the very thin Gwen had made a comment about Ivy being plump. At once, the rot had set in. From then onward, Gwen was the enemy. And Ivy was in corsets for life.

'What has Joan's *mother* got to do with all of this?'

'Oh, she'll be saying things to Joan, trying to turn the girl's head. Talking about us.'

'But Mrs Fairchild *wants* me to marry her daughter,' Andrew said patiently. 'Why would she cut off her nose to spite her own face?'

'Probably because she'd look better without that beak,' Ivy retorted, her tone razor-sharp. 'Anyway, Andrew, I don't know why you brought that woman up; we were talking about Joan.'

Andrew didn't bother arguing. 'Perhaps if I stepped back, ignored her for a while?'

'Oh, I don't think that would work,' Ivy replied, her back as straight as a down-spout. 'She might meet someone else. You'll have to woo her, buy her a present.'

'But I've bought her loads of things and that doesn't seem to work,' Andrew replied, sitting beside his mother and dropping his voice to a conspiratorial whisper. 'What about you and Dad?'

'What about us?'

'Well, how did he make you fall in love with him?'

Dreamily, Ivy thought back. 'He was very romantic.'

'Like how?'

'He wrote . . .' to Andrew's amazement, he could see his mother blushing, 'poetry.'

This was hard to digest. Andrew blinked slowly as he thought of his harassed, overworked, ever-anxious father. He had seen early pictures of Duncan and knew that he *had* once been young – with a full head of hair – but the fact that his business-minded, bookworm father could actually have written *poetry* was a revelation.

'Was it good?'

'No, terrible,' Ivy replied frankly. 'But that didn't matter. It was the fact that he had taken the time to write it for me.'

'So you think I should write some poetry for Joanie?'

'It might work.'

'What if it doesn't?'

'She'll laugh at you.'

'Great,' Andrew said shortly. 'That's all I need.'

'But if it *does* work,' Ivy replied, winking impishly, 'she might find herself falling in love with you.'

Andrew considered this for a long moment. 'I'm not sure I *can* write poetry.'

'Then crib something from someone else! God knows there are enough love poems to filch ideas from.'

'Isn't that cheating?'

'Oh, really, Andrew! You'll never get ahead in life with that attitude.' Standing up, Ivy moved to the door, then turned. 'Steer clear of Tennyson, though, and Keats. I had a terrible letting-down with Keats once.'

TEN

Tucking his latest drawings into his jacket pocket, Micky made for the school gates. For the second time that week, Kat wasn't waiting for him. He didn't mind really, he hardly needed to be walked home, it was just that he missed hearing about her day and laughing when she mimicked Mr Unwin. She was mischievous but kind about the grocer. As she was kind about everyone – unless they did her family a wrong turn. Walking on, Micky found himself frowning, anxious suddenly. His small enclosed world – although at times hard – was reasonably safe. His home, his school, his family. But before long, all that was going to change, and he felt weak with the dread of it . . . He thought of the conversation he had overheard the previous evening when Ma Shaw had called round. She had been whispering, but her strong voice had carried up the stairwell to where Micky was listening. He knew he shouldn't eavesdrop, but sometimes it was the only way to find out what was going on. Most of the time people protected him, made allowances. But not Ma Shaw; she wouldn't have made allowances for God.

'Micky will have to start work sooner than we thought,' she had said. 'Yer going to need another wage coming in, Anna.'

'Not yet,' his mother had countered bravely. 'He doesn't have to leave school for another six months.'

'Why keep him on? Poor lad can't amount to anything—'

'Ma! Keep your voice down!' Anna had admonished her mother-in-law. 'Yer don't want the boy to hear you, do you?'

'Yer soft with him,' Ma Shaw had replied, a little less sternly in the face of Anna's spirited defence. 'Micky could work down the docks, or in the mill. They're looking for a lad in the weavers' shed . . .'

'It's not what I want for him.'

'I know that, luv, but the poor boy can't do anything else,' Ma Shaw had responded, her tone sympathetic. 'Face it, Anna, we'd be lucky to land him a good job in the mill with his drawback. We have to be realistic about it; no point giving the lad false hope. It's not like he's anything special to offer.'

Pausing, Micky felt in his jacket pocket, his fingers closing over the drawings. His grandmother didn't know what she was talking about. No one knew about his talent. They just thought of him as poor Micky, but he had something extra. And one day they would all know . . . But his spirits plunged suddenly as he walked on. Talent he might have, but it wasn't enough to keep him out of the mill or off the docks. And that was where he was bound for now. Of course Billy would look out for him, and his father would be there if he ended up at the Albert Edward, but if it was the mill . . . God, Micky thought desperately, he'd be on his own there: runt of the litter again. Pushed around, bullied.

Deep in thought, Micky stepped off the kerb without looking, then heard the blast of a car horn. Jumping back, he lost his footing and fell on to the pavement, the car missing him by only inches. Shaken, he was just clambering back to his feet when a man got out of the car and approached him.

'Why don't you watch where you're going!'

Cowering, Micky looked at the stranger. The striking face was vaguely familiar.

Sorry, he signed.

'You what?' the man said, grabbing Micky by the collar and shaking him slightly. 'What's the matter with your voice?'

Wriggling in the man's grasp, Micky pointed to his mouth and then shook his head.

A slow look of understanding came into the man's eyes. 'Dumb, hey? There's only one dumb boy round here that I know of. You Micky Shaw?'

Dread swept over Micky. He knew enough about cruelty to sense it in a person, and he could feel the brutality of this man immediately.

'Well, are you Micky Shaw?'

He nodded.

'Silky Shaw's nephew?'

He nodded again.

'I know your uncle,' the man said, letting go of Micky's collar and smiling wolfishly. 'We go back a long way.'

Micky was feeling clammy, fear making him sweat as the man kept talking.

'Looking at you, it seems like times are hard. Not exactly dressed and ready to impress, are you? I bet you could use a shilling, hey?'

Micky didn't respond.

'Half a crown?'

Still, Micky didn't move. He couldn't. He was mesmerised by the man like a snake would be mesmerised by an alligator. He understood one thing, and one thing only – he was terrified.

'I'll tell you what, Micky Shaw, you do something for me and you can have this half-crown.' He waved the coin in front of the boy's wide-open eyes. 'I just want you to run an errand. Now that's worth half a crown of anyone's money, isn't it?'

Micky continued to stare at him.

'I'll take your silence as agreement. Now you go to your uncle's and tell Silky Shaw that an old friend of his is back in town. Tell him Robin Wells said hello.' He smiled coldly. 'You got that? Robin Wells said hello.'

About to put the coin into Micky's hand, Wells suddenly

noticed the pieces of paper poking out of the boy's jacket pocket and grabbed them. Panicked, Micky tried to snatch them back, but Wells laughed as he held them out of the boy's reach. Slowly he unfolded the pages and then paused, his glamorous smile fading. The images were crude, but clever. He even recognised the grocer, Gregory Unwin, from his caricature.

Surprised, Wells looked down at the cringing boy, his tone pure ice.

'You'll not make yourself any friends with these, lad. People don't like being made a fool of. They don't like being laughed at – especially by some creepy little mute. You should know that only too well, you being a dummy.' He glanced back at the drawings, then burst out laughing as he came to the caricature of Ma Shaw. 'Now, if I were to show your grandmother this – this *is* your grandmother, I remember the old bitch very well – what d'you think she'd say? How d'you think she'd feel about her little grandson drawing such a cruel picture of her? You should be ashamed, Dummy Shaw, you should really.'

Distressed, Micky tried to grab the drawings again, but Wells held them out of reach, taunting him. 'You could upset your gran, Micky, break her heart. If the old cow had one.' He paused, tucking the drawings into his own pocket, Micky watching him helplessly. 'Now run along and deliver that message to your uncle.'

Hesitating, Micky stepped back, then put out his hand, pleading with his eyes for Wells to give him the drawings. But instead Wells put the half-crown into Micky's palm and then walked off, whistling.

Dragging on his cigarette, Billy sighed. He was – he was only too willing to admit – a happy man. Not angry about anything. At peace with the world, in fact. He could see the vaulted roof of the warehouse overhead, the stacks of wood and timber piled up around him, Jane Rimmer resting her head on his shoulder. Not the best place to make love, but not the worst either, and it was wonderfully quiet. Billy took another drag of his cigarette. He could tell from her regular breathing that Jane was asleep and gently nuzzled the top of her head, surprised by his own tenderness. Now this was more like it, Billy thought, this was living. Not working, or being chivvied about on Amber Street, but here, with his own woman and his own life. Nothing else. His own little world, banked around with Siberian pine and Russian oak, his little calm hollow of tranquillity which was his alone. Alone, with only his girl to share it with.

Outside, Billy could hear a ship's hooter sounding eerily through the November fog. Soon it would be Christmas, but the timber deliveries would keep coming up the River Ribble, the Albert Edward kept busy over the holidays, the docksides manned round the clock. But no one would come into this warehouse, Billy knew only too well. This one was stocked up, no room for another plank to be added. Just the little space in the centre, hardly six feet by twelve, left for Billy Shaw and his girl . . . Sighing, Jane moved against him, her arm lying across his chest. All her taunts about Billy having to give his wage to his mother were forgotten. Billy had had a taste of being independent, and he liked it. After all, he reasoned, he had won the money on a dog race. It was his to spend how he wanted . . . In truth, he had felt a momentary pang of guilt, but it hadn't lasted, and when he had given Jane her present she had been so pleased. Billy smiled to himself. To think that winning on a dog had got him lying with Jane Rimmer. That was what money did for you, got you respected, got you women.

Not that he was too concerned about other women, just Jane. His uncle might change his girlfriends every six months, but that was Silky, he was like that. Billy was made of different stuff. At least he was now. The realisation surprised him, but he had fallen hard for Jane Rimmer and was determined to keep her. He had given his heart to her and no one else . . . He nuzzled Jane's hair again, feeling an uncharacteristic stillness inside. All his tension and aggression had gone; as though their lovemaking had released a steam of anger inside him. His fists had uncurled, his spine relaxing, the muscles of his torso and face losing their tautness. For once, Billy Fists wasn't in the mood for fighting, and wondered if – he smiled inwardly at the thought – he was falling in love.

Outside, the ship's hooter sounded again, the melancholic noise echoing in amongst the banks of Russian timber and skimming the still black water of the Albert Edward. Soon the cold hours would settle over the warehouses, night foxes skirting the vast coils of steel anchor chains and the crates. And overhead the dormant cranes would loom ominously out of the mist, their sleeping heads drooping down, like giants on watch.

But for now, there was only Billy and his girl. Only a man in love with a woman, only the promise of a present to believe in. And a future sweeter than the past.

Having finished work late, Kat was surprised to see Micky up in the centre of town, looking upset and hovering around Tulketh Street. Crossing the road, she approached him. Micky backed off as she came closer, and surprised, she caught hold of his arm.

'What's the matter, luv?'

He looked at her, then shook his head, turning away. Anxious, she tried again.

'Micky, look at me, what is it? Has someone done something to you?' She studied his face, knowing she was on the right track. 'Did you have a bad day in school?'

He shook his head violently.

'So was it something after school?'

He nodded, signing to her hurriedly. She watched his

hands, then motioned for him to slow down. 'What? Do it slower, so I can follow. What d'you mean – *you can't tell me*. What is it, Micky? Come on, trust me, you know you can always trust me. What are you doing here? Why aren't you home?'

He didn't respond.

Surprised, Kat looked around at the shops that surrounded them: a pawnbroker's leaning against a bookie's, and a grimy hardware store barred at the windows and uninviting. A place everyone knew was owned by the biggest liar in Preston. All of them were already closed for the night – apart from a light burning in the window of Silky's tattoo parlour. So *that* was who Micky had been coming to see.

She turned back to her brother. 'Did you come to see Silky?' Micky flinched, and Kat pressed him. 'It's OK. Did you want to see him about something?'

Slowly Micky took the half-crown out of his pocket and showed it to her.

'What's that for?'

Hurriedly Micky moved his hands, signalling, Kat watching him intently, her expression bewildered. 'You've got a message for Silky?'

He nodded.

'What message?'

Micky signed the answer twice. The second time, Kat understood.

'Robin Wells said hello?'

At once, she paled. The shadow of Robin Wells had loomed over Preston for many years, and especially over the Shaw family. In whispers she had heard about the feud between Wells and Silky, and the threat that had been issued – and never fulfilled. Kat thought of Ivan, of the violent, crude tattoo on her uncle's arm that had never faded. Just as Ivan's fear had never lessened. All through her childhood, Robin Wells had been the bogeyman, used to scare her into obedience, then later regarded with awe. But that was just what he had been until this moment – a bogeyman, a creature of stories and nightmares. Some dark force with no reality. Until now.

Uneasy, Kat clutched his brother's hand. She could see how terrified her brother was. How typical of Wells to pick on Micky. How typical and how despicable. Catching her brother's arm, she hurried him over to her uncle's shop and knocked loudly on the door. Silky opened almost immediately, smiling as he showed them in, although he was more than a little surprised to see an anxious Kat with a clearly terrified Micky following behind her.

'This is a surprise,' he said kindly. 'I just have to finish off a customer and I'll be with you.'

Gesturing for them to sit down, Silky moved back to his client, a wiry man, stripped to the waist, sitting astride the chair as Silky tattooed his back. Having never seen her uncle at work before – or a semi-naked man – Kat was fascinated, flushing as the client winked at her. Avoiding his gaze, she couldn't, however, help noticing the spread eagle on the man's chest, and the skull and crossbones on his left arm. And underneath, the name GORDONIA.

'It's a ship.'

'Pardon?' Kat replied, Micky shrinking further behind her.

'The *Gordonia*,' the man went on to explain. 'It's a ship. Been coming backwards and forwards from this port for years. I served me apprenticeship on 'er.' He winced as Silky began to tattoo the upper part of his back. 'We went up to Siberia before winter last year, got caught just before the real cold came down. But it were so bleeding bitter even then that if yer didn't wear gloves, the skin on yer hands would stick to the railings.' He glanced over his shoulder warningly. 'Go easy, Silky, that's hurting.'

'You have to suffer for beauty, you know that,' Silky replied wryly, dabbing at the tattoo to take away the blood.

Fascinated, Kat watched her uncle, remembering what Ma Shaw had told her about the tattoo parlour. After Ma's grandfather had died, her father, Percy Clegg, had inherited the parlour. Apparently he had been tall, stringy and mean as a water rat. All the haphazard charm of the business had changed the day Percy took over in 1871. Painting the windows black so that only the top third was clear, he had printed TATTOO PARLOUR – QUALITY ARTWORK on the glass. And underneath he had written in smaller letters: No Drunks.

'I remember growing up over the shop, in that cramped flat smelling of damp,' Ma Shaw had told Kat many times, the recall sour. 'My mother bad-tempered; moody old Percy crouched like a suited crab over his customers muttering to himself . . .'

Apparently Percy had never been a man to come out directly with what he thought; instead he had mumbled his grievances into his shirt front. And although the dockers and factory workers were his chief customers, Percy loathed them with a passion. But he was a gifted tattooist and his thin fingers, stained with blue and green ink, worked adeptly and quickly.

'Mind yer, if any poor sod cried out in pain, my father would step back and glower at them,' Ma had gone on. 'Yer've never seen anything like it. He were *terrifying* in his funereal black, his sleeves protected with white cuff guards.'

Kat remembered one evening when Ma Shaw had had a beer. It was the first time Kat had ever since her grandmother drink, and although it didn't affect her adversely, it made her unusually confiding, almost wistful. Relaxed, she had told her granddaughter even more about her past. About how she had been a tomboy, smashing the window of Mrs Grimsby's tripe shop. But although she had been good-looking, the lads had never tried anything on with Ma – she was too terrified to let anyone take liberties, because God only knew what would have happened to her if she had come home in trouble.

'It were a grim place, that flat,' she had gone on. 'I used to wait fer my father to light the gas lamps in the tattoo parlour before going upstairs to dodge him. Always kept out of his way. Miserable sod . . . Then my mother died and I were left alone with him.' Ma Shaw had stared into her glass bleakly. 'From then on, I had to starch those blasted shirt protectors, bleach the towels, scrub the lino in the shop, and empty the bucket under the tattoo chair – the one filled with bloodstained cloths and sometimes vomit . . .'

Kat was staring at that bucket now. But Silky's was clean, covered with a white cloth, no echo of Percy's dark, melancholic reign.

'Tom Shaw came into the tattoo parlour one late winter afternoon and winked at me,' Ma Shaw had continued, smiling wryly, 'and I fell in love. On the spot, in that instant. Three months later I married him. And my father didn't attend the wedding. Not that I bloody cared.'

Curious, Kat looked around her, trying to match her grandmother's memories to the present. The parlour had changed since Percy's day, and Silky had added his own kind of north-west glamour. Portraits of movie stars like Douglas Fairbanks hung alongside photographs of tattooed men, whilst underneath advertisements for Brylcreem and Black Cat cigarettes hung edge to edge, like monochrome washing. And along the wall at the back Silky's designs were displayed. Kat studied them with interest. Her gaze settled on a pattern of a pair of wings, then moved to a snake curled around a staff. To her surprise, she found them unexpectedly beautiful.

Turning to Micky, she pointed to one impressive design. *Bull's head*, she signed to him. *Good, hey*?

Although obviously uneasy, he signed back, *Clever*.

In the chair, the client was watching the exchange, intrigued. So intrigued that he barely winced as Silky began to tattoo his left shoulder blade. Still looking at the designs, Kat stood up and began to walk around, Micky's gaze never leaving her. Throughout her childhood she had often visited

Silky, but had always gone in at the back. It had been drilled into her by her father that the tattoo parlour wasn't any place for a female. When she had asked why, he had mumbled something about it being common. He didn't elaborate any further, but Kat had noticed that neither her father nor Silky had tattoos. Apparently it was something beneath even the likes of them.

But now her interest had been caught and she was curious. Slowly she continued to walk around, glancing into the back room off the parlour and then moving closer to the chair where the customer was sitting. As he leaned over his client, Silky's floppy dark hair fell over his forehead, his slim arms exposed where he had rolled up his sleeves. And in his hand he held the tattoo needle delicately, with an impressive, unexpected dexterity.

'Does it hurt?' Kat asked suddenly, out of the blue.

The customer glanced up at her. 'Not bad. Yer get used to it.'

'Does it last?'

'I bloody hope so,' the sailor replied, laughing.

Unable to resist for a second longer, Kat leaned a little closer towards the man to study the tattoo. Although surprised, Silky said nothing and carried on working, and Kat found herself admiring her uncle's work. The drawing of the panther was amazing, the animal's crouching form taking shape amongst the running ink and bloodied skin. Pleased by her interest, Silky dabbed at the tattoo, the image emerging sharply for an instant before the blood began to flow again.

'It's incredible.'

'Good, hey?' the sailor asked, grinning over his shoulder. 'I'm glad the first to see it is a pretty girl.'

'That's my niece you're talking to; mind your manners!' Silky teased him.

'She'll be married soon,' the man replied, looking at Kat again. 'The pretty ones are first to go.'

Dabbing away the blood again, Silky stood back. 'That's

it for tonight,' he said, helping his customer to straighten up. 'Sleep on your stomach and I'll see you next week to finish off.'

Slowly the sailor stood up, pulling on his shirt and jacket and wrapping a scarf around his neck. Finally putting on his cap, he paid Silky, then turned back to Kat.

'Yer've lucky eyes. Cat's eyes.' He spat on his hand, then offered it to her. About to intervene, Silky watched, impressed, as an unfazed Kat took the sailor's hand and shook it. 'Aren't I the lucky one?' the man asked, smiling and walking out, Silky locking the door behind him.

'Before you say another word,' he said hurriedly, 'don't mention any of this to your mother. Jesus! She'd go mad to think of you seeing half-naked men.'

Kat rolled her eyes and beckoned Micky over. 'My brother's got a message for you.'

Surprised, Silky turned to his nephew and ruffled his hair. 'That so, lad? What is it?'

Kat answered for her brother. 'Robin Wells said hello.'

She could see her uncle tense and waited for a long instant before Silky spoke again. 'You saw him?'

'He nearly knocked Micky over.'

Silky turned to the boy anxiously. 'Are you OK?'

Micky nodded, but kept his gaze averted.

'Did he hurt you? Micky! Did Robin Wells hurt you?'

Micky shook his head, then wandered off into the back of the shop. A moment later they could hear him putting water into the kettle and setting it on to boil.

'What happened?'

Kat shrugged. 'Micky just said that Wells gave him half a crown to give you the message. But I think there's more to it. Micky looked terrified when I saw him, and he's been acting oddly ever since.'

'If that bastard even touched him . . .'

'I don't think he touched him,' Kat replied, 'I think he *said* something. Something that frightened him.'

Dropping his voice, Silky turned to the work table next to the chair and began to tidy up.

'That shit . . .'

'Why send a message?' Kat asked. 'Why didn't Wells come here himself?'

'He likes to drag things out, keep the suspense going,' Silky replied, dropping the end of the drill into some water. The metal gleamed for a moment before the blood muddied the bowl. 'Did he say where he was staying?'

'You're not going to see him!'

'I'm not afraid of Robin Wells, and I want to give him a message of my own – keep away from my bloody family.'

Impressed, Kat studied her handsome uncle. She found it difficult for an instant to imagine that a man as sleek as Silky could be tough. But tough he was. Ivan was bigger, her father was wirier, and Billy was the meanest fighter, but Silky had a quiet menace about him. A steel under the charm that was unexpected and deadly. If you wanted a bloody nose, take on Billy Fists, but if you wanted a knife in the guts from a source you suspected the least, Silky was your man.

Kat wondered then if that was why Robin Wells had kept his distance, waiting for the moment when he stood his best chance. Because in her uncle he had met his match.

'I don't want you involved,' Silky said, motioning for Micky to come towards him. 'What else did Wells say to you?'

Micky shook his head.

'Nothing,' Kat interpreted.

'So what else did he do?'

Micky paled. Kat saw the response and so did Silky. 'Hey, kid, listen to me. There's just me and your sister here and neither of us is going to repeat anything you say. All right? It stays *here*, inside these walls, and goes no further. What did Wells do, Micky?'

There was a long hesitation. Finally Micky reached into his pocket and brought out a slip of paper. His hands were sweating so much that some of the pencil marks were smudged when he handed it over to his uncle. Frowning, Silky looked at the drawing, then passed it over to Kat.

'Did you do this, Micky?'

He nodded, terror in his eyes. Surprised, Kat glanced back at the rough piece of paper. On it there was a caricature of their father, holding his nightwatchman's lamp aloft. Jim's expression was perfectly observed – the look of a good man blundering through life. And a bottle of beer was tucked into the back pocket of his trousers.

Silently, Micky began to sob. Kat put her arms around him and laughed.

'But it's good!' she said, holding him at arm's length and nodding. 'It's so real. So like him. Why didn't you tell me you could do this, Micky? You're a clever boy, a very clever boy. To think you had this talent all along and never said anything.' She could see him flushing with pleasure and hurried on. 'You have a gift, Micky, a real gift.'

'She's right. Looks like I'm not the only artistic one in the family,' Silky said, looking at the drawing again. 'This *is* good, Micky. Have you done others?'

Urgently the boy signalled to Kat. She understood and turned back to her uncle.

'He had some others. But Robin Wells took them.'

Micky was still signalling, his hands moving so fast that Kat had to concentrate to translate accurately. 'What, Micky? What about Ma Shaw? Oh,' she said, suddenly understanding what her brother was afraid of. 'Don't worry, luv, she won't see it! And if she did, she'd know it was a joke.'

'Want a bet?' Silky said drily.

Suddenly Micky's face fell.

'What is it?'

I did others, he signed to his sister. *Mr Unwin, Mr Pickles and Uncle Ivan.*

Laughing, she hugged him to her. 'So what? They were just drawings.'

They would be cross, Micky signalled back.

'No!' Kat told him firmly, 'If they had any sense at all, they would see that you had talent. They would know what we now know – that you're gifted. God, Micky, you could be an artist. You could make your name with this ability. And that's what *really* matters now.' She hugged him again. 'I'm so proud of you, Micky. You have to work on your talent now, do more—'

He took the others, Micky signed to her helplessly.

'So what? He can't do anything with them!' Kat replied reassuringly. 'Stop worrying, luv. They can't get you in any trouble. They're *drawings*, that's all. Clever, but not dangerous.'

Looking on, Silky felt an overwhelming anger that Robin Wells could pick on someone as weak as Micky. That he would try to get at his old rival via his nephew. The memory of Ivan's bloodied arm came back to Silky at the same time. Twice Wells had threatened him through members of his family. Twice he had thrown down the gauntlet indirectly.

And it was twice too often.

I think of that evening and everything comes back to me, in intense, almost surreal detail. The tattoo patterns on the wall, the metallic smell of the drill, and Micky almost weeping with fright after his run-in with Robin Wells. Of course Silky played the threat to himself down – that was his way – but the thought that my little brother had been intimidated by a thug was too much for me.

I hated Wells from that moment on – as I had never hated anyone in my life.

Later, as we walked home, Micky kept asking me if he would get in trouble, and all I could say was how proud I was of him. How impressed by his talent. Then I told him that if our grandmother was insulted by a caricature, it was her choice. We all knew that Micky never did anything from malice . . . When I think of him now – flushed with achievement and the first realisation that he had something special – the thought makes me ache. As we turned into Amber Street, he made me promise that I wouldn't tell anyone about his drawings.

I promised. But in all honesty, I knew it was one oath I doubted I could keep. In time, when he was ready, I would make sure that everyone knew how brilliant my brother was. There would be no more hiding for Micky. He was worth noticing, worth recognising. Of course I never realised how *he would become known.* How *he would eventually claim his time in the limelight.*

We never know how our lives will pool or divide. How the people we think of as threats prove to be weaklings – and those we think of as benign can inflict the greatest injury.

ELEVEN

Summer 1930

The slump was hitting cotton; exports were down. All over the country, and particularly in the north-west, the hard times were beginning to bite. The Labour government spoke of a new phase of industrial depression and told people to expect some hardship. And daily the unemployment figures rose. In the mills of Preston, the takings dropped. Some fall-off was due to a decrease in demand, and fierce foreign competition; some was almost laughable. The new shorter skirts that had heralded freedom for women also meant the demise of the petticoat. In the past, women had bought ten or twelve yards of cotton; by 1929 it had fallen to three. The government even engineered a National Cotton Week, encouraging over 10,000 shops around the UK to try and revitalise the slumping industry.

On the docks, work was available, but not plentiful. Now the father of another daughter, Jim was sticking to his promise and had remained off the beer. Mellowed by his ongoing romance with Jane Rimmer, Billy had kept his fists to himself and his nose clean. He was in love and relishing the feeling, almost immune to the encroaching turn of the industrial tide. And spending more and more time away from Amber Street.

'I think he's serious about that Jane Rimmer girl.'

'Never!' Kat laughed, taking the new baby from her

mother and nursing her. 'Billy's never serious about anyone for long, you know that.'

Anna frowned. 'He's gone very quiet.'

'That's a blessing, surely,' Kat replied, laying the baby, Christine, in the repainted cot and sitting down on the side of her mother's bed. 'What about Micky, then? God, he must have grown three inches in the last week!'

Delighted, Anna laughed. Although Kat was exaggerating, the recent physical changes in her younger son had been remarkable. Suddenly the whey-faced boy had started to develop, and was now as tall as his father. Still thin, admittedly, but he was no longer a child. In fact, although he still had his pinched, haunted look, he was – to everyone's surprise – about to start shaving.

'Time passes so quickly,' Anna said, her tone reflective. 'I can remember so clearly when he was a baby.'

It had been folly for her to have another child. She would never have said so, but others did regularly. Like their neighbour, Mr Armitage at The Horse and Cart, and of course, Ma Shaw, who had banged on so relentlessly about it that Anna found herself lying, covering up her own weakness to convince her mother-in-law that the birth had been easy for her. In reality, the arrival of Christine had all but caved in Anna's resilience. Within weeks of her confinement, her heart weakness had presented itself as a worrying quickening rhythm. Only Kat was privy to the reality of the situation, arranging an expensive, but vital, doctor's visit when Jim was at work – and Ma Shaw nowhere in sight.

Then Anna had seemed to rally, still relying on Kat to help her, but beginning to regain a little of her strength. Until she had caught a cold and ended up back in bed. Jim blamed himself, said that he had brought it from the docks, that the sailors off some Danish ship had imported it into the Albert Edward. That it was some extra-fierce version of foreign flu. It wasn't extra fierce; it was just too much for Anna, and it laid her low for almost a month. But now, once again, she was rallying.

'I was thinking about the baby's baptism,' she said suddenly, 'but I think it'll have to wait for a bit. We've not got the money for the priest, but don't go mentioning it to your father, luv. I said we'd see to it when I was up and about.'

'It's not important.'

'Oh, it is!' replied Anna, always a fervent Catholic. 'The baby should be blessed. Otherwise anything happens to her she'll go to hell.'

Kat had no time for that view, and said so. 'People only go to hell when they've been wicked, Mam. She's a baby, she's not done anything.'

'The Pope says—'

'The Pope can say what he likes, but he's not paying for her baptism, is he?' Kat countered; then, seeing her mother's horrified face, she softened her tone. 'Anyway, nothing's going to happen to the baby, so why are we even talking about it?'

'You should believe,' Anna said gently. 'Religion is a great comfort in life.'

'I can't believe in something I can't see.'

'Don't you love the baby?'

''Course I do!' Kat replied, horrified.

'But you can't see love, can you? And yet you know it's real.' Anna paused, shifting the pillow against her back. Her education might be patchy, but she had a firm grasp of logic. 'Did I tell you about how your father proposed?'

Kat smiled. 'Tell me again.'

'He went down on one knee – and it was winter then – and said, "I can't live without you, Anna. Marry me."' She dimpled with pleasure at the memory. 'Can you imagine that? What nonsense, saying that he couldn't live without me.'

'He means it,' Kat said quietly. 'Dad loves you very much.'

'One day someone will love you like that,' Anna replied,

sensing a subtle change in Kat. Now that was interesting, wasn't it? Another thought followed on almost at once. 'Oh my word, I don't believe it! You've got your eye on someone.'

'I have not!'

Anna leaned forward, excited. She had longed for her daughter to be old enough for romance. After all, Billy didn't share his emotions with anyone, and it was such a pleasant diversion from her illness. 'Who is it?'

'No one!'

'I know there is!' Anna insisted, clapping her hands like a child. 'Don't you trust me?'

'Oh Mum, it's not that. I trust you more than anyone in the world,' Kat replied, glancing down. 'It's just silly, that's all.'

'Is he good-looking?'

'I think so.'

'Smart?'

'Very.'

'Does he like you?'

Kat's face flushed. 'He's not interested! And what makes it worse is that he's engaged to someone else. Well, virtually.'

Her face crimson, Kat picked at the threadbare coverlet on her mother's bed. She felt so stupid, but how did you stop thinking about someone? Dreaming about them? Making up silly scenarios in which you were the heroine and he was besotted with you? Falling in love and carrying you off into some distant pastel sunset away from Amber Street. Christ, Kat told herself, infuriated, she was such an idiot.

And although she had tried to deny it to herself, it was obvious. After all, hadn't Horace Armitage guessed? Hadn't he teased her? Thanked her – laughing – for standing up to Andrew about the flaming red door? And hadn't it been Horace who had tipped Kat off when Andrew was due round to collect the rent the following week? And then the month after that, when he had called the landlord's son in to check the roof?

Each time Kat had shrugged the information off, but it was no good.

'What's it to me?'

Horace had glowed with mischief. 'I can see that Andrew Pitt's taken a shine to you, and you like him. Be honest now, Kat, he's a fine young man.'

'Too fine for me. And too old.'

'Must be all of twenty-three!' Horace had teased her delightedly. 'Did I ever tell you about The Monkey's Tail? The public house I had when I were in my thirties?'

She had feigned indifference, but was dying for him to continue.

'Nah.'

'Well, I were married then, to Mrs Armitage – God love her – and we knew this young man who fell in love with the vicar's daughter. And they got married. Even though everyone was against it, and they all said it wouldn't work, it did.'

'She was a vicar's daughter; that's respectable,' Kat had countered, not unreasonably. 'My uncle's a tattooist.'

'Well, yeah, that's a bit different . . .'

'And I'm *not* after Andrew Pitt! I'm not after anyone. I wouldn't be stupid enough to overreach myself and make myself look a fool all over Preston.' She had paused, curious despite herself. 'Anyway, I suppose Andrew Pitt's already spoken for.'

'Rumour has it he's going to marry Joan Fairchild, but there's been no announcement in the paper and the romance has been going for a long while now. Strikes me that a man who's keen would have had a ring on her finger by now.'

Startled out of her reverie by her mother taking her hand, Kat sighed.

'Honestly, if I tell you, you'll laugh.'

'Go on. Who have you taken a fancy to?'

'Andrew Pitt. You know, Old Man Pitt's son.'

'Our landlord?'

Kat nodded. 'I said it was silly!'

'Not silly,' Anna replied, squeezing her hand tightly. 'But not sensible. People stick to their class, Kat. You have to accept it, and live with it. Rich men who go out with working-class girls are just leading them on. They play around with them, but they don't marry them.' She paused, anxious for her daughter and slightly embarrassed. 'You've not been with him?'

'Oh Mum, whatever do you take me for!' Kat replied, horrified. 'You can trust me, you should know that.'

'I never thought I couldn't, luv. It's just that you're so young, and men can be very persuasive . . .'

'No man will persuade me of anything, unless I'm good and ready to be persuaded,' Kat snapped back, her voice falling off again. 'Anyway, he's not interested in me. I'm just being a fool even to think about him!' She turned to her mother anxiously. 'You won't tell anyone, will you? Not Dad. Not Billy, for God's sake!'

'I won't tell a soul,' Anna assured her. 'But I'd put Andrew Pitt out of your mind, luv. Keep your sights set around Amber Street and find a decent lad of your own ilk. Don't go hankering after the Andrew Pitts of this world – there'd be nothing but misery for you there.'

An unexpected late spring chill was washing over the dockside, the Albert Edward grim in the fast-falling night. Rubbing his hands together, Jim hurried into the shed and poked at the indifferent fire in the stove, banging his feet to get some warmth into them. Bloody hell, he thought, it was colder than a witch's tit. With his mittened hands he checked the rota, then realised that he had left his sandwiches and billy can at home. Damn it, he thought impatiently, how had he managed to forget them? It wasn't like him; he enjoyed his grub too much to risk missing a meal. Glancing round, he felt in the old tin on the shelf and then realised that greedy Stanley had finished off the last of the biscuits. Not that they had been good ones anyway. Just odd-shaped broken biscuits that Mr Unwin sold off cheap . . . But thinking about them made him hungry, and he wondered just how he was going to keep watch all night with only tea for sustenance.

Of course he could go home quickly . . . No, he told himself, if he was caught out he would be fired. And besides, he wasn't reckless these days. He was a sober, reliable husband, father and employee. The kind of man who wasn't going to take stupid chances. Not with a family to support and a new baby to feed. He would just have to keep himself busy, he decided, picking up the lamp and walking back out into the foul night. The weather would take his mind off his stomach. To add to the cold, a bitter rain had started to fall, the big ships in the dock shifting like ancient mammoths, their holding ropes creaking eerily. Thank God for Billy's wages, Jim thought, walking along. Without his son's pay to support his own, they would be in a right mess. Especially now there was talk of all this unemployment; even some wages being docked at the mills. Who the hell would have imagined that? Herricks, the biggest cotton supplier in England, cutting back? And how long before there would be men laid off on the dock?

Shaking aside the depressing thoughts, Jim walked on purposefully, holding his watchman's lamp aloft. It cast a long, warm light on the dock in front of him, his own shadow elongated and unreal as he made his way towards the first of the big warehouses. He would try the locks and then do the dockside, checking around the backs of the ships for stowaways. Walking along, the lamp flickering in the wind, Jim thought suddenly of Missie Shepherd, and realised that the working girls had been thin on the ground since her death. Good thing too; God only knew who was hanging around in the shadows.

'Dad!'

Surprised, Jim turned at the call. Kat was running towards him, waving his billy can.

'You forgot your dinner.'

'What the hell are yer doing here?' Jim asked, seeing with relief that Micky was with her. 'Yer shouldn't be down the docks, neither of yer.'

'I'm all right with Micky,' Kat said, gesturing to her brother and then wrapping her coat around herself more tightly. 'Be honest, you're glad to see me, you know you are. How could you have gone all night without something to eat?'

Falling into step beside her father, Kat linked arms with him. Micky trailed behind them, deep in his own thoughts, occasionally stopping to skim stones across the dock.

'I haven't been down here for ages,' she said longingly. 'I miss it.'

'I miss yer being around, luv, but it's not the same since Missie Shepherd were killed. Too dangerous for you.' Suddenly Jim paused, holding up his lamp and peering into the distance.

'What is it, Dad?'

'I thought I saw a light, over by Warehouse 3. But it can't be, the place has been closed up for months.' Again he peered into the darkness, then shrugged. 'Just my imagination.'

'Ma Shaw's sitting with Mum.'

'Blimey.'

Kat laughed. 'She was reading and Mum pretended she'd fallen asleep.'

'Smart woman, your mother.'

Content, they walked on, Jim pausing to check the locks on the first warehouse, and chalk the door, and then dropping back into step with his daughter. He seemed very efficient, very keen to look the part, Kat realised, smiling to herself. Obviously he was making the point that he was taking his job very seriously, eager to impress on her that he was not the feckless man he had once been. Suddenly Kat remembered Micky's caricature and realised how clever it was; how accurately her brother had caught the kindness of their father – and his ever-present effort to remain on an even keel. The drawing had been done with skill, and something more important: empathy.

Behind them Kat could hear the sound of men laughing, some sailors coming back to their ship after a visit to one of the dockside pubs. Just how hard was it for her father to pass those places and not walk in? Just how difficult was it for him to fight his instincts nightly? Proud of him, Kat squeezed his arm.

'What's up?'

'Nothing, Dad,' she said lightly. 'Just glad to be with you.'

He stopped short. At first Kat thought it was a reaction to her words. But then she saw her father raise the watchman's lamp and stare across the docks towards the warehouses in the distance. Following his gaze, she could just make out the faintest light, and then a loud rumble, like thunder, but not thunder. A sound unlike any other. Low-pitched, unearthly, a roar that reverberated like an animal's death throes.

'Jesus,' Jim said suddenly, beginning to walk towards the noise.

'What is it?'

'I'm not sure,' he replied, beginning to walk faster, the watchman's lamp casting their shadows huge in front of them. 'It's the old warehouse . . . Oh God, I think there's been a fall!'

Beckoning for Micky to follow them, Kat began to run to keep up with her father's quick pace. The light, held high, illuminated their way, its beam swinging backwards and forwards erratically.

'Stay here!' her father suddenly commanded her. 'Stay here.'

Then, without another word, he hurried on alone, Kat and Micky watching him. As they did so, the sound grew in volume, swallowing up the dockside and reverberating around the Albert Edward, some of the sailors coming out on deck to watch as Jim hurried onwards. Following the watchman's light, Kat could see her father's figure as he crossed the gap between the working warehouses and the storage buildings.

The noise stopped, and a dense silence followed. The watchman's light held steady as Jim paused and lifted it aloft again. Then, slowly and purposefully, he walked towards the warehouse.

'Dad, don't!'

'I know what I'm doing!' he called back. 'I think there's been a fall inside. The timber's shifted.'

'Dad!' she called after him, beginning to run forwards, Micky following.

'Stay back!' Jim shouted, wrenching open the door of the warehouse and stepping inside. 'You hear me? STAY BACK!'

Immediately there was another gigantic rumble. Kat screamed and hurled herself forward, Micky hot on her heels as they ran into the warehouse after their father. As they entered, Kat paused, flinging her arm protectively across her brother's chest to stop him going any further. Around them in the dim light they could just make out the gigantic slabs of timber lying where they had fallen; huge felled trees like some eerie primeval forest.

The silence burned in her ears.

'Dad?'

'Stay back!'

'Dad,' she pleaded into the dim light, 'what's happened? Dad!'

'Stay back!' he called hoarsely. 'For Christ's sake, stay back!'

Something in her father's voice terrified Kat and made her move, Micky following her lead. Clambering over the timbers, she made her way towards the watchman's lamp, only yards in front of her, its light dim but steady.

'Dad!'

No reply.

Crawling over the fallen wood, Kat struggled on, the

lamplight growing brighter as she dragged herself over the uneven banks of wood. Once she lost her footing, but she didn't stop, scrambling back to her feet and pausing only when she came within the beam of the lamp.

Breathing heavily, she saw her father first. Jim was standing with his head bowed, in a ghastly, protracted stillness. He seemed immobilised, transfixed. At his feet – crushed to a bloodied pulp under the crippling weight of Siberian timber – was Billy. Only his face was left exposed and unmarked, his arms still wrapped around his girl, his eyes open and looking blankly upwards.

We never expected that Billy would be the first to go. Everyone had always watched out for Mum, especially after Christine was born, and Micky had always been delicate. But Billy? Wasn't he supposed to be the tough one? He didn't look so tough when I saw him that terrible night. He looked like a smashed-up child, Jane Rimmer tiny in his arms, blood everywhere. And his eyes wide open . . . I could see the expression on my father's face and almost feel the vibration of shock that went through him. When he turned to look at me he was changed. I can't tell you how, only that he was lessened, as certainly felled by that timber as Billy had been.

The days that followed had their own time. Everyone will tell you that. After a death there is a cessation of normality, a stiffening of hours, a turgid, hollow ring of overlong days. So it was with us. Mr Armitage next door at The Horse and Cart sent condolences and, without thinking – for I know there was no malice in the action – brandy.

He came in with the bottle and put it on the kitchen mantelpiece. Ostensibly for my mother, but she didn't touch it. Instead my father looked at it as though drawn to some horrible sight he could neither run away from nor avoid. I couldn't move the bottle out of his reach – that would have been a way of saying I didn't trust him – but I wanted to. At the same time I prayed he would be strong enough to resist. That the watchman would stay on watch over all of us.

For days the brandy bottle stayed on the mantelpiece, untouched. Every day I looked to see if the seal had been broken, but even on the morning of Billy's funeral it remained intact. For months afterwards, every time my father left for work I checked to see if he had taken the bottle with him. But he always resisted. Instead it sat on that mantelpiece like a hand grenade, waiting for someone to do something which would finally make him pull the pin.

PART TWO

It is not that their arrogance wounds me
But that each heady action of theirs
Peels at my heart and delivers
Blood, blows and labyrinth tears.

Anon (Italian, eighteenth century)

TWELVE

Summer was sticky that year. It came with the increase of national unemployment, the ache of Billy's death and Jim Shaw's slide into depression. Anna – bereft at the loss of her firstborn – weakened, and a week after Billy was buried, Ma Shaw came to stay at Amber Street. Kat had wanted to keep her grandmother away, knowing how she would take over and undermine her parents, but there was no avoiding it. Uselessly she tried to insist that she could look after her mother and the baby.

'Don't be daft! You have to work,' Ma Shaw said crisply. 'We need yer wage.'

'I can still work and look after the baby in the evenings . . .'

'And Micky will have to get a job too.'

'Not yet!'

'Yer got a money tree in the back yard, girl? Because if yer have, I'd like a few leaves off it myself,' Ma Shaw replied tartly, then modified her tone. 'We all have to pull together now. I mean, it were a tragedy about Billy, but life goes on.' She moved to the foot of the narrow staircase and looked up. 'No one's cleared out his things, I suppose?'

'I will, in time. I just haven't got around to it yet,' Kat replied, although she knew only too well that it was one job she couldn't face.

Whilst Billy's possessions remained upstairs, he was still

with them. When they went, he would have been banished from the house. As though he had never existed . . . Kat felt her throat tighten at the thought. They had all avoided the clearing out. Anna had murmured something about doing it in time, and Micky had carried on living in the room without changing anything. At times Kat had heard him crying and knew how much he missed his protector. But to actually *remove* Billy's things would be like shutting the door on his memory.

Ma Shaw had few such qualms. Having organised a number of funerals for the poor and buried two husbands of her own, she was more than capable. Within minutes of her arrival, Kat could hear the sound of her grandmother moving around upstairs, the creak of the springs as Billy's bed was stripped and the scrape of the wardrobe on the lino as Ma Shaw gathered up his things. So few things, Kat thought, trying to dislodge the memory of her brother's dead face. So few simple things, so little to show for a lifetime. Jesus, she thought desperately, trying not to cry, you were so strong, Billy. What happened? How could you die in a stupid accident? What a pointless, futile way to go.

'Micky!' came a sudden roar from upstairs.

Kat jerked to her feet and ran to the bottom of the stairs. 'Ssh! Mum's asleep. What is it?'

'I imagine yer mother might like to see these!' Ma Shaw snapped back, pounding her way downstairs. In her hand she was waving some papers, ominously familiar to Kat.

'Those aren't Billy's!' Kat replied quickly. 'Those drawings belong to Micky.'

'Hidden away behind the wardrobe! And I can see why!' the old woman said, her colour flushed. 'Yer little brother's been laughing at all of us behind our backs. Little sneak, look at these!' she said, slamming the caricatures down on the kitchen table. 'Jokes! He's been making fun of people. Bloody hell, there's one of me here!'

Trying to snatch the pages out of her grandmother's

hands, Kat rose to her brother's defence. 'They're just pictures . . .'

'They're flaming cheeky! That boy's got too much time on his hands if he can waste money and paper on this rubbish.'

Then, without another word, Ma Shaw gripped the drawings firmly and ripped them all in half.

'What are you doing!' Kat cried, horrified. 'They're all he has, for God's sake!'

'For God's sake? I'll say it's for God's sake. That flaming kid should have been doing something worthwhile, not dawdling around with crayons like a big jessie.' Ma Shaw had been shaken by finding the caricature of herself. Another time she might have laughed, even seen the funny side, but in the face of Billy's death, Micky's artistic efforts seemed almost an insult. Didn't the boy realise that he had to work and get a wage in, especially now that Billy wasn't around? Didn't he understand that the likes of the Shaws had to do the mill and factory jobs just to exist? *Christ, didn't he see it?* There couldn't be any day-dreams, any wasted time. Micky Shaw's future was already mapped out for him, and he had to stick to it.

Seeing her grandmother's anger, Kat tried to calm the situation down. 'Ma, I think you're being too hard on Micky. It's just a few drawings . . .'

The old woman didn't seem to hear her. 'Tomorrow your brother can get a job in the mill. There's one still going – which is a miracle in itself with this unemployment. He can do something worthwhile, contribute to the family. Poor lad can't help it, but him being a mute's not helping—'

'How can you call him a mute!' Kat shouted, beside herself. 'Micky can't help being handicapped. You're just jealous because he's got talent—'

'Talent!' Ma Shaw replied, her tone steely. 'What good is talent at drawing? What food does it earn? What rent does it pay? What good is being an artist when yer need to bring in a wage?' She was hating herself for her hardness, and yet she knew she was right. There was no point living in the bloody clouds. The Shaws lived on Amber Street, only a short walk from the slums. 'Wake up, Kat, and think. There's no time for art around these parts, and yer'd do well to remember that. And it's no use getting uppity with me; yer brother will have to work and pay his way because yer mother needs looking after and God knows how long yer father will keep sober now.'

'I HATE YOU!' Kat shouted suddenly.

Ma Shaw's mouth fell open. Never before in her life had anyone dared to stand up to her. 'Don't you talk to me like that! You need me; this family needs me.'

'We don't need you!' Kat threw back. 'We can manage.'

'I'd like to see it.'

'Well stick around and watch,' Kat replied, amazed by her own bravado.

'Yer've quite a mouth on you, girl,' Ma Shaw said coldly, 'and I have to say I admire that. Yer need to be strong to get on in this world. But as fer these,' she pointed to Micky's ruined drawings, 'they're no good to anyone. Yer might think otherwise, but I love that lad. I've been sorry fer Micky since he were born. But being sorry and being practical aren't the same thing – he has to forget all this rubbish and work for a living.'

'He could work at his drawings. He's different . . .'

'If yer going putting ideas in his head, yer'll wreck his life,' Ma Shaw countered, her voice losing its hard edge. 'This family's no money fer art school; we have to pull together or go under.'

Tears in her eyes, Kat stared at her grandmother defiantly. 'I'll never forgive you for this. They aren't just drawings, they are all Micky has. What harm were they doing to anyone? Why couldn't you just leave them? Pretend you hadn't seen them?'

'But I *did* see them.'

Her voice even, Kat shook her head. 'No, they were just

something you didn't approve of. Something you wanted to clear out. You didn't *see* them at all.'

But later that night, as Kat lay in bed and listened to the queasy silence of the house, she realised that her grandmother was right. Oh, Ma Shaw had overreacted, but her response hadn't just been because of Micky's drawings. It was *fear* that had made her act that way. Fear that any recognition of Micky's talent would encourage it. That he might really believe he had a future, a career, in art . . . Sobbing, Kat turned over and buried her face in her pillow. The shock of Billy's death had shattered the family, but for her there was something equally painful to come. She dreaded seeing her little brother turned out into the workplace. Dreaded seeing Micky – mute, timid Micky – trying to hold his own in the hell of the mill.

The looming spectre of unemployment was growing, even beginning to affect shopkeepers as customers cut back on their purchases. Profits suffered. Gradually people like Gregory Unwin began to limit their small stock of speciality goods and stuck to the utilitarian ranges. No one was buying treats any more. There was a slow but uneasy change in the air, and rumours were beginning to circulate about another war. Many around Amber Street, Friargate and Priory Road remembered only too clearly the carnage of the Great War, and the mill owners, steelworks and industrial firms all dreaded more upheaval and bloodshed. So they consoled themselves with the thought that the rumours were just that, nothing more. No real threat . . .

War, however, was the last thing on Andrew Pitt's mind as he walked into his father's office and sat down, sighing expansively. Duncan studied his son over his bifocals. It didn't really suit Andrew to be tough; he was too eager to believe a sob story, too pliable in some ways for rent collecting. But then again, he was learning. He had to, if he wanted to inherit the business.

'Finished already?' Duncan asked him, raising his sparse grey eyebrows. 'You were quick.'

'No, 128 Amber Street are behind with the rent, but I told them they could have another week to pay.'

'That's my money you've got on such a long rein!'

'They've never been behind before, Dad,' Andrew replied evenly. 'Give them a chance.'

'Why couldn't they pay?'

'Mr Howard's been laid off work.'

'Ah . . .' Old Man Pitt sighed, leaning back in his seat. What his son needed was a good wife, someone with a bit of character. Someone who would keep him on his toes. 'How's Joan?'

'Down in London.'

'Are you *ever* going to ask that girl to marry you?'

'When she gets back.'

'Which is?'

'Soon.'

'Dear God,' Duncan replied sarcastically. 'You really *do* know how to sweep a girl off her feet. Get her bagged, Andrew, before someone else does. I tell you, Joan Fairchild comes from a good family with money, you could do a lot worse. A *lot* worse. And besides, her father and I are old friends.'

'Only because you don't need corsets,' Andrew replied drily, thinking back to his mother and Gwen Fairchild's old feud. 'I can't imagine those two ever getting on.'

Suddenly Andrew saw a flicker in his father's eye and leaned forward. 'What?'

'What d'you mean, *what*?'

'You were thinking of something in the past, Dad. I could see it in your eyes.' He paused, having the satisfaction of seeing his father flush. Obviously the dark horse hadn't spent all his life between the pages of a book. 'Tell me, I won't breathe a word.'

'Well,' Duncan began, looking round and dropping his

voice, although they both knew that Ivy was out at her bridge evening, 'I knew Gwen before I knew your mother. Went out with her, actually.'

'You're joking!'

'We were engaged . . .'

'Does Mother know?'

'I meant to tell her, Andrew, I really did. But there was never the right moment. And then Gwen went and made that comment about your mother's weight and I didn't dare.'

Biting his lip, Andrew suppressed a smile. 'Were you in love with her?'

'We're not talking about me!' Duncan retorted hotly. 'We were talking about you and Joan Fairchild. It's obvious you're in love with her, so what's stopping you?'

'Nothing,' Andrew said, his tone emphatic. 'When she comes back, I'm going to propose.'

'You are sure?'

'Positive.'

'No more excuses?'

'None.'

If it hadn't been for the fact that Arnie Glover owned Jim a favour, he would never have considered taking Micky on at the Gull mill. A bullish, but surprisingly soft-voiced man, Arnie looked at the slender youth in front of him. Was this really his idea of a mill worker? Hardly. Now if Billy had still been alive . . . there was a man anyone would have hired. Built like a brick shithouse and not the type to be pushed around. But this lad . . .

Well aware of the unprepossessing impression he was making, Micky stood with his hands behind his back, his face expressionless. Around him he could see the monochrome shadow of his future. The mill had no colour, just light and shade, with an absence of life and breath. Even the cotton was colourless; interminable lengths of white, blank and expressionless as a winter sky. And as endless. No strokes of oil crayons here, no joyous yellow, no ruinous blue, or soul-scraping red. Nothing . . . In that instant Micky wanted to strike out at Arnie Glover, run away from the Gull mill and the noises echoing behind him. The slam of the looms, the clatter of hundreds of bobbins and the overloud, deafening shouts of people trying to make themselves heard over the machinery. It was like some suffocating, screaming hell of cotton dust and engine oil, and people – none of them mute . . . And who had put him here? His grandmother, Ma Shaw, the same woman who had ripped up his drawings. For once Kat had been wrong. Ma Shaw *had* been insulted by his caricature. So insulted that she had used it as an excuse to destroy his work.

Micky paused, knowing that that wasn't the whole reason for his predicament. It had been Billy's terrible death that had sealed his little brother's fate. With Billy gone, it was inevitable that Micky would have to work and bring in a wage. Closing his eyes for an instant against the tearing memory of seeing his brother dead, Micky calmed himself. He would do what he had to do. After all, the family was only just coping. His father's nightwatchman's wage, coupled with Kat's, was just about meeting the rent, but there was nothing left over. Except goodwill . . . Mr Unwin had come up trumps, putting aside some bits and pieces for Kat to take home. Broken biscuits, a torn half-bag of sugar and some cracked eggs. Like their mother said, it was so kind of him. But Kat's expression had been mortified and Micky knew how much she dreaded anyone finding out. In fact rather than accept charity, she had offered to work longer hours, but Mr Unwin had declined. Grocers – even the kind ones – didn't do overtime.

Watching Arnie Glover bark some orders to a foreman, Micky tried not to think about his ruined drawings. His grandmother's spite had winded him, but he consoled himself with the fact that he could do more. Or could he? Ma Shaw had taken his paper and oil crayons and there were no more coming his way. Not now he had left school. Of course it served him right, Micky thought blankly. He should never have believed that he could escape Preston, that he had talent enough to make up for his handicap. Kat had just been encouraging him, that was all. Giving him hope. Which had turned out to be almost as unkind as Ma Shaw's act of vandalism.

'You can start tomorrow,' Arnie Glover said, turning back to Micky.

He nodded in agreement.

'Yer have to do the running and fetching, and clean under the looms. Yer'll be taught how. But yer've got to be quick, lad, it's dangerous work.'

Wary, Arnie Glover looked the lad up and down. Well, he was small, and light on his feet, but was he smart enough? It was hazardous work cleaning under the looms, but it had to be done, otherwise the machines would jam. He thought of the lads who had previously done the job, their skinny legs disappearing under the slam and bang of the looms opening and closing only inches above their heads as they cleared and swept out the cotton dust. When Arnie had first started work there had been a little kid who hadn't been quick enough. He had been caught in the loom as it swung back, taking his left arm with it. Arnie could still remember the screams as they struggled to stop the machinery, the kid rattled backwards and forwards like a bloodied rag.

'Are yer fast on yer feet?'

Micky nodded.

'Good. Yer'll need to be.' Arnie paused, feeling sorry for the lad. But what choice was there? He knew that with Billy's death the Shaws needed money, fast. And there was nothing going at the docks. 'Micky,' he said suddenly, touching the youth's shoulder, 'I want yer to know that yer can come to me if there's any trouble. What with yer being mute an' all. I'm a good friend of yer father's and I'll see yer right.'

Mouthing *thank you*, Micky turned and began to walk away. Behind him he could hear the ominous, gobbling shuffle and rattle of machinery and felt his throat tighten as his footsteps quickened. Then he broke into a run, his breathing accelerating, his feet slamming on the pavement as he fled from the sounds of the hated mill and the realisation of where he would spend the rest of his life.

THIRTEEN

'But you're like a *brother* to me, Andrew!' Joan Fairchild said, winking. She was sitting on the edge of her parents' sofa, looking amused and astonished, her pert way captivating. 'I mean, thank you for your proposal, but I never realised . . . I didn't think you were so fond of me.'

Andrew was horrorstruck, stammering, 'You . . . you must have known . . .'

Shrugging, Joan paused, taking a quick glance at the clock on the mantelpiece. The thing about being pretty, spoiled and very rich was that men liked you effortlessly. All kinds of men. And why not? Joan knew she was good company and always light-hearted. But then again, what was there to be *depressed* about? she thought, chewing the side of her fingernail and keeping her gaze averted from Andrew Pitt.

Who was, at that moment, seeing Joan Fairchild as everyone else did. Superficial, skittish and cute – very appealing to any man who wanted to marry well and dodge deep conversations. Embarrassed, Andrew stared at the carpet. It wasn't Joan's fault. She had never been denied anything in her life, and had been the focus of her parents' complete devotion. Everything had come easily to her. And because of that, Andrew realised, it meant very little.

'But I really care about you,' he went on, feeling a sinking sensation in his guts as he looked at her. She was bemused. Obviously he was just another acolyte.

'And I like you too,' Joan replied, frantically hoping that the phone would ring to break this smouldering embarrassment.

After all, she couldn't really consider marrying Andrew Pitt, even if he was attractive and a thoroughly nice man. It wasn't that she hadn't *tried* to like him. She had, and she did. In fact she liked Andrew a good deal more than most of the men she knew. But he didn't excite her. And however much her mother and father might want it, she wasn't going to marry him. Besides, it was too easy. *He* was too easy. Too predictable, too boring . . .

'I'm sorry I embarrassed you.'

Kindly, she touched the back of his hand, then heard a sound outside the door. Her parents were listening! Damn it, wasn't that just like them? Joan could imagine their reaction – what the hell was she doing turning down Andrew Pitt? They would be infuriated, but she could talk them round. They loved her, after all. And she was their only daughter; they wouldn't be angry with her for long, Joan was sure of that.

'Andrew . . .'

'Oh, let it drop!' he said angrily, getting to his feet and walking to the window.

His humiliation was complete. All his hesitation and sleepless nights had been a waste of bloody time. The girl didn't want to marry him after all. In fact, it looked suspiciously as though she didn't even want to spend time with him . . . Fingering the edge of the curtain absent-mindedly, Andrew wondered if there was any way he could come out of this mortifying experience with his dignity intact. But even if he managed to persuade Joan to keep quiet, he knew that the Fairchilds would be on the phone to his parents the moment he left.

'Andrew, don't be angry,' Joan said, walking over to him, her voice lilting, trying to coax him back into good humour. 'We've always been friends.'

'And of course *friends* never marry.'

Surprised, she looked at him, seeing a sparkiness she had never expected. Perhaps she had been a little rash; perhaps he wasn't that predictable or boring after all. He looked so different annoyed, a sudden toughness coming through that was a revelation. Maybe she shouldn't just brush him off.

'We could—'

'We could what?' Andrew countered, his temper further roused. 'Be civil? Remain good friends? Go boating, perhaps?' He stared into her surprised face, amazed at his own venom and knowing that the whole embarrassing scenario was being overheard. 'No, I don't think we could remain friends! I've made enough of a fool of myself, I won't lay myself open again.'

His voice was taut, unlike him, and Joan was suddenly impressed. Hadn't he always been so careful around her before? So attentive, anxious to please? Yet now here he was, out of temper, and irritable, and looking more attractive than he had ever done. Then another thought hit her – *how dare he talk to her like that!* She was Joan Fairchild, and everyone was nice to her. Every man wanted to be with her, to take her out. Every man wanted her.

'Andrew, let's not fight . . .'

'Well I'm not being bloody civilised,' he replied, unexpectedly indifferent to her feelings.

The thought was galling to Joan, especially as the whole dreadful scene was being overheard by her parents. She *had* to turn the situation round, to save her face. After all, hadn't her mother and father told her that she could have anyone she wanted?

'Andrew,' she crooned, 'please don't be angry.'

'Perhaps you want me to ask you again?'

'You could,' she replied, her tone light, encouraging. Now this was more like it. This way *she* would be the one to choose. She wasn't going to have any man walk away from her. Even if she had rejected him.

'I don't think so, Joan.'

She blinked, wrong-footed.

'I won't ask you again. In fact, I won't ever come back here – for any reason,' Andrew said shortly, moving to the door. 'I wouldn't want to embarrass you, or myself.'

Beware the fury of a patient man, Joan thought, remembering the quotation as she looked at Andrew. Perhaps she hadn't taken him seriously enough. But how could she, when he had been pussy-footing around, hiding his feelings for so long? Suddenly petulant, she found herself baffled. So what if he had been devoted to her for years? Other men felt the same, but they hadn't ended up shouting at her and saying they were never going to see her again. Suddenly Joan was experiencing something of what Andrew had tolerated for so long. Suddenly *she* was being rejected, and it hurt.

'Please, Andrew,' she said, smiling her sweetest kitten smile, 'don't go . . .'

'Why? You want me to stay and have a brotherly chat with you?'

She reached out. 'Andrew—'

Turning from the door, he stopped, his fury threatening to overwhelm him. Then slowly he walked back to Joan. For a long instant he studied her face, then he grabbed hold of her and kissed her hard on the mouth. Finally, without another word, he left.

And Joan could only stand in the middle of the room, her fingers pressed to her stinging lips, calling hysterically for her mother.

Smoking a cigarette at the front door of the tattoo parlour, Silky watched the street. He had had a good week and was wondering how he could pass a little of his stash over to Amber Street to help out. Of course he could give the money to Ma Shaw, but that wasn't the answer. His mother was getting on everyone's tits and any monetary help from her would stick in Jim's craw. Checking his glossy reflection in the window, Silky thought about Kat. She was a bright one, he could give the money to her, she would know how best to use it. God knows it would help, with Anna getting sick again. Silky knew she needed someone more skilled than Mrs Soley. You couldn't hold back on medical help.

Frowning, Silky inhaled again. At least Jim had stayed off the drink. What a hell of a mess they would have been in if he'd lost his job at the docks. Jesus, Silky thought, now that *would* have been a disaster. But Jim was holding on. No one was sure for how long, but he was holding on. As for little Micky . . . Poor bugger, Silky thought, remembering the night he had seen the caricatures. The kid certainly had talent, but what good was that? Micky Shaw could have been Michelangelo and it still wouldn't have got him anywhere in 1930s Preston.

Watching a young woman pass, Silky nodded to her, returning her smile. He wondered momentarily if he should pursue the matter, but left it. He ran on instinct, did Silky, and it had served him well. Instinct and secrecy. The word around Preston was that he was a hard man, but not in the usual way. He wasn't like Pa Gallager, a violent thug, over in Hanky Park, or Noel Lyle, a ruthless businessman, in Salford. Silky was a fixer. Someone who knew everyone, but kept himself above them all. His contacts were legion – burglars, thieves, politicians, upmarket whores and heavy men – but he never used their services for himself. Instead he acted as a go-between. People came to him for advice, or to sort out their troubles, and he would help them, just because he could, and because it paid to have heavyweight friends. But he never – *never* – let himself become personally involved.

Aware that a big dark saloon car had pulled up at the corner, Silky kept smoking. He had been waiting to hear directly from Robin Wells for weeks, but no word had come. But now – unless Silky missed his guess – Wells was watching him. Come on, you bastard, he thought, his left hand sliding into his pocket and closing around a Stanley knife. I'm ready when you are . . . Still smoking, he watched the road, his immaculate hair and clothes making him stand out, a polished icon on the grimy street.

'Is that 'im?'

Ignoring his narrow-faced companion, Robin Wells studied Silky in the doorway opposite. 'Fucking ponce. Look at him – standing there like the Prince of Preston. You'd think he owned the town.'

Impressed despite himself, Wells scrutinised his old rival stonily. There was something dangerous about Silky Shaw, something only another violent man could recognise. A coldness, a lack of fear that was unnerving. At another time, Wells would have hired Silky. A lot of men thought they were hard, and some genuinely were. But the ones who had mercury in their veins instead of blood you could count on the fingers of one hand.

'Does 'e know yer 'ere?'

' 'Course he does,' Wells replied. 'That's why he's standing there. So I can see him – see that he's not afraid of me.'

'Wot yer going to do?'

'What's that to you?' Wells replied sharply, turning to his companion. 'Since when did I have to let *you* know my bloody timetable?'

The man backed down. 'I didn't . . .'

'No, you didn't,' Wells replied. 'Now, drive on. I've seen everything I want to see tonight.'

Hearing a tapping at the back door, Kat hurried to answer it. In the cool night air, Horace Armitage was standing on the back step, looking harassed.

'Whatever is it?' she whispered. 'I'd ask you in, but Mum's sleeping in the kitchen and I don't want to wake her.'

'How is she?'

'Not too good,' Kat replied, pulling her shawl around her shoulders and moving out into the back yard.

A whey-faced moon shone down on them, a neighbour's dog barking as a tram passed in the distance. Unshaven, Mr Armitage seemed preoccupied, distracted.

'Can I help you with something?'

'No, Kat, no! I wanted to have a word with you. It's about the rent.'

'What about it?'

'I wanted to tip you off. Old Man Pitt's clamping down a bit. You know there's been some layings-off and people who can't pay. I'll not knock the man, he's been reasonable – God knows – but he wants paying this week. In full.'

'Oh hell . . .' Kat said, making sure the back door was closed behind her. 'You heard that we couldn't make the full rent last week?'

'News travels, luv. Not that I'm one to gossip! But yer hear all sorts in a pub. And besides, yer not the first. And it's not from yer own doing. I mean, Billy dying like that – it were a tragedy.'

'Micky's gone to work now,' Kat replied defensively. 'We'll have three wages coming in next week.'

'Aye, but that's not *this* week, luv.'

'Surely Mr Pitt will let us have a little more time?' she asked anxiously.

God, not this now, Kat thought. Hadn't it been hard enough for them to pay the doctor's shillings? And to buy Anna's medicine? It hurt Kat to remember it, but they had had to grub around to raise enough for Billy's funeral, and if Silky hadn't made up the difference her brother would have ended up in a pauper's grave. Not that a penny had come from Ivan. Oh no, his money was his own, and never a farthing went elsewhere. Even to his half-brother . . . Shivering, she glanced down at her feet. At least the brandy bottle remained untouched, that was something. Her father might be remote, melancholic, but he was sober.

'I'd lend yer some cash if I could . . .'

'I know you would, Mr Armitage,' Kat replied, touching his shoulder briefly.

'But we're all struggling at the moment. I just wanted to tip yer off. Make sure yer were prepared fer Friday, yer know.' He moved to the back gate, then paused. 'If it's the old man, yer got problems, luv. But if it's young Pitt, yer'll be all right.'

Kat flushed. 'What?'

'Oh, I mean nothing bad, luv. I know yer respectable. It's just that Andrew Pitt likes yer, and he might be disposed to doing yer a favour. Nothing more, luv, nothing more. It's a tough life, Kat, and yer have to use what yer've got. And sometimes a pretty face can work wonders.'

FOURTEEN

Thursday night was bitterly cold, the wind rattling the back door and snaking through the cracks at the window. Too weak to climb the stairs, Anna had been sleeping on the old sofa in the kitchen, next to the fire, the baby beside her. The cold she had caught previously had weakened her system so much that she was virtually bedridden – and in no position to argue with her mother-in-law. Having moved in, Ma Shaw had swiftly made herself at home, hanging a partition curtain up in Billy's old bedroom to separate her bed from Micky's. *Share with me*, Kat had said, but her grandmother had been emphatic. Kat's room was hardly big enough for one bed, let alone two. No, she and her grandson would have to share. It would work perfectly with the curtain to divide the room in two. What was the problem?

Kat could only imagine how difficult it was for her brother, missing Billy and knowing that in his place was the grandmother he had come to loathe. Because he did now loathe Ma Shaw, and fear her in equal measure. He had explained as much to Kat, his face animated with anger when he talked about the ruined drawings and the loss of his materials. What right, he signed to his sister, did Ma Shaw have? Why couldn't she leave his things alone? She had what she wanted – he was in the mill now. Why did she have to destroy his pictures too?

And now he was sharing a room with her. Kat paused. Did

he listen to her low snoring in the night? Look at her hair rags – those pieces of cloth his grandmother pressed into service each night – and wince? Used to hearing the vital murmurings and, at times, hurried confidences of his brother, what comfort was an old woman? Short of temper, her corset creaking as she undressed behind the partition, the chamber pot in use sometimes in the early hours. With his protector gone, how intimidating was life for Micky now? Kat wondered, still angered that he had been forced into work so soon, thrown in at the mill before an opening occurred at the Albert Edward . . . And yet she knew there had been no choice.

They needed money fast, needed Micky's wage desperately. Her thoughts turned to what Mr Armitage had told her about the rent. Dear God, how *could* they pay it, together with the shortfall from last week? Unable to sleep, she went downstairs into the kitchen, the clock showing one thirty. Her mother was asleep, but Christine was stirring. Kat picked her up and began to nurse her. Thank God she was a quiet child; a fretful baby would have been too much for Anna to manage . . . Nuzzling the top of her sister's head, Kat suddenly noticed the parcel on the table.

Her father had forgotten his supper again. It took no effort for her to remember the last time he had forgotten it, on the night of Billy's death. Outside, the sounds of night were echoing, the footsteps of the men coming off a late shift at the mill and the quick, hurried shout of a woman calling from the shadows, either hurrying her husband home or kicking him out . . . There and then Kat decided that she would take the food to her father on the docks. She couldn't sleep, and if she was honest, she was looking for something to occupy her mind.

Tucking a drowsy Christine back with her mother, Kat moved upstairs. She dressed hurriedly, then left the house, taking care not to wake anyone. She wasn't afraid of the streets, had known them all her life, and followed the route to the Albert Edward automatically.

The cold was here to stay, she realised. No more balmy autumn days, making even an industrial town like Preston look picturesque. From here onwards the winter would begin his long stretch, pulling the days shorter, the nights long and limp as a broken reed. Then the winds would follow, her father coming home and telling the family about how they had had to tie up the boats in the dock, and how the cranes creaked and growled in their metal casings. Or would he? Kat wondered. Her father hadn't been telling any stories lately, too preoccupied with Billy's death and Anna's deterioration.

Many times Kat had watched her father staring at his wife from the kitchen doorway as she slept. After a while he would put out his hand – and then withdraw it suddenly, as though afraid he would wake her up. And later the inevitable conversation about Billy would begin again.

'Why was he there?' Anna would ask, over and over again, although she knew the answer only too well.

'He were with his girl, luv, yer know that.'

'But why?' Anna would reply, dazed with grief. 'Why there?'

'It were quiet there, luv. Yer know how young couples are, they like to have time to themselves.'

She had nodded, as though she had understood. 'But why there? Why amongst all that stacked timber? He must have known it was dangerous.' Her voice always rose at this point, Jim taking her hands in his. 'He must have known!'

'No one knew, Anna,' he'd reply patiently. 'No one knew.'

'The kids didn't see him, did they?'

And the lie would follow, as it had from the night of Billy's death, their father making them both promise: *Don't tell yer mother yer followed me. Don't tell her yer saw him.*

'No, Anna, they didn't see anything. They were behind me, a long way behind. I stopped them before they entered the warehouse.'

She would sigh, temporarily comforted. 'Thank God, thank God . . .'

Thoughtful, Kat hurried along, pulling up her collar to keep out the cold. The street lamps were lit, a light still burning in a window over The Grapes and Fox on the next street. So Mr Armitage's competition was up, was he? Kat thought, hurrying past. Not that anyone respectable went to The Grapes and Fox, a watering hole for many of the petty thieves of the area. Even her father, in his heavy drinking days, had avoided it. The pub wasn't a spit-and-sawdust place like some around the docks, but it was a meeting place for villains. If you were planning a robbery or any other illegal piece of work, you went to The Grapes and Fox. There you would find crooks of every description propping up the bar, a whole bargain basement of choice. And most of them fresh from Strangeways.

Crossing the street, Kat kept her head down. It was cold and she was avoiding eye contact, just in case someone mistook her for a working girl. Unlike many, she had sympathy for the prostitutes – her father had taught her that, telling her about Missie Shepherd and showing the compassion she admired. And that Ma Shaw took as weakness. But wasn't that typical of her grandmother? Kat thought, walking on. Ma Shaw found fault with everyone, and God knows it wasn't difficult to criticise a whore.

A sudden noise behind her made Kat stop walking and turn. A man was coming towards her and for an instant she tensed. Then she realised that he was passing her, intent on his own journey.

It took Kat another fifteen minutes to reach the Albert Edward. She turned towards the old office hut, where a light burned. With luck her father would be in there and she could avoid going around the dockside or – she shuddered – the warehouses. The giant slumbering carcasses she had played around so happily when she was a child now resonated with the terrible rumbling sound of the timber falling and the sight of Billy lying broken on the floor.

Lifting the latch, Kat walked in. Thank God, her father was sitting in the chair in front of the stove.

'Dad,' she said, touching his shoulder. 'You forgot your sandwiches again.'

He turned, surprised to see her. And in that instant – even before she saw the bottle – Kat knew. Snatching the beer from his hand, she looked down at her father, Jim smiling with a mixture of sheepishness and helplessness. His eyes went in and out of focus as he tried to concentrate on her.

Kat locked the door and shook him by the shoulders. 'Dad! Dad, how many have you had?'

He couldn't focus at all. Jesus, Kat thought, he was *drunk*. Completely, utterly drunk. No wonder he had forgotten his sandwiches; he had probably had a pint before he reached the docks, and then all thought of food would have gone from his mind. Who needed to eat when you could drink? Kat could imagine how his reasoning would have gone. First one quick pint to keep out the cold, and then another. And another.

Her expression hardened as she looked at him. 'Have you been drinking since you came on duty?'

'Hello, luv, how's yer mam?'

She wanted to hit him, but resisted. 'Dad, look at me and answer me. Have you done your rounds?'

There was no expression in his eyes. They were a drunk's eyes. Time and work were no longer in his world; he was absolved of reality, of responsibility. The watchman had turned in his watch.

'Dad,' Kat repeated, 'have you done your rounds of the docks?'

His head lolled forward, his breathing changing. He was, Kat realised with horror, fast asleep. Out to the world, in a drunk's oasis. Hurriedly she looked around, then reached for the ledger. There were no ticks against the dockside or the warehouse listings. And she knew what that meant – her father hadn't done the rounds. She tried to steady her thoughts. What if the boss walked in now? What then? The answer was obvious: her father would be fired. And with his wage gone, how would they pay the rent at Amber Street?

Kat knew they couldn't manage it on her wage alone, and they would have to wait another week for Micky's first pay.

With fury, she looked at her sleeping father. How could he? How could he now, when he knew what state they were in? How could he be so selfish, so reckless? Throwing down the ledger, she looked around her. Should she go home and get Micky? But that would be too much for him; he had to be at work himself at six. Was there anyone else she could turn to? She thought of Ivan and shuddered. God, no, Ivan couldn't find out. What about Silky? He would help, Kat thought, Silky always helped. But how long would it take her to get from the Albert Edward to the heart of Preston, wake Silky, and return with him? The answer was obvious – *too long*. By the time she had done all that, the morning watchman would be here. And would find her father drunk. No, there was only one thing for it – she would have to do the rounds herself. The thought unnerved her. It was dark, and the dock looked different, full of shadows. God only knew what – or who – was out there. Her thoughts slid back to Missie Shepherd, then to her dead brother. Come on, she urged herself, shaking away her nervousness. The rent's due tomorrow. If you don't do this, the whole family will be sunk.

Breathing steadily to calm herself, Kat looked around her. The clock showed two thirty-five. If she hurried, she had time to check round, mark up the warehouses, fill out the ledger, and get her father home before the foreman came on duty. Quickly she banked up the stove and then picked up her father's coat. Jim wasn't a big man, and Kat was quite tall; from a distance the coat wouldn't seem too big, and it would cover her own skirt and jacket. She gathered up her hair on top of her head and pulled her father's cap over it. Not one blonde strand was left out to give her away. After all, if someone came checking, they couldn't find a girl making the rounds. They had to think it was a man. Finally she lifted her father's watchman's lamp, a memory coming back to her of the time he had first brought the light home, glowing with pride. To Kat, the lamp had been a constant reminder of her father's sobriety, a symbol of his responsibility. Its light didn't illuminate only the docks; it seemed to light Jim Shaw's own way.

And now it would have to illuminate hers . . . Struggling to light it, Kat was successful on the third attempt and closed the latch, the lamp glowing as she walked out of the hut and raised it to shoulder height. Surprised, she realised how much light it threw around, and how much it illuminated its bearer. Taking a deep breath, she headed for the dockside. On her left, two huge old storage ships from Germany and Russia slumbered on the cold tide, the vast iron chains curled like sinister metallic snakes on the quayside. Picking her way around them, Kat headed towards the next dock.

Every noise danced in her head, each sound echoing and skimming the water, or playing hopscotch around the ships. She prayed, as she had never done before, that the man who had killed Missie Shepherd wasn't waiting behind some wall. Keep calm, she told herself; if there was anyone watching, they would think she was a man, not some vulnerable woman, skirting the shadows. Keep calm . . . Looking left to right, she moved along. The Albert Edward was very quiet, only the sounds from a far-off pub coming low and muffled on the night tide. A few times she heard splashes, but knew it was only rats, disturbed and making their getaway. On and on she walked, then she turned towards the warehouses, the vast looming bulks silhouetted against a sullen moon.

Concentrating, Kat walked round, marking each doorway to show that all was in order. A couple of times she stiffened as she heard men's voices, a whistle piercing the darkness. But she carried on. An hour turned into a second, the lamp moving from hand to hand as Kat's arms began to ache. Finally she came to the farthest warehouses and stopped, her courage momentarily faltering as she remembered the sailors' tales and the dockers' reminiscences. About Missie Shepherd, and the old sailor who had been killed for his measure of tobacco at the turn of the century. Many said that the old man – a Norwegian – walked the docks at night, pausing to light up his tobacco at the entrance to Warehouse 5. Kat had her own memory, one she knew would join the legion of others. Of her brother under the timber. Would someone see Billy Shaw one day? Would they come back to their ship trembling, recalling how a ghostly man had stopped them and warned them about a timber fall?

It's only Billy, Kat told herself, it's only Billy. How could I be afraid of my own brother? Slowly she began to walk on, passing down the side of the first warehouse, the lamp marking her way. Chalking the doorway, she moved on to the second. In the distance there came the sound of a fight, then silence. In front of her, the light caught a huge shadow, her body hardly recognisable, just some nocturnal being walking through the early hours. She realised then how lonely the nightwatchman might feel. How exposed, the only lighted, moving figure in the night. Around her, sounds swelled and noises trembled. Her imagination turned the innocent creak of wood into a trapped animal; the clatter of the anchor chain in the distance into the strident calling out of someone lost. Perhaps, Kat thought, it wasn't so hard to understand how a man might take a drink to steady his nerves. How her father, having seen his son dead, might find it nearly impossible to walk the docks sober.

Pausing, she leaned against the side of a warehouse, putting the lamp at her feet. She was tired, her nerves exhausted; she still had one more warehouse to check and then she had to return to the hut. Listening, she caught the chimes of St Harlow's church – five o'clock – and, picking up the lamp, hurried on. No one must catch her. Not Missie Shepherd's killer, or the foreman – who, at that moment, she feared more. Her father must not lose his job. The Shaws could not survive unless she finished the round and covered up for him.

Later, when she got him home, then she would have time to

think. But not until then . . . Moving on quickly, she rounded the last warehouse and began to retrace her steps. Around her the metal bulk of the ships shifted in the lifting night, the first rays of dawn breaking as she arrived back within sight of the hut. In the distance she could see a light flickering on the water and heard footsteps echoing behind her. Her mouth drying, she hurried on, almost running the last yards to the hut, then locking the door behind her. Her father was still asleep. Her hand shaking, Kat looked at the ledger; then, copying her father's initials, she signed beside each entry to say they had been checked. If she was caught, not only would her father be fired, she might well be charged with fraud.

Finally, she turned to her father.

'Dad! Dad! Wake up!' she said, shaking him. There was no response. Aware that they had hardly any time left, she found the remainder of his cold coffee and – after a moment's pause – threw it in his face.

Shaken, Jim jerked awake. 'What the hell!'

'Come on,' Kat urged him, pulling him to his feet. 'We've got to get out of here.'

He looked at her, bemused. '*Kat?*'

'Yes, Kat,' she agreed, leading him out of the hut, the unlit lamp over her shoulder.

'What yer doing here? Yer shouldn't be here! It's not safe fer a girl!'

'Dad, calm down.'

'The docks are dangerous! Yer shouldn't be here – is Micky with yer?'

'Not this time,' Kat answered, helping her father along. He was obviously still quite drunk, and confused about what was happening. Luckily he didn't resist and followed her out, his arm linked through hers. Then he paused, staring at her. 'Whatever are yer doing, luv! That's my coat and cap yer've got on!'

She shushed him hurriedly. 'Quiet. Be quiet, Dad. We're going home.'

Half dragging her inebriated father, she helped him along the dockside, turning round occasionally to see if the foreman was following them, or if Ivan had come on early for his morning shift. But there was no one about – only a couple of sailors who laughed as she passed.

'Hey, lad,' one called out to her. 'Yer want to get him home to sleep it off.'

She nodded, keeping her face averted. They had taken her for a young man, she thought with relief.

It took her an hour and a quarter – including an early tram journey – to get herself and her father home. By the time they were within reach of Amber Street, Jim was sobering up. Realising something of what had happened, he began to talk in staccato sentences.

'I weren't meaning to get drunk . . . Yer know, Kat, what it's been like. All the worry . . . Yer know. Billy and yer mam.'

'Yeah, Dad,' she said, stopping and turning to him. 'Can you walk on your own now?'

'Sure, sure.' He looked sheepish, close to tears. 'Did I lose my job?'

'No, but that's only because I did it for you, Dad.'

'Yer what!'

'I covered for you. And I signed the warehouse lists and the ledger.'

'Yer can't do that!'

'What else should I have done!' she hurled back, tired and agitated. 'Left you there, out cold? Until the foreman found you? Drunk on the job! I thought you'd stopped drinking. I thought . . . *God, why do you do it?*' She sighed. 'You can't, Dad. You *have* to keep this job, or we'll be in real trouble. Don't you understand? I know how it hurt you about Billy; it hurt me and Micky too. But you can't let it cloud your brain. Think of Mum,' she said pleadingly. 'She relies on you.'

He was staring at her, ashamed. 'Yer didn't *really* do the watch, did yer?'

She ignored the question. 'You have to keep this job. We

need your wage, or we'll be thrown out of Amber Street. We can't make the full rent this week – do you understand? If you lose your job, we're finished.'

'It won't happen again.'

'You've said that in the past.'

'No,' Jim said hurriedly, straightening his jacket and smoothing back his hair. 'This time I swear on my life – it won't happen again. Now, luv, give me back my coat and cap.'

'You have to see that it's not just your life,' Kat replied, passing her father his uniform. 'It's Mum's and Christine's and Micky's. Keep off the booze, Dad, please, or it'll finish you. And the rest of us.'

FIFTEEN

'I never thought I would say it about my own child, darling, but you're a fool!'

Joan Fairchild was beginning to think that her mother might well be right. It had been two weeks since Andrew had stormed off, and although Joan had expected him to come back, he hadn't shown his face. Suddenly her cosy world seemed out of synch, her stability threatened. She hadn't really wanted Andrew – until he left. And then she wanted him very much indeed. Besides, no man rejected her – even if she had rejected him first.

Surrounded by the leafless winter trees that lined the road, Joan could just see the thick clumping of vegetation that bordered Avenham Park. The house and the location shouted money; a wadding of prosperity that kept the poor at bay and the downtrodden streets of Preston at arm's length. Gareth Fairchild's business was in trade. All kinds of trade. Electrical, plumbing, heating, lighting. He had an instinct for what could make money and could spot an up-and-coming idea virtually as soon as it left the drawing board. Intellectual he was not, and had seldom been known to read a book, something Duncan teased him about mercilessly, but as a businessman he was sharp. Gwen might try to put a gloss on her husband's workmanlike interests, but she had known from the start that Gareth was never going to be a doctor or a solicitor. And as time had passed and she had seen their bank account swell handsomely, she had found a peculiar admiration for nuts and bolts.

Joan had never really been interested in how her father made his money; she was only interested in the lifestyle and opportunities it brought her. The chances in life that she took for granted and relied on. Like the Andrew Pitts of the world being always there to dance attendance on her.

'What shall I do?' she asked her mother sullenly.

'There's nothing you can do,' Gwen replied, walking over to her daughter and studying her. Pretty girl, very pretty. 'He'll come back.'

'What if he doesn't?'

This wasn't a route Gwen wanted to take, even in theory. She had decided a while back that the Pitts and the Fairchilds would be a good match, and besides, she had her own reasons for wanting the marriage. Like getting one over on Ivy Pitt. The way that woman had treated her! Gwen thought, still smarting from what she saw as Ivy's protracted disdain. And all over a silly little joke . . . Well, perhaps it hadn't been a *joke*, but what was so wrong about telling your best friend the truth? Ivy had an arse on her like the milk float's horse, and that was that. It was clear for everyone to see – but somehow, just because it was Gwen who had mentioned it, Ivy had taken offence. And *stayed* offended.

What was worse, the Fairchilds had been doing rather better than the Pitts lately. In truth, both families were hardly pressed for cash, but Duncan had been pretty smart with his investments and was putting away some handy money. Of course, if Gwen had been the peevish type, she could *really* have set the cat amongst the pigeons. If Ivy was insulted now, how would she feel if Gwen told her about her little fling with her husband? For a moment the temptation was like toffee on her lips, but Gwen resisted. That would just be a quick triumph; she must wait and play the long game. Be patient. After all, the smartest people never showed their hand.

Which brought her to the subject of bridge . . . Gwen smouldered for a long, smoky instant. She and Gwen still attended the same bridge club they had belonged to since they were young women. Only now they avoided each other. They would nod a greeting, but that was all. Never play at the same table. Never exchange conversation – until the last eighteen months, when the realisation that a marital bonding between their children was possible had necessitated a reunion. Personally Gwen would have liked to restrict her communication to red ink on an unsigned note, but she was prepared to swallow her feelings for the sake of Joan's good match. As for Ivy, she was pleasant, but unbending. Which could, of course, Gwen thought meanly, be due to her corset.

So now they smiled at each other, two social corpses locked in rictus grins. And exchanged pleasantries; Gwen noting with delight that Ivy's arse was straining against its whalebone confines; Ivy relishing the fact that Gwen's face had more lines than the local tram route.

'Mother, I'll say it again,' Joan wailed, 'what if Andrew doesn't come back?'

'He has to, darling.'

'Perhaps I should call him? Or write to him?'

'No, darling!' Gwen replied fervently. 'The woman *never* chases. You want him to think that you miss him?'

'But I do.'

'Yes, but he mustn't know that.'

'But how will he find out, unless I tell him?'

'He has to find out himself.'

'How?'

'In his own way. That's what romance is all about.'

'But if he doesn't find out, and I don't tell him, he might think I don't care.'

'Joan, darling,' Gwen said, between clenched teeth, 'you should have thought of that earlier. After all, you were the one who rejected him!'

'But I didn't want him then,' Joan replied, close to tears.

'But he looked so different when he was angry. So tough, so attractive. So *not* like Andrew. And now he's gone, and I want him back.'

Crossing the sitting room, Gwen poured two sherries, drinking one off straight away and then refilling her own glass before passing the other to her daughter.

'Couldn't you talk to his mother?'

Gwen's plucked eyebrows rose. 'What!'

'You and Ivy Pitt were good friends once . . .'

'With the best will in the world, darling, we aren't exactly chummy now.'

'Well, what about his father?'

An old memory stirred inside Gwen. Duncan hadn't been quite so keen on his books when they were in their teens. In fact, literary leanings had been rather low down on his list then. She remembered the Duncan Pitt of old: how they had sneaked off for the day to Southport and spent the whole time laughing on the fairground and chasing each other down the pier. Later they had walked out on the long empty shore, the sea a mile away, lapping somewhere on the horizon. In those days a natural romantic, Duncan had bent down and picked up a shell, wiping the sand off on his handkerchief and passing it to her.

'It's not much of a present, but it's lucky, Gwen. One day I'll buy you diamonds and mink, but I'll never love you any more than I do at this instant.'

She had taken it from his hand, warm from the sun, and then slid it into her pocket . . .

'Mother!'

Gwen's thoughts left the sea, the shore and the shell. Suddenly she was a middle-aged woman again, married to another man.

'What on earth were you thinking about?'

'Nothing important,' she replied, looking at her daughter coolly. 'Nothing important at all.'

* * *

Coughing, Anna leaned over the side of the sofa and spat into the basin Kat was holding. Covering the thick sputum with a cloth, Kat helped her mother back against the pillows. She was worse, anyone could see that, and it was risky for the baby to be with her so much whilst Anna was restless, sleeping fitfully. What if she rolled over on to Christine in the night? Kat had tried to bring up the subject, but Anna had been adamant: she was looking after her baby.

The previous evening Kat had managed to have a private conversation with the doctor that Silky had so kindly paid for.

'Will she get better?' she had asked him.

'It's not a question of her getting better; your mother will always be weak. I can't do anything to make her heart strong. There's no medicine I can give her; it's her condition and it won't change.'

'Isn't there anything that can help?'

'The shock of Billy's death set her back a lot. She can't take worry. Can't take any more anxiety. You have to keep her calm.'

The doctor had looked at Kat and sighed inwardly. Who was he kidding? He knew how hard life was on Amber Street, how tight money was. Worry was part of everyday life. Most people got by, learned to live with the tragedies. Trouble was, any more tragedy could kill Anna Shaw.

Remembering his words, Kat knew only too well what the doctor was telling her. *Protect your mother, and that way you'll keep her alive . . .* Sighing, she pulled a kitchen chair up to the side of the sofa and started to brush Anna's hair.

'Oh, I like that,' Anna said, smiling as she handed Christine over to Ma Shaw.

'You have lovely hair.'

'Not blond, like you.'

'I like dark hair,' Kat said firmly, taking a surreptitious glance at the mantelpiece. The bottle of brandy was still sitting there. Untouched. Without realising she had been holding her breath, she relaxed. Her father was keeping his word.

'I thought we should get some black pudding for your father when he gets home. That bread's dry eating now, and we've not got enough for cheese,' Anna said, thinking aloud. 'I only wish we could afford a bit of jam.'

'Mr Unwin said he might let us have some old stock,' Kat offered, thinking of her considerate employer. So considerate that he hadn't even scolded her when she had fallen asleep at work. Covering for her father had cheated her not only out of one night's sleep; for the following week she had found herself unsettled, waking frequently, wondering if the watchman was on watch. Please, Dad, she had prayed, stay sober. Please . . .

Kat began to brush her mother's hair again. Within the hour, one of the Pitts would call for the rent – and they hadn't raised enough to meet that week's as well as pay off what they owed. Her glance moved to the clock, next to the bottle of brandy. In a few minutes she would make an excuse and go outside, catch the landlord on the corner so that Anna wouldn't overhear the exchange. Or her daughter begging for extra time.

Shaking away the thought, Kat bent down towards her mother. 'You know something?'

Anna smiled up at her. 'No, what?'

'Mr Unwin said that he was going to visit his sister this Christmas.'

'I didn't know he had a sister.'

'Neither did I, until yesterday. She lives in Liverpool, and she has a son. Which makes Mr Unwin an uncle.'

'A good uncle, I bet.'

Kat nodded. 'Yeah, he's a kind man.' She glanced at the clock again, hearing Ma Shaw's heavy footsteps overhead. 'What's she doing?'

'Nosing around,' Anna replied, her voice automatically lowered. 'I know how helpful your grandmother is, but it's not like it was, not with her around.'

'You can say that again.'

Guilty, Anna hurried on. 'I'm very grateful for her help . . .'

'But you wish she'd go home?'

Both of them laughed, covering their mouths with their hands. 'Is she going to stay for ever?' Anna asked.

'No, not for much longer,' Kat replied, knowing that she was probably lying and that Ma Shaw was a fixture – for the foreseeable future, at least. After all, Kat was working all day, as was Micky; who else could help Anna tend the baby?

Kat could hardly believe that only a year ago her mother had been well enough to look after her home and family. Now she was reduced to a semi-invalid on an old couch, watching the world go by. Not that Anna was miserable; far from it. She had Christine, and although she still grieved for the loss of Billy, she comforted herself with the fact that she had the rest of her family around her.

'I'm going for a breath of air, Mum.'

Surprised, Anna looked at her daughter. 'It's cold tonight.'

'Nah, it's not. I'll be back in a minute,' Kat replied.

She stepped out on to Amber Street and looked round, then, nodding to a neighbour, walked to the end of the street. The noise of the piano came from The Horse and Cart. Nervously she tried to compose what she would say. How she would state her case so that she couldn't be refused. But her mind wandered. Was it true what Horace Armitage had told her? That Andrew Pitt admired her? No, she told herself sharply, no point thinking stupid thoughts. He didn't even know who she was. Hadn't he walked right by her the other week without even noticing her? Some impact she had made . . .

Glancing down the street, Kat suddenly spotted Micky sauntering down the ginnel towards her. He was yawning, whey-faced, his wrists bony and large from a sudden growth spurt. He was still intermittently bullied, but for how much longer? Kat wondered. Before long – if he continued growing at this rate – he would outstrip his bullies. The thought appealed to her. Waving, she beckoned to him, signalling her welcome.

He signed back: *Hello, what are you doing?*

'Waiting for the landlord,' Kat told him. 'I don't want Mum overhearing anything.'

I get paid on Monday, Micky signed hurriedly.

'I know, it's not your fault,' she reassured him. 'How's the job going?'

He shrugged. *All right.*

'Worse than you thought?'

To Kat's amazement, Micky shook his head. *I've made a couple of friends.*

'That's great,' she said, then dug deep into her coat pocket, bringing out a brand-new pencil. 'I told Mr Unwin how clever you were, how good your drawings were, and he said that every artist needs his materials. And I got this paper for you too. Not the best, but good enough.'

Touched, Micky stared at her, then signed: *Thanks. I've missed drawing.*

'I know.'

Don't tell Ma Shaw.

Kat laughed, nudging him. 'No, I won't! But don't hide anything behind the wardrobe again.'

Smiling, he walked on, into the Amber Street house.

It was nearly ten minutes later that Kat noticed a man making his way towards her. For an instant she was so nervous that she almost hoped it was Old Man Pitt – but then she saw it was Andrew, and felt a queasy, nervous sensation in her stomach. A mixture of apprehension and excitement.

Waiting until he crossed over, she walked out under the lamplight.

'Mr Pitt, can I have a word with you?'

For an instant he didn't recognise her, then he smiled stiffly. 'You want a word? What is it?' he asked, his tone sharper than he meant.

'Sorry . . . I was just wondering . . .' She hesitated. Andrew, watching her, was attracted and yet angry at the same time. Another bloody woman; what favour did *this* one want?

'Yes?'

'We owe your father a little rent from last week, and of course, this week's . . . It's just that we're a bit behind . . . You know my brother was killed in an accident at the docks, and Micky – my younger brother – has only just managed to get a job because he's handicapped. But very reliable. I mean, he wouldn't let anyone down.' She paused, out of breath, feeling embarrassed and ill at ease. To have to beg, to this man, the one she had such a liking for . . . it was so humiliating. And he was looking at her with such an odd expression on his face.

'What are you asking me?'

She was surprised by the harshness of his tone. He had been so easy-going before, but now he was brusque and short-tempered.

'We need another week to pay.'

'Another week!'

'Please . . .'

At any other time Andrew would have agreed, but his heart had been stapled shut by Joan Fairchild. Unable to take out his feelings of folly and rejection directly on her, he chose to strike out at the person standing in front of him. It wasn't anything to do with Kat, or her situation; it wasn't any fault of hers. It was a reaction, an explosion – and she took the brunt of it.

'You think you can sweet-talk me into this?' he asked her coldly. 'You think I'm that big a fool?'

She stepped back, flushing. 'I just wanted another week to pay . . .'

'You and your family are like all the rest! On the make. You think I don't know about your father, Miss Shaw? You think it isn't common gossip that he can't stay off the drink?

Can't hold down any job for long? I suppose you want me to subsidise his next drinking bout, do you?'

Her voice rose. 'My father's not drinking at the moment.'

'You said it – *at the moment*,' Andrew countered. 'Well that's not good enough. I suppose he sent you to me thinking that his pretty daughter would swing it for him—'

'How dare you!' Kat snapped. 'How dare you talk to me like that!'

His eyes narrowed, unknown malice coming from somewhere deep within him.

'How dare I talk to you like that? How dare *you* talk to me! I'm the landlord; you have to do things my way. Not the other way around.' He was beside himself, his voice bitter. 'You think I'm a soft touch, just like everyone else does. Well, one word from me tonight and I could have you thrown out. You and your family. I just have to report back to my father and it's over for you.'

Stunned, Kat stared at him. 'What happened to you? You're not like this.'

'How would you know what I'm like!' he blustered, moving after Kat as she began to walk away, mortified.

Her face was burning with shame and humiliation. He thought she was a scrubber, a woman trying to con him, cajole a favour out of him. Her cheeks were on fire. *She wasn't like that, she wasn't like that at all.* But he thought she was. And of all people she hadn't wanted *him* to think badly of her. It was all so unfair. She had tried to help, and had failed. And made herself look cheap in the process.

'You don't know me, Miss Shaw!' he called after her. 'No one knows what I'm really like.'

She turned at the end of the street to face him. Desperation made her brave, and humiliation made her outspoken. She might have lowered herself in his eyes, but she was damned if she wasn't going to say her piece.

'No one asked me to talk to you; it was my own idea to try and appeal to your kindness. To ask for one week – seven days – to raise the rent.' Her voice was calm, controlled. 'I know you can go home to your father and I know he can turn us out. I know many families who've ended up on the street. It happens every day. And I don't suppose you – or your like – ever think about where those people end up. Or whose lives you ruin. After all, it's not your fault, is it? We can't pay the rent, so you're within your rights. Only sometimes, being right isn't enough, Mr Pitt. Sometimes being right is just an excuse for being cruel.'

She stopped short. Her temper had got the better of her, and she was bitterly regretful. Who did she think she was talking to? This was Andrew Pitt, the son of their landlord, the man who could have them thrown out. His threat hadn't been an idle one; he could evict the whole Shaw family and no one would blame him. They *were* behind with the rent, and now she was telling him what she thought of him. The very person she should be appealing to, she was insulting. God, Kat thought, stunned at her own stupidity, what was this loss of temper going to cost?

Waiting for his response, she thought of her mother – hadn't the doctor reiterated, over and over again, that Anna was not to be worried? And wasn't there reason enough to worry already? About the fall in employment? The shortage of money? The way the Shaws were existing on the edge? But Kat had forgotten all that. Instead she had stood her ground, saying her piece. Utterly, completely, selfishly reckless . . . Perhaps, she thought dismally, she was more like her father than she'd thought.

'Mr Pitt . . .'

Putting up his hands to silence her, Andrew took in a breath. 'What I said was unforgivable.'

'But . . .'

He stopped her again. 'I was rude, very rude. I'm sorry.'

Astonished by the unexpected apology, Kat said nothing, just stood looking at him.

'I was using you as my whipping boy,' Andrew admitted,

ashamed. 'I shouldn't have spoken to you like that. And I admire you for saying so.'

'Maybe we both spoke out of turn,' she replied, her voice hardly audible.

'No, you were right. I *was* cruel – and I had no reason to take it out on you.' He moved to walk away, then turned back to her. 'You can have your seven days, Miss Shaw. But perhaps you would pay me next week?'

'Of course,' she said hurriedly. 'I'll settle in full.'

'Will you pay in person?'

She hesitated. 'If you want me to.'

'I would consider it a favour.'

SIXTEEN

The question was, should he invest some money in the tattoo parlour, or would it be a waste of time? Silky rinsed his needles and pondered. It was an odd fact, but even though people were cutting back, there were always men who wanted a tattoo and were prepared to pay for it. Not that it cost a lot – and Silky knew only too well that on the docks and in the mills and factories, tattoos stood for something. A man over twenty without one was suspect in some area. It was a kind of social shorthand. You had your tattoo to mark a rite of passage, from being a boy to being a man. What you *chose* had another meaning. Lads sometimes had MOTHER put on their arm, usually quickly followed up with the name or initials of their girlfriend. Sailors had a liking for ships, fair enough, and anchors. Mill workers for some reason liked the Union Jack, and as for the blue-collar factory workers, their taste ran to hearts pierced with arrows, or dragons.

The villains were the best. Silky still treasured a note from Pa Gallager from Hanky Park – who would have believed he could write? – saying that everyone in Strangeways had liked his snake tattoo. That was lucky, Silky thought, because tattooing the local hard men was a risky business; you had to keep a steady hand and a cool head. If they didn't like it, you wouldn't get paid and you might lose a couple of front teeth into the bargain. But if you pleased them, they sent you custom – and there was another advantage. People wouldn't mess with you if they thought you were connected.

Still thinking, Silky tapped his front teeth with one of his needles. His last apprentice had been a dead loss, scared off too quickly by three dockers who had all come in at once and taken bets on who would get the best tattoo. Unnerved in the presence of a combined weight of around sixty stone of muscle and drunk flesh, the lad had buggered up a simple skull, and only Silky's intervention had prevented him from having his arse tattooed by three amateurs. After that, Silky never saw his apprentice again.

But despite that, Silky liked the hard men. And they came to him not because he was in the roughest area of town, but because he was good. Percy Clegg – the mean bastard – had been talented too. Silky thought about his grandfather and winced. The place had been grim then, but the man had been an artist, and by watching him Silky had learned what made a reasonable tattoo into a masterpiece. After all, Percy always said, you had the damn thing on your body for life, so it had better be good. Silky thought of the brutal tattoo on his half-brother's arm and grimaced. That sod Wells hadn't had the guts to come for him, so he'd gone for Ivan. And Ivan had never let him forget it.

Silky's eyes narrowed. One day he would get even with Robin Wells for that ham-fisted bit of savagery. He would just wait, that was all. Slow and steady . . . But he *couldn't* wait for another apprentice, and so once again he thought about Micky. Well, why not? Wasn't it the perfect solution? God knew, the family needed more money coming in. Micky could help out part time, and he'd be doing what he liked. Being an artist. What did it matter if you were drawing on paper or flesh? Besides, Ma Shaw couldn't tear up skin. Trouble was, Micky was handicapped. Dumb. A mute . . . Silky thought about that for a long time, sliding into the tattoo chair and studying his shiny shoes. Could the lad cope? With the work, yeah; Silky was sure he could teach Micky all he knew. But could he manage the customers? Not the mill hands or even some of the dock workers, but the villains?

Of course the tattoo parlour *could* be the making of him, Silky mused. Micky was growing physically, not a runt for much longer. Some meat and muscle on him and he'd be a fair size. What held him back was his timidity, his shyness, which invited bullying. But then again, if you couldn't talk, you were up against it from the word go . . . He thought of the sign language between Micky and Kat and smiled. Now there was a girl! He could see his niece holding her own with anyone.

The answer was suddenly obvious to him. Silky didn't have to convince Micky he could do it; he had to convince *Kat*. If he sold the idea to her, it would work to everyone's advantage. More money would be going into the Shaw household. Money earned, not charity. Micky would be able to develop his talent. And Silky could toughen up his nephew at the same time . . . Silky was fond of his brother, but he knew that Jim was only a reasonable father, and Billy wasn't around any more to protect his little brother. So now Micky had to learn to protect himself.

The wage wouldn't be much – but the experience would be invaluable.

The following Friday, Old Man Pitt came for the rent in his Daimler. Disappointed, Kat handed him the money and glanced quickly into the back seat, hoping that Andrew was with him. But the old man was alone. Well, she thought, watching the car drive off, what had she expected? That it would really matter to Andrew Pitt if she kept her word? Did she seriously suppose that he had even remembered what he had said? Still, there was one good thing about it, she consoled herself: they were up to date with the rent. They were safe. Until next week.

'Hello.'

Kat stopped walking, glancing over the back gate of The Horse and Cart. A round-faced girl with an amused expression was looking at her quizzically.

'Are you Kat?'

She nodded. 'Who are you?'

'Mary Armitage, Horace's niece.'

'I didn't know he had a niece,' Kat replied, glancing over Mary's shoulder into the back of the pub. 'He never said anything.'

'My father and he fell out a long time ago,' Mary replied. 'I've come to live here now.'

'In the pub?'

She nodded, cheerful in a cheap wool dress. Interested, Kat studied her. There was something appealing about Mary Armitage; she looked like she had a bit of mischief about her. 'Mum died a long while back, but my father's only just passed on and I've no one else. So I had to come here.'

'I'm sorry about your parents.'

Nodding again, Mary sighed. 'Well, that's life.' Then she brightened up. 'We could be friends.'

'I'd like that,' Kat said truthfully. 'It'll be nice having someone my own age living next door. I could do with some company.'

Putting her head on one side, Mary studied her. 'I should get a job, you know. But my uncle said that I can keep the house tidy for him instead.' She laughed suddenly. 'A pub! Can you imagine! My parents wanted me to be a teacher, but I wasn't clever enough.'

'You don't look stupid to me.'

'Oh, I'm not really.' She laughed again. 'Anyway, I'm hoping I can get married soon.'

'Married!' Kat replied, stunned. 'Aren't you a bit young for that?'

'*No!* I think I would make a good wife, for some kind man. He would *have* to be kind, you know. And anyway, it would be nice to have a man to look after me. Take care of me.' Mary changed the subject deftly. 'Uncle Horace told me all about you and your family. Sorry about your mum being ill and all that . . .'

Touched, Kat nodded. 'She's not so bad at the moment.'

'Losing your brother, that was awful.'

'Did your uncle tell you everything about us?'

'Everything,' Mary replied, 'and he thinks you're marvellous. Said that some local rich boy admired you—'

'That's not true!' Kat hurled back, more sharply than she meant. 'Your uncle's very kind, but he's wrong.'

Nodding, Mary stepped back, but she looked unconvinced. 'I should go in now. Help out . . . We could go to the pictures, if you like. There's a Douglas Fairbanks film on at the Roxy.'

Hesitating, Kat wondered how she could tactfully refuse. Money was too tight for luxuries and she hadn't been to the cinema for over a year.

'Well, I could, but . . .'

'Uncle Horace said he would treat us,' Mary said, smiling. 'I think he wants us to be friends.'

Horace Armitage *did* want his niece to make friends with Kat, primarily because he was a childless widower and had no idea how to deal with the young woman who had suddenly arrived in his life. At a stroke, his previous steady existence had been overturned, his nocturnal wanderings in his longjohns curtailed. No more listening to the radio with his feet in a bucket of Epsom salts, no more putting newspaper on the table as a makeshift cloth. Oh no, Mary had arrived and overnight life had changed.

It was not that she was demanding; far from it. She slid into The Horse and Cart easily, cheerful and helpful, always trying to find ways to be of use. But she also liked to chat, and Horace didn't know anything about girl talk. Mary's innocent ramblings about Douglas Fairbanks and her wry observations about some of the pub customers had him panicked, ushering her into the back, out of sight. After all, she could be cheeky – and men would be men. Wincing, Horace remembered the petticoats and underwear left to dry on the overhead rack. Dear God, he thought, glancing away, what if someone looked through from the pub and saw them? A drunk man could be carried away by less than the sight of a pair of drawers.

Mary's casual enquiry about her father had been the last straw. Everyone but his daughter knew that Glyn Armitage had been a womaniser, carrying on around the north-west like he was going for some sort of record. With his wattles and his beer belly, Horace had never attracted women, but Glyn had been a seducer in his pram. In fact Horace had a theory that if anyone could die of sexual exhaustion, his brother would. Bed-hopping from Preston to Burnley, from Oldham to Bolton and back again, Glyn made love to more women and sired more bastards than anyone had a right to. And now Mary was asking questions . . . Which was when Horace came up with his master plan. He had to find his niece a confidante, and who better than Kat Shaw next door? To hurry their friendship along, Horace was even prepared to invest some of his meagre earnings. In fact, he had come to the decision that the two girls would benefit from a weekend in Blackpool. Nothing fancy, mind, but a change, some sea air and time to get to know each other.

'Are yer off yer mind?' Ma Shaw said, stomping into the pub by the back door. Hands on hips, she looked at Horace, who was standing horrified, like a recalcitrant child.

'Er, what's this, Mrs Shaw?'

'Letting them two girls go off to Blackpool fer the weekend! Have yer lost yer senses?'

'I said I'd pay fer the little trip. If they stay in a bed and breakfast, I can stump up fer it. No spending money, mind, they'd have to find that fer themselves.'

'Well that's typical of a man, isn't it?' Ma Shaw replied,

leaning towards Horace warningly. 'What kind of trouble are they going to get into on their own? What kind of decent girls go away on their own?'

Horace hadn't considered this. 'I thought they might like it . . .'

'Like it!' Ma Shaw snapped. 'I'll say they'll like it. And all the young men out to get girls into trouble will like it too!'

Horace flushed. 'I never thought of that.'

'Well it's obvious to anyone with half a brain!'

'I just wanted to treat them. Mary needs a friend, and to be honest, yer Kat could do with a holiday herself.'

'Well they can't go alone!'

'Aye, I see . . . I see that . . .' Horace's voice staggered to a halt.

'They need a chaperone.'

'I can't go!' Horace said, desperate to avoid his niece and her new friend. 'I've a pub to run! I can't leave here!'

'I'll go.'

He blinked, very slowly. 'Mrs Shaw, I mean . . . I mean . . . I can't pay fer yer too. I've not the money . . .'

'I don't mean fer yer to pay fer me!' she snapped. 'I'll pay me own way. Those girls can't go alone – but I'll not stop them having a treat.'

Horace was thinking that Ma Shaw accompanying them would stop any treat in its tracks. But then again, he wasn't in a position to argue.

'We'll pick a weekend when Jim's not working; he can help Anna with the baby. Do him good. And Micky will lend a hand. They'll cope.' She walked to the door, then turned back. 'Did I say thank you?'

'Er, no.'

'Well thank you, Mr Armitage, fer yer kindness. Times are hard, and yer being right generous. Like yer say, Kat could do with a break. I reckon both girls will have a right good time.' She paused. 'As fer me, I'll keep an eye on them, but not get underfoot. Oh no, I know my place. Always have.'

Three weeks later the trip was organised, and despite Ma Shaw acting as chaperone, Kat and Mary were transported by the idea of visiting Blackpool. As for Anna, she was looking forward to being alone with Jim and the baby, out of Ma Shaw's scrutiny for the first time in what seemed like years. Having saved a little money, and with a food parcel from the kindly Mr Unwin, Kat sat on the train between Mary and Ma Shaw, watching as they left the urban streets of Preston and headed for the coast. She had never left her home town before and was almost faint with anticipation. Only one thing worried her – Micky. It would have done her brother so much good to come with them, but she could hardly mention it, as Mr Armitage was paying. And besides, Micky wasn't eager to spend any more time than necessary with his grandmother.

'Look!' Mary said suddenly, pointing out of the window. 'I can see the tower!'

'See one tower and yer've seen them all,' Ma Shaw replied, putting away her book and grabbing the suitcase. 'Well come on, girls, time to start our little holiday.'

Behind her back, Mary rolled her eyes, Kat trying not to laugh.

Horace's planning had gone no further than the trip itself. It had been left to Ma Shaw to arrange accommodation with an old friend of her second husband. For many years Beatrice Aldenshaw had been running a bed and breakfast in one of the cheaper areas of Blackpool, her manner grand, her voice artificially refined. Greeting Ma Shaw at the door, she ushered her into the poky hotel, the girls following.

'Of course I don't have to tell ladies like yourselves,' she said, her voice strained with the effort of sounding middle class, 'but there's no going out late, or bringing gentlemen back—'

'There'll be none of that!' Ma Shaw barked, Mrs Aldenshaw jumping.

'I serve breakfast at eight, and high tea at seven. No washing in your rooms, mind.'

'I've no mind to wash, we're on holiday.'

'So,' Mrs Aldenshaw said, looking Kat up and down. 'Is this your granddaughter?'

Kat smiled, introducing her friend. 'I'm Katherine and this is Mary.'

Ma Shaw intervened. 'I came here with the girls because yer were a friend of my late husband, and he spoke well of yer. But I need to know about the kind of guests yer have here. No single men, I hope?'

Mrs Aldenshaw blinked again. '*Pardon?*'

'Single men are trouble. With young women around. They get ideas.'

'There are no single men staying here. I think you will be very comfortable,' the landlady concluded, taking in a deep, patient breath. Really, what a person did for friendship, and to think Nobby had been *married* to this tartar. 'I want you to think of this place as your home for the little time you have here.'

Ma Shaw nodded, making a mental note to check that the linen on the beds was dry. After all, a woman who could put on a voice like that was trying to cover up something.

The following afternoon, Ma Shaw was fast asleep on her deckchair, a copy of *Picture Post* open on her lap. Catching Mary's eye, Kat jerked her head towards the pier, then together they crept away. With any luck, the old lady would be asleep for a couple of hours. Mary ran on ahead across the sands as Kat turned her face up to the sun and breathed in the strange ozone scent of the sea. Behind her she could hear the sound of laughter and voices, but no sinister echo of a mill hooter, or clatter of clogs on cobbled alleyways. Here the sky was searingly blue, the clouds distant. And although the beach was busy, the weather wasn't good enough for crowds. There *were* people, but not the breathless press of Amber Street, or the sweaty push and pull of the factories or the mill. Not cheek-by-jowl living . . . Suddenly Kat felt a longing for room to move, enough space to stretch her limbs and breathe in clean air. Another girl might want to go to Blackpool for the funfair or the lads, but for Kat the intoxication of space was breathtaking. Glancing across the sands, she waved to Mary, who was watching a Punch and Judy show. As Kat walked towards her, she made herself a promise. One day she would have space, acres of land around her. Freedom, under a high sky.

'Let's get some ice cream,' she said, linking arms with Mary and drawing her towards the pier.

'Wait a minute! I want to have my fortune read,' Mary replied, pointing to a hut with MADAME ZORA written on the side.

'It's rubbish!'

'Oh come on, it's only sixpence.' They walked over – then noticed the sign: CLOSED.

'So much for the future,' Kat said wryly, urging Mary further down the pier towards the big dipper. 'Now *that* would be fun.'

'I don't like heights.'

'How d'you know?'

'I know I get giddy on the top floor of a bus,' Mary replied.

They crammed a whole holiday into the next hour, the big dipper, the ghost train, candyfloss, even going on the dodgems, Kat screaming and laughing alternately. Finally, reluctantly, they began the walk back down the pier, a couple of boys wolf-whistling as they passed.

Shyly, Kat looked down, Mary laughing.

'Can you imagine what it would be like if we were here on our own?' she said, watching as a few other lads passed. 'Mind you, I suppose you're thinking about Andrew Pitt.'

'No I wasn't!' Kat replied, wondering if she had been wise telling Mary about her romantic fantasy.

But then again, who could you tell apart from your best friend? And Mary was always so interested in emotional matters. Didn't she love to give Kat advice – culled from her penny-dreadful romance books? Stealing a furtive look at her friend, Kat found herself imagining a walk along the pier with Andrew Pitt . . . Her thoughts stalled suddenly. How could she walk along the pier in her shoddy clothes? Another thought followed on – in her fantasy she had wonderful clothes. One of those expensive drop-waist silk dresses, her hair bobbed to her chin, and make-up: a touch of powder and some lipstick . . .

'What *are* you thinking about now?' Mary asked, drawing Kat's attention back to the present.

'Nothing much.'

'You were smiling.'

'Yeah? Well I was smiling at nothing much,' Kat replied archly, leaning over the iron railings to look into the water.

Below, a discarded straw hat sailed past, followed by a sweet wrapper. Further away, the water was clear and blue, the birds calling overhead, the sun making light ribbons on the tide. Inhaling, Kat breathed the salt air and realised how much she *had* been thinking of Andrew Pitt. But surely it wasn't just wishful thinking any more? Oh, it was true that she had been infatuated with him in the past, but she was older now, and Andrew Pitt seemed finally to be noticing her as a girl, not just as a tenant. After all, hadn't he smiled at her as he walked past? And then, a week later, called by to ask after her mother? Now, who did that unless they were interested? And then there had been the time only two days previously when he had bumped into Kat on her way home from work. Talking had been strained, forced for a while, but then Kat had mentioned there was a rumour going around that Charlie Chaplin was a woman in disguise – something that made Andrew pause and then laugh outright. They had relaxed from that moment on and Kat had decided that she liked his laugh – full and genuine, a sound she would like to hear more of. Finally, when they reached Amber Street, Andrew had walked Kat to her door and then paused.

She had thought for a moment that he might kiss her, then flushed when he said a hurried good night and walked away. But there *had* been something there, she had sensed it . . . Horace Armstrong might tease, and Mary could be merciless, but Kat was actually beginning to allow herself some hope. Albeit very faint, and very tentative.

'Are you in love?' Mary asked quietly.

'He's out of my league,' Kat replied, her voice low. She was trying to be logical, but at the same time was desperate that Mary would buoy up her hopes. 'He's supposed to be marrying Joan Fairchild. From another rich family. How could I compete with her?'

'You should be more confident.'

'Oh come on, Mary, be honest – what have I got to be confident about with a rival like that?'

'You're good-looking, smart and . . .'

'Yeah?'

'. . . good-looking.'

Laughing, Kat looked back down into the water. 'Like I said, Andrew Pitt is out of my league.'

Mary sighed, pushing her hair back with her hands. 'What would be your ideal man?'

'I dunno,' Kat replied, glancing over to where her grandmother was sitting on the beach. She was still asleep, unmoving. 'Ma Shaw's been married twice.'

'Blimey!' Mary replied, stunned.

'What about you? Who would be your ideal man?'

Musing, Mary jumped up on to the railings, the wind ruffling her hair as she swung one leg. 'Someone very kind. Someone who thought the world of me. Who worshipped me. I wouldn't mind if he was older than me.'

'I would! I don't want an old man.'

'Don't be so sure. You should think about it,' Mary said reasonably. 'An older man would be a father figure, someone more patient. More experienced.'

'And older,' Kat said smartly.

'I wouldn't mind if he wasn't that good-looking either.'

Kat stared at her friend, nonplussed. 'Oh, I want someone good-looking.'

'Handsome is as handsome does.'

'Huh?'

Mary rolled her eyes. 'My mother used to say that all the time . . . You know that my father was very handsome?'

'Was he?'

She nodded, warming to her theme. 'Women loved him. Of course my parents didn't think I knew, but I could hear them arguing all the time. About his affairs . . .' She dropped her voice, Kat listening avidly.

'He had affairs?'

'Lots. And other children, apart from me.'

Stunned, Kat stared at her. 'You mean . . . ?'

'Bastards.'

'Mary!' Kat exclaimed, astonished. She looked round. 'You can't say that!'

'I can, because it's true,' she replied, unfazed. 'He was awful, really awful. Uncle Horace goes pale every time I mention his name. If I want to be alone, I just have to make some comment about home and he runs off.'

'You're evil,' Kat replied, laughing. 'You really are.'

Smiling, Mary nodded, then glanced over at her friend. Kat might not admit it, but she was obviously falling in love with Andrew Pitt and unable to see anyone else. Mary had noticed the boys staring at Kat. And why not? She was unusual, stunning. Half urchin, half siren. And totally unaware of her appeal.

'I know one thing. I don't want a cruel man,' Kat said suddenly, Mary leaning forward to hear her more clearly.

'That's a funny thing to say.'

'Yeah, I know. But it came into my mind just then when you asked me what I wanted in a man. I didn't know, but suddenly I knew exactly what I *didn't* want. Cruelty. Someone unkind.'

'Why would you pick anyone like that?'

'I wouldn't,' Kat answered enigmatically. 'But maybe they would pick me.'

SEVENTEEN

Coughing, Micky held a handkerchief over his mouth and then ducked under the clattering loom. He was painfully thin, and too tall for the job, but then again, it paid well so he was going to keep doing it. Just inches over his head the loom banged closed, then swung open again, giving him the chance to run underneath. The idea was to sweep up the cotton dust and wastage whilst avoiding being hit by the heavy machinery overhead. Timing was all-important. There had been many accidents, one young lad being struck on the side of his temple and killed several years earlier. The owner explained that that was an accident. That the lads were carefully trained and the boy hadn't been concentrating. But that wasn't entirely true. Twelve years old, the lad had been at school all morning and then sent on to the mill for the afternoon shift. He hadn't been careless, he had been asleep on his feet.

Micky knew the story. And he knew about the others too. The broken arms and the dislocated shoulders. All of which made him very careful and very quick. Under the loom he held his breath as long as he could, timing the slam and clatter of the machinery. Breathe in, sweep along, breathe out, run for the break. It was easy, if you kept thinking, and holding your breath . . . Ten minutes later Micky completed his last run on the shift and excused himself, making for the outside privy. The rain had stopped, he saw with relief, noting a break in the clouds. After relieving himself, he glanced round and took out a scrap of paper from his pocket. Smoothing it against the brick wall of the privy, he began to draw an image of Arnie Glover, the foreman, with his pork pie hat and ginger eyebrows. His hand moved over the page quickly, with complete confidence. And as it did so, the mill disappeared, the slamming of the loom fading, the factory hooter turning into a poised, empty well of silence. Micky drew from the heart, from that space inside him that was certain and clever. He drew and grew. Began the size of a snail, with an empty page, and by the time he had filled it he was taller than the Blackpool Tower, bigger than Jupiter, smarter than the man who came round trying to flog the *Encyclopaedia Britannica* at the door. At such times Micky felt – for an instant – his breath melt in his chest. As though the act of creation was more than the act of living. And he knew without doubt that he was in the space God had made for him. Not under the loom, not shuffling and bullied in Amber Street, not dumb as an ox, but in the sweet home of his mind and his talent.

Turning into the mill yard, Kat saw her brother in the distance and moved towards him. Trade had been slow at Unwin's and she dreaded what she was sure would soon come: the inevitable laying-off. After all, times were hard, and Gregory Unwin, for all his kindness, didn't really need her any more. Disconsolate, she had dropped in on Silky, anxious to avoid going straight home and facing a grilling from Ma Shaw. And there, in her uncle's tattoo parlour, Kat had heard Silky's proposal. Which was madness, she thought at first. Then thought again. Micky working with her uncle. *Micky* . . . Well, why not? How rough was it in a tattoo parlour? Any rougher than dodging machinery that could tear off your arm?

'What are you doing?

Turning, Micky automatically stuffed the paper into his pocket, then sighed, seeing Kat approach.

'Drawing, hey?' She smiled, leaning against the wall next to him. Overheard the welcome snap of blue had gone, clouds grey and restless as white horses balking the afternoon sky.

What you doing here? he signed.

'It's late, Micky. I've finished work and I've just been over to see Silky. He was telling me about an idea he had. About you.'

His eyebrows rose, then he signalled: *What idea?*

'Silky's apprentice has gone. Another one.' She smiled wryly. 'He needs someone in the parlour to help him out. Learn the trade. He asked about you. If you'd like to.'

Pausing, Kat wondered if she was doing the right thing. Was the tattoo parlour really the place for her brother? But then again, Micky would be with Silky; he would be safe. And more importantly, he would be able to develop his talent.

Micky was staring at her in silence.

'So, what d'you think?'

He said nothing.

'Silky could train you, and pay you. Not much, Micky, but it would be a wage and you'd be doing what you want. In a way.'

She stopped talking, surprised to be getting no reaction. Was her brother alarmed by the idea? Or offended? Surely he couldn't be. But then again, was tattooing *art*? God, Kat thought, feeling her stomach lurch, she had been mad even to consider it. How could her mute brother mix with the likes of Silky's trade? And who was she kidding, thinking that tattooing some docker was equal to creating a picture? She had just allowed herself to be persuaded, so worried about the lack of money coming in that she would consider anything. But Micky, a tattoo artist? God, she was a fool, a bloody fool!

'Forget it, it was stupid . . .'

Hurriedly he touched her arm. *He would pay me?*

'Yeah, not much, but a wage.'

For drawing? Micky shook his head, struggling with the words, then signing: *For tattooing people?*

'Yeah,' Kat agreed, hurrying on. 'I didn't say yes, Micky. I just said I would ask you.'

He would pay me?

Kat nodded. 'You couldn't do it full time. Just part time at first.'

You said yes?

'I said it was up to you, Micky.'

But what do you think?

'I think you're brilliant. I think I'd like to put you in some posh art school, give you paints and canvases and watch you impress the world.' She paused, her tone even. 'I don't think a tattoo parlour is good enough for you, Micky. I don't think it's really where I want you to be. But if you're asking me if I think you could do it – yes, of course you could.'

It's not real.

She flushed. 'Well I know that, Micky. It's not real art—'

He cut her off, signalling and slapping his arm. *It's on flesh. Flesh and blood.*

'On the skin, yes.'

For keeps.

She frowned, not understanding what he meant. 'I know it's not on paper. Not real drawing . . .'

It stays.

'What?'

It stays for ever.

And then she understood. 'Yes, Micky, it stays on, it's permanent. Anything you did would be on that person for life.' She could see a faraway look come into her brother's eyes. My God, Kat thought, he was excited, he wanted to do it. He wasn't offended, he was overwhelmed. The thought that something he created would last for ever was intoxicating to him. 'Do you want to do this?'

He nodded, then caught her arm.

He wasn't joking, was he?

Her heart shifted. 'No, Micky,' she replied, 'he wasn't joking. Silky wants you to work for him. You'll be his new apprentice.'

And you think I can do it?

'No one could do it better.'

He nodded, his eyes momentarily closing. And then he kissed her gently – ever so gently – on her cheek.

EIGHTEEN

1932

Thing was, if you had a reputation for being a villain, you had better live up to it. And if there was one thing Robin Wells prided himself on, it was being a villain. Not your common-or-garden thug – but a smart villain. A heavyweight. Wells paused, checking his reflection in the glass in his dressing room. Lately he had expanded, making money from running a Manchester casino, selling the business on and investing the profit in property. All well and good, but money wasn't the be all and end all for Wells. He liked the frisson of fear he inspired in people, and the attraction he had for women. Of course his background helped. Women liked to fool themselves that sleeping with him wasn't like sleeping with another crook; Wells had class, they reasoned, he had come from money. The fact that he was as rancid a thief and bastard as could be found in any dive in Salford was smoothed over by the happy fortune of his birth.

Wells stared at his reflection, at the smart suit and well-groomed hair and nails. Always do the nails, he told his cohorts; women noticed nails. Keep them manicured and a woman would take you for a gentleman. Slowly Wells studied his face, and was pleased to see that his expression gave nothing away. His eyes were – as always – unreadable. Although his smile was welcoming, sensual even . . . He thought suddenly of Silky Shaw and found himself irritated.

Shaw had been an annoyance for years, but Wells wasn't a man to be hurried into revenge. He liked to toy with people – and particularly grudges. Never a hothead, he realised that by drawing something out, you got the advantage over your enemy. People loathed waiting. They feared it. They would run to a fight, but it was the slow, grinding uncertainty that undermined them, got them worn down. It was then that Wells would strike. Long after anyone else, when his enemy was bloody knackered.

Like the Komodo dragon. Wells thought of the film he had seen at the cinema about the giant lizards that lived on some God-forsaken island. Apparently they could kill anyone with a bite, there and then, but they preferred a different approach. They would simply bite their prey, then wait. The bacteria in their mouths did the rest. It took two weeks for the infection to kill. Two weeks for the stricken animal to sicken and then die in agony. A long, measured death. A time when the victim knew it was over for them, but had to go through the prolonged end. Wells admired that. Liked to fashion himself on the lizard. Liked the wait. Because the wait could be better than the kill.

He had grown tired of London and Manchester and come back to Preston on a whim, thinking he would stay for a while and then move on. But he had stayed longer than anticipated, finding himself reluctant to leave his home town. His parents had heard of his return, but never pressed their son for a visit, and Wells didn't want any reunion. The only reconciliations he desired were with old adversaries. And there were a few of them. Like Silky Shaw. And Duncan Pitt . . . Wells wondered how surprised people would be to find out that he and Old Man Pitt were acquainted. But that was the thing about being well connected; his father had known Pitt in the past and little Robin had overheard plenty in his childhood. Confidential conversation that his father presumed would stay in the family. Titbits that a cunning child stored away for future reference.

Like how Old Man Pitt had made his money. Not the way everyone in Preston believed, not by hard work. But by deliberately destroying the legal document of another man and thereby taking over a property that wasn't, by rights, his own. The truth never came out, because Wells's father had been tight with Duncan Pitt and because the victim had committed suicide a month after the fraud was perpetrated. With his death, the truth was buried. *But not forgotten.* The whispered conversation little Robin had overheard so many years earlier had joined various other pieces of knowledge he would use when the time was most apt. Like now. Now, when he had decided he would stay in Preston. And of course if he stayed, he had to stamp his mark on the place.

Pulling on his jacket, Wells smoothed his hair again. Old Man Pitt might have spent the rest of his life respectably, donating to charity and generally being honourable, but his fortune had been based on another man's blood, and no amount of charity work could obliterate that. He might buy and collect fine books, but he was as big a villain as the illiterates in the steaming slums. He might be kindly, not press too hard for his rents, be a little more reasonable than some landlords, but it was his conscience he was trying to assuage, not his tenants. And if – over the years – there had been times when Old Man Pitt believed he had paid for his sin, that the dead man's suicide was accounted for, he was wrong. An old sin, like a corpse, stank – and sooner or later someone smelled it.

In Duncan Pitt's case, it was a shame that his nemesis would be Robin Wells. But the latter had had his eye on Pitt's property for some time and didn't take too kindly to the assumption that Andrew Pitt would inherit it after Duncan died. No, Wells wanted Ratcliffe Row, Hover Terrace and Amber Street. Liked the idea of having a cosy little pocket of streets he could make into his own playground. Liked the thought of putting his own kind of tenants in, and his own kind of pubs. So much for The Horse and Cart; he would make the place pay for itself, make the weak move out and bring in the hard cases. Maybe run a whorehouse in one of the streets. Make some real money.

And no one was going to stop him. Wells would just call by and explain the situation to Old Man Pitt, and he would roll over and Andrew would be out on his ear. Duncan Pitt wasn't going to risk exposure, that much was certain. It was worthwhile giving up a few terraces to keep a corpse underground. Well worth the sacrifice of Ratcliffe Row, Hover Terrace and Amber Street to avoid being publicly denounced. And jailed.

Of course the fact that some of the hated Shaw family lived on Amber Street was just a bonus to Wells. He thought of Silky and imagined his face when he found out about the new landlord. He would be wondering when Wells would come for him. But Wells liked the idea of picking the family off one by one. First Ivan, then Jim Shaw, then Silky . . . The reason for Wells's hatred was something he found difficult to admit, even to himself. But he had loved the woman Silky stole from him. Loved her totally, even considered going straight for her. She had been the one sweet presence in his stinking world, and for a time he had come to believe that she might offer him a way out of the mire. Until Silky Shaw had come along and she had chosen him. Turned her back on Wells, his money, his promises, his real bloody affection, for some greasy-haired smarmy bastard with a tattoo parlour. If Silky had married her it wouldn't have been so bad, but the affair had broken up soon after and somehow that had made it worse. Wells had been dumped for another man – and then his ex-girlfriend had left the other man and moved on. She hadn't come back for forgiveness or to beg. No, she had got on with her life. Goodbye, Robin Wells, and bugger you.

Taking a deep breath, Wells steadied himself. Think of that bleeding Komodo dragon, he told himself. Wait. Revenge will be all the sweeter when it comes. Meanwhile he had to get on with the matter in hand . . . Leaving the house, he made for his car and slid into the driver's seat, starting the engine and smiling imperceptibly. His excitement was almost sexual. The moment had arrived for him to draw blood. To lance the boil that had festered throughout Duncan Pitt's life. And damn anyone that got in his way.

Thirty minutes later, he was parking outside the Pitts' luxurious house on the edge of Avenham Park. He headed for the front door, knocking twice and waiting. A moment later a harassed-looking woman answered, struggling to hold on to an obese Pekinese dog.

'Hello?'

'Is Duncan Pitt at home?'

'Who wants to see him?' Ivy replied, letting go of the dog and trying to look composed.

'Is he in?'

'I asked you a question,' Ivy retorted, disliking Wells on sight.

He was equally enamoured. She would be sorry she'd taken that tone with him when her housekeeping was cut back.

'My name is Wells, Robin Wells. I know your husband. Or rather, I should say that my father and he were old friends.'

This was safe ground, so safe that Ivy immediately smiled and stood back. 'Do come in. Sorry if I sounded curt, but you can never be too careful who you let in these days. You hear such stories. Thieves, even murderers, roaming the streets. And they look respectable . . .'

Wells smiled reassuringly, walking in.

'I'll go and let my husband know you're here, Mr Wells. If you would like to wait in the study.'

Oh, he would like to wait, Wells thought, walking into a comfortable room filled with Duncan Pitt's impressive collection. Thoughtfully he studied some of the books on the shelves: *On the Origin of Species*, Freud's works, and *How to Get Ahead in Business*. Wells smiled to himself. How to get ahead indeed! Old Pitt had got his victim's bloody head on a spike. Slowly he continued his survey, hearing the sound of a door slamming in a room overhead, followed by footsteps coming down the stairs.

A moment later Duncan Pitt walked in. His complexion was so waxen Wells wondered if he was ill. Certainly he was a lot older than he remembered, but then he must be pushing seventy.

'Robin Wells,' Duncan said slowly, as though the name itself was difficult to pronounce. He seemed not to know how to behave; not welcoming, not hostile. And although he had no idea what Wells was visiting him about, he had the look of someone sensing catastrophe. 'Your father was a good friend of mine.'

'Too good.'

'Pardon?'

'I've not come here to chat. I've got a business proposition for you.'

Stunned, Duncan sat down at his desk. He was trying to look in control, but he was, in fact, intimidated and his legs were about to fail him. A long time had passed since he had seen Robin Wells, but he had heard all about the little boy he remembered from so long ago – and his reputation was frightening.

'I ask you not to take that tone with me.'

'I shall take any tone I like,' Wells replied, sitting down opposite Duncan. 'I want your property: Ratcliffe Row, Hover Terrace and Amber Street.'

'Are you mad!'

'I want them within the week. You can keep the other two streets you own, I don't want them. Think yourself lucky you got off so lightly.'

Duncan was finding it hard to breathe. 'I've heard about you, Wells. I was talking to your father only the other week and he said how ashamed he was of the way you've turned out. You've got a reputation.'

'I should think I have, I worked hard enough to get it.'

'A reputation that no decent man would want. You're a known liar and a thief and God knows what else.' Duncan could feel his hands shaking and clenched his fists. Jesus, Wells was terrifying, sitting there so composed. To come into his house and demand his property, his income! How dare he! As though he was entitled to it! 'I think you should leave!'

'I think you should shut up,' Wells responded evenly.

'Get out of my house!'

'Change your tune, or it won't be your house for much longer,' Wells replied, Duncan paling. 'Oh, and I'd ask your wife to move away from the door; you don't want her eavesdropping on our business, do we?'

'I have nothing to hide.'

Raising his eyebrows, Wells leaned forward and dropped his voice to a whisper. 'Stanley Gorman.'

The effect was cataclysmic. At once the fire went out of Duncan and he seemed to shrink, his body ageing with the impact of his old sin. Staggering to his feet, he moved to the door, then hesitated, trying to get a grip on himself. Outside he found Ivy listening – just as Wells had surmised.

'Go upstairs, sweetheart.'

'But that man! What is he talking about? He wants your property! He can't do it!'

'Go upstairs.'

'We need Andrew here.'

Uncharacteristically harsh, Duncan caught his wife's arm, his voice lowered. 'Listen to me, don't tell Andrew about this. Don't tell anyone.'

'But . . .'

'*But nothing!* If you want to help me, stay silent and trust me.'

Taken aback, she studied her husband's face. She hadn't heard the mention of Stanley Gorman's name, only Wells's demand for the property, but she knew enough to realise that her husband was afraid. And now she was too.

'Go upstairs,' Duncan went on, 'and let me handle this.'

Unnerved, she put her hand over her mouth as though to stop any sound coming out to give them away. All the years of Duncan's protection and her domestic comfort seemed suddenly under threat. There was an atmosphere in the house that had never been there before – and it had entered with Robin Wells. And she had let him in. This man who had changed her husband, overturned their lives, made the air turgid around them: *she had let him in.*

'Are you in trouble?'

She saw her husband hesitate as though he was about to confide, then he shrugged. 'I can handle this. Go upstairs and wait for me.'

Walking back into his study, he found Wells by the window, looking out.

'Nice house. I used to think I would buy a place like this, settle down, have a family. But that's not for me. I enjoy business too much.'

'What do you know?' Duncan asked, his voice hoarse.

'I know about Stanley Gorman.'

'Who?'

'I'm not playing games with you. I know what you did, and if I tell everyone else, you're finished. You'll end up in jail, even at your age. And your life will be over. Think of it, Mr Pitt: your son will be the inheritor of nothing but a bad name, and your family will be outcasts.' He put his head on one side. 'Not quite what you had in mind, is it? But it can all be avoided by just giving me some property.'

'That's blackmail.'

'Better than murder.'

'I killed no one!'

'As good as. Your fraud made Stanley Gorman take his own life.'

'I made him a good offer for his property.'

'You're a bloody liar,' Wells replied phlegmatically. 'You knew those buildings were worth a fortune, but you wanted to get them off Gorman for as little as possible. So you got your surveyor to lie, to tell him that they were unsafe, that the underpinnings had gone, that he would have to sell cheap to get anyone to buy them.'

'He could have got his own man in to check on the survey.'

'Stanley Gorman believed you,' Wells replied. 'You were friends. He had no reason to doubt what you said. No reason to think you would cheat him, that you would ruin him. Gorman had a family to support; he was desperate for money, he was ill . . .'

'I didn't know he was ill!'

'So it would be all right to cheat a healthy man, would it? You were lucky Gorman killed himself.'

Defeated, Duncan slumped into his chair. 'How do you know about Stanley Gorman?'

'Your wife isn't the only one who listens at doors, Mr Pitt. I used to, when I was a bored child. You would be amazed what I learned about the good citizens of Preston. People don't notice a child, have you ever realised that? They don't take much mind of them. And if they did, who would think a kid would be interested in business? Or remember what he heard?' Wells walked back to his seat, looking at Duncan. 'You're sickly. Shock does that, makes a man a bad colour.'

'I can't—'

'Yes you can. You can hand over the property and I'll say nothing.'

'What's to stop you coming back for more?' Duncan asked, his voice breaking.

'Nothing. I could come back, if I wanted. Or I could go elsewhere, remind someone else of something they would rather forget. Don't try to evoke pity in me, or negotiate. I don't feel for you, Mr Pitt. Or your family. I don't understand all these emotional ties; they're . . .' he paused, waiting for the right word, '*clutter*. What matters is this – you're a cheat and so am I, and that means we can do business.'

'I can't—'

'Oh, you can.'

'All right . . . I'll hand over the property.'

Duncan was a spent force. His past had caught up with him, overtaken him, and was now waiting, dark and inescapable. With one last futile attempt to excuse his actions, he said pathetically, 'I didn't kill Stanley Gorman.'

'Dear God,' Wells replied. 'Who cares?'

NINETEEN

It was a well-known fact that every Thursday night there was a card game at The Grapes and Fox. No one actually mentioned it; no one had to; everyone who was interested already knew about it. A couple of times Silky had gone for a flutter, lost a bit and won once. But he never took it seriously. Ivan, however – for all his puritanical streak – liked the cards. He was good, too. Good enough to get a bit of a name, good enough to take Jim once or twice. But Jim had no head for booze, or cards. And Jim had too much to lose to risk courting the tables again.

So when Ivan hit a winning streak at around nine fifteen that Thursday night, he was trying to concentrate and irritated by the chatter behind him. Irritated – then unnerved when the name Robin Wells came up.

'What about Wells?'

'You playing or what, Ivan?'

He waved his companion silent with a brusque gesture. 'What about Wells?'

An old man with a stained moustache and beer breath bent down towards Ivan. Around his head the fug of cheap smoke circled him like a halo.

'I 'eard he'd taken over some streets round 'ere. 'Eard he'd got Ratcliffe Row, Hover Terrace and Amber Street.'

Ivan flinched. 'Amber Street?'

'It's yer turn, Ivan, get on with the bloody game!'

Impatiently Ivan threw down a card and lost the point. Leaning over the back of his chair, he returned to the old man.

'I don't believe it! Those streets belong to Old Man Pitt.'

'Not any more. Yer've got family on Amber Street, haven't yer?'

Uneasy, Ivan nodded, then threw in his hand.

'Hey, yer can't leave now,' his fellow player snapped. 'Yer were winning.'

'I were winning until I heard about Robin Wells,' Ivan replied, his tone sour as he made for the door.

In moody silence he walked down the street, crossed Friargate, passed the Harris Library and the Guild Hall, heading for Amber Street. Usually he was unwilling to get involved with the family, but this was different; this time he was making sure that everyone knew he wasn't paying for anyone else's trouble again. The sooner Jim knew about Wells, the better. Thoughtful, Ivan passed under the few blossoming cherry trees, the vegetation thinning out the nearer he got to the poor area of town. Finally he turned into Amber Street and paused. The sun had set and the impoverished terrace looked worn down and dank, a man smoking a pipe on the corner, a couple of kids pushing an old cart full of kindling. Storing up for the winter weather early, Ivan thought. Or maybe they were anticipating one of those late cold snaps in May, coming full throttle to catch out the sickly or the newly born.

Knocking hurriedly on the door, Ivan walked in, Kat looking up from the kitchen table. 'Oh, hello there.'

He nodded, mumbling, and looked round. He had heard that Anna was weak and was now mostly confined to bed, Kat and Ma Shaw looking after the house and the baby. Or rather the toddler. Staring at the cheerful little girl on Kat's knee, Ivan touched Christine briefly on the forehead, then cleared his throat as though embarrassed by the merest show of affection.

'Is yer dad home, Kat?'

'You've just missed him.'

'Ivan!' Ma Shaw said, walking in at that minute from the back yard. 'What brings yer here?' She knew already. Not the whole story, but she understood her son well enough to anticipate doom. Ivan wasn't a man who brought good news; he had been born to pass on trauma.

'I were wanting to see our Jim.'

Ma Shaw's eyebrows rose. 'Oh aye?'

'Yer heard about Wells?'

'Yer get water out of them,' she replied wryly, unable to resist teasing her son.

'I mean Robin Wells.'

'Robin Wells?' Kat echoed, remembering the shadowy figure who had hovered – on and off – in their backgrounds for years. 'What about him?'

'I should talk to yer dad . . .'

'Oh get on with it!' Ma Shaw barked. 'What's up?'

'Old Man Pitt's given over Ratcliffe Row, Hover Terrace and Amber Street to Robin Wells.'

'Never!'

'I've just heard.'

'But why?' Kat asked, her voice shocked. 'Why in God's name would he give them over to that man?'

'Money, I suppose.'

'But the old man's rich, and if he wanted to sell, why sell to someone like Wells?' Kat queried.

She was more than a little uneasy, fully aware that while the Pitts might be lenient at times, Wells was quite another matter. Watching Ivan pull his sleeve down over the crude tattoo, Kat glanced automatically at the mantelpiece. The brandy bottle was still there, untouched. But for how long now? she wondered. If they fell behind with Wells as a landlord, they were finished. Her heart thumping, she thought about her father. He had stayed off the booze for months, kept to his job, but it hadn't stopped her checking up on him every few weeks. Not saying anything, just spying – she hated the word *and* the action, but it needed to be done.

No one else knew about it. She would sneak out of the house, make her way to the Albert Edward, and watch the watchman. Then, when she was satisfied, she would return home. It was a miracle no one had caught her, but so far her secret – and that of her father – had stayed safe.

'Bugger,' Ma Shaw said simply, sitting down. 'I have to say, Wells is the last landlord anyone would want. I heard all about him in Manchester when he bought some property there, running off decent people and putting all sorts in. Whores and flop houses . . .'

'Don't let Mum know. She'll only worry.'

'She wouldn't be the only one,' Ma Shaw replied shortly, picking at the cuticle on her forefinger. 'Good job Micky's helping out at Silky's as well as working at the mill. We need to make sure the rent's paid up in full and on time from now on.'

'Wells might find another reason to evict.'

Ma Shaw looked up at her son, faking bravado. 'Really? Like what?'

'Like Silky.'

'Pah! That bother were over years ago.'

'If yer believe that, yer'll believe anything,' Ivan replied sourly, slumping, uninvited, on to a chair.

The atmosphere was oppressive, Ivan remembering the old injury, Ma Shaw suddenly faced with what she feared most – the headlong fall into the slums. Meanwhile Kat was wondering if the news would destabilise her father or galvanise him. Gently she stroked Christine's hair, rocking the toddler on her lap. The job at Unwins wasn't bringing in much of a wage, but there were precious few other opportunities. She had tried the mills and factories, but the jobs were going to the men first, then the women with families. Not the single girls with no dependants.

'We'll not cry before we're hurt,' Ma Shaw said finally,

standing up and hauling her lanky son to his feet. 'Ivan, get yerself home. Thanks fer coming, but we'll take it from here.'

Together the women watched him leave, then turned back to each other. 'It's not good,' Ma Shaw said.

Kat nodded. 'I know.'

'Wells could get nasty, and though I pooh-poohed it to Ivan, he's been waiting to settle the old score with Silky.'

'He wouldn't throw us out!'

'He might try,' Ma Shaw replied, walking to the door and reaching for her shawl. 'I'm going to have a word with yer father.'

Alarmed, Kat was on her feet in an instant. 'I'll go,' she said hurriedly. 'You sit with Christine. It's a long way . . .'

'I'm not an old fool!' Ma Shaw snapped, Kat wondering for an instant if she realised why her granddaughter was so concerned. 'I'm not worn out yet! I can catch a tram and walk the rest of the way.'

A sudden noise from upstairs interrupted them: Anna calling out. Kat took her chance and ran to the door.

'You see to Mum, I'll go and tell Dad,' she said. She took in a deep breath of relief as she hurried down Amber Street. If her father had fallen off the wagon again, she didn't want Ma Shaw to know about it. Not tonight. Not ever, if she had her way.

Stupefied, Andrew stared at his father. '*Robin Wells?* Are you mad!'

'I have my reasons,'

'They'd better be good ones,' Andrew replied sharply.

Grey-faced, Duncan sat at his desk. His legs were still shaking, the confrontation with his son almost as draining as his run-in with Wells. Nothing, no words, could explain his actions. Unless he confided the real truth – and he could never do that. Couldn't risk his son's hatred and distrust. Or that of his wife. Better that they think him misguided, or a fool, than know the truth. But the trauma of the situation had undermined Duncan Pitt and he was losing weight quickly, his reassurances to Ivy that he knew what he was doing falling on deaf ears.

'The deal is done.'

'But why?' Andrew replied, shaken. 'What possessed you?'

'It's my business to do as I like with!' Duncan barked back, his colour high on his cheeks, his attitude close to frenzy.

Uneasy, Andrew studied his father. 'What is it?'

'What's *what*?'

'Come on, Dad, you wouldn't have done this unless there was a bloody good reason. You know what Wells is like, you know what he could do with your property.'

'It's his property now.'

'But why?' Andrew replied, baffled. 'Just explain it to me, Dad, just tell me why and I'll understand. I know you must have your reasons, I know you must think it's the right thing to do – just tell me and I'll accept it.'

'I don't have to explain myself to you!'

'What's the matter with you?' Andrew countered. 'This isn't like you. You've done a deal with a thug. Someone a decent man would cross the street to avoid.'

Duncan kept his eyes averted. He knew that people were talking, and he could understand why. Oh, he had put the story out that he had been short of money – *that* people understood. That was business. What they couldn't come to terms with was *who* he had done business with.

'You'll not go short, Andrew, we have other property . . .'

'I'm not talking about my inheritance! This isn't about the property, Dad! It's why you sold it to Wells.'

'I'm not going to discuss it,' Duncan replied, stiff-necked.

'Fine,' Andrew said, his tone quiet. 'Obviously you don't trust me.'

'Of course I do!'

'No you don't. Otherwise you would explain.'

'Some things you have to take on trust.'

'But in this I don't trust your judgement,' Andrew replied sadly. 'Mother thinks I should talk to our solicitor. She said you won't explain the deal to her either and that you might have been confused . . .'

'I'm not senile!'

'Well you're acting it!' Andrew replied. 'Anyone selling property to a villain for God knows what purpose isn't acting in their right mind.' He paused, dropping his voice. 'Has he got something on you?'

A long moment unfolded between them, Duncan looking down at his desk and noticing a scratch on the leather he had never seen before. His mind went back and he remembered Stanley Gorman, with his wiry blond hair and his barman's laugh, thanking Duncan over and over again for taking the property off his hands. No one else would have helped him out like that, he had said. Now he would be able to marry his sweetheart. Jesus, he had laughed, what would he have done without his old friend? . . . Go on, Duncan told himself, go on, remember . . . Stanley Gorman, wiry blond hair slicked with blood from where the train had hit him, barman's laugh silent. Stanley Gorman, who had been like an echo in Duncan's conscience for years, until good living and good loving had made the sound less and less resonant. Until finally the dead man's echo came only at night, and then Duncan would turn over and rest his head on his wife's breast and forget. But no longer. Now Stanley Gorman was everywhere; he was in every tram, every car, his voice was in every radio programme. The faint echo Wells had rung like a dinner gong, and now the sound was drumming incessantly in Duncan's ears.

I built my money and my life on a fraud. It cost me a man's life, Duncan thought, looking at his son blindly. How in God's name can I tell you that?

'Dad,' Andrew said again quietly, '*has* Wells got something on you? Is he blackmailing you? If he is, tell me, we can sort this out. We can sort anything out together.'

No, Duncan thought, turning away, that's what you believe when you're young, but it's not true. There are some things in life that nothing can ever sort out.

The news reached Joan a day later and left her, like everyone else, baffled. Honestly, she thought, what on earth was Old Man Pitt playing at? Then again, perhaps this was the perfect opportunity for her to reopen her relationship with Andrew. She could, as a friend, offer condolences. *Condolences?* she thought, frowning. What the hell was she talking about? The old man had made a suspect business deal, he hadn't died.

Probably better if he had done.

'The man must be mad!' Gwen said simply. 'The way things are turning out for that family, they'll ruin their name. I mean, people judge you on who you do business with. And doing business with a crook is not going to help anyone socially. Frankly, darling, it's a good thing you never got back with Andrew.'

Joan's head shot up. She had wanted to get back with Andrew and had tried to effect a reconciliation, but all her planning had been futile. Their paths didn't cross and Andrew wasn't playing any more. Instead he had been seeing another girl, and Joan had pretended that her own affections were occupied elsewhere. But she was lying to herself. As had been the case all her life, she wanted precisely what she couldn't have. And this time not even her parents could get it for her.

'Everywhere you go, you can hear people gossiping about Duncan Pitt trading with a villain,' Gwen went on mercilessly. 'Of course no one can predict mental illness—'

'*What!*'

Gwen glanced at her daughter. 'You don't sell property to a gangster, darling, unless you're mad.'

'Or ruthless.'

Both women turned to look at Gareth, slicing the top off

his boiled egg. 'Duncan Pitt could just be ruthless and not care about his good name. And he can't care too much about his son's either. Those streets took a sizeable part out of Andrew's inheritance.'

'Money isn't everything,' Joan replied, on the defensive.

'Maybe Duncan's teaching his son to be ruthless too,' Gareth went on blithely. 'Times are changing; honourable men are throwing in their lot with villains to make money. Where's there muck, there's brass.'

'Andrew isn't like that.'

'How d'you know?' her father replied evenly. 'He might be his father's son.'

'I don't believe Andrew is immoral!'

'Well whatever his son is like, Duncan Pitt's name is ruined,' Gwen replied coolly. 'People won't talk to him any more, and as for Ivy, I feel sorry for her, but she's not welcome at the bridge club. I heard the other day that she was snubbed at the hairdresser's.'

'You lie down with dogs, you get up with fleas,' Gareth replied enigmatically. 'Duncan Pitt is a changed man, with a ruined reputation. Shame he had to take his wife and son down with him.'

The news came down Hover Terrace even before his footsteps sounded, people scurrying for their houses and closing their doors. Driving his car slowly along the terrace, Wells caught a few anxious faces watching him from windows and then turned towards Amber Street. Parking, he walked over to The Horse and Cart and pushed open the door. Spotting him, two older men backed off to a far table. Horace glanced up from his stool. Having seen it all, he wasn't fazed by Wells and nodded resignedly.

'You want a drink, Mr Wells?'

'A pint.'

Slowly Wells looked round, then moved over to the piano

and sat down. It was a little-known fact, but he had played in a trio in London, in a club off Beak Street. It was a little quirk of his, a talent he couldn't resist. All the diligent tutelage that had been forced on to him as a child had paid off. In every other fibre of his body he was a hard man, but something about music reached him. He could – when alone – play Bach and Handel. He could – when he wasn't trying to seduce a woman – play the darkest portions of Rachmaninov. He could – when he was solitary, in the early hours – play Mozart like a pro. But not in public. When he was watched, he played jazz, flashy show tunes, Gershwin . . . Slowly Wells's fingers moved over the keys, and then he began to play. Surprised, Horace watched him, wondering how a bastard like Wells had such talent, then turned as the door opened again and Kat walked in.

She came in smiling, glancing over to the piano and then looking at Horace.

'I heard the music.'

Swivelling round on the piano stool, Robin Wells took a long look at her and liked what he saw. Liked the unusual face, the intelligent eyes, the voluptuous figure. Who would have thought there was a woman like this on Amber Street? His jaded interest, usually slow to ignite, was caught by Kat. She was young, he realised, but not girlish, not silly. This was no stupid kid. This was a woman. Intelligence radiated from her, along with something else: a patina of natural style. This was a woman who could wear expensive clothes, who could be transported from the back streets with ease. An orchid hiding under a heap of dung, just waiting to be replanted.

'How d'you do?' he said, fascinated. 'Miss . . . ?'

'Shaw, Katherine. But everyone calls me Kat.'

'Mary's out the back,' Horace said urgently, hoping Kat would take the hint. He had seen Wells's interest and wanted to protect her. But didn't know how to. And for once, Kat didn't scent danger. She had heard the music, that was all. Come inside to listen to a ragtime tune. And now she was talking to a stranger who had a fascinating presence about him. She didn't see the lizard hiding inside the expensive suit.

'You're a good player, Mr . . . ?'

'Wells. Robin Wells.'

The colour went from her face immediately, all friendliness closed off. Turning, she made to leave, but Wells called out to her.

'You know of me then?'

She nodded, unwilling to trust her voice.

'I know your uncle.'

Her eyes closed, then opened again as she turned back to face him. Around her the customers waited, listening.

'Which one? I believe you know both.'

'Oh yes, of course,' he said, smiling. 'Ivan Lomax is your uncle too. I was thinking of Silky Shaw, though . . . I suppose he's talked of me?'

'Not much.'

Now all her instincts were alerted and she had the sensation of being pulled underwater, every cell in her body straining to escape drowning. The violence others had sensed in Robin Wells was palpable in the very air around him, and yet she didn't dare to insult him. He was their landlord. Kat had a mother to protect, a roof to keep over the Shaw family's head. Showing her true feelings might well result in disaster.

'You shouldn't believe everything you hear about me,' he went on. 'People like villains, like to build things up. You know what I mean?' His fingers ran over the piano keys again, a melodic tune swinging sweetly through the stuffy pub. 'I don't have any ill feeling towards you, Katherine . . .'

She nodded, making for the door.

'But your uncle Silky is another matter.'

Stopping, she turned again.

'You want me to run an errand for you, Mr Wells? Like Micky did? Or Ivan? You wrote a message on Ivan.'

Behind the bar, Horace coughed warningly, and Kat realised she was pushing her luck.

'You have a temper,' Wells said, amused. 'Well cut your teeth on someone else, Miss Shaw, because I bite back.' Rising to his feet, he moved past her to the door, then turned, touched her shoulder momentarily, and walked out.

Exhaling, Horace moved to the window in time to see Wells drive off. Then he turned back to Kat. 'I admire your guts. But I'd keep away from him. I didn't like the way he was looking at you.'

She shivered. 'He's frightening,'

'Yer not the first one that's said that.'

'Did he say anything about the street?'

'No, luv.'

'This place?'

'No.'

'So we're safe?'

'No, Kat. We stopped being safe the day that man took over.'

TWENTY

The first two months passed without incident, but in September Jim's hours were curtailed and his wage cut. Still working at the mill and part time for Silky, Micky developed an ear infection and was laid off for a week, his wages docked. Desperate, Kat turned to the only person she could rely on.

'I can help out here,' she said.

Silky raised his eyebrows. 'You have a job.'

'It's not bringing in enough of a wage.'

'But you can't come here, Kat. A girl working in a tattoo parlour? Are you joking? It's only one up from going on the streets.'

'It's respectable. You're my uncle.'

'Kat, everyone will talk. You'll be pointed out, you'll be an outcast.'

'And since when was I going to Buckingham Palace anyway?' she shot back. 'Silky, we need the money . . .'

'I'll loan it to you.'

'No, I want to work for it,' she replied firmly. 'When Micky's better, he'll come back. But for now, let me do this. If I work with you, you can do twice as much, that means twice as much money. We need to pay the rent. There are no excuses. We've managed so far. But you more than anyone know what this is about. *We have to pay Wells.* He's got rid of three families in Ratcliffe Row already, and he's gunning for us.'

'Because of me,' Silky said thoughtfully. 'I'll go and talk to him.'

'That won't do any good! He'll not listen to reason. Oh come on, Silky, if you let me work here with you, I could back up the rent. See us all safe.'

'What about your father?'

'His hours have been cut back.' She looked away. 'He's taking it badly.'

'Like how?'

'Like he might do something stupid. Bet on the horses . . .'

'You're joking!'

'Yeah, maybe. I don't know, Silky, I honestly don't. You know Dad, he's unreliable. And the other day I overheard Ma Shaw banging on at him about being a lousy provider. I know Mum heard, and that's bad for her.'

'You can't carry everyone, Kat, it's not your duty.'

'I'm not carrying everyone!' she replied heatedly. 'I just want us to get over this bad patch. And we will, Silky, when Dad's hours go back up again and Micky's better. It's just temporary. Ma Shaw said she had some savings put away. Not much, but I don't want to take it from her. Not unless we really need it.'

'Working here is not a job for a woman.'

'You don't think I can do it!'

Rolling his eyes, Silky picked up a tattoo needle and held it in front of her face.

'This is the needle. One of several. Which have to be sharp, and clean. You have to make a design on flesh, press the needle into the flesh so that the ink goes under the skin and stays there to make the tattoo permanent. You can't make a mistake, and people move around because it hurts. They moan, they complain. Most of them are men – drunk men sometimes – and they don't trust women. Or else they'll make a pass at you. Either way you'll have your hands full. When people hear that you're working here, they'll gossip and say you're a scrubber. They'll assume you're rough, and your reputation will be shot. Because no one – *no one* – will ever forget that you worked in a tattoo parlour. You could live to be one hundred and seventy-five years old and no one will forget. You'll be mixing with factory workers, sailors and dockers. They'll try and put their hands up your skirt and their tongues down your throat. Micky gets by because he's got talent, but he finds it hard going. And he's a young man. I'm around, but I can't nursemaid you, Kat. You have to look out for yourself – and know how to handle trouble.'

'All right.'

'It will only be temporary.'

'OK.'

Resigned, he stared at her. 'You can only do the basics, you hear me? I'll do the outlines of the tattoos, you fill in.'

'OK.'

'It's not a joke, Kat.'

She nodded grimly. 'I know that, Silky, honestly. I know that.'

Having never been anything but accepted all his life, Andrew was finding the gossip difficult. He was, he realised almost at once, caught between two stools. His inherent honesty made him want to leave, but his loyalty to his father – and his bewildered mother – forced him to stay. Daily he waited for an explanation from Duncan that would make sense of the situation. Daily he longed for the breakthrough, the means by which he could defend his father from the world. But as the weeks and months passed, it never came. Instead he found himself living with a father he loved but despised. At times he wondered if he should move out, take his mother with him and start his own business, but his love for his father stopped him. Endlessly he wondered if Duncan was ill, mentally impaired. If he was honest, he wanted the excuse of sickness to prove that his father's action had not just been ruthless business greed. But was it greed? Andrew asked himself again and again. With full access to the accounts, he had searched for the payment from Wells for the property – and never found it.

So where had the money gone? Or was there any money in the first place? And if not, that suggested only one thing – his father was being blackmailed by Robin Wells. The thought was horrendous, but infinitely more palatable than thinking Duncan was voluntarily dealing with scum. Yet always a further thought followed on – *what exactly had his father done?* What could a man do that was so bad he would risk his family's love and his good name to conceal it? Duncan Pitt's reputation had been tarnished by his involvement with Wells, so how much worse was the secret he was sacrificing so much to preserve?

And then Andrew realised he knew nothing about his father. That the man he loved and admired was a stranger. That the kindness he had taken for granted, the safe home, the financial buffers, were illusions. The future he had anticipated was insecure, as hard to hold down as smoke. And the rejection, the social cold-shouldering, hurt. Only one person had been really supportive: Joan Fairchild. The woman who had rejected him was now offering friendship. But the love Andrew had felt for Joan had long since faltered. Faced with a disgraced father and an anxious mother, he was hardly able to remember the romantic anguish he had once felt so acutely. Time and trouble had aged Andrew Pitt, whilst the woman he had longed for had remained the same. He now felt about Joan as she had once felt about him: sure of her, certain of her affection, of her constant love.

And he knew now it wasn't enough.

TWENTY-ONE

'She's doing what!' Ma Shaw said, her voice ringing throug the house on Amber Street. 'Working at Silky's! The world' gone bloody mad! Bloody mad!'

Hurriedly Anna reached for her mother-in-law's hand t calm her. 'She likes it there. Don't take on, Ma, she's onl helping out for a while, until Micky's better.'

'A tattoo parlour!' the old woman exclaimed, pullin Christine on to her knee as she sat down on the side of th bed. Hurriedly she brushed the toddler's hair, Christin mewling. 'Sit still!'

'You know Kat . . .'

'Oh, I know her all right!' Ma Shaw replied, tyin Christine's hair into a ponytail and fastening a ribbon aroun it. She would have to calm down, she told herself, it wasn' good for Anna. But honestly, hadn't she offered her saving to tide them over? Her granddaughter was crazy; peopl would talk about this one. God above, how people woul talk . . . Preoccupied, she undid Christine's hair and began t brush it again.

'Ma, you've already done that,' Anna said, putting her fee over the side of the bed.

'Where are yer going?'

'I thought I could make some dinner . . .'

'Yer not well enough!'

'I'm not an invalid,' Anna said quietly. 'How difficult d

you think it is for me to lie here, overhearing how worried everyone is? I'm not strong, but I'm not deaf. I know what's going on. I know Jim's hours have been cut back; and as for Micky, he's really suffering with that ear infection, I could hear him in the night.'

Retying Christine's ribbon once again, Ma Shaw exhaled slowly. 'It's just a bad patch we're going through. I put a poultice on Micky's ear and it'll be good as new soon.'

'He's in pain.'

'It's on the mend, Anna, stop fretting.'

'I know there have been cutbacks at the Albert Edward. Jim must be so worried. Poor thing, he does his best.'

'Yer've always said that, but I know what he's like – unreliable. Always has been.'

Weak she might be, but Anna had overheard too much to be totally ignorant, and she understood something of how precarious their situation had become. Much as the family might try to protect her, she had snatched at titbits of news and noticed the changes in routine. She knew that Jim's hours had been cut – not because he'd told her, or because she'd overheard, but because he was a bad liar. Trying to cover up, he had pretended to go out to work at the same time and return as usual. But she knew that he had, in fact, merely sneaked downstairs, whiling away the hours until he crept out for the shorter shift . . . All that time and trouble, just to stop her worrying.

And now here was Ma Shaw grumbling about him. Again.

'You've never had a good word for Jim. You always preferred Silky. I think you even like Ivan better than Jim.'

'I love them all the same.'

'That's not true,' Anna said, her frustration turning to uncharacteristic anger. 'Jim has never been able to please you.'

'It's obvious why.'

'I'm not arguing with you – and not in front of Christine.

She's only little. I don't want her to hear you calling her fathe names.'

'She might as well know the truth. And I don't call hin names!'

'You never stop!'

'And you see him as some kind of hero!' Ma Shaw sho back. 'Yer want to take off the rose-coloured glasses, Anna and see Jim Shaw fer what he really is.'

'You can't talk about him like that! He's my husband!'

'And he's my son, and I reckon I know him best.'

'You reckon you know everything!' Anna said sharply, Ma Shaw reeling. 'Well you don't! Jim's a good man. He's just no been lucky.'

'People make their own luck.'

'What fool believes that!' Anna replied, suddenly catching her breath and leaning back against the cushions.

At once Ma Shaw's anger faded and she was all concern. Illness she could cope with, but not rebellion. 'Now look what yer've gone and done. Got yerself all worked up.' Carefully she tucked Anna back on to the bed. Thank God her daughter-in-law didn't know about the new landlord. 'Nothing will be helped by yer getting ill and worrying. We'll come through, we always do. You have a little rest now, whilst I take Christine to the shops. It'll all be fine, Anna. It always is.'

Frowning, Andrew pulled up at the kerb and then rolled down the car window. The light was on inside the tattoo parlour, illuminating Silky and his customer. And someone else. Someone Andrew knew, but could hardly imagine being there: Kat Shaw. Surprised, he turned off the engine and stared. Of course he knew that Silky was her uncle, but it looked – that couldn't be right, could it? – like Kat was working in the place. Fascinated, he watched Silky begin to map out a tattoo on a man's arm and then stand back, Kat picking up the needle, dipping it in ink, and filling in the design.

Good God, Andrew thought, the world was full of surprises. It seemed like only yesterday that he had been talking to her about Horace Armitage's red pub door. He had been impressed by her then, even more impressed when later she had asked for his help and he had been so churlish. Although fully aware of the fragility of her situation, she had not backed down. Had even told him off . . . He had admired her for that. Thought about her, on and off, in the months that followed. Then found himself talking to her, asking after her mother, making bloody silly excuses to hang about near where she worked. He wasn't smitten, he told himself. He wasn't smitten. But he'd been very close to kissing her a week or so ago. And he was very sure that he was going to kiss her soon . . .

He looked back through the tattoo parlour window. Kat Shaw had become even more striking, Andrew thought. Unusual, composed, so unlike all the whey-faced girls he had known. And all those girls, who had been so keen to know him, had gone now. Scared off, warned away, by Duncan Pitt throwing in his lot with Robin Wells. There were no more virgins on offer, no more eager mothers pressing would-be wives on the Pitt heir. Not now he was tainted by his father's sin. No one cared what his father had done, only *who* he had done it with . . . Smiling grimly, Andrew realised that he was no longer the eligible bachelor. That the social attention he had taken as a right was now denied him.

So preoccupied was he that half an hour passed while he sat in the car and thought. And at the end of thirty minutes he was no nearer to understanding anything and startled when a door banged closed nearby. Jumping, he saw Silky and Kat come out of the tattoo parlour and lock up, Kat walking off in the direction of Amber Street.

A whim forced him out of the car, crossing over and calling her name.

Surprised, she stopped, then frowned incredulously as sh saw him approach. 'Andrew?'

'Hello there. I saw you in the tattoo parlour . . . Well, saw . . .' he blundered stupidly. 'How are you?'

She smiled, welcoming. 'I'm fine.'

'Are you working at your uncle's place?'

It was Kat's turn to be embarrassed. This was Andrew, th man she liked so much – and he had seen her working in tattoo parlour. She looked away. Bugger it, she though furiously. She had wanted to tell him herself, to explain whe they had one of their conversations. To slip it into the chat a though it wasn't really so dreadful for a woman to b working in a tattoo parlour. But instead Andrew had caugh her out, seen her at Silky's, and by the look on his face, h was stunned. As well he might be, Kat thought, her fac burning with fury and disappointment. God, how stupid wa she? How could she *really* hold out any hope for a relationship with Andrew Pitt? Silky had been right. Apparentl working in the tattoo parlour *was* only one up from walkin the streets; in the few weeks she had been there, Kat had bee snubbed, insulted and even called a whore. Ma Shaw ha worked herself into a lather as well. Telling Kat that she ha ruined her good name and that no decent man would wan her . . . And now here was Andrew, staring at her.

'*Are* you working for your uncle?'

She nodded, trying to sound light-hearted. 'Yes, shocking isn't it? I'm surprised you're even talking to me.'

He raised his eyebrows. 'I'm surprised you're talking to m – after what my father did. Have you heard?'

She nodded. 'Oh, we heard. Couldn't help bu hear . . . Why did your father sell out to Robin Wells?'

'To tell you the truth, I don't know.' He looked round uncertain. 'Would you like me to walk you home?'

'But you've got a car,' Kat said, gesturing across the street

'OK, can I *drive* you home?'

She smiled. 'I'd like that. In fact, I'm glad to see you.'

For a moment he seemed taken aback, then he smiled warmly. 'I'm glad to see you too, Kat. I wanted to talk to someone.'

'You can talk to me.'

'I know that,' he said, the atmosphere between them relaxing as he held the door open for Kat to get into the passenger seat. She wasn't used to cars, and once inside, she perched uneasily on the seat, her hands on her lap. As she waited for Andrew to get in, she noticed a darn at her heel and crossed her ankles hurriedly.

'Is there anywhere you'd like to go?'

'Wherever you think,' Kat replied, noticing that her other ankle also had a darn, and hoping against hope that Andrew wouldn't notice. It was dark, she reassured herself, no one would see her stockings. Or her coat, which was worn at the hem. Suddenly, in the comfort of Andrew's car, she felt both envy and frustration. She could *never* be a part of this, however much she day-dreamed about it.

'I have to say,' he said, drily, 'that talking to you is always refreshing. You do speak your mind.'

'I think you mean I have a temper.' She pulled a face. 'Gets me into trouble sometimes.'

'I don't mind it. You just say what you think,' Andrew replied, starting the car, Kat gripping the sides of her seat.

She was uneasy, and yet praying that someone would see her, that the gossips would say, *We saw Kat Shaw driving around with Andrew Pitt.* She almost wanted her mother to see her. Just so Anna could feel pride in knowing that her daughter had managed to catch the interest of such a man. But most of all Kat was happy to be there, so close to Andrew. And because he was preoccupied driving, she could steal greedy looks at his profile, at his hands on the wheel, at his suit. And she could smell him too, the odour of good tobacco and expensive clothes. Not Amber Street cast-offs. Not suits a man could get for next to nothing from a house clearance.

'We could go out for dinner.'

Immediately Kat panicked. *Dinner?* Where? How? She couldn't go for dinner in darned stockings . . .

'Well . . . I should really get home.'

'OK. We don't have to eat,' Andrew replied, picking up on her anxiety and suddenly desperate to make her feel comfortable. 'We could just talk. Let's stop for a bit.'

He parked the car by some closed shops and turned off the headlights. The evening was mild, and Kat wound down her window and breathed in.

'Will you carry on working for your father?' she asked.

'I have to.'

'For the money?'

'No, because he's my father – and because of my mother. I can't just up and leave . . . I wish he'd explain, though.'

'And he won't?'

'No,' Andrew said simply, turning to her. 'Why are you working at your uncle's?'

'We have to pay the rent. We daren't fall behind – not with our new landlord.'

He flushed. 'I'm sorry.'

'It wasn't your fault. It wasn't your decision.'

'No . . .' he said simply, turning away. 'Other people change your life, don't they? Have you noticed that? Sometimes it's not your own actions, it's something or someone outside. Something that has nothing – but *everything* – to do with you.'

She knew exactly what he meant. 'I suppose that's the way it is for most people.' Unless you're Ivan, she thought, thinking of her solitary uncle. 'I mean, that's what happens in families, isn't it? One person's bad luck, or bad judgement, colours everything.'

'But I don't know why my father did it,' Andrew said dully. 'He won't explain. I mean, he says we needed the money – and that's fine. But he could have sold to anyone. Why Robin Wells?'

Kat glanced at him carefully. 'Why do you think?'

'I don't know. My father was always so honest before – why would he throw away his good name?'

Hesitating, Kat wondered what to say, and then wondered if she should stay quiet. But speaking her mind was Kat's strong suit.

'No one throws away their reputation unless they have more to lose than their good name.'

He turned, looking at her with admiration. 'You make it sound honourable. As if my father did something good.'

'Maybe he did.'

'So why won't he explain?'

'Maybe he can't.'

'You do realise that we are both outcasts, don't you?'

She laughed softly. 'But you're a *rich* outcast!'

'I don't feel rich. I feel shabby.'

The depth of the conversation was catching them both unawares. But their situations – so outwardly different – were, in fact, very similar. Andrew had indirectly lost his status and Kat was trying desperately to hold on to the tiny amount of control she had, forfeiting some of her good name in the process. Both had made sacrifices for their families, and in that instant, both recognised the value of the other.

'We could buy a bell and ring it to let people know we were coming.'

Kat laughed again. 'The Preston lepers. Of course there is another solution.'

He looked at her, smiling. 'What's that?'

'We could kill Robin Wells.'

'Very good. How?'

'It would have to look like an accident,' Kat went on, mock serious. 'Perhaps we could stun him and then throw him into the dock at the Albert Edward.'

'He'd float.'

'Not if we weighted down his pockets.'

'Nice . . .' Andrew replied, smiling. 'What with?'

'Bricks.'

'What about cement? They do that in the films, don't they? I saw James Cagney do it to a gangster.'

'He *is* a gangster.'

'No, Cagney's an actor.'

She grinned. 'But Robin Wells is a real gangster.'

'A very good one too.'

'So what makes a good villain?'

'No conscience and a sharp suit.'

They both laughed, the atmosphere in the car easy, comfortable. For the first time in her life Kat was really enjoying a man's company, and Andrew was entranced. She was stunning, smart and easy to talk to. So unlike the stilted women he had known before. Joan Fairchild seemed so spoiled, so lightweight, by comparison to Kat Shaw. He felt at that moment as though he could have stayed in the car with her for ever.

Kat felt the same too. But flattered as she might be, she was no fantasist and she knew there was no future for them. This would be a one-off, a happy schism in normal life, a glimpse into a world off limits to both of them. A memory she would enjoy – but only that. A romance that could never get off the ground because it was earthbound, locked into social rigours and bank accounts.

'I have to go,' she said, smiling and getting out of the car.

'Let me drive you all the way home.'

'It's only the next street,' Kat replied, bending down at the window. 'Thank you.'

He was genuinely puzzled. 'For what?'

'For a nice time.'

'Next time we'll have that dinner,' he called after her.

Pausing, Kat turned back to the car and bent down again, her tone light. 'Even outcasts have their pecking order, Andrew. You're an upper-class outcast; I'm working class.'

His expression was suddenly urgent. 'Don't say no . . .'

'I have to!'

'All right,' he said. 'Say no now. But one day you'll change your mind. Outcasts have to stick together.'

'Bye, then . . .'

He called her back. 'One other thing . . .'

'Yes?'

'I don't why I'm saying this, or if you'll laugh at me, but I have to tell you: if you need me, Katherine Shaw, I'll be there for you. I swear I will *always* be there for you.'

TWENTY-TWO

Unsteady on his feet, Jim weaved down towards the dockside and the hut. He would make it inside and have a rest, clear his head. He was crazy to have had another drink, but God knew he had to do something. His feet moved erratically, the watchman's lamp swinging backwards and forwards, now lighting the side of a boat, then the swallowing black water. Nausea overwhelmed him suddenly, and he doubled up, vomiting into the dock and then slumping against the rope block. He could never explain what he had done, even to himself. It was unforgivable – his wife sick, no money in the pot for the rent, and Wells breathing down his neck like a bleeding vampire.

Pushing himself upright, he lumbered on, trying to hold the lamp steady. He would do his round somehow, and tomorrow he would explain and never touch a drop again . . . Except *how* could he explain? He thought of Ma Shaw, of her disgust. What had prompted him to steal her savings? He knew he was no good at cards. He should have given the money to Ivan, let him take the hand. But he had been a fool, taken the drink they'd offered him and then started showing off. Of course they'd let him win at first, and Ivan had – to his credit – tried to pull him away from the game. But Jim had had it all sussed. He would win a fortune. Enough to pay the rent not just that week, but every week for months. Enough to *buy* the bloody house off Wells. He might be on short time, with cut wages; his son might be laid off sick, and Kat working in a flaming tattoo parlour, with everyone gossiping about her; but he was the head of the Shaw family and he would sort it all out. He thought clammily of how he had taken his mother's savings. She might think no one knew, but it was common knowledge in the Shaw household that she kept her money in an envelope rolled up in an old corset in her top drawer. He had flushed with shame – at taking the cash and rummaging in his mother's private things. But hell, he had told himself, she would never even know! He would win so much that he'd put back double the amount. And then she'd have to change her tune! No mocking him then, no showing him up in front of Anna and his kids, even little Christine. Oh no, he'd be on top, in charge – and he would have enough money to get a nurse for Anna and send his mother packing.

So he'd sat down to play, and won. And won again. And had another drink. And another. And getting pissed, he hadn't noticed the dealer exchanging glances with the other players and the landlord of The Grapes and Fox nudging the watchers. Because he'd been stupid, and drunk, and getting silly with the booze, it had taken Jim a while to realise that the neat little wedge of his mother's money had dwindled to a few pence, and the greedy white hands of the dealer were pulling the rest towards him like a corpse making a last jerk at life.

Throwing up again, Jim wiped his mouth with the back of his hand, the lamp swinging madly. He couldn't bear to think of his wife's face, of poor Anna, who had always stood up for him. And Kat . . . Oh God, what would he say to Kat? Jim felt nothing like the same remorse for his mother. Ma Shaw had been riding him all his life; he was only – in a way – fulfilling her expectations. But he loved his wife and elder daughter, and he knew he had let them down so badly that even Anna would find it hard to excuse him. Worse, it might cause her to collapse . . . He stopped walking. Jesus, his actions might cause Anna to have a heart attack. Hadn't the doctor warned them that she hadn't to be worried? And after the death of Billy and the birth of Christine, her resistance was low. Just how many more traumas could she take?

If only he had been lucky with the cards, like Ivan. Ivan, who had no dependants, no one who relied on him. He won every time – why was that? Just one more example of life being stupid, pointlessly stupidly wrong. Jim stopped walking again, trying to get his bearings. Warehouse 8, he thought; he would walk the perimeter and then double back, do the dockside and sign off. No one would be any the wiser.

All he had to do was keep walking, keep on watch, keep awake.

Still smiling after her encounter with Andrew Pitt, Kat walked into the kitchen in Amber Street and paused. Nothing was different. But everything was. The clock ticked slowly on the mantelpiece; the sound of a radio came from upstairs. On the table was a note: *Have taken Christine to Mrs Howard's.*

At nine o'clock at night? Kat wondered, surprised. But then again, Ma Shaw was a good friend of the stout Mrs Howard and sometimes called by, leaving Christine with her for a change, so that she could have a break from Amber Street. Looking forward to the prospect of a quiet night, Kat read the rest of the note: *Micky gone to the mill for the night shift. Said he felt up to it. Yer mother was tired, having a rest. Get yerself something to eat. I still think yer shouldn't be working round at Silky's.*

And then she saw it. Or rather, she didn't see it. The brandy bottle had gone . . . Catching her breath, Kat looked round, hoping someone had moved it, and yet knowing that only one person had taken it. Her father.

'Jesus,' she said softly, under her breath.

Why now? Why now? She was bringing in enough money: even with her father working half-time, they could meet the rent. And poor Micky had dragged himself back to the mill. So why would her father go back on the booze now? Another thought followed on, and without pausing Kat made for the door again. Hurrying down the street, she jumped on a late tram, heading for the docks.

The Albert Edward was in darkness, no moon shining that late September night, as she moved further into the meshing of warehouses and quays. The water was lapping slowly, like an old cat, as she turned towards the shed. She could see a light burning inside, and prayed that her father was in there. Perhaps he wasn't drunk at all; perhaps he had thrown the bottle of brandy away and would be surprised to see her. Sober, on his toes . . . But she doubted it. Opening the door, Kat walked in. There was no one there. Her father had signed in, but the handwriting was a scrawl and told the story only too clearly. The solution was obvious: Kat had to find her father before the foreman did, or before Jim fell down, dead drunk, on the job. If he was found that way, he would be fired. And she knew only too well what that would mean.

Pulling her shawl over her head, she left the hut. She knew the docks well, but without a moon she still struggled for a few moments to adjust to the lack of light. She was surprised to find her nerves jangling and wondered if it was the docks or trepidation about what was to come that was making her so afraid. And then she realised that there *was* something different. The atmosphere was thick, overhung with some kind of premonition. As she had done before, Kat walked round the warehouses and signed each of them off. But this time it seemed that she didn't walk alone, that the ghosts of her brother and Missie Shepherd walked behind her, and often she turned, catching her breath. There were no ghosts, she told herself, just the living.

Trouble was, someone living was following her . . . Keep moving, Kat told herself, surprised by her own fear. Keep moving . . . Memories of Billy's death came back uninvited and brutal, the horrible sound of the timber fall making her pause. God, it was dark. Around her shadows flitted between the warehouses, lingered on the quayside, Missie Shepherd walking out with her throat cut.

'God,' Kat said, spooked. Keep calm, she told herself, it was just imagination, that was all. But it wasn't. There was something watching her. She could sense it. Hurrying on, her footsteps sounded louder and louder – and she realised that whoever it was would hear her coming long before she knew they were there. And no one had ever caught Missie Shepherd's killer . . . There was something bad in the air that night. The Albert Edward was too quiet, too deserted. No sounds came from the boats, no men singing. No breath of wind to ripple the water or even the sound of the occasional rat plopping off the quayside into the depths of the Ribble below. Just silence. Spinning round, Kat peered into the darkness, trying to see. But she couldn't make out where she was and began to panic. Round and round she went, her feet turning on the quayside, her ears straining for the sound of her father's voice. Or the sight of the watchman's lamp.

And then, suddenly, she heard something and began to run. Towards the sound, towards what she thought was a faint light. *It was!* Kat saw with relief. It was the watchman's lamp. She had found her father . . . Breathlessly she ran on, turning towards the far quayside, towards the soft draw of the lamp, towards safety. The lamp was getting brighter – *she had found him.* Everything was going to be all right now. Even if he was drunk, she would cover for him. Take the lamp, do the round herself. No one would know.

Running the last few yards, she stopped, bewildered. The lamp was there – but on the ground beside it lay her father, in a stupor, asleep where he had fallen.

'Dad,' she said sharply. 'Wake up!'

It was obvious from his breathing that he was dead drunk. Using all her strength, Kat grabbed him under the armpits and began to drag him along – realising after only a few feet that it was impossible. But if she couldn't get him to the hut, she couldn't cover for him . . . Breathing heavily with the effort of trying to move him again, Kat swore under her breath, fighting tears. Perhaps if she left him here, did his round and then came back for him, he might be awake and they could still get away with it.

'Dad, how could you, you bastard!' she said, beyond reason, standing on the quayside with her drunken father at her feet.

And then she heard footsteps coming towards her. Running softly, purposefully. For a second Kat's hopes rose, then fear took over. No one called out a greeting, no one made a sound to herald their coming. Why was that? she asked herself, clammy with terror. Because they weren't coming to help – *they were coming to hurt her*.

Responding instinctively, she blew out the lamp. In the darkness she wasn't so obvious a target. No longer visible to her attacker. They were on equal ground now. Jesus, who was it? All the hairs on the back of her neck rose as she stood motionless in the black night and listened to the approach of the threatening footsteps. Someone had been watching her. Someone out there had seen her illuminated in the lamplight – and although she wasn't alone, her father couldn't defend her. Her legs shaking, Kat stood immobile on the spot. She didn't know whether to run or stay. If she ran, she would leave her father defenceless, but if she remained, she was a ready target . . . The night tide shuffled under the dark sky, the quayside silent. Only the sound of the footsteps broke the malignant quiet.

Coming closer, ever closer, towards her.

TWENTY-THREE

Waking, Anna glanced at the clock beside her bed. Eleven thirty, and the house so quiet. Getting up, she made her way downstairs carefully and read her mother-in-law's note. Good, she thought, she and Kat would have the house to themselves for a while. And then she realised that Kat's coat wasn't hanging on the peg by the back door, where she always put it when she came in.

Uneasy, she walked to the bottom of the stairs.

'Kat! Kat!' she called up, expecting a reply, but not getting one.

Puzzled, she moved back upstairs, shivering in her nightgown and opening the door to her daughter's room. There was no one there, and the bed hadn't been slept in. There was no note either, and the curtains were open. Suddenly anxious, Anna realised that Micky was on the late shift – and that her daughter hadn't come home. Kat, who was always so careful, so considerate. Kat, the daughter who would never worry her. Glancing at the clock again, Anna sat down on the side of the bed. She was alone and she was uneasy, almost afraid. For the first time in years there was no one in the house, no one there to help.

And then she remembered Horace Armitage and began, firmly and rhythmically, to bang on the partition wall.

PART THREE

Thou hast committed —
Fornication? But that was in another country:
and besides, the wench is dead.
Christopher Marlowe, *The Jew of Malta*

I would always look back and remember the terror of that night, long after I forgot other terrors in my life. I stood by my father's body and braced myself, not knowing where the attack would come from, but trying to anticipate the blow. Or the pain that would follow. Trying to prepare for the unpreparable.

Time, that most audacious of recorders, played tricks with the night. I know that I was not standing there for years, that centuries did not pass whilst I waited. I know – with my logic – that it was not an aeon but some little insignificant scrap of minutes. But in those minutes I lived numerous times. I saw Amber Street, the pub, the back gate, Micky's drawings and Ma Shaw's second-best hat. Trivia, in the face of terror, enjoys its moment of mockery.

I don't remember if I had a fear of death, but I had a fear of the initial impact. Of the blood or disfigurement to follow. Of being injured and not recovering. Of being, somehow, spoiled. I wanted, in that brief impasse between safety and danger, to grab at the memory of being whole, to keep a mental image of myself before I was changed for ever.

And I wanted to live.

TWENTY-FOUR

Grabbing her arm, someone swung Kat round, holding on tightly as she struggled. In the darkness, neither of them could see what was really happening, Kat biting down on her attacker's thumb, a strange, muffled grunt of pain following. But it took the person only a moment to recover, and then they struck out, a heavy blow coming out of the darkness and striking Kat full on the side of her head. She fell like a dead weight. And she knew in that moment that she had to keep conscious, that if she blacked out, she was finished. Staggering to her knees, she tried to get back to her feet, but the blood kept pumping in her ears and the sound of someone's breathing came loud and ominous on the night air. Stretching her hands out in front of her, as a blind man might, she reached into the darkness, suddenly feeling an arm loop around her neck and haul her up and off her feet.

Terrified, she struggled for breath, her legs and arms flailing, her airway shut off. Then – in the moment she was about to collapse – she was released. The arm lost its grip and she fell to the ground. In the dense night she could only see the outlines, but now there were *two* figures – and after a hurried scuffle, the larger one ran off. Immediately she felt a hand reach down to her. A hand she knew.

'Micky! Oh Christ, thank God it's you.'

Scrambling at her feet for the watchman's lamp, Kat

hurried to light it, Micky standing looking at her and signalling frantically.

Are you OK?

'Who was it?' she asked, her voice hoarse, her throat aching as she held up the lamp and tried to see into the gloom. But there was nothing to see; she could only hear footsteps fading away in the background. Someone running away. Urgently she looked around. 'Did you see who it was?'

Micky shook his head, signing. *It was a man, but I don't know who he was.*

Her heart still banging, Kat swallowed painfully, her throat swollen. Hadn't everyone said the docks were dangerous? No place for a woman? They had been right. God only knew what would have happened if Micky hadn't come along.

'They never caught the man who killed Missie Shepherd,' she said finally, her voice shaking. 'You don't think . . .' Holding up the lamp, she looked into her brother's face. 'You don't think it was him, do you? Jesus, Micky, thank God you came along . . .'

He stared at her, then carefully signed: *I came to find you – the bottle's gone.*

So he had noticed too, had he?

'I know,' she replied, stepping back and holding the light over their father. Jim was still unconscious, lying in a foetal position. In silence, his children regarded him, Micky touching his sister's arm to make her look at him.

You shouldn't be here. You could have been killed.

'I had to cover for him! If Fleetwood finds out he's drunk, he'll fire him. Someone had to do the watch.' She paused, her temper rising. 'God, he's really let us down this time.'

But why would he get drunk?

'Who knows?' Kat replied, shaken and trying to sound calm. 'I thought he meant it when he promised me he would stay off the booze. I believed him – and now look at him, dead drunk, without a care in the bloody world.' She paused again, took a deep breath. 'No one can find out about this, Micky, or we're sunk. Mum can't know either, you hear me? We *have* to make sure the watchman's pay keeps coming in.'

How?

'We have to keep a watch on the watchman,' she explained evenly. 'We have to make sure that if Dad can't stay sober, *we* do the round. Check the dock and the warehouses, and then forge his signature on the work sheet – without anyone knowing it was us. I've done it on my own on and off, and it was hard work, but between the two of us it should be easier. Will you help me? After your shift?'

Her brother nodded vigorously, signing: *I'm better, back at the mill, and I can be back working with Silky tomorrow.*

'We'll share the work, Micky. We'll share the work at the tattoo parlour *and* the responsibility of checking on Dad.' She hesitated. 'I don't want to drag you into this; maybe I should do it on my own . . .'

No! This place is dangerous!

'I'd certainly feel a lot safer with you around,' she admitted. 'But there'll be trouble if anyone finds out, Micky. We'll be taking wages under false pretences. Fleetwood would fire Dad and he might even ask for the money back. We have to keep this a secret.'

Maybe Dad won't get drunk again.

'God forgive me, but I don't trust him any more,' Kat said, her tone resigned. 'I love him, but I don't trust him. He knows how sick Mum is, how we need the money since his hours were cut back. He knows about Robin Wells, and yet he *still* got drunk. I don't think there's anything in the world that could stop him.'

Horace Armitage – with Mary in tow – had responded immediately to Anna's frantic knocking. Using the spare key that had been entrusted to them for emergencies, he had bumbled into the back kitchen to find Anna distraught and short of breath.

'Oh my word, Mrs Shaw, don't take on. Calm yerself,' he said, gesturing for Mary to get some water.

Round-eyed, she passed it to Anna and then sat down on the old sofa next to her. 'Are you OK?'

'What kind of question is that!' Horace replied. 'She needs a tot of brandy. Find the bottle, luv, will yer?'

Looking round, Mary found some ginger beer, and a little dandelion and burdock, but no brandy.

'There is none,' she said calmly.

'There is!' Horace replied, turning as the door opened again and Ma Shaw walked in. As usual, her expression was irritated. Even more irritated when she saw the little group of people in the Amber Street kitchen.

'Now then,' she started, 'what's this?'

'Anna's had a bad turn,' Horace began, his rotund form immediately levered out of the way by Ma Shaw's sturdy left arm.

'Anna!' she said, looming over her daughter-in-law. 'What's the matter, luv?'

'Kat's gone.'

'Gone where?' Mary asked, her tone expressionless.

Ma Shaw silenced her with a look. 'What d'you mean, Anna? She's probably just gone out for a breath of air.'

'Past midnight?' Anna replied bleakly. 'I knew she should never have gone to work at Silky's, and now someone's kidnapped her on the way home. Or worse . . .'

'It could be a docker,' Mary offered. 'Or a drunk sailor . . .'

'If you can't think before yer open yer mouth, keep it closed!' Ma Shaw barked at the girl, then turned back to Anna. 'Yer fretting fer nothing, luv. Our Kat will walk in any minute. Just like I did. Couldn't stay at that Gertie Howard's a minute longer, although Christine wanted to stay. God, but Gertie can talk. On and on about her son, and he's dimmer than a toc 8 lamp. Not that yer'd believe it to hear her tell it . . .'

'I thought a glass of brandy might help Mrs Shaw,' Horace ventured bravely, looking round. 'But I can't seem to find it. I saw it on the mantelpiece only yesterday.'

'Then it must be there now!' Ma Shaw replied, turning to look.

As though she wasn't quite sure if she was seeing clearly, she moved over to the space where the bottle had been and stared for a long instant at the dust ring. So he'd given in at last, had he? she thought. Trusting, loving Kat might believe that her father could resist the lure of liquor, but Ma Shaw had known that one day he would succumb. The only thing she didn't know was why.

God, she thought, sometimes it was horrible to be right. Horrible to see your suspicions fulfilled . . . Glancing at her shaken daughter-in-law, Ma Shaw considered the facts. Kat was missing; Jim had fallen off the wagon. Were the incidents related?

'We should call the police.'

'Oh, police!' Mary said, thrilled. 'In *uniforms*.'

'No, in coaches drawn by white mice,' Ma Shaw retorted drily, turning to Horace. 'Yer got a phone at the pub – could yer ring them fer us?'

Nodding, he was about to leave when they all heard the sound of footsteps coming down the street. Not one person, but two, maybe more. And then they realised that one person wasn't walking, but being dragged along . . . Cursing under her breath, Ma Shaw went to the front door and looked out. Suspended between his son and daughter was Jim, still unconscious. Still dressed in his watchman's coat, the unlit lamp hanging over Kat's shoulder.

'Get the bugger in!' she snapped to her grandchildren, stepping back and throwing open the door of the front room. With one final effort, Kat and Micky dropped the dead weight of their father on to the couch, Ma Shaw shoving them out of the door and then closing it after them.

'Kat!' Anna cried out in relief from the kitchen. 'God, I was so afraid something had happened to you when I woke up and you weren't there.'

'We thought a sailor had got you,' Mary volunteered mischievously.

Kat walked over to her mother and felt her forehead.

'You're burning up.'

'I'm fine now,' Anna insisted, relief making her colour return. 'Mr Armitage was going to call the police . . .' Her gaze flicked to the closed door of the front room, her expression hopeless. 'Is your father . . . ?'

'Dad had a fall,' Kat said, Horace Armitage watching her suspiciously. 'Mr Fleetwood called by at Silky's and asked us to bring him home.'

'Is he all right?'

'Oh yes,' Kat lied, avoiding the publican's gaze. 'He will be fine in the morning.'

Relieved, Anna relaxed – and then glanced at her son. 'But why is Micky here? Why didn't Silky help you?'

'Micky called for me at the tattoo parlour before his shift, so it seemed obvious for us to go together for Dad.'

Kat paused, her glance moving to the mantelpiece. Was her mother believing the story? It was so far-fetched, but then again, Anna was ill and always desperate to think the best of her husband.

'No sailors then?' Mary said, standing up and smiling.

'No sailors,' Kat agreed, returning the smile. 'But thanks for coming over, and thanks to you, Mr Armitage. Sorry you were bothered.'

'No bother, luv. Always happy to help in a crisis. Lucky yer dad's going to be all right in the morning.' He glanced over to the mantelpiece knowingly. 'Falls can be nasty things sometimes.'

In the silent front room Ma Shaw was staring at her son, repulsed. Drunk as a prince, and how come? she wondered.

How could he *afford* to be that inebriated? Hadn't the local pubs refused him tick for years? So how exactly had he paid for his stupor? Leaning down, she smelled the booze on his breath, and the vomit, and winced. Drunken, useless bugger, she thought, checking his pockets. Jim stirred but didn't wake, and his mother continued her search. The watch she had given him had long since gone, along with her grandfather's guard. She'd been a right fool there, should have given it to Silky. But Ma Shaw was all too aware of how much she had always favoured Silky, and had tried to be even-handed with the other two. Difficult as it was, with Ivan being such a lanky Job and Jim being such a bloody ass . . . Emptying her son's pockets, she studied the motley objects – two mints, a tram ticket, a box of matches, a crumpled card – the 8 of diamonds – and an old envelope.

She frowned, smoothing out the envelope and then staring at it with incredulous recognition. And then, to her astonishment, she felt tears smart behind her eyes. Hurriedly she looked inside. Of course it was empty. Jim had paid for his booze with her savings. Slowly her gaze moved to the playing card. No, she thought despairingly, don't say he had *gambled* her money. Her bloody money that she had saved so hard for. Her money – worked for, grubbed around for – hidden away for emergencies. Usually Jim's emergencies. Because Jim was the one with the sick wife, the low wages, the four children. And because he knew his mother would always bail him out.

Flopping heavily into the seat beside her son, Ma Shaw looked around the shabby room. Everything – Jim's home, his wife's health, his kids – had been jeopardised; balanced on the fall of a card. Or poured down his throat and then pissed out the other end . . . Inflamed, she suddenly leaned forward and struck him on the cheek with all the force she could muster. He winced, mumbled in his stupor, and then fell back into sleep. She couldn't hurt him! Ma Shaw thought, almost laughing. Jesus, he was too drunk even to hurt.

In silence she sat in that front room, watching her son. If it took all night, she wanted to be there when he awoke. She wanted him to see her face before any other, so that he would know at the instant of consciousness who he had betrayed . . . Listening to his heavy breathing, Ma Shaw stayed on watch, the terror of poverty snickering in the dim light around her, teasing her, making inroads into her turgid imagination. There was no money left for the rent, and Robin Wells to pay. No money, no excuses. And a man with an old grudge, just longing to turn them out . . . An ancicnt remembrance of the Poor House came back to Ma Shaw in vivid, eerie hostility.

And with it came her endless, enduring fear of the slums – now snapping at their unsteady heels on Amber Street.

TWENTY-FIVE

Of course Joan knew that her parents would hardly approve of her going to a nightclub, but how would they know? Sipping a glass of wine, she looked around her, smiling at her companion and feeling cocky, full of herself. This wasn't one of her parents' gatherings, or an evening with the dull sons of Preston's elite. This was different, exciting. Almost dangerous. Glancing quickly at her companion again, Joan studied the well-made-up face of Ginny Arthur. The perfect powdered skin, the arched brows, the Cupid's bow of a mouth, the pristine garnet nails. She was impeccably hard, and cold as charity, no longer a virgin and eager to induct Joan into sex. Any reputation Ginny had once had had been exchanged for thrills. She wasn't a whore, just a young woman who liked presents and the good life. One day, she told Joan, she would marry a banker. Someone too dull to know about her past. Someone who would inherit his father's thriving business. Someone kind, but not exciting. Someone, Joan thought, like Andrew Pitt. But then again, she told herself, she wasn't going to moon around crying over him any more. She was going to show him how attractive she was, what a catch Joan Fairchild was for any man.

Taking another drink from her glass, Joan smouldered. She had seen Andrew a few times, but their friendship had never got off the ground. Even her extended kindness had been met with a lukewarm response. Andrew was bearing the brunt of Duncan's bad business moves with considerable steel.

'I think there's nothing worse than someone pining over a lost love,' Ginny said suddenly, as though she had magicked herself into Joan's thoughts. 'It's so pathetic.'

'Some people take a while to get over things,' Joan replied. She was remembering how she had met Ginny, at the hairdresser's. A voice had cut through the noise of her hair dryer and she had looked up to see a customer squealing with delight. Apparently Ginny had just had her hair dyed to deepest black, and a fringe cut, so that she looked like Claudette Colbert. It was so new, she was saying, turning her head from right to left repeatedly, so irresistible.

Her high spirits had appealed to Joan, and they had started chatting. Ginny had mentioned something about having just broken off her engagement to some Leeds businessman, and Joan had told her about Andrew Pitt. Together they had commiserated, and by the end of the week they had gone shopping and to the cinema together. It had quickly become apparent to Joan that Ginny Arthur was fast, the kind of companion her parents wouldn't like. But her recklessness, her boldness and her sexual confidence struck a chord in Joan, and she found herself wanting to emulate her friend.

And then Andrew would hear about her adventures . . . He would be intrigued, maybe even jealous to know she was seeing other men. Maybe he would see her differently and realise that he missed her. Maybe it was her one last-ditch chance to win him back. And if she didn't, she would have fun anyway. She had a right – when he had been so cruel to her.

'Oh my God,' Ginny said suddenly. 'Do you see who has just come in?'

Joan glanced over to the entrance of the club. A nightclub in the middle of Manchester, a league away from a Preston drawing room. She had lied to her parents, saying she was going to the cinema, and then stopped and changed in the ladies' toilet at the station. Swapping her smart clothes for a beaded dress, then hastily applying lipstick, she had gone on to meet Ginny . . .

'Where am I supposed to be looking?' she asked, staring over the heads of the seated customers.

'At him! The sexiest male in the north-west!' Ginny cried, gesturing for the man to come over to their table.

Without smiling, he approached, his dinner jacket perfectly tailored, his expression flat. Behind him followed two other men, who hung back a little. Ginny pointed excitedly to the seat next to her.

'My God, Robin Wells! I haven't seen you in ages.'

He shrugged, out of temper, looking round. He glanced across to Joan and she blushed. Smiling fleetingly but mesmerically, he turned back to Ginny. 'You've got a new lamb with you.'

'Joan Fairchild,' Ginny replied, putting her head on one side. 'I'm showing her how to have a good time.'

'And get a bad reputation.'

'You're so sour, Robin,' she teased him. 'Be careful, or I might remind you how I got that reputation.'

'Not through force, darling,' Wells replied. 'Not through force.'

She laughed, nudging him, and then put her mouth to his ear to whisper something. Embarrassed, Joan looked down.

'We're making Miss Fairchild uncomfortable, Ginny,' Wells said, admonishing her, and then turned to Joan. 'Would you like to dance?'

'I don't think you can, can you?' Ginny asked, infuriated.

In the pause that followed, Joan knew she had to make a decision. She wasn't going to be left out of anything, or pitied by anyone. Smiling her most dazzling smile, she took Robin Wells's proffered arm, delighted to have got one over on Ginny. Obviously the time had come for her to be more worldly, Joan thought. She wasn't a baby any more. She wanted admiration. To be longed for. Desired again, as Andrew Pitt had desired her. But he wasn't in love with her – and suddenly anyone else would do.

So she stood up, sizzling with charm. 'I'd love to dance, Mr Wells.'

And he smiled with his lizard's eyes and took her hand.

Grunting, Jim opened his eyes and winced. The early daylight from the window blinded him momentarily as he tried to focus, the dark outline of a figure watching him making him jump.

Startled, he sat up. 'What the—'

'Where's my money?' Ma Shaw said, her tone warning.

The memory of the previous night came back to Jim at once. Christ, he thought, his mind bleary, his stomach churning with nausea. He had taken his mother's savings, lost most of them at the card game and then boozed the rest. Every penny in his pocket. He could smell the vomit on his jacket and tried stupidly to wipe himself down. Ma Shaw grabbed his arm so tightly he winced.

'WHERE IS MY MONEY!'

He thought of lying, but just shrugged, trying to remember how he had got home. And how he had done his job. He could vaguely remember walking down the docks, but nothing else . . . Christ, had he been fired? Had Fleetwood found him?

'WHERE IS MY MONEY!' Ma Shaw persisted, hauling her son upright.

'I . . . I lost it.'

'Yer thieved it off me, yer own mother. And then yer lost it!' She slapped him hard across the face, Jim's head jerking to one side. 'That were all I had, yer bugger! All I'd saved fer emergencies. And yer took it.'

'I were going to give it back. I were going to win at cards. Give yer back double! I were going to win—'

'Yer never win at anything!' she snapped, dropping her voice ominously. Quiet, Ma Shaw seemed more threatening than ever. 'If it hadn't been fer yer own kids yer'd be fired now. Some bloody watchman yer turned out to be! They brought yer home – after they did yer round fer yer,' she hissed at him, beyond disgust. 'Yer piece of filth! Yer worthless, useless piece of filth! I'm sorry I ever gave birth to yer.'

Cowed, Jim winced as she carried on, relentless.

'Yer never were any good. Always a stupid kid, easily led, bloody silly. Got yerself wed as a boy and had no more sense than to fill up yer wife with more and more kids yer couldn't afford. And her sick – but that doesn't matter to yer, does it? Jim Shaw thinks of nothing. Too stupid to keep his trousers fastened and his hands off the bottle.'

'I'll pay yer back, Mam.'

'Yer right yer'll pay me back. Yer'll work every day fer the rest of yer life, if that's what it takes. Yer'll work and keep sober . . .' She paused before delivering the body blow. 'And hope yer wife doesn't die because yer so worthless.'

Jim paled at the thought. God, had he *really* endangered Anna? Was she going to die on him? Without her there was nothing. He loved her more than anything – had he risked her *that* much?

'Mam,' he said, panicked, 'is Anna all right?'

And then Ma Shaw knew she had him. Had found a way of getting – and keeping – her son under her thumb. Had found the instrument of emotional terrorism she could wield in revenge for the trauma he was causing her. Jim's greatest fear was to lose his wife; Ma Shaw's greatest fear was to lose her fight against poverty. In that instant she saw a permanent way to move herself into Amber Street and into the running of the household. A way of recovering some of the security her son had stolen from her. No one was going on the skids in the Shaw family – it was her duty to make sure of that.

'Anna's health is up to you, Jim. She's very weak, and she

should never have had so many kids. You were stupid there.'

Ma Shaw bent down towards her son, whispering into his ear, terrifying him. Making him need her. Not want her, not love her. Need her. She was fighting for her life and all their lives. Otherwise she could see the future only too easily – their unavoidable, terrifying descent into the slums. If she didn't watch out, Jim would drag them all down – and might even kill his wife in the process.

'I can help yer, lad,' she said, her tone calm. 'I'll look after yer wife from now on. She'll need me to watch over her, protect her from a bleeding fool like you.'

'I'll do anything yer say!' Jim blathered, heartbroken. 'Just don't let her die.'

'Yer have to give me every penny yer earn,' Ma Shaw went on. 'Yer can't be trusted, so yer have to pass yer home and wife over to me. Yer hear me, Jim? Yer already a thief; yer don't want to turn out to be a murderer, do yer?'

TWENTY-SIX

While one of the greatest political monsters the world had yet seen started to build his power base in Germany, *King Kong* went on general cinematic release. Playing to enraptured audiences everywhere, the story of the gigantic gorilla being defeated by ignorance became a symbol of the times. Then, as unemployment continued to rise around the country, the unthinkable happened in what had been the stronghold of the northern mills. Cheap foreign cotton was affecting imports, and that had a knock-on effect at the docks. The Albert Edward was still busy, but the torrent of ships and cargoes was beginning to fall off. No job was safe. Men who had worked in the same positions as their fathers and grandfathers were suddenly aware that they might well not have a job for life. Or even for the next year.

The press began to call it the Depression. Fights were reported, clashes between workers and bosses; lay-offs; husbands and fathers no longer providing and families losing their homes. Robin Wells had picked his time well. As the hardship began to bite, he evicted the slow payers and replaced them with his own kind. Within months the atmosphere of Amber Street had changed. What had always been a poor area was now sleazy, inviting comparison with the likes of Kirkham Street. Flop houses where petty thieves and destitutes paid a penny for a few hours' sleep on a straw mattress nudged dark houses where the curtains were always drawn. The street, which had been rough but safe, altered, and by early spring of the following year no respectable woman walked around after dark.

The old residents cursed Duncan Pitt. And he in his turn looked on and saw his poor but reputable property become sordid. At times he would catch his perplexed wife staring at him and wonder if he could risk telling her the truth; wonder if it would be as damning as he feared. But he knew he never would. If the story of Stanley Gorman came out, he was finished. Not just financially, but morally. No one would do business with the Pitts when they found out how the money had been made. He would be shunned, imprisoned – and his family would be finished too.

As for Andrew, he had watched his father's decline – mental and physical – and assumed increasing control over the business. He had often asked for the explanation he wanted so much, but his father was never forthcoming. Instead Andrew determined to recover as much of the Pitt reputation as was possible. They might have lost Ratcliffe Row, Hover Terrace and Amber Street, but nothing else was going to Robin Wells.

For all the trouble he had caused him, in some strange way Andrew was grateful to Wells. Otherwise the affection that was building between Kat and himself would never have come about. Although reluctant at first, Kat had gradually believed him when he told her that they weren't *so* different. That he wasn't the amazing catch she had believed him to be.

'Well if that's so,' she said, mocking him, 'I'm not sure I'm interested. I mean, you do realise I could have my pick of Preston?'

He laughed, sliding his arm around her shoulder. They were in Avenham Park, on a cold, quiet March evening, walking together as they often did now.

'I didn't say I was a nobody!'

'Good thing too,' she replied, snuggling against him. 'I want a hero, Mr Pitt. A real, honest-to-God hero.'

Together they walked on, slowly. From their first initial talks, they had developed a strong bond. Initially Kat had been nervous, reluctant, but Andrew had won her over with his determination. Having had no reason to call except to see Kat, he had visited the house on Amber Street regularly. He had known that the neighbours watched and gossiped, but he had had nothing to hide – even though he ran the gauntlet being Duncan's son. It was worth the abuse. He had wanted to be with Kat Shaw and had been proud to be seen with her.

'You know something?' he said suddenly, pausing in their walk. 'Why don't you come for dinner, meet my mother?'

At once Kat stiffened. It was one thing to walk with Andrew and pretend they were equals, quite another to visit his home off the park. A home whose chimneys she could just see over the tops of the winter trees. A handsome home, light years away from Amber Street. Especially the changing face of Amber Street.

'No, I don't think so.'

'So why are we seeing each other?' Andrew asked, suddenly serious. 'Are you ashamed of me?'

'*What!*'

'You act like you are.'

'Oh, Andrew! How can you even think that – me ashamed of you! It's just that we're . . . we're . . .'

'Don't say *friends*,' he replied coldly. 'That is the one thing I couldn't bear to hear. I care about you, Kat, and I need to know that you care about me. I could . . . I could love you.'

Stunned, she stared at him. She had never even allowed herself the fantasy of hearing those words. He might believe it, but she knew that the difference in social class was all-important. Or if not class, money. Andrew had been disgraced by proxy, but the Pitts were still well off, and in time people would forget Duncan's actions. Besides, the tenants could rail for ever and still nothing would change. There was no power in poverty.

'Andrew, I can't meet your mother.'

'Because of what my father did?'

She shook her head. 'What he did is not your fault, and you're trying to make things better, I know you are.'

Andrew had told her his plans; about how his father was gradually passing responsibility for the business over to him. The metalworks would bring in the usual stable income, but in other ways money would be harder to find. Because Andrew had promised to hold on to the other property the Pitts owned, even if the rentals hardly broke even. The only thing he could assure his tenants was that he wouldn't sell out to Robin Wells. He had made an oath and he was going to keep it.

Kat admired him for that, but at first she wondered if it would turn out to be his choice. If Duncan would pull another devious trick and break his son's oath by default. But that New Year Duncan Pitt had fallen ill, developing some kind of kidney problem, and was soon too incapacitated to leave the house. So there he had stayed for the last few months, physically improving, mentally detached.

'I thought about going to see Robin Wells.'

'What!' Kat exclaimed, startled.

'Talk to him, try and find out how he managed to get that property off my father.'

Kat took a deep breath. 'I wouldn't do that, Andrew.'

'Why not?'

'Because you're a decent man. Because my family has suffered – as yours has – because of Robin Wells, and I know what that man is like. Because you're good and trusting and you couldn't deal with him.' She put her hand over his mouth, momentarily silencing him. 'Silky is the type who can deal with Wells . . .'

'I'm not a bloody weakling!'

'I didn't say you were,' she replied gently. 'There's nothing weak about you. You're all heart and courage – but you're not slum fodder. Not back-street poor. Not gutter sly. And Robin Wells is. It's not enough to want to set a trap, you have to know *how* to set it.'

'I tell you, I can deal with him.'

'One day, yes. But not today or tomorrow. Don't go up against Robin Wells. Not yet. Not until you're ready.' She reached out, touching his face, realising suddenly how much she wanted to comfort, protect and love him. 'Even David needed a sling when he took on Goliath.'

Moved, Andrew bent down, kissing her gently on the mouth, Kat's arms going around him tightly. There was no pretence any more. They loved each other – and were ready to admit it.

Ivy was staring morosely at the clock, thinking about the quietness of her life. Upstairs was her husband, already retired to bed, reading. Or pretending to. They had separate rooms now, Ivy unable to sleep with a man she could no longer understand or trust. Her temper tantrums, her tears, her reassurances had come to nothing – Duncan would not tell her why he had given over the property. In the embarrassing darkness of ignorance, Ivy found her life unravelling like bad knitting. The reassuring stitchwork of afternoon tea, drinks parties and bridge nights had steadily fallen apart – and she didn't know why. Friends she had thought she could rely on had turned their backs, or kept their distance. And what did she have as a defence for her husband's actions? Nothing. She couldn't even begin to explain or excuse it. Her existence had been upended and she hated her husband more for his lack of trust than for her own social decline. A few times she thought of leaving him, but decided against it. She had nowhere else to go, and besides, she had Andrew. And her son had more than proved himself.

'Mother,' Andrew said, walking in at that moment and throwing his coat over the back of the nearest chair. 'What are you doing?

Reaching for the book she had tried to read several times, Ivy shrugged. 'I was reading. Your father's already gone up to bed.'

'How is he?'

'The same.' She patted the sofa next to her. 'Come and talk to me.'

Smiling, he sat down. She could tell at once that he was excited about something and longed to share it. Anything that would take her mind off the suffocating deadness of her existence.

'You seem happy.'

'I am,' he replied, looking into his mother's face. 'I'm in love with Katherine Shaw.'

Blinking, Ivy heard the sound of footsteps moving overhead. Duncan was walking around . . . In the past she would have called him down to discuss the matter, and then later talked with him about it in bed. Would have clucked about how misguided young people were and then laughed as they remembered their own youth. In the past they would have discussed the merits of Joan Fairchild and how they could prise Andrew away from Kat Shaw. In the past . . .

'*Katherine Shaw?*' Ivy repeated, trying to sound composed. 'You mean the girl you've been talking about lately? I thought that was just friendship.'

'More than that now.'

Having become very close to Kat, Andrew had already confided in his mother. Ivy had been stunned, but cynically she had hoped that time, which would restore their good name, might also restore her son's eligibility. Apparently, though, Andrew had no time to waste.

'You have to think of your status, darling.'

He raised his eyebrows. 'I have no status. I'm the son of a wily old businessman who trades with Robin Wells. Kat is an honest girl.'

'But she's so . . . ordinary.'

He looked at his mother with amazement. '*Ordinary?* Yes, maybe her background is ordinary. But she's extraordinary in other ways.'

'But to pick a girl from Amber Street,' Ivy replied, aghast.

Rising to her feet, she began to pace up and down frantically. 'This is your father's fault! I'll never forgive him for what he's done to us!'

'But I *love* Kat,' Andrew replied firmly. 'I'm *glad* about what Father did. Otherwise this wouldn't have happened.'

'*Glad!*' Ivy echoed, enraged. 'Oh, and I'm delighted! Thrilled! Overcome with joy!' Her anger had festered for months and now burst. 'I have no standing in this town any more, and your father won't even take me into his confidence. Making me look like a complete fool. As if *I* had done something wrong! And now you – my only son – come home and tell me that you're in love with some girl who works in a tattoo parlour! The watchman's daughter!' Infuriated, Ivy picked up an expensive cushion and hurled it across the room, smashing it into a display case in the corner.

Andrew watched her, amazed. 'Mother . . .'

But Ivy wasn't going to listen to anyone any more. Pushing her son out of the way, she ran to the bottom of the stairs and shouted upwards: 'Duncan! DUNCAN! You bastard, come down here and see your handiwork now. See what you've done to us.' She then dropped heavily on to the bottom stair, sobbing.

'Mother,' Andrew said gently, catching hold of Ivy's hands and trying to placate her. 'Calm down . . .'

'Calm down! Why couldn't you marry Joan Fairchild?'

'She didn't want me.'

'Why couldn't you have pursued her? She's a spoiled brat; she's probably aching to take you back now she thinks she can't have you.' Ivy paused, her anguish suddenly lessening as she saw a way out of their predicament. 'You know, Andrew, Joan *is* still very fond of you. Never held what your father did against you. I'm sure she would love to hear from you, even if her blasted mother snubbed me in the street. We aren't good enough for Gwen Fairchild now. Oh no, but she was all over us before, when she wanted her daughter to marry you.'

Sighing, Andrew sat beside his mother on the stairs. 'I don't want Joan Fairchild, I want Kat.'

'A girl from a tattoo parlour!' Ivy repeated, laughing mirthlessly. 'I suppose she could ink a nice Union Jack on your chest. Or you could display your initials on your forearm. That would be nice. K and A intertwined with a snake. We could have a tasteful wedding at The Horse and Cart and invite her drunken father and her dumb brother along . . .'

Breathing in, Andrew fought to keep his temper. 'Don't say something you'll regret later, Mother. You're upset—'

'You're right I'm upset!' Ivy snapped, her mouth tight. 'The world's gone mad! And you expect me to be pleased for you? Why don't you just shoot me and put me out of my misery quick?'

Infuriated, Andrew walked upstairs, slamming the door of his room, the house falling back into silence. Still at the bottom of the stairs, Ivy wiped her eyes, rigid in her unbending corset. She might have seen her own life falter, but she wasn't about to let her son's destiny be overturned by anyone. Not Duncan, and certainly not some Amber Street slattern. Awkwardly she got to her feet. She had been helpless too long, too much at the mercy of men's decisions. Now it was time for her to sort out the mess herself.

TWENTY-SEVEN

Kissing Andrew on the cheek, Kat turned to go.

'What's the rush? I thought we could go on to the pictures.'

She hesitated, wondering if this was the time to confide about her father. But then again, could she risk it? God knew it was a miracle that Andrew had chosen her and was standing up to his mother; how much would he feel was too much to defend?

All through that summer Kat and Micky had kept an eye on their father. The watchman's children standing watch. They knew only too well what their father had done, but not even stealing from Ma Shaw had warranted her gradual and corrupting torture. Having always belittled her son, she now added the piquancy of guilt and the intimation that his actions might cause the decline of his wife. And he believed her. Gradually the previously foolish but happy-go-lucky Jim had altered, become a hesitant, nervy shadow, his mother always present, having moved permanently into the Amber Street house.

Whilst pretending to offer security and nursing, she actually undermined her son to the point that his home was no longer his, and he felt like an interloper there. Pitying her father, Kat was waiting for the inevitable falling off the wagon, but a terrified Jim stayed firmly sober. As that spring turned into summer, brother and sister continued to check on him, ready to do his watchman's round. To make his marks and forge his signature. At first they went nightly, then on alternate nights. And finally, as June came in, their hopes rose . . . Jim never knew they watched him. Never knew that Micky called by on his way to the night shift at the mill, and that Kat gave over a portion of her evenings to go with him on watch. Sometimes their arrangements didn't go so smoothly, Kat being held late at Silky's whilst Micky cooled his heels waiting for the late tram on Friargate. Both became over-tired with the extra responsibility and tension and with keeping their secret. But both knew it was imperative to keep tabs on their father. If he lost his job, it was over for all of them.

Then, just as they had begun to relax, Jim faltered. Ma Shaw had been at him endlessly, berating him about not making enough money, about how she had to ask Silky to make up the rent. *Again*. About how Ivan had said Jim wasn't fit to have a family. About how such a useless son was never going to amount to anything and might drag all the Shaws into the gutter with him . . . However much Kat tried to reassure her father, Ma Shaw's words held sway over him. And that night he fell off the wagon again.

Once again his children were there to catch him. Together they did the watch, and then Micky forged his father's signature on the ledger.

'Wait, look at this,' Kat whispered, pointing at the book. 'It's different tonight.'

Holding the watchman's lamp over the ledger, Micky stared at the note pinned to the top of the page.

Jim

Let me know which warehouses need new locks. And I want a list of the new ships that came in on the last tide.

Fleetwood

'Hellfire,' Kat said simply. 'I'll have to go and count them. You take the warehouses, Micky, and I'll do the boats.'

He nodded, both of them glancing over to their father, asleep in the chair. For a moment Kat wanted to walk away, to say that she had had enough of looking out for her father. That she was tired and weary of the creeping around and covering for him. But she couldn't, and instead she picked up the lantern again.

'You take the other light,' she told Micky. 'If we hurry, we can do this in an hour and then get home.'

She felt uncharacteristically nervous, as if that night their luck might finally run out. And then what would follow? Don't think about it, Kat thought, you're just spooking yourself. But she made sure she put on her father's coat and cap and disguised herself thoroughly. After all, it wasn't just Fleetwood she wanted to dupe. There was always the threat of running into her unknown attacker again. In fact, Micky had become so nervous for his sister that they had devised a special form of communication as they worked the dock. A series of whistles every few minutes or so. They would alter the whistle often; different pitches, different notes, but it was their way of making sure each knew where the other was. And that they were both safe.

Luckily, Kat's premonition had been misplaced. An hour later they had met up again safely at the hut, where Micky had painstakingly forged a reply to Fleetwood's note. His creative abilities didn't cover just drawings and tattoos; he was adept at copying, and when he had finished, Kat looked at the note, then at her brother, with admiration.

'That's perfect, Micky. Just like Dad's handwriting.'

She glanced back at their drunken father. Experience had told her that he would wake around six, an hour before his shift was due to end. An hour in which he had time to regain his senses . . . She often wondered what he thought when he realised that his watch had been done for him. He must have known that his children had stepped in, but was too shamefaced to ask them. Too embarrassed, too humiliated. Instead he colluded with them in silence. They kept his secret, and he kept theirs . . . But could Kat confide the same secret to Andrew? Could she risk his disapproval, knowing he wouldn't want her walking the Albert Edward even with Micky in tow?

'So, *are* we going to the cinema?' Andrew repeated, bringing her thoughts back to the present.

'I can't, love, I have to baby-sit Christine.'

'I thought your grandmother did the baby-sitting?'

'She's going to see Mrs Howard tonight,' Kat replied, linking arms with him.

'We should talk about the future . . .'

'Andrew!' Kat admonished him. 'We're *always* talking about the future.'

'Then why don't we get engaged?'

Pausing, she studied him. 'Not yet.'

'Why not?'

'You know why not: your mother doesn't like me.'

'I do, and that's all that matters.'

Kat glanced away. 'Mum's not been too good and Dad's worried. You know how it is at home. I want things to be better when we tell them. And I want your mother to have come to terms with the situation.'

'No,' he said kindly, '*you* want to come to terms with the situation.'

'Maybe I do,' Kat agreed. 'I love you, Andrew – I've never been so sure of anything – but I have to wait until it feels right.'

'There will never be the *right* time. There will always be something to worry about, wait for, mull over.' He stared at her, willing her to agree. 'The trick about life is to stop waiting for the right time and make time right for you.'

'Is the time right for us?'

'Do you have to ask?'

Laughing, she flung her arms around his neck and clung

to him, relieved that he had made the decision for her. Her passion for him was intense. And even though they had never made love, Kat wanted him as much as he wanted her. They would wait, he had told her, they would belong to each other completely if they waited. And he had been true to his word . . . How had she been so lucky? Kat thought, resting her head against his chest, stupidly, blindly happy. How had she managed to win the love of Andrew Pitt, the young man she had first seen years before, collecting the rents on Amber Street? The man she had told her mother about, had fantasised about. How could she have won him? And who cared about what the world said? Who cared about his father's disreputable dealings? God knew, her own family had problems enough. All that mattered was that she was going to marry the man she loved. Everything else was secondary. Once married, she could help her family in ways she had never thought possible. She could curtail Ma Shaw's tyranny and get Micky out of the mill. She could snap her fingers at poverty and the tyranny of the rent. And if she could rise above it, so could her family.

'You mean it?' she asked Andrew breathlessly, looking anxiously into his face.

'I mean it. Eight weeks on Saturday.'

Surprised, she looked at him. '*What?*'

'Two months from Saturday, we get engaged.'

'Oh, really?' she asked, stunned and amused at the same time. 'This is the first I've heard of it. And anyway, what kind of a proposal is that, Andrew Pitt?'

He paused, frowning. 'OK,' he said, taking her hand and counting off the fingers. 'One is for my devotion, two is for my loyalty, three is for my faithfulness, and four is for my promise that I will love you until the last breath leaves my body.'

Moved, Kat teased him, 'But what about my thumb?'

'That's for taking the lid off jars.'

Laughing, she balled up her fist and punched him

playfully. 'And that's for not asking me to marry you properly!'

'So will you, my love?' he asked, his tone urgent. 'Will you marry me?'

Unable to trust her voice, Kat nodded, then lifted her head. 'But why announce our engagement two months from now?'

'That's when we tell your family and my family,' Andrew went on, tensing himself for the difficult news he had to impart. 'I doubt my father will be bothered; he hardly seems to take an interest in anything any more.'

'But why wait two months?' she asked, suddenly anxious. 'What's so special about eight weeks on Saturday?'

'I have to sort out some business first.'

'Must be a lot of business.'

'It's abroad, sweetheart.'

She looked stunned.

'Abroad?'

'My father has concerns in Australia.'

Her eyes widened. 'Australia! That's the other side of the world.'

'That's why it's going to take me a while to get there, sort things out and get back.'

'Australia . . .' Kat repeated, achingly vulnerable. She had her man, but in the moment she had him, he was going to leave her. 'Do you have to go?'

'Yes, darling, I have no choice,' he said patiently. 'I don't want to, but I have to. My father's passing everything over to me, I have to go over there and talk to people. He wants to close the factory down, but I think there's a future out there.'

'But Australia. It's so far away,' Kat said again. 'Why can't someone else go?'

'There *is* no one else . . . Perhaps you could come with me?'

'How!' Kat replied incredulously. 'I can't just up and leave my family, my home. You know that.'

'I know. I know . . .'

Sighing, he pulled her towards him and stroked her hair, realising how close she was to tears. For days he had dreaded telling her about the trip, then decided that he would allay any fears she might have by proposing. That way she would know he was coming back. For her. And their future together. If he had had more time, he would have married her first, but that would have proved to be complicated. And besides, he wanted a proper wedding for Kat. Not some hurried job that would be bound to have people talking.

'I have to sort everything out and settle some sales. I reckon – with the travel – it will take me eight weeks. But when I get back, we get engaged, Katherine Shaw.'

'Don't go,' she said brokenly, terrified for some reason she couldn't fathom. 'Please don't go.'

'It's only two months, darling, only eight weeks. What can happen in two months?'

The man looked familiar to Silky, even though he couldn't quite place the narrow, sinister face. Slowly he wiped his customer's wiry upper arm with a pad of cotton wool soaked in disinfectant, studying the unflinching expression and the heavy under-eye bags.

His instincts were alerted, but nothing in his manner betrayed his unease. 'So, what would you like?'

The man turned his cold eyes on to him. 'Wot's yer speciality?'

'We can do pretty much what you ask for.'

Nodding, the man pointed to a pattern on the wall. 'I like the bird.'

'Good choice,' Silky replied. Kat walked out from the back room, the man watching her curiously. 'This is my niece Katherine, she helps me.'

The man made no comment. Silky drew out the shape of a bird and dabbed away the blood as the needle cut into the skin.

'I heard yer had a young man working here.'
'My nephew, yes.'
'Where is he?'
'He works in the daytime,' Silky replied, glancing over to Kat and gesturing for another cloth.
'I heard he were good, right good.'
'He's the best,' Silky agreed generously. 'You want to wait until Micky's working?'
'Nah,' the man replied, glancing at the outline. 'Perhaps *Micky* could do my other arm? Yer know, I could have a pair of birds. One male, one female. Love birds.'
'Whatever you want,' Silky replied, concentrating. 'Micky's here every afternoon from two until five.'
'Blue and green.'
'What?'
'The lovebirds,' the man said coldly, resting his head back against the seat. 'I want them blue and green.'
True to his word, the man returned three days later. Silky's tattoo had almost healed, only a few scabs still covering the wingtips of the bird. Otherwise the design was clean, with no sign of infection. Not that anyone would get infected at Silky's. But although the tattoo parlour was hygienic, many customers failed to follow even the basic principles of cleanliness. Some never thought to keep the tattoo clean; others fingered it, or let dirt enter the open wound. Silky had seen his fill of festering tattoos and even lanced a couple of abscesses another tattooist had caused by using dirty needles. Fleas and bed bugs could be a problem too. If the customer got bitten in his sleep he would scratch relentlessly and the newly broken skin of the tattoo would get infected. Sometimes part of a tattoo was lost for ever where the skin had been eaten away by bacteria.
But this customer had no such problems. Walking in, he nodded to Silky and sat down, staring curiously at Micky.
'Yer Micky?'
Micky nodded.

'I heard yer were good.'

Again Micky nodded, then pointed to his mouth and shook his head.

'Oh aye, I remember, yer a mute.'

The insult passed over Micky's head. It was the truth; he *was* a mute. But he could talk with the inks, Micky thought, flattered that he had been asked for personally. Slowly he began his design, drawing it on paper and showing it to the man first.

'Sure, yeah, nice. Do it.'

Then he bent down over the man's wiry arm and began. After a couple of minutes watching his nephew work, Silky felt confident enough to go into the back, sitting down and thinking about Molly, his latest girlfriend. He would see her tonight, bring her back to the flat over the shop, have some fun. Stretching his immaculately tailored legs out in front of him, Silky yawned. He would have a few minutes' kip whilst Micky was working. Get up his energy for the evening to follow.

An hour later Micky stepped back for the last time and studied his design critically. He had excelled himself. The bird was perfect. Not that Silky's hadn't been good, but Micky's creature was exotic, taking flight, blue and green, a seabird shimmering against the man's pale skin.

'Fuck me.' Micky frowned, watching the customer as he looked at his tattoo. 'The bugger looks like it's really flying. I heard yer were good and they weren't kidding.'

Thank you. Micky mouthed back.

The man's gaze held his. 'I heard it weren't just tattoos yer were good at. I heard yer could draw and other things . . . I have a friend who needs a bright lad, someone creative, *artistic*. Some young man who might have ambitions beyond Amber Street. Might fancy a bit more money, bit more of life. I mean, even a dummy can get a girl when he has money to spend.'

Uneasy, Micky stared at the man, a creeping sense of dread overtaking him.

I don't understand, he mouthed.

'I think yer do, lad,' the narrow-faced man replied, dabbing at the tattoo with a piece of wadding. 'I think yer know that forging ledgers at the dock – and taking money fer a job to cover fer yer father being drunk – isn't right. I think yer know that Mr Fleetwood would sack yer father and might well ask fer his wages back. Seeing as how they were got illegally.'

Panicked, Micky glanced to the door, but Silky was impervious, fast asleep in the back room.

I don't understand, Micky mouthed again.

'Then I'll spell it out fer yer,' the man went on. 'My boss, Mr Robin Wells, wants yer to do some work fer him. In return, Mr Wells will keep his mouth shut about what yer and yer sister have been up to at the docks. If yer *don't* agree, he'll shop yer. Which means that yer family will be out on the street. Now, is *that* fucking clear enough?'

TWENTY-EIGHT

Horace Armitage was looking at the blocked downspout in the back yard of The Horse and Cart and wondering if he dared report it to Robin Wells. Better not, he decided. Better try and have a go at cleaning it out himself, rather than disturb the landlord. After all, Horace knew he was on borrowed time. That several of the other pubs Wells had taken over had had their respectable landlords ousted on the flimsiest of excuses. He eyed the downspout thoughtfully. Best keep quiet, hope Wells would leave him alone. Why invite attention for a downspout?

Of course Horace, being rotund and out of condition, wasn't going to be able to fix the pipe himself; the question was, who could he ask? If Billy Shaw had still been alive, he would have been the obvious choice. Billy would help anyone out for a pint and a meat pie. But Billy was long gone. Like so much of the old days . . . Taking a deep breath, Horace pulled out a rusty old ladder from the lean-to. He propped it against the damp back wall and then, very timidly, began to climb. But his feet had only just left ground level when his head began to swim and he scurried back to earth and into the dim, stuffy safety of the pub.

Mary was leaning against the bar, reading one of her cheap romances. Still panicked from his recent elevation, Horace smiled distantly, wiping his forehead with the back of his sleeve.

'Yer reading, luv?'

She nodded, showing him the title – *Love's Embrace*. Dumbfounded, Horace regarded the cover, with its demure female turning away from her hirsute admirer. Having never counted romance as one of his interests, he was immune to the machinations of some of his single or widowed customers who considered him a catch, despite the beer belly and wattles . . . So he had had little interest in his niece's innocent flirtations, and only became aware of her romance with Trevor Blaggett when Ma Shaw teased him about it.

'It's not a very good book,' Mary went on blithely, Horace's gaze still glued to the cover.

'*Love's Embrace*? That's sounds a bit . . . racy, luv.'

'Oh no,' Mary replied. 'It's just about a girl who falls in love with this rich man. He thinks she poor, because she's working down the pit . . .'

'Down the pit?'

Mary frowned, rolling her eyes. She frequently played dumb with her uncle because she knew he was afraid of smart women. 'No, maybe it wasn't the pit.'

'I mean, there's not many women working down pits, luv.'

'Maybe it was a mill.'

Horace had to admit that although he was very fond of his niece, she wasn't bright. But she *was* pretty, and that made him think of her boyfriend – and the offending downspout.

'How's Trevor?'

She shook her head. 'He doesn't read much.'

'No, well, he wouldn't,' Horace agreed. 'Busy working at Hallards.'

He thought of Trevor again, a plumber employed at Hallards in town. A good worker, people said, a lad who could turn his hand to anything. Like a downspout.

'Why don't yer bring him in fer a pint, luv?' Horace offered. 'I'd like to meet him.'

'You *did* meet him, Uncle,' Mary replied evenly. 'He came in last week. You shook his hand and said he was welcome here any time he wanted to call. And that he had better treat me right.'

The memory slowly inched its way back to the forefront of Horace's brain, through the worry about Wells and finding the rent. Gradually, as though fog was clearing, he recalled a young man with greased-back hair, a gap between his front teeth, and bony arms.

'Oh yeah. Of course . . . Terry.'

'*Trevor.*'

'Trevor,' Horace agreed, nodding and trying to make up lost ground. 'So when's he coming in again?'

She shrugged. 'I dunno. We had a falling-out.'

This was bad news. 'I'm sure it was nothing serious, luv . . .'

'He's seeing another girl!' Mary replied shortly. 'Well, I *think* he is. He might be . . . He didn't deny it when I asked, so that says something, doesn't it? Mind you, she's from over Holland Street and you know what it's like there. And I heard she had bad skin.'

Horace was struggling to keep up, his niece just hitting her stride.

'I can't let him treat me badly, can I? You said so, you said he had better treat me right. So I thought I'd refuse to see him for a while.' She paused, looking guilelessly to her uncle for romantic advice. The last thing Horace could give her. 'You're a man, what do you think he's doing?'

'Well . . . well, I . . .'

'Would you like a girl with bad skin?' Mary went on. 'I mean, she's got a reputation too, I heard. Which makes sense, because then you'd know why he wouldn't care about her skin.'

'Well . . .' Horace stammered hopelessly.

'I heard she'd been seen with a group of boys in Avenham Park, late at night, and that only means one thing, doesn't it?'

'Ah . . .'

'That she's no good. And if he wants someone like that,

then he can have her. But not me. Oh no. Like you said, Uncle, he's going with her for one thing and one thing only . . .'

Horace couldn't remember saying anything like that, and was trying desperately to back away. Even the ladder and the downspout were preferable to these feminine confidences.

'. . . she was laughing and giggling. Even went with one lad on the handlebars of his bike, and her skirt blew up . . .'

'Is that someone coming in the yard?' Horace said, stepping back. 'I think I heard someone coming in.'

Having successfully made sure that her uncle would not be interfering in her romantic life, Mary sighed and picked up her copy of *Love's Embrace*.

'Like you said, Uncle,' she concluded deftly, knowing that this would be the first – and last – intimate conversation she would have with Horace, 'you can't trust men.'

Sitting beside a tipsy Ginny Arthur, Joan sipped her own drink and then replaced the glass on the table. She felt uneasy, suddenly not quite so confident. The life Ginny offered wasn't her way, and after spending one evening with Robin Wells, Joan had discovered that she didn't have the makings of a party girl. She was fascinated by his aura of menace, but intimidated by his sexual advances and turned him down when he made his move. After all, flirting was one thing, but seduction was quite another . . . Amused, Wells had passed on the information to Ginny, who had then pressed Joan for details. Which went something like: *he's very attractive, but I can't sleep with him.* Ginny wondered what exactly Joan was intending to do with any man, if not sleep with him. And then realised that Joan – with all her social standing and money – was a spoiled tease.

Not in the least affronted by her show of decency, Wells surmised that Joan might turn out to be useful to him, and decided to cultivate her. Not in the way he had cultivated

Ginny, but by giving her just enough attention to keep her hooked. After all, her father was a wealthy man, and powerful in the town. The kind of man who had always given him short shrift – and Wells never forgot a slight. So perhaps, via Joan, Gareth Fairchild might be brought to heel at a later date.

Apologising to Joan for his boorish behaviour, Wells flattered her into thinking he was a gentleman. Perhaps not entirely the villain he was perceived to be; perhaps even prepared to change for her . . . She allowed herself to be fooled, because lately she had heard some unwelcome news. That Andrew was in love with some woman from Amber Street named Katherine Shaw. A woman with no money, working in a tattoo parlour.

Some two-bit scrubber, Gwen had told her daughter delightedly. 'Now aren't you glad you didn't marry that fool of a man? Look what he turned out to be.'

'Andrew wasn't a fool,' Joan had replied, smarting. 'And I rejected *him*, remember?'

'Oh, could I ever forget! You've been moping after him for years now. For God's sake, Joanie, snap out of it. You overplayed your hand; now move on.' Seeing her own daughter rejected in favour of some slum girl had been too much for Gwen to stand. Her invective – unable to be turned directly on the Pitts – had targeted Joan. 'You need to find a husband quick, settle down and have some children. I mean, you *must* have met someone else you like. You don't want to hang around too long, or you might find yourself on the shelf. And then what? Being pitied for the rest of your life, still hankering after a man who's in love with someone else. I mean, you don't want to look like a fool, do you?'

Joan's mouth had fallen open with shock at the words, and she had immediately thought about Robin Wells. I wonder what you would make of *him*, Mother? Andrew would look like a saint next to him . . . Her pride hurt by the mention of the words *on the shelf* and *being pitied*, Joan had vowed there and then to cultivate Robin Wells. If only to spite her mother.

Her thoughts came back to the present as Wells passed her the nightclub menu. Affecting concern, he then made some comment about the fish and told Joan that she had to eat well, that it was good for her and would keep her fit. Young people, he said, thought they were invincible. But even they shouldn't try and burn the candle at both ends . . . Used to being petted and spoiled, Joan sunned herself in his concern, blithely unaware of how she was being duped. Tonight her companion had decided to be paternal. Obviously the lover role hadn't gone down too well, so it was time to change tack. Robin Wells could read people better than a priest read the Latin Mass.

Amused, Silky was watching his niece through the back door of the tattoo parlour. Although Kat was working, her thoughts were obviously a long way away from the anchor she was tattooing on to Harry Yates's arm. Her concentration was there, but her expression was distant. Silky knew that look only too well. He loved that look, loved to wear it himself. So Kat was in love, was she? No prizes for guessing who with . . . Only a few years earlier it would have been unthinkable that his niece and Andrew Pitt could be a couple. Too much would have separated them: money, status, experience. Only a short while back, the Pitts had had power, their son the most eligible of bachelors. How impossible would it have seemed to think of Andrew Pitt visiting Amber Street for anything other than collecting the rents? But so much had changed since Duncan Pitt had thrown in his lot with Robin Wells.

Silky thought of his old rival, intrigued that Wells had never taken revenge. But then again, Wells had a reputation for spinning things out. And Silky had a reputation for being relaxed. So they had shadow-boxed each other, both aware of the other, both waiting for the first punch. Which hadn't come. Wells hadn't struck and Silky hadn't wasted time worrying about it. Let other men wear themselves out; he wasn't going to ruin his work and his nights with Molly by giving Wells any power over him. When – or if – the time came, Silky would deal with it. But if Wells was hoping to grind him down with suspense, he had picked the wrong man.

'Yer a pretty girl,' Harry Yates said suddenly, looking up into Kat's face. 'I wish I were twenty years younger.'

She smiled. 'I bet you had the pick of the girls, Harry.'

'I had some good 'uns, and that's fact,' he said, leaning back in the chair, the tattoo needle making its metallic drilling sound. 'I were a fine-looking man in my prime. Yer'd not think it now, but when I were fighting in the Great War I had three women writing to me. I had to dodge them all when I came home to Preston station, because they were all waiting at the barrier fer me – and not one knew about the others!'

Laughing, Kat stepped back to check her work.

'I 'eard yer were walking out with Andrew Pitt.'

'Is that what you heard, Harry?' Kat replied, smiling inwardly. Just wait until they knew about her engagement.

'Make a good-looking couple, yer would. And he's rich. Even if his father's a bad sort. Mind you, if Old Man Pitt hadn't blotted his copybook, yer'd never have stood a chance with his son.'

The truth of the comment hit Kat forcibly. It was true: Duncan Pitt's fall from grace had made an otherwise impossible relationship possible. Andrew's father could hardly contest an unsuitable match, given his own shortcomings. And as for Ivy, much as Kat might hope to win her over, Andrew did not have to obtain his mother's approval.

'I mean, yer a fine woman,' Harry went on, 'but there's many who'd say that working in a tattoo parlour's not respectable. I know, I've heard them talk.'

'I've heard them talking too – but behind my back, not to my face.'

'Some said this work might have lost yer a few chances in the marrying stakes.'

Listening, Silky frowned by the door. Hadn't he said the same? Hadn't he worried about his niece's reputation? But what could he do? She needed the work and the money.

'But hey, what's the worry now?' Harry Yates went on. 'No more hard times fer yer, Kat, not if yer marry young Pitt.'

The temptation was almost too much to bear. For an instant Kat wanted to bend down to Harry Yates and tell him all about the forthcoming engagement. But she didn't. Instead she wiped his arm and told him, 'Keep the tattoo dry and don't let any dirt get in it, and then come back next week and we'll finish off.'

Ten minutes later she was rising out the needles and taking the dirty cloths into the back. At first she had found some of the work distasteful, but she had soon got used to it. As for Micky, Kat knew only too well that the blood and dirty cloths horrified him; just as she knew he would never let on. He was indebted to Silky and determined never to show his uncle anything that might be misconstrued as ingratitude. Frowning, Kat picked through the cloths. The bloodied ones she dropped into a pail, and then walked out of the back door with them. Making her way over to the rubbish bin, she turned and glanced over the back gate. On the other side of the alley was a parked car, the man inside watching her. A man she knew – Robin Wells. And it wasn't the first time she had seen him there either. Unnerved, she realised that Wells had been visiting more and more regularly, always parking in the same spot. Watching, waiting – but for what?

Tossing the rags into the bin, she moved back inside. What the hell was Wells doing? she wondered uneasily. Was he spying on her, on Micky, or on Silky? Pushing the remaining cloths under the cold water, her thoughts wandered in the still September air, a fly beating against the window. Although she had managed to keep her job part time with Gregory Unwin, he had been forced to expand his business to bring in trade.

Now the carefully arranged shelves were cramped, an assortment of hardware, nails and bolts cluttering the grocer's shop. The refined gossip he had loved to entertain had been curtailed; now the shop played host to workmen as well as matrons. To handymen who bought little and said less. Unemployment and uncertainty were undermining everyone and every trade.

Returning to the parlour, Kat glanced up as her uncle came in, reading the evening paper, his oiled wavy hair immaculate, his appearance mortally dashing.

'I was just reading about America,' he began. 'Not quite the land of opportunity it was a while back. Not after that Wall Street crash and the fallout that followed it. They say it's having a knock-on effect over here.' Slowly he put down the paper, his eyes amused. 'So, when were you going to tell me?'

'Tell you what?

He gestured for Kat to sit down opposite him, which she did. Her apron was folded on her lap, her expression unreadable, except to Silky.

'You're in love.'

She flushed. 'Hey!'

'Oh, come on,' he teased her. 'This is your uncle Silky; there's nothing I don't know about love. Has he proposed?'

Automatically Kat dropped her voice, as though she hardly trusted her words.

'We're going to announce our engagement on the twenty-first of October.'

Silky reached out, taking Kat's hand and kissing it. 'Well done, sweetheart. He's a lucky man.'

'Don't tell anyone, will you!' she said hurriedly. 'Please, I don't want anyone but you to know. We have to wait a bit longer because Andrew has some business to sort out in Australia . . .'

'Australia!'

'I know, it's a long way away. But when he comes back we're going to tell everyone. He's leaving tomorrow for two months. I can hardly bear to think of him being gone so long.'

'It'll go quick.'

Her face was suddenly glowing, her happiness palpable. 'I love him, Silky, I really love him. You know how that feels? Like you could melt . . . just sink to nothing without that person?'

He nodded, understanding perfectly.

'I *couldn't* live without him. I wouldn't want to.'

'You won't have to. He loves you as much as you love him.'

'How do you know that?'

'He's told me,' Silky replied, smiling knowingly. 'You don't think your uncle would let you marry just anyone, do you?'

She laughed, already thinking ahead. 'Mum will be so pleased, and it'll help Dad, I think . . . I mean, he's not been the same since Ma Shaw moved in. She's at him all the time.'

'I've told her to come here, stay with me for a while.'

Kat shook her head. 'She won't come. She believes we can't cope without her. Maybe she's right,' she admitted, 'but she didn't have to move in, give up her own flat and take over at Amber Street. I know Mum finds it difficult, having to be grateful all the time. And Dad . . .'

'I know.'

'No you don't, not really,' Kat said without censure. 'Ma Shaw drives Dad all the time. Never gives up on him. Never stops. I know he's unreliable, but she's making him worse.'

Alerted, Silky kept his voice steady. 'Is he drinking again?'

'No.'

He nodded, sensing the lie. 'You've had to worry about your family for a long time, Kat. It's time you had your own life now.'

'But I've got dreams for *all* of us, Silky,' she confided, suddenly wanting to share. 'I want Micky to take art classes, Christine to go to high school, when she's older. As for Mum, she can have the best medical care and they'll never have to worry about making the rent again, because I can help with the money. Oh, I know how much you've helped us; we'd have sunk without you – but you won't have to bail us out again, Silky. When I'm married, we'll be safe.'

'Make *yourself* safe first,' he said quietly. 'The rest will follow.'

They sat together in silence for a while. On the mantelpiece was a photograph of Molly, Silky's latest love, and a note from Anna. Beside that was an old photograph of Ma Shaw with her three sons, lanky Ivan scowling into the camera, Silky as glossy as ever, and Jim, jovial and open-faced, grinning at the good fortune of being alive. Before long there would be another photograph, Kat thought: of her in her wedding dress, standing next to Andrew, her new husband. She closed her eyes, revelling in the dream of her future. How people would talk, envy her. Katherine Shaw from Amber Street marrying into the Pitt clan. Well, some would say, they're made for each other, both suspect. Him with his dodgy father and her the watchman's daughter, making ends meet in a tattoo parlour . . .

Ten minutes later Kat roused herself, said a hurried goodbye to Silky and made her way home. No time to day-dream; life had to go on. And she had promised to take Christine over to Mrs Howard's that evening . . . The mild September air nuzzled her cheek as she headed home, thinking of Andrew about to leave for Australia. It had been so hard to say goodbye. She had clung to him tightly, as tightly as he had clung to her. And he'd promised her he would write, telling her over and over again that in two months' time they would be engaged. And never apart again.

'This is the last time I'll ever leave you,' he had said, kissing her urgently. 'When I get back, we'll never be apart again. Just wait a little while, my love, and then the world is ours for the taking . . .'

Passing Gordon Street, Kat suddenly saw Micky running towards her. Smiling, she waved, then tensed. There was something wrong. Short of breath, Micky pulled up next to her, his face drawn, sweat on his forehead.

'What!' she said, instinctively afraid. 'What is it?'

We have to talk.

'Is it Mum?'

He shook his head.

'Dad?'

No, it's worse.

Glancing round, Micky drew his sister into a ginnel, checking there was no one about to overhear them. His breathing was laboured, his hands moving so quickly Kat could barely make out what he was telling her.

'Slower!'

I've been looking for you. We've been found out. They know about us doing the nightwatchman's round for Dad.

She could feel her legs weaken and leaned against the wall. 'Who knows?'

Robin Wells.

'What?' Kat said breathlessly. 'How? What's it got to do with him?'

Wells wants me to forge some documents for him, then he'll keep quiet.

At once she remembered the compelling man in The Horse and Cart, picking out a tune on the piano. Sinister, frightening. The same man she had seen watching her. Just sitting in his car, watching. *That* man.

'He told you this?'

He sent someone, Micky signed, patently terrified. *If I don't work for him, Wells will turn us out of the house.*

'Micky, slower, slower. Tell me more slowly.'

His hands kept moving, speeding up with his panic. *But if I work for him and anyone finds out, I'll go to jail . . .*

'You're not doing anything for that man,' Kat replied, her tone deadly. 'Tell him you refuse.'

He'll throw us out! Get Dad fired, tell everyone what we've done. Micky's expression was desperate. *But I can't forge things for him, Kat! I can't. They'll put me away.*

'No one's putting you away. No one's going to make you do anything illegal, Micky.'

Her tone was firm, but her heart was pumping. Christ, Wells had them over a barrel now, for sure. What was she going to do? What *could* she do? Catching hold of her brother's hands to steady him, Kat felt her own shaking. God, of all people, Robin Wells . . . Her mind turned back to the old feud between Silky and Wells. Was this his revenge? Certainly Wells had the upper hand. If Micky didn't do what he said, he would expose them. And that would be the end. Their father fired, his children's forgery uncovered. No wage. No money. No rent. And God only knew what the shock would do to their mother . . .

Trying desperately to gather her thoughts, Kat stared ahead. What could she do? What *was* there to do? Go and see Mr Fleetwood at the docks, tell him what had happened, that they were being blackmailed? Throw herself on his mercy? No, Kat realised, she couldn't do that. She had to keep their secret. So what *was* the solution?

What are we going to do? Micky signed again desperately, close to panic. *Jesus, what are we going to do?*

Kat was also fighting panic. Could she go to Andrew for help? No, she couldn't even reach him. What about Silky? No, not her uncle, there would be God only knew what reprisals for his intervention. There was only one thing she could do – go and talk to Robin Wells herself. The thought chilled her. Could she face him? Could she really take on a man like that? But what was the choice? She had to go and plead her family's case. Surely there was some arrangement they could come to? He couldn't seriously want to ruin the life of a nineteen-year-old youth? To make Micky into a criminal?

Or could he? Kat thought of the way Wells had branded Ivan. How he had frightened Micky when he had first returned to Preston. How he had sent messages to Silky by terrorising members of the Shaw family. Rumours had abounded about Wells's ruthlessness. And she had seen plenty herself. His evictions, the way people ran when they saw him coming. He frightened his tenants and he frightened her. But she had to pretend otherwise. She had to try and reason with him, reach a compromise with a hard man who wasn't above anything – if the rumours were to be believed.

She was going to bargain. Her hands shook, her mouth drying. Could she do it? Could she? She had no choice. She was going to face someone who frightened her, someone who could ruin her and her family. *And she had nothing to bargain with.*

TWENTY-NINE

Checking her watch for the third time, Kat heard the town hall clock strike eight. Slowly she counted the chimes, trying to calm herself. Then, as the last note faded, she began to walk towards the end of Friargate. It had taken her a while to calm Micky down enough to take him home, and when they arrived back at the Amber Street house Kat had hurried him upstairs. Composing herself, she had then walked into the kitchen, little Christine running into her arms, Anna sitting by the table. The long, warm summer had served her mother well. Gone was the look of strain, and Anna had recovered so much that she had started to help Ma Shaw with some light chores again.

Looking up, she had smiled at her daughter. 'Hello, luv, had a good day?'

Kat had nodded, avoiding Ma Shaw's eyes. Ma Shaw could always pick up on a lie. 'We were quite busy in the shop and Silky had a new customer.'

Ma Shaw had harrumphed behind her. 'Tattoo parlour!'

Fighting annoyance, Kat had sat beside her mother. 'I saw Mary just now, with Trevor Blaggett.'

'He wants to get those teeth of his fixed.'

You want to get that mouth of yours fixed, Kat had thought, returning her mother's amused smile.

'D'you think they'll get married?'

'Everyone's marriage mad!' Ma Shaw had snapped,

banging down a pan of peeled potatoes. 'You'd think life began and ended when yer got wed.'

Anna had given her daughter a warning look. It had said: *let it go, don't provoke her*. And normally Kat would have backed down, but that night her nerves had been on edge and she had been in no mood for her grandmother's incessant carping.

'*You* married twice.'

'And lived to regret it! And yer can watch that tone of voice with me, young woman. Yer not too old to get a good slapping.' Ma Shaw had looked round, suddenly wanting to pick another fight. 'Where's that brother of yers?'

'Upstairs. He had a headache.'

Immediately Anna had been full of concern. 'Oh, I hope it's not another infection. I heard—'

'He's a strapping lad now, big enough to get over anything,' Ma Shaw had said, interrupting. 'Yer don't want to make the boy soft.'

Infuriated, Kat had ignored her and turned back to her mother. 'I'm going out with Micky later, walk with him over to the mill. The fresh air will do him good before he goes on his shift.'

'Ah, it's not too bad! The late shift's never as hard as the day—'

Kat had spun round on her grandmother. 'Micky works the afternoons too, remember? God knows how we'd manage without his wage from Silky's.'

'Well yer'd not meet the rent on what yer father earns, and that's a fact . . .'

Before Kat could respond, she had felt her mother catch hold of her hand and squeeze it in a silent request for patience.

'He went sloping off a while back. Long before he's due on watch. God knows why he left so early . . .'

In that instant Kat had wanted to grab Ma Shaw and hurl her out into the street, slamming the door behind her. Then she had wanted to sit with Christine and her mother and tell them all about how she and Andrew were going to get engaged. Of course everyone knew he was going to Australia, but no one knew what would happen when he returned. In that moment Kat had felt impelled to confide, to share her happiness. To push back the thought of what she had to do, if only for a little while. Just to see the look on her mother's face. The joy. Just to give Anna the present of hope.

But Ma Shaw hadn't been about to leave and she hadn't been about to stop talking.

'Of course it's all right for yer brother to work fer Silky. But you shouldn't be there.' She diced some carrot and threw it into the pan. 'Mrs Crompton were saying only the other day that it's not a job fer a woman. Mixing with all types.'

Ignoring her, Kat had looked back to her mother. 'I wonder how long it'll be before I get a letter from Andrew.'

'Hah! Now there's a case in point. I wonder what he'll get up to when he's on the other side of the world.'

'Nothing!' Kat had exploded, standing up. 'He loves me, and he's honest.'

'Yer fooling yerself.'

Incensed, Kat had been about to retort when she had checked herself. Why worry about an old woman when she had to face Robin Wells? Ma Shaw was a complaining, angry sod without a good word to say for anyone, and she had always been the same. So instead of replying, Kat had sat with her mother for a while longer, and then she had called upstairs for Micky and together they had left the house.

Wells's cohort had told Micky to be on the corner at eight, and now Kat was standing beside her brother, both of them waiting. She had no fixed plan and had not decided on what she would say. She would just react to what Wells said. It would be simple. *It would be* . . . She could feel her heart banging in her chest, Micky tapping his foot nervously.

Finally a car drew up beside them, Robin Wells winding

down the driver's window. 'You've got a big mouth, Micky – for a mute.'

Giving Kat a cold look, he gestured for her to get into the passenger seat, Micky climbing into the back. The interior of the car smelled expensive, the leather dark and glossy as a horse's flank. And Wells was wearing aftershave, bitterly sweet.

'I think we'll have a talk in my office.'

Kat frowned. 'Why can't we talk here?'

Ignoring her, Wells pulled away from the kerb and drove along in silence. Behind her, Kat could hear Micky's rapid breathing and resisted the impulse to look at Wells. About ten minutes later, he stopped the car outside a factory and ushered them in. The place was small, filled with boxes and shelves, workers eyeing them uneasily. In the background Kat could hear the soft shuffle of machinery and the thud of the door as Wells showed them into his office.

'Sit down.'

They both did as they were told, Wells lighting a cigarette and staring at Micky. 'You really are a wet week, running to your sister like that.'

'He can't work for you,' Kat said simply. Wells turned to her, his gaze steady and unblinking. 'He can't do what you want. It's against the law.'

'So is taking a wage under false pretences,' Wells replied, studying her.

Aware of the scrutiny, she glanced down, then looked up again and held his gaze. Well, she had nerve, Wells thought. Her brother might be a weakling, but Kat Shaw certainly wasn't. And good-looking – but he already knew that. Handsome enough to attract Andrew Pitt. Now *that* had been interesting gossip, Wells thought, taking some credit for the romance. After all, if he hadn't done that bit of business with Duncan, who would have put money on any Amber Street offspring hooking old money? But then again, Kat had something about her that was fascinating to men. Fascinating to *him* . . . Another thought followed on, enticing. Wells was within a finger-length of taking his revenge on Silky – by ruining his nephew. But now an even sweeter revenge came to mind. Something far more damaging and enjoyable for him.

At the same moment Kat was staring at her hands. She felt afraid, but in some strange way almost excited by being with Wells. Oh, she hated the man, but there was something confusingly compelling about him.

'We didn't take money under false pretences,' she said, trying to keep her voice steady. 'We worked the watch—'

'That your father should have done.'

'We only filled in for him now and then.'

'Fleetwood won't be interested in whether you did it once, or every night for a year.' Wells paused. 'You know that, and so do I. He'll fire your father. And even if he doesn't take any further action, there's goes the watchman's wage.'

'My father can find another job.'

'Who's hiring drunks these days?'

'*He isn't a drunk!*'

'Don't lose your temper, Katherine,' Wells said, his tone patient. 'You're fooling yourself and you know it. You have to be realistic and see things for what they are. I'm offering a simple solution – if your brother does some work for me, I'll keep my mouth shut. Otherwise, your family is in trouble.'

'I'm sorry, but Micky won't work for you. You don't really want to do this,' Kat said, thinking on her feet and trying to appeal to Wells's chivalry. But she couldn't look at him. 'Please don't make my brother into a criminal.'

'He *is* a criminal.'

'No,' she said imploringly. 'He only came to the docks because of me. It was my idea. He only did it because I asked him to. Look, he's just a kid; don't wreck his life.'

'I'm giving him a job, not throwing him to a pack of wolves.'

'But that's not true, is it?' Kat replied, facing him, her temper flaring. 'You might as well be throwing him to the wolves if he works for you. If you make him into a forger.'

Wells was coolly unmoved. 'He's already an *amateur* forger; I would simply be making him into a professional. Think of it as a promotion.'

She took a deep breath to steady her nerves. 'This isn't about Micky, is it?'

'Enlighten me.'

'It's about Silky.' Kat could see his eyes flicker. 'I know you two have unfinished business, but that's not Micky's fault.'

'I'm getting bored,' Wells said suddenly, annoyed that Kat had seen through him. 'Either that brother of yours works for me, or I expose you both.'

Panic came quickly, Micky grabbing at Kat's arm.

I'll do it.

'There you are,' Wells said, smiling, as he lip-read Micky's words. 'Problem solved.'

'He's *not* doing it!' Kat retorted, her temper rising. 'No one in our family is a criminal. And Micky's not going to be the first.'

'You're in no position to argue. *I'm* the one who's holding all the cards.'

'All right, *I'll* work for you instead.'

He almost laughed. 'You can forge?'

'I could clean your house, your office. This factory . . .'

Frowning, Micky caught hold of her arm. *No!*

She shook him off, turning back to Robin Wells. 'There must be a job I can do.'

The trap sprang shut. Pausing, Wells looked at her for a long moment, the implication obvious. Oh, and she caught it. She caught it and tensed and knew what he was thinking. And knew that on some level – subconsciously – she had anticipated it.

'Well there is *something* you could do for me, Katherine. Something that might make me inclined to let your brother off the hook. Something a lot easier than housework and a lot more pleasurable . . .'

Before his sister had time to react, Micky lunged towards Wells and struck him. Falling backwards in his chair, Wells lost his balance, the right side of his forehead striking the edge of his desk. The pain knocked the air out of his lungs, winding him momentarily, blood gushing from the wound as he struggled to his feet.

'Jesus,' he said, gasping, his fury uncontrolled. 'You fucking little shit!'

Kat didn't hesitate. Pushing Micky out of the office, she ran after him, making for the side door, Wells cursing and shouting after them.

'I'll bloody kill you! You *and* your fucking sister! I'll get all your family for this! You're finished! FINISHED!' Still partially dazed, Wells made it to the office door and then slumped against it, shouting so loudly that the workers came out to watch. 'Go on, run, you little bastard! Some good it'll do you. Wherever you go, I'll find you, Micky Shaw, and when I do, you're dead!' He shook his head, blood fizzing in his ears, his voice menacing. 'As for you, Katherine, you think about my offer. You think about it good and hard, you hear me? And if you've any bloody sense, you'll take me up on it – because if you don't, I'm going to make you wish you had. I'm going to get your bloody brother, then the rest of your bloody family . . .'

Kat paused next to Micky. They were out of sight of Wells, but they could hear every word he said. He was marking her card, Kat realised; he was threatening her, making sure she knew what was in store for them all.

'You hear me? I'll get every one of your family. Turn them out on the street, see them dead. Take my offer, Katherine – YOU HEAR ME? It's the only chance you've got.'

THIRTY

Woken by a banging on the back door of the shop, Silky glanced at the clock beside his bed: two thirty. Disturbed, he got to his feet and threw open the bedroom window, looking down. Overhead, a moon lit the ginnel and the back yard, a figure ducking suddenly into the shadows. Uneasy, Silky pulled on his trousers and reached for the hammer he kept under the bed. If it was a burglar, he was going to regret breaking in . . . Silently he turned the handle of his bedroom door, moving out on to the landing. The moonlight illuminated the area eerily, the sound of whispered voices drifting up from below.

Silky's hand tightened on the hammer. So there was more than one of them, was there? he thought, keeping to the darkness as he edged out further. Come for the bloody takings, had they? Cautious, he edged a little further out. It never occurred to him to run. He had never backed down from anyone and wasn't about to start now. Slowly he descended the back stairs, making sure he avoided the steps that creaked, his bare feet making no sound. At the bottom, he paused outside the door. So they were in the shop, were they? he thought, listening to the indecipherable whispering. What the hell did anyone want in the shop?

'Creeping around your own place, Silky,' a voice said suddenly, someone grabbing hold of him and taking the hammer from his hand.

Uselessly Silky tried to shake them off, but there were two of them and he had no choice but to be manhandled into the tattoo parlour beyond. Almost thrown through the doorway, Silky found himself momentarily blinded by the shop light. Blinking, he stared ahead, a figure coming into sharp focus. Robin Wells.

'I wondered when you'd call by,' Silky said, impressively calm, his gaze moving to the deep gash on Wells's forehead and the darkening bruise around it. 'You bump into something when you were breaking in?'

Despite himself, Wells couldn't help but admire his old rival. Even faced with three men at two in the morning, Silky hadn't broken out into a sweat. In other – maybe better – times, Wells would have liked someone like Silky working for him. You didn't meet many real hard men.

'You see this?' Wells said, pointing to his forehead. 'Your bloody nephew did this.'

'Micky? Good for him. I always thought the lad had guts.'

'You watch your mouth.'

'If Micky hit you, you must have done something to deserve it.'

Taking a breath, Wells moved closer. Silky could sense the two men behind him, and although he didn't show it, he was nervous. He had no weapon and Wells was obviously enraged. Jesus, he thought, why on earth had Micky hit him? He could see the cold heat in Wells's eyes, and knew then that he was going to get a beating. Not just for the injury his nephew had inflicted, but for the old injury, the humiliation from long ago.

'I've had enough of you and all the bloody Shaws. In fact, *Silky* – what kind of a stupid fucking poof's name is that? – you've been an irritation for years. I've never forgiven you for what you did.'

'The lady made her own choice. And she chose me,' Silky replied, tensing for the blow he knew would follow at any moment. He almost wanted it to come, for the revenge to be over after so long. In truth, he was bored with waiting, and ready to take Wells on in a fair fight. Not that it would come to that. Fairness was not Robin Wells's strong suit. 'You should have looked me up earlier, instead of sending messages through my brother and nephew,' he went on, goading Wells. 'I've not been hiding.'

'You've got some balls, I'll give you that,' Wells replied, walking over to the table next to the tattooing chair. Slowly he moved around the parlour, peering at the designs on the walls and at the needles and drill Silky used daily. Picking up the drill, he fingered the end gently.

'Your nephew has talent. And your niece too. Good-looking girl, Kat. Feisty . . . I like that in a woman.' He paused, looking into Silky's face. The light overhead lit up the ragged end of the wound on his forehead, blood beginning to seep out again.

'Stay away from Kat—'

The punch hit Silky full in the stomach, knocking all the wind out of him. Dropping to the floor, he doubled up, gasping for breath. In the background he could just make out one of the men filling the kettle, and wondered for one insane moment if they were all going to have a cup of tea together. Hauled up on to his feet, he was then thrown into the chair. But before he had time to respond, the men had tied him down with rope, binding his arms and chest and legs so that he couldn't move a muscle. In that instant Silky realised he was defenceless. And in the background, he heard the whistle on the kettle beginning to sing, like some strange night bird, plaintive and sad, its weird metallic sound distorted in the clammy atmosphere.

'Where's your nephew?'

'I don't know,' Silky said honestly. He could hear the kettle whistling more loudly and fought panic, looking into Wells's eyes. 'I don't know where he is.'

'If you did, would you tell me?'

'No,' Silky said, smiling his most urbane smile and jerking

his head towards Wells's wound. 'Does it hurt?'

He would never forget the pain that followed. First there was a short silence, complete and queasy, Wells looking away as though repelled at the thought of what he was being forced to do. From the back room Silky heard the kettle whistling through its hot metal throat – then silence. Then footsteps. One of the men came into the tattoo parlour holding the kettle handle with a cloth. Wells took it, and held it over Silky, so close he could feel the heat from the metal. Over his head he passed it, taunting him, then over his legs, then over his genitals. Finally, in the instant when it seemed he had changed his mind, Wells suddenly tipped the kettle, pouring the boiling water over Silky's right hand, the skin reddening and burning, his fingers curling inwards as he screamed.

When Wells had emptied the kettle, he dropped it and walked out, leaving Silky unconscious in the chair, his hand a bloodied pulp.

Outside, he stood on the pavement opposite, staring at the tattoo parlour.

'Set fire to it.'

His cohort, the narrow-faced man, flinched. 'What!'

'Set fire to the shop.'

'But . . .'

'Oh, just do it,' Wells said wearily, as though irritated by some minor, trivial matter. 'But only the back – we don't want to kill him, do we? And make some noise when you do it. Enough to tip off the neighbours so they can raise the alarm.'

The man looked at the shop, baffled, and then turned back to Wells.

'But why?'

'Because I don't like tattoos. That's why.'

A nervous autumn wind was blowing down the River Ribble, making the water shimmy in the dock, the lights from the boats darting about on the night tide like liquid glow worms.

Inside one of the dock pubs, some Russian sailors mooched over a late drink, a couple of girls around Missie Shepherd's age coasting listlessly for trade. The full moon had scuttled itself, temporarily beached behind clouds, its glow only partially illuminating the dockside. On the far side, Jim had begun his round for the night. Sober, he moved along purposefully, pretending to feel what he did not – in control. Driven out of his own home by a harpy of a mother, Jim dreamed of the day when he would have a full-time job again and could push Ma Shaw out. Then he and Anna could be alone with little Christine and Micky and Kat. Like it used to be.

Of course he knew he had only himself to blame. His actions had caused the change in circumstance, had made his mother his gaoler, his children his guards . . . Mortified, he thought of the times he had woken at the docks to find his watchman's round done for him. His own son and daughter turned into criminals to save him. Humiliated and embarrassed, he had never mentioned it, and together the three of them kept their secret, Ma Shaw never finding out, Anna in blissful ignorance, believing her husband was holding down his job responsibly. The thought made Jim itch for a drink, his discomfort making him thirsty. He would do the next couple of warehouses and then double back, call in at The Moon Shadow and get some beer. The landlord didn't take tick, but he *did* take the odd piece of timber or metal that Jim skimmed off an incoming load. Stealing for a drink . . . Jim paused, disgusted by how low he had sunk. He was a liar and a petty crook who would end up in the gutter. In his mind, he was already there.

And as their father mapped out his round on the far part of the Albert Edward, Kat and Micky were making their way along the dark side of the warehouses, keeping to the shadows. Repeatedly Kat turned, listening for footsteps or the sound of a car. Anything that would tell her they were being followed. From the way her brother was breathing, she could tell how afraid he was, how panicked. But she didn't stop for long, and after another couple of moments urged him to follow her again. Her whole mind was concentrated on one thing and one thing only: getting Micky to safety. Because if Robin Wells found him, he might well carry out his threat. And kill him . . . Turning, she beckoned for Micky to catch up, ducking back again when the moon sauntered out from behind the clouds. Its big yellow face grinned down on them like a ghoul, Kat looking round to check that the coast was clear before moving on, Micky behind her. At first she had considered hiding him in the town, but where? She wasn't going to endanger her uncles, and she certainly couldn't take him home. The next option was the obvious one – the Albert Edward. But at the docks there was only one place she could think of to hide her brother – the deserted warehouse where Billy had died. It was the only place she could be certain that no one would look. Ever since the accident, the place had been cordoned off – THIS PROPERTY IS UNSAFE. But that wasn't strictly true. The timber had long been moved out, and now the warehouse stood half empty, only broken-up boxes and crates and rusty machinery left abandoned there.

But luckily the warehouse had a bad reputation. Even the whores didn't go there because of the ghosts; because poor Billy Shaw came back in the night hours and walked the place of his death. Or so the rumours went . . . And for once Kat was glad of the superstition. Indirectly, Billy, who had always kept his little brother safe in life, would still keep him safe after death.

'This way,' she said suddenly, pulling Micky towards the warehouse. He looked ahead – and back to her – alarmed. 'It's all right,' Kat told him. 'Come on.'

Watching her, he winced as she broke a small panel of glass and slid her hand in, turning the lock, the key inside. Pushing open the door, she motioned her brother to follow her, the moon lighting the entrance like the opening of a tomb. Inside, the warehouse was dusty, the indistinct outlines of boxes and machinery rearing up menacingly around them as they moved further inside. As quickly as she could, Kat got her bearings, and then took hold of Micky's hand.

'Up here, follow me,' she said, leading him towards the ladder in the corner.

Urging him up, she followed, both of them crouching down as they reached the platform and shuffling to the back. There they finally sat down on some sacking, Kat lighting a lamp she had brought with her. The light was very dim, Micky's face ghostly, terrified.

Sorry. I shouldn't have hit him.

Her hand went out, clasping his. For all the trouble they were in, she couldn't admonish him. Micky had attacked Wells for *her*, because she had been insulted, propositioned. Because he had been the good brother and wanted to protect her. Because he was an honourable man; not a lad any more. The poor runty kid people had once teased had turned out tougher than anyone had suspected.

'You have to stay here, Micky. You have to hide – until I can work out what to do. Until I can move you somewhere else.'

Go to Silky.

She nodded. 'I've already decided to do that,' she reassured him. 'You know you'll have to go away for a while, don't you?'

Aghast, Micky stared at his sister.

No.

'Yes, love, you have to. You can't stay here indefinitely and you can't come home. Wells is crazy. He would hurt you, Micky, if he found you . . . We'll find somewhere better for you to go. But for now, you have to stay here. You'll be safe, I promise.'

He glanced away, down into the belly of the warehouse. She knew only too well what he was thinking. Remembering the night of Billy's death; the way their father had found his son crushed under the timber, blood coming from his nose and mouth, and Jane in his arms. It was as though it had only just happened, Kat seeing the whole tableau again.

It's eerie.

'No it's not,' Kat reassured him. 'Billy's here. You can't be afraid when he's around. Billy always looked out for you, remember? I'll leave the lamp with you. But don't turn it up, keep it low. And if you hear anyone coming, blow it out. If it's me, I'll whistle like we always do, OK?' She hugged her brother suddenly, as if he was a child again, and Micky clung to her, frightened, gradually realising the enormity of what he had done.

'I have to go . . .'

No! You can't go out there on your own.

'Micky,' Kat said, pulling back and looking at him, 'I *have* to go. I'll come back later with some food for you. But you have to stay here – do you understand? *You have to stay here.*'

He nodded, trembling.

'I'll get this all sorted out. I'll go and see Silky,' Kat went on, feeling the first shimmer of hope. 'He'll know what to do. Silky always knows what to do.'

Without another word, she climbed down the wooden ladder and made her way back on to the dockside, passing by the Moon Shadow pub and hearing the sounds of an argument coming from inside. Hurriedly she pulled her coat tightly around her and scurried on. She prayed that her father would stay sober that night and do the watchman's round; prayed that Silky would be at home; and most of all she prayed that no one had followed her and Micky to the docks. Looking round, she could see no one. No cars, nothing. Perhaps Wells would let the matter go – but she knew otherwise. He was going to make them pay for what they had done, and if he couldn't find Micky, someone else would suffer.

Catching a late tram, Kat got off at Friargate and walked hurriedly towards the tattoo parlour. She was composed, confident that her uncle would help her, that somehow the redoubtable Silky would have the answer. So when she drew closer to the street where her uncle lived, she was surprised to find a number of people gathered around. Why would so many people be out at night unless something had happened? Instinct made Kat start running, turning the corner to see the tattoo parlour black with smoke, an upstairs window still smouldering from the recently extinguished fire.

'*God!*' she screamed, running forward, a fireman catching her arm to stop her.

'Yer can't go any further, miss.'

'That's my uncle's place. That's Silky's—' She stopped, turning to the fireman. 'Is he still in there?'

The fireman exchanged a glance with his colleague, then looked back to Kat.

'We got your uncle out.'

'Is he OK?'

'He's burned. His right hand's very bad.'

She flinched. 'Where is he?'

'In hospital, miss, Preston Royal Infirmary. Maybe yer should have a word with the doctor there. He'll be able to tell yer.'

A sudden thought overtook her. It came blinding, white hot.

'How did the fire start?'

The fireman shook his head. 'Lamp, something like that. Maybe your uncle fell asleep and a coal rolled out of the fire, set the rug alight. Yer'd be amazed how simple things start fires off.'

Nodding dully, Kat appeared to accept what the fireman said. But she knew how the fire had started. Someone had set it. Someone sent by Robin Wells. So finally Wells had taken his revenge on Silky – and Micky had been the excuse. She knew then that Wells was keeping his promise and had declared war not just on her uncle, but on the entire Shaw family. And he had only just started. He could turn them out on to the street at any moment. Without a home, they would be destitute. After all, Wells would have no compunction in exposing what she and Micky had done – and then their father would lose his job at the docks. No money, no home. As for poor Silky, the fire had wrecked his shop and damaged his right hand – ending his career and his means of making a living.

Wells was picking them off, one by one . . . Kat's eyes closed for an instant, almost as though she couldn't bear to see what was coming. How could the family survive so many body blows? How could her mother withstand the shock? One man had them completely in his control and there was nowhere – and no one – to turn to for help. Helplessly, Kat thought of Andrew, longed for him. But he was out of reach, out of touch from this sooty northern town, this burned-out wreck of a shop, the paper patterns curled and blackened on the walls and Silky's tattooing chair smouldering from the firemen's hoses. It had been a rough place, Kat thought. Nothing much at all, just a tattoo parlour in a run-down part of town, but it had meant so much to Silky. It had been a landmark, visited by the hard men from the docks and the nervous white-collar clerks, tipsy after a night out.

How people had talked when she went to work there, Kat remembered, and how trivial it all seemed now. How they had clucked on and on about her ruining her reputation, but she hadn't. Andrew had still loved her. Andrew had still wanted to marry her. But now that she needed him most, she couldn't reach him. Couldn't ask for his help. And God, and how much he would have wanted to help her, Kat thought longingly. How much he would have supported her, tried to sort things out. But then again, how *could* he sort this mess out? No one could.

But that wasn't strictly accurate, was it? Kat thought, staring blindly at the burned-out shop. There *was* a solution, and she knew it only too well. It had been spelled out for her. Wells had explained it, given her the way out. There *was* a means to ensure that her family kept their home on Amber Street, that Anna was looked after, that Silky was left alone and Micky untouched. There *was* a way to ensure that no one ever found out about the watchman's daughter doing the watchman's job. There *was* a way.

It would protect her family and keep them safe. But it would destroy her.

Rain had started falling by the time I arrived at the Preston Royal Infirmary. Silky was sedated, his right hand heavily bandaged, his face composed. I remember looking at him, at the long glossy eyelashes and the perfectly formed mouth, and realising how handsome he really was. I had always known he was brave, but had never seen his real beauty before. Or maybe it was a quality that shone through that night, from under his skin, from that part of us that is honest and kind. Whatever it was, it was rare and I doubt I will see it again.

When I left my uncle, I returned to the tattoo parlour and stood outside, just looking at it. The rain had been falling on the burned-out shop for a while by then, making it smoulder, the exposed wooden beams of the upstairs room looking like a rib cage torn open. And overhead, the same ghoulish moon that had spied on me as I hid my brother on the docks watched and waited with me.

I knew where he would be, and of course he was there. In his car, parked at the back entrance of the tattoo parlour, where he had watched me many times. He just sat there, looking at me, his expression unreadable as I walked over to the car. For one stupid moment I imagined that I could will myself away; that I could join Andrew, away from this grimy northern town and the acrid smell of the smoke. But I knew I couldn't.

Getting into the passenger seat, I stared ahead for a long moment before I could trust my voice.

Then finally I said: 'If I go with you now, will you leave my family alone? Will you promise not to hurt them?'

He nodded.

His eyes were dead. Oddly without triumph. I had expected to see some gloating, but there was none. Or maybe he didn't show it. Was I afraid of him? Terrified. Was I afraid for myself? No, I just thought of Andrew, of the Australian sunshine and the wide new country. And I felt my heart empty, knowing I would never see it. Knowing that after this night, I could never be with him, or love him, again. He had gone away promising that when he returned we would become engaged. That we would tell everyone we were in love.

What can happen in eight weeks? he had asked me.

Life happened in those weeks. Robin Wells happened in those weeks.

We do what we have to. Not what we want, or choose. Not what we hope or wish for. We do what our experiences and our consciences dictate. So I sat in that car, dry-eyed, as Robin Wells drove me away from Amber Street, my family, and all I had known. I left behind the girl I was and became the woman people talked about in whispers, without using my name.

So notorious did I become that I was only referred to by a title: The Watchman's Daughter.

THIRTY-ONE

Docking in Liverpool at the end of October, Andrew collected his bags and immediately began the journey back to Preston. He hadn't been too worried at first that his letters to Kat hadn't been answered, but by the third week he began to feel anxious that he had received no reply. Perhaps, he consoled himself, there was a hold-up with the postal system. After all, from Preston to Sydney was a long way. But there was more to it than that, he felt instinctively. There was something wrong. Had Kat changed her mind? Had she met someone else? It's only two months, he had said, what can happen? The unthinkable could happen . . .

No, Andrew told himself, picking up his car from his father's Liverpool office, he was panicking, that was all. He would get home and Kat would be overjoyed to see him and they would announce their engagement at the weekend. He would tell her about Australia, about Sydney in particular, and describe the size of the place and clean smell of the air. No hurried terraces, no smog, no dingy back alleyways. A new country, he would tell her, looking for new people . . . He moved out into the traffic, taking a while to get accustomed to the narrow streets, the dark overhang of October weather. Still, it was home. But maybe not for ever . . . A dream was tickling against his heart. For a while he had been unsettled in Preston, embarrassed by his father's actions and irritated by his mother's patronising attitude towards Kat. If he emigrated with his new wife, no one would judge them. No background to criticise, no social differences to juggle, just a new beginning.

He liked the thought of that and hoped Kat would like it too. Once they were married, he would see to it her family wouldn't go short, and his own parents were more than a little well off. When everyone was settled and safe, what would there be to hold them? Andrew could honestly say that he was going to look after the family's business in Australia; it wasn't as though he was leaving anyone in the lurch by emigrating.

So his thoughts went on, as he drew closer and closer to Preston. As he drove, the last of the clear weather faded. Within moments the sky had darkened overhead and the rain began, making the streets greasy, a mean wind rapping the overshoot of clouds. In the Albert Edward the boats shifted in their moorings, and a few sea birds skirted the dockside, driven in from the shifting sea.

The weather was turning, and a chill had come into the air.

Wincing, Silky limped along the pavement, then paused outside his deserted shop. He had been kept in the Preston Royal Infirmary for three weeks. For the first week he had been unconscious, his lungs damaged by smoke, but then he had rallied. And as he had done so, the burns on his back and legs had healed, although his right hand had been so severely injured he only had very limited use left.

The doctor in charge had been mystified by the difference between his bodily burns and the injury to his hand, but Silky was giving nothing away.

'I fell asleep with a cigarette in my hand. Must have dropped it and set the place alight.'

'But the wound is a *hot water* burn, Mr Shaw,' the doctor had gone on, 'not a fire burn.'

'Nah! You've got it wrong, Doctor. After all, I should

know,' Silky had replied, winking. 'I was the one that was there.'

Yes, he was the one who had been there, and he played and replayed every moment of that night in his head. Even asleep, he had dreamed of the kettle being swung in front of his face, and felt the agony of the boiling water . . . Coming back to consciousness, he had found Ma Shaw asleep by his bedside, her hat tipped over to one side, her mouth slightly open.

'Ma,' he had said, waking her.

She had come to with a jolt. 'Silky . . .'

'Is Micky OK?'

Nodding, she had reassured him. 'He's fine. Kat hid him at the docks. But she told everyone she got him away to London.'

'Wells will find him!' Silky replied anxiously.

'No he won't. He believes Kat.' Temporarily avoiding the questions that would naturally follow, Ma Shaw had touched her son's good hand. 'Wells set the fire, didn't he? He did this to you?'

Silky had nodded. 'But you tell no one. You hear me, Ma? Tell no one.'

'What about yer hand? The doctor said it were a hot water burn.'

'Let it be, Ma,' Silky had said quietly. 'I fell asleep, right? I fell asleep and dropped my fag. That's how the fire started. That's the story I want you to put about. It was an accident. You understand, Ma? An accident.'

'So the bugger's got away with it, has he?'

'Only for now,' Silky had replied, leaning back against his pillows. 'Only for now.'

He had found out about his niece a week later. When he had been considered strong enough, better able to cope. It had been Ma Shaw who had finally told him the truth, on one of her visits to the hospital. She had been evasive to begin with, making him anxious. Then finally she had told him what Kat had done.

'I know why she did it,' she had said, folding her arms, as though protecting herself bodily from any further criticism. 'Micky went for Wells and she did it to get the lad safe. But it's been weeks now. I try asking her about Micky, but she won't tell me anything; she just says she'll sort it out.' Ma Shaw had paused, wiping her nose roughly with a cotton handkerchief. 'Of course, Jim's drinking, but he doesn't get drunk these days. It's like he's finally learned how to handle the booze – some achievement. Anyway, whatever happens, the house is safe, rent paid – I suppose it will be, seeing as how Wells owns it.'

Stunned, Silky had looked at his mother. 'You're not criticising her!'

'How could I!' she had snapped back. 'There's plenty of others doing that. I know why she did what she did: she did it fer us. I just can't bear to think about it. Her with Wells, and him crowing like a bloody cockerel on the top of a midden.' Ma Shaw had been close to tears. 'I could kill him fer what he's done.'

No, Mother, Silky had thought. *I* will kill him for what he's done.

Clumsily lighting a cigarette, Silky gazed now at his ruined business, his mind returning to the present. He remembered Kat coming to watch him work, and the way she had laughed when he chased her with the tattoo needle. And then he thought of her with Micky, their heads close together as they talked, Micky using sign language, his sister responding. Tied together in their own secret world . . . Inhaling, Silky kept staring at what was left of his shop . . . He thought about Kat when she first came to work for him, and the way people talked about her, even Ma Shaw going on and on about how she would ruin her reputation. Moved, he closed his eyes for a moment, thinking of the night she had admitted her love for Andrew. She had been so young, so unspoiled. Brave, caring, putting her family first. As she always had done.

And then Silky thought of the last time he had seen her,

driving past in the passenger seat of Robin Wells's car, wearing expensive clothes, a hat with a veil half covering her face. Beautiful, remote. Like a replica of herself, a perfect copy, but one without life . . . Christ, Silky thought, he had let her down so badly. He hadn't been there, hadn't protected her when she needed help. No one had been there for her when she made her decision. When she realised that the only way to protect everyone was to become the mistress of Robin Wells.

The thought made Silky draw in his breath. There had been no quick affair, no one-night stand. Wells had wanted a drawn-out, public revenge. So instead of seducing Kat and then leaving her, he had made her his mistress. Moved her into a flat off Avenham Park, put her on show. His whore . . . Silky winced, remembering what he had overhead.

. . . Katherine Shaw's no good. Just gone with Robin Wells for an easy life. Fancy, a man like that. Mind you, he's got plenty of money. Not that she hasn't ruined herself. And she used to think she'd bag Andrew Pitt . . .

He had written to her several times, but she had only replied once. She said she had heard that he was better and sent her love. She said she was sorry . . . *she was sorry*, Silky thought incredulously. Shaking his head, he thought about the future. His business was ruined, but he would build it up again in time. He was better now, and he would call in some old favours, borrow some cash to get the tattoo parlour up and running again. Not as good, but workable. Rough, but enough to bring in a bit of money . . . He glanced at his ruined hand, the fingers claw-like, turned into the palm. He knew that it was useless, that he couldn't even hold a pencil with it, but for the last two weeks he had been practising with his other hand. At first he had struggled – but he had also been determined. *He would learn how to work with his left hand.* He would start again. In time he would put the shop sign back up and open the doors. He would re-educate his brain and his left hand, and claw his way back. Wells might think he had finished him, that Silky was beaten – letting his niece keep the family afloat. But he wasn't lying down for anyone. He wasn't giving up. He was Silky Shaw. He was going to fight back for himself. And for Kat.

And he was going to get Robin Wells.

Waking, Kat took a moment to realise where she was, and then felt the familiar lurch in her stomach. She was in the flat by Avenham Park, the flat Robin Wells had bought for her, the place he visited often. Tentatively she climbed out of bed, not wanting to wake her lover. For a moment she stood looking at him, and then she turned, fighting the memory of their first night together. Walking into the kitchen, she made herself some tea and then moved into the living room. It was obvious that Wells had thought a lot about his mistress's home and had decorated it to his own sensual taste. The curtains were heavy, expensive, the sofas covered with velvet, the Italian glass coffee table perched on its opulent base. He would have bought it in London, Kat realised, the same place he had bought her clothes. Sighing bitterly, she sipped her tea, fighting a cynical laugh. When she had lived in Amber Street, hadn't she longed for pretty clothes? For costly underwear and leather handbags? For silk stockings without darns? But she had never realised how much they would turn out to cost. Far more than they were worth.

Shaking her head, she still couldn't dislodge the memory of Wells taking her into the bedroom that first night. He had guessed that she was a virgin and had obviously been titillated by the thought, whereas she had felt only panic and revulsion. She had known then that there could be no going back, just as she knew it would be pointless to put up a fight. After all, she had made a bargain with him . . . So she had let him undress her very slowly, promising as he took off her shabby clothes that he would buy her the best outfits in England. And then he had pushed her back on to the bed . . . Her face burned with the memory of his long, slow look at her body, of the way his hand had traced her face, her legs, her stomach, her breasts and then slid between her legs, stimulating her.

Although initially repulsed, she had found, to her shame, that his touch excited her. Her confusion at that moment had been complete – how *could* she feel anything? This wasn't Andrew, the man she loved, *this was Robin Wells*. But if her mind rebelled against it, her body did not, and Wells was a clever lover who had learned to take his time. He also knew about how a woman's body worked. So he had stroked her slowly, touched her, and talked to her, kissing her tenderly until finally he entered her almost before she had time to realise what was happening. Even though it had been painful, Kat had felt something completely unexpected – her body caught up uncontrollably in the sexual sensations. And although he would never know it, the feeling of his penis moving inside her and his tongue licking and caressing her nipples unlocked something inside Kat. It was the moment when she realised that she might be afraid of Robin Wells – but she was also fascinated by him.

But it was a weakness he would never discover.

'What do you know about it!' Mary snapped at Trevor Blaggett. 'You can't come here and badmouth my best friend.'

'Kat Shaw is a slut, and everyone knows that now.'

'Get out!' Mary replied furiously. 'Go on, get out!'

'Yer can't be siding with her!' he said, incredulous. 'She's sleeping with Robin Wells, fer God's sake.'

'And she has her reasons.'

'Aye, money,' he said, pulling a face. 'That's the reason most women go with villains.'

Pushing him out of the door, Mary slammed it shut, then sat down at the bar, ignoring the few regulars who were sipping their drinks at the tables a little way off. Sitting alone was a lanky, morose-looking man who had come in only minutes before. Ivan Lomax had watched the exchange between Mary and Trevor Blaggett and found himself curious as to why the young woman would defend his niece so vociferously. He had some recollection about their being friends, but being a stranger to close relationships, he didn't realise friendship extended to such a vocal defence.

Unaware of his scrutiny, Mary ran her fingernail along the wood of the bar top, Horace walking in and watching her.

'I heard yer arguing with Trevor.'

'He was horrible about Kat.'

'Well, luv,' Horace said carefully, 'people see things in black and white around here.'

'I don't believe she just went off with Wells, not just like that,' Mary replied, animated. 'That's not like her. And anyway, where's her brother?'

Ivan was listening carefully, hugging his pint to himself. He had been interested in Mary for a few weeks and had begun to day-dream about ways of making her notice him. Having been nervous around women for years, he had a very welcome and instinctive feeling about Mary – that she might just be the kind of girl who wanted a man to look after her. And he *really* wanted to look after her. But how could he win her over? Was it possible?

'I can't believe that Micky upped and left, just moved to London,' Mary was continuing, her tone heated. 'Seems odd to me – he's dumb, for God's sake! How could he survive in London on his own?'

'He's not on his own,' Horace replied, trying to stop her worrying. 'He's with friends.'

'What friends?' Mary queried. 'Micky didn't have any friends, apart from the lads at the mill and Kat. How likely is it that he would know anyone in London?'

Stealing a glance at Mary, Ivan noted her round flushed cheeks and realised she was unexpectedly pretty. But not *too* pretty, not completely out of his league.

'How can you say it makes sense, Uncle?'

Horace coughed. 'Didn't someone say Micky had a cousin down there?'

'Oh, that would be his father!' Mary replied, her tone dismissive. 'But since when has *he* got anything right? It's just so odd that Micky would go away like that.'

'Well I don't know anything else about it,' Horace replied carefully. He didn't fully accept the story either, but didn't dare to delve any further into it. Wells had been round The Horse and Cart a few times lately, questioning the profits and intimating that he might get another landlord in. Hardly the time to start ruffling feathers, Horace thought cautiously. 'We should stay out of it.'

'Oh, everyone's staying out of it, Uncle. No one wants to say a word in Kat's favour.'

'Yer can't blame them, luv.'

'Yes I can! They want to believe the worst. They want to despise her and look down on her – when everyone knows that she's keeping the roof over her family's head. Because her father certainly couldn't manage it.'

'Mary, yer have to mind what yer say!'

'Join in with the rest? No, Uncle, I won't. I don't know what made Kat act the way she did, or why Micky went off like that. But I do know she had to have a good reason to go with Wells. I'm not knocking her! People just want to say what a scrubber she is, what a disgrace – and you're just like all the rest. She's finished to you, isn't she? Ruined her life. Hardly worth thinking about any more. Well, I miss her,' Mary said tearfully, walking to the door, 'and whatever anyone else says, I still think she's the most decent person I've ever met.'

Sipping at his pint, Ivan watched her go and then stared deep into his glass. He felt something that warmed him. Mary's outburst, so intense and deeply felt, had impressed him. It was so fearless, Ivan thought, wondering what it would be like to have someone stand up for *him* that way. He flushed at the fantasy. Who would ever stand up for Ivan Lomax? Who would want to defend him? What had he ever done to inspire affection or devotion? He had seen his family struggle and deliberately ignored their difficulties. Too fond of his own money and company to offer help – financial or emotional, he had ended up exactly where he deserved to be. But that wasn't true, Ivan thought. Secretly he had always fantasised about being a hero, doing good. That was what he *really* wanted . . .

Suddenly he saw the coldness of his life; felt the real depth of its chill when he saw it held up against the fire and heat of Mary Armitage's outburst. Her defence of Kat had been noble. Ill-considered, maybe. But grand. Ivan hung his head, struggling with the feelings he had had for weeks. The feelings which had now come to a head. The publican's niece had provoked an unexpected sea change in him. He didn't know how to go about it, but he knew what he wanted.

To *matter* to someone. To matter to her.

THIRTY-TWO

Avoiding the mirror, Kat picked up her bag, then walked back into the bedroom and changed it for a smaller, less expensive one with a gilt clasp. Late-afternoon sunshine lit the perfume bottles on the dressing table and reflected off the silver photograph frame. Wells had been generous, but then he could afford to be. He had won . . . She looked with detachment at the bed, at its piled cushions and soft plush covers. In truth, she couldn't deny that she liked the beauty of her surroundings and the rows of new clothes and shoes. The flat had room to move in; in Amber Street, space had been limited, the living conditions cramped, without privacy. There were other compensations too: the knowledge that her family was safe, and the growing hold she had managed to achieve over Wells.

Her mind moved back to the previous night. As he did most evenings, Wells had come to the flat after work, tossing down the newspaper and greeting her warmly.

'I have something for you,' he had said, passing her a large box. 'Go on, open it.'

Obediently she did so, taking out a mink coat. *A mink coat*, Kat thought, her face expressionless. How many months' rent could you buy with a mink coat? How many doctor's visits? How many art school lessons for Micky? How much building work to restore Silky's shop? But she was getting it for just one thing – sleeping with Robin Wells.

'It's lovely. Thank you.' She knew she had to keep walking the fine line between distance and dislike. She could remain cool, but not too cool – otherwise Wells would get angry, and might renege on their contract. So both of them shadow-boxed around each other. And whilst Kat knew that he would never suspect that her feelings about him were in any way ambiguous, Wells realised that his growing affection for Kat had to be controlled, or it might give her the upper hand.

'Sit with me,' he had said, patting the velvet sofa beside him. 'I bought some new records, jazz. D'you like jazz?' His hand moved slowly down the line of her neck.

'Yes, sometimes.'

'We could go out for dinner and then come back, listen to some music and . . .' He leaned forward and began to kiss her.

Having been initiated into the art of lovemaking by an upper-class whore, Robin Wells was a skilled lover. He knew what to do, and how, and no detail was overlooked. Even the practical ones. From the first, he hadn't wanted Kat to get pregnant and had arranged for her to see a private doctor in Liverpool to arrange contraception. The whole episode had been mortifying for her. The doctor knew she was Wells's lover, and making sure she didn't conceive was obviously a chore he was used to . . . But still, Kat had thought as she dressed herself later, any humiliation was better than being pregnant with her lover's child.

'You look so beautiful tonight,' Wells had murmured, kissing Kat's face and neck, his hand moving inside her blouse.

Fighting any unwelcome feelings of excitement, Kat had let her mind drift. She thought about the past, about The Horse and Cart, about Micky's drawings. In her imagination she left the mistress's life and walked Amber Street again, running to the corner to meet her father, as she had done when she was a child. And later, meeting up with Micky at the Albert Edward, covering Jim's watchman's round. She thought about Christine and wondered how quickly her sister was growing, and if she could risk a visit home . . .

Drawing back, Wells had looked deep into her eyes. 'Do you really like your coat?'

She smiled remotely. 'I said it was lovely.'

'Want to show me *how* lovely?' Wells asked, leading her into the bedroom.

Of course Robin Wells didn't understand that possessions and gifts meant nothing to Kat. That he could buy her every dress in Paris and it would be futile. Where the likes of Ginny Arthur had taken him for all they could get, Kat asked for nothing. And accepted nothing for herself. Only his silence. And his reassurance that every member of her family would be safe. In return for her sacrifice, Kat became an outcast. Her neighbours in Avenham Park all knew who she was – the Watchman's Daughter, Robin Wells's mistress – and avoided her. There were no friendly greetings, no casual exchange of gossip; when they saw Kat entering or leaving the building, they snubbed her. Widows and middle-aged matrons who had worked long and hard for their position in life saw her as an immoral, selfish young woman. A slut. They might have accepted Wells because he was rich and from a good family, even though they heard rumours of his dealings – but they couldn't accept Kat's fall from grace. She might think she was living the high life now, but when she lost her looks and Wells moved on to someone else, who would pay her rent then? No Avenham Park in the future, they intoned, more like some slum in the back streets. After all, what decent man would even be seen walking down the street with the Watchman's Daughter?

Bringing her thoughts back to the present, Kat walked out of the flat and left the building. The day she had dreaded had come. She was going to meet Andrew, the man she loved, the man she had hoped to marry. A long time ago, a lifetime ago, she had been excited, clinging to him the night he proposed. They only had to wait for two months and then they could announce their engagement. Just two months . . . But what bitter months they had been. Months that had brought savagery, horror, violence and her own disgrace. Eight weeks in which Katherine Shaw's life had run out of control. Become another woman's. Someone she hardly knew. And didn't like.

People might talk about how life had changed for women, Kat thought bitterly, but it was a fallacy. Even in the progressive 1930s there were only two types of women: respectable and amoral. Revered or despised. Clean or soiled. There was no middle ground. No partial seduction. No small affair. If a woman fell from grace, she stayed fallen. There was no way back . . . Sighing, Kat pulled on her gloves. Whatever it had cost her, she had succeeded. Having enjoyed seducing a virgin and making her his public property, Wells had rewarded her with the promise that he would provide for her family and leave Silky alone. But making sure that he wouldn't go after Micky had been more difficult. Eventually she had convinced him that her brother was in London.

'London?' he had replied, stroking her throat. 'Why London?'

'We have a cousin in Blackheath. Micky went there.'

Surprisingly, Wells had accepted her story, even though Micky was still hiding in the deserted warehouse on the docks. Kat flinched at the thought. God, if Wells ever found out where he was, and that she had lied to him . . . But she had had to get Micky safe, and the lie that he had gone to London had done the trick. All she had to do now was to find a way to really spirit her brother out of the north-west. And out of Wells's reach for ever . . .

In the distance, the town hall clock chimed, Kat pausing on the street beside the park. She couldn't go, she couldn't see Andrew . . . Her courage failed her momentarily, making her want to run. And then she calmed herself. This was something she had to do. Just as before, there was no choice. Besides, it was obvious that there was no chance left for her to be with Andrew. Even if he still wanted her – which he couldn't, when he knew what she had become – she could never see him again. The line of respectability had been crossed. She was on the wrong side now.

Having picked their meeting place well, Kat spotted Andrew waiting at a table in the cafe on Friargate. Her mouth dried, anguish coming like a pinch to the heart. She had forgotten how much she loved him. And now she knew she had lost him. Avidly she searched his face: the pale skin grown tanned, the long nose, the thick shock of hair. He looked so healthy, so full of vigour and plans. So out of place in that tea shop. So ridiculously happy . . . Slowly, Kat walked over to him.

He sensed her and turned, smiling, his hands going out for hers. And she just stood there, without moving or responding. His smile flickered, a question in his eyes, and then some kind of terrible realisation changed his face.

'Kat?'

Sitting down, she reached for the menu, read something about toasted tea cakes and then fiddled with a paper napkin.

He was watching her, noticing the expensive clothes, the perfume, the subtle coldness of her manner. A feeling of intense fear washed over him. Hadn't he thought he had overheard someone talking about her? They had been whispering – and then he had lost interest, realising they were talking about another person. *Another* Kat.

But were they?

'What is it?'

'You look well,' Kat said simply, tears at the back of her throat, bile in her mouth. 'Australia agreed with you.'

'Jesus,' he said helplessly. 'What is it?'

'I can't see you again.' His hand went out, Kat withdrawing hers, her chest so tight she was finding it hard to breathe. 'Things have changed, Andrew.'

'No . . .'

She nodded, smiling oddly, as though someone was

moving her mouth, her expression, her face working independently from her heart, which was screaming inside.

'Sorry, Andrew, I didn't mean to hurt you . . .'

'I don't believe it.'

'I've met someone else.'

'What?' His voice was a whisper. 'Who?'

'It doesn't matter.'

His hand shot out so fast he knocked the teapot off the table. It fell with a clatter, cold tea splashing over the floor. 'Leave it!' he snapped at the waitress as she came over. 'Leave it!' Anguished, he turned back to Kat. 'Who is it?'

'I have to go . . .'

'No,' he said firmly, 'you owe me a name at least. You owe me that. We were going to get married. I thought you loved me. I thought we were in love. We were, I know we were, when I left . . .' His voice dropped, helpless, low. 'So now I want to know who took you away from me. I *have* to know.'

'Robin Wells.'

He laughed hoarsely, Kat getting to her feet to avoid the look of distaste in his eyes. 'Robin Wells? Are you mad?' He was trying to remember what he thought he had overheard, but the words wouldn't come back. Just the realisation that they had been terrible. And true. 'Robin Wells – why didn't you choose the Devil, Kat? Why stop at Wells?'

Fighting tears, she turned to go, Andrew catching her hand desperately.

'Don't go! You can't want him. *You can't.* I don't understand. Explain it to me. Make me understand. I can't lose you to him, I can't. Why? Why, Kat?'

She could feel his hand around hers and wanted to turn and cling to him. To say: why did you go away when I needed you so much? When he threatened my brother and nearly murdered my uncle? Where were you when I cried out for you? When I needed someone to stop me from going to Wells? *Where were you?* And then she realised it wasn't Andrew's fault. That it had been fate, timing, bad luck. That some cruel spite of nature had parted them, and now it was too late. There was no hope, no chance of a reconciliation. To pretend otherwise would be to cheat Andrew, to make a fool out of him and prolong the pain. He deserved to know what she was; she owed him that much at least.

The break had come – and it had to be final.

'Why can't you come back to me?' he asked her, his eyes pleading. 'I still love you. I still want you.'

'No,' she said simply. 'You don't want Robin Wells's whore.'

PART FOUR

They'll smile in a glassless reflection
And pick at the word, not the bread;
So that, when they're sated, they'll hunger
For the laugh – and the life – of the dead.

Anon (translated from the French)

THIRTY-THREE

Micky rubbed his chin, feeling the stubble, then reached for the lamp. Lighting it, he shone the dim illumination around his cramped hiding place and looked for his razor. He would shave, but then again, maybe not. He needed water to shave, and he couldn't risk going out yet. From the beginning, he had taken care that the tiny window at the side of the warehouse was covered with sacking, just as he had made sure that he did not venture out unless it was in the early hours; between three and five, when the dockers weren't active and the pubs were closed. Even the prostitutes didn't work the Albert Edward then, and especially not when it was cold. And it was getting cold now.

Huddling further into his blanket, Micky glanced at his watch. Only another hour to go and he could stretch his legs . . . He thought momentarily that he might draw something, but for once even that comfort wasn't appealing. Instead, he listened to the water lapping outside and tried to imagine being home again. Back in Amber Street, before he had gone into hiding. Kat had explained to him all about the London story, Micky amazed that Wells had believed it. But there was something about the certainty with which his sister reassured him that made him suspicious. *How could she be so certain of Wells?* Stretching his legs further, Micky let them dangle over the edge of the platform. He could only see a little way into the darkness below, but his sister had been right about one thing – he did feel safe in the warehouse. Maybe Kat was right. Maybe Billy *did* watch over him.

But how long did he have to stay here? Micky wondered. He had been here for over a month, hiding out, Kat bringing him supplies whenever she could. But not regularly. Not every night; maybe every other night. When he questioned her, she told him that she had to be sure that no one was following her. That she didn't inadvertently tip anyone off about his hiding place. At first lonely, Micky longed for the sound of his sister's step, followed by the turning of the key in the lock and then her voice calling out a soft welcome. Laden with food and newspapers, she sometimes brought him a bit of tobacco, though she always told him to be careful when he smoked and not risk a fire. Apparently there was no detail his sister hadn't considered. How he got rid of his own waste, how much paraffin she could give him for the lamp, and how long it would last if he was frugal with it. She told him that she had to be very careful when she visited – and she also told him that she was going to get him away. Far away, where he would be safe for ever. Where he could take drawing lessons . . .

Micky liked the idea of that, though he wondered how likely it was. He had had a lot of time to think, hidden in that warehouse, and after a while he had become friends with the silence. It didn't bother him that he wasn't working at the mill; he just wondered how the family was managing without his wage, and if his father was holding down his watchman's job. A few times Micky had been tempted to go out at night to check on Jim, but had resisted. He had caused enough problems without risking further upheaval. But now and then he heard footsteps in the early hours, and blowing out his own light he would peer through the high window to watch his father pass. Sometimes he could see from Jim's gait that he was drunk; at other times his father would be mumbling to himself as he crossed the dark shadows between the warehouses, a night cat darting for shelter as his lamp's beam swung into view.

If only he knew I was up here, Micky would think, tempted to make a noise to force his father to look up. If only he knew . . . But he never let on, just stayed quiet, like Kat had asked him to. And then he began to draw again: caricatures, landscapes, the outlines of the warehouses and the boats in the dock. He looked out from his hiding place and saw the high sky and the sea in the distance, and dreamed of the day he could leave as a free man. Without spending the rest of his life looking over his shoulder for someone following him.

And at night, as Micky slept on the platform, he dreamed of canvases and paints, of Mr Pickles, his old teacher, and the crayons he had stolen. He dreamed of his mother and father, of Ma Shaw and the hated mill. Asleep, he dodged the hammering machinery as it clattered over his head, and then he relaxed, dreaming of his sister and the tattoo parlour. Silky was there, dapper as ever, smiling and winking at him.

But in the darkest night hours his dreams often shifted to something more sinister. And then he dreamed of Robin Wells, climbing noiselessly up the ladder to kill him where he slept.

Checking the tea tray for the third time in a minute, Ivy glanced out of the window. Upstairs, Duncan was asleep, sedated. The doctor had told her that he was deteriorating. That what had appeared to be a kidney infection was in fact something more sinister. Perhaps cancer . . . To her surprise, she had hardly responded to the news. Merely asked the doctor to confirm the diagnosis when the test results came through. But if it was cancer, how long did her husband have to live?

'A few months. Sorry, Mrs Pitt, but it progresses very quickly.'

Nodding, Ivy had decided there and then on her next course of action. If she was soon to be a widow, she had better secure her future. Financially she was well off, but emotionally she was poverty-stricken. When the doctor had left, she composed herself. She could see the solution in front of her, as clear as a cinema screen. There was a way she could secure her own emotional progress: by arranging her son's future happiness. She was fully aware that at present, Andrew was bereft, but maybe that would help her plan, not hinder it. A person was at their most vulnerable when they were in pain. And her son was certainly in pain.

Again Ivy checked the tea tray, rearranging the spoons as she heard the front doorbell ring and waited for her old rival to be shown in. She greeted Gwen Fairchild with a wan smile. Gwen was – Ivy noticed, even in her state of advanced plotting – still chronically slim.

'Gwen, how nice to see you again.' She gestured to a seat. 'And thank you for responding to my invitation.'

Smiling automatically, Gwen sat down. Her curiosity had propelled her to the Pitt house, Ivy's enigmatic note forcing the encounter.

'I wanted to see you, as an old friend,' Ivy went on. 'Despite our differences, Gwen, you and I were once close. And I have some very sad news to tell you – Duncan is dying.'

Gwen's eyebrows shot upwards, her face flushing. Why would Ivy tell her this – did she know about the old affair?

'I'm . . . so sorry.'

Ivy nodded. 'We've been estranged for a while, since Duncan's odd business decision regarding Robin Wells . . .' She let the matter hang in the air just long enough to rattle the old bones. 'But I'm going to miss him when he's gone, Gwen. You can understand that. And I miss my old friends.' She reached for her rival's bony hand. 'Of course when Duncan passes on, Andrew will take over the business and I will have nothing to worry about. You know how honourable my son is. How good a man he is.'

Gwen was getting the picture fast. Duncan was on his way out, Andrew coming into power. And Andrew and her daughter had once been very close . . .

'I have to tell you something in confidence now,' Ivy went on, her voice dropping. 'Andrew was in love with someone very unsuitable.'

'I heard.'

I bet you did, Ivy thought to herself.

'He was misguided, fooled by the woman. You know how these things go . . . But he and Joan, they were very fond of each other once, and I dare say your daughter still has some feelings for him?'

My, my, my, Gwen thought delightedly, this was turning out to be an interesting visit. Now if she and Ivy could get Joan and Andrew together, that would be a coup. And with poor, unfortunate Duncan dead, there was no scandal to hinder the union any more.

'Well, I can't speak for Joan . . .'

'Can't you?'

Gwen's expression was momentarily glacial. '. . . but it would be wonderful to see them together again. They made such a well-matched couple. So handsome, so suited.'

Ivy could hardly resist slapping Gwen, but managed it.

'So perhaps if you had a word with your daughter? And I had a word with my son?'

Gwen nodded. 'Poor Duncan, has he got to suffer long?'

'Only weeks at the most,' Ivy replied deftly, seeing Gwen's ruthlessness and hating her for it. 'The happy couple could be married by spring.'

Entering through the back, Kat paused then moved on into the kitchen. Anna was asleep, Christine – smiley and good-natured as ever – running over to her as Ma Shaw walked in from the front room. For an instant Kat looked at her grandmother, and then Ma Shaw nodded, the slightest imperceptible nod, but both women knew what she meant.

'Kat! Kat!' Christine said excitedly, Anna stirring and then waking. Seeing her elder daughter, she smiled and sat up in the day bed beside the fire.

'Oh, love, how wonderful to see you,' she said, holding out her hand. 'I was just dreaming about you.'

Touched, Kat moved over to her mother and sat down next to her. She had taken care not to wear make-up, or expensive clothes, but something in her demeanour tipped Anna off.

'Are you all right?'

'I'm fine, Mum,' she said, clinging to her little sister and feeling Anna stroke the back of her hand. In that moment she wanted to move, to say: *Take my sister away from me, don't touch me. I'm dirty, you don't want me any more.* But instead she leaned over, resting her head against her mother's chest, Ma Shaw watching them.

'So, how's the new job going?'

Kat tensed, but her grandmother continued calmly, talking to Kat, but also explaining what was going on to Anna. Or rather, her version of what was going on.

'Yer've been right busy with that new dress shop, haven't yer, luv? I were telling yer mam this morning how they were working yer so hard. Good thing yer can stay with Silky, him living so close by an' all . . .'

Pressing her face against her mother's shoulder, Kat nodded in agreement with the lie.

'It's fine.'

'I mean, we miss yer, God knows we do, but we understand. Business being business and jobs being hard to come by.'

Anna smiled wanly as she stroked her daughter's hair. 'I just worry about you staying with your uncle.'

'It's OK there,' Kat said. 'Silky's place is so close to the dress shop, it makes life easy for me. And I can help him out a bit. You know, whilst he's recovering.'

'He's always been very fond of you,' Anna said tenderly. 'But we miss you here.'

Still clinging to her little sister, Kat kept her face buried. She knew that soon she would have to pull back and talk normally. That she would have to cover her feelings and perpetuate the story Ma Shaw had made up. But surely *someone* would expose her? Surely they couldn't go on with the lie and not expect Anna to find out?

'I miss you too,' Kat said finally, sitting up and kissing her mother's cheek. 'Sorry I haven't been round for a while.'

'All my children are leaving me,' Anna teased. 'Micky in London, and you staying with Silky.'

'Both doing well,' Ma Shaw said emphatically.

It seemed to Kat that she was in some kind of trance, and that if she concentrated and stayed very still, she could remain there. That these ridiculous lies – made up by the most stolid woman she knew – might magically become reality. She *would* be staying with Silky at the tattoo parlour. And Micky *would* be thriving in the capital, not holed up in a deserted warehouse, jumping at shadows.

'Yer staying fer yer supper?'

Kat looked over to Ma Shaw. 'I'd like that.'

'Tea and flat cake?'

She nodded again, walking over to her grandmother and standing beside her. 'Can I help?'

'Oh, yer've helped more than anyone ever could,' the old woman said simply, turning to put the kettle on.

An hour later, Anna had fallen asleep and Christine was in bed. Kat moved over to the back door and sat down on the step, pulling her coat around her. A moment later, her grandmother joined her.

'I used to sit here shelling peas,' Kat said quietly.

'And eating them too.'

She nodded. 'I should be going.'

'In a bit,' Ma Shaw replied, lowering her own bulk on to the step. 'God, I haven't done this fer a while.'

'You used to say it would give us a chill on the kidneys.'
'I used to say a lot of things.'
Kat paused. 'Thanks.'
'Fer what?'
'The story about the dress shop. I suppose someone will tip Mum off and I'll have to tell her the truth eventually.'
'Yer mam only sees a few people now, and they're all going along with what I've said. No one wants to tell her about you and Wells.'
Kat flinched, moving to go. 'I should get back . . .'
'Yer don't have to be ashamed,' Ma Shaw said hurriedly. 'I've badmouthed people all my life, but I'm not judging yer. I've no right. If it weren't fer what yer've done, the whole family might have gone under.'
'Thanks . . .' Kat paused, staring ahead. 'I want to go and see Silky.'
'He wants to see yer too.'
'I know what really happened to him.'
'But we don't tell anyone, do we?' Ma Shaw asked, her eyebrows raised. 'It were an accident with a cigarette.'
'His hand was no accident.'
'*It were an accident*,' Ma Shaw repeated again. 'That's what my son said and it's what he wants people to believe. He'll deal with it in his own way, in his own time. When he's recovered. Yer know Silky. He'll get his own back.'
Rising to her feet, Kat glanced down at her grandmother. 'I don't want to, but I have to go.'
'Yer go, luv, and come back soon. Don't mind what people say. The day will come when yer can tell the truth. And then it won't matter what people think.' She shook her head. 'I'll watch out fer yer mother. Doctor calls by every other day now, thanks to you.'
'What about Dad?'
'Given up,' her grandmother replied dismissively. 'Drunk when he can be, though he holds his booze better than he ever did. Must be years of practice. But whatever your father does

or doesn't do, it's thanks to you that he's managed to hold down the watchman's job.'

'You're all safe here,' Kat said, her voice unreadable. 'The rent's covered.'

'But at what cost, luv?' Ma Shaw replied. 'At what bloody cost?'

'. . . So this is your chance,' Gwen finished, looking over to her daughter and nudging Joan's foot with the toe of her shoe. 'Are you listening to me?'

'Yes,' Joan replied, trying to gather her thoughts. 'You said that Andrew wasn't interested in Katherine Shaw any longer. That she was Robin Wells's mistress.'

'Slut.'

'*Mistress . . .*' Joan repeated, confused. Katherine Shaw, the woman who had been her rival for Andrew's affections, was now the lover of Robin Wells. Joan thought back to how Wells had courted *her*, made her think he was interested in her. Oh, she had rejected his sexual advances, but that hadn't seemed to cool his interest. Just made it rather more paternal. She had been sure she fascinated him – but she had been wrong. Just as with Andrew, she had misread the signs. God, was she *that* stupid? What the hell was happening? she thought, outraged. She was Joan Fairchild – no one treated her like that! As for Katherine Shaw, what was it about this woman that made her so appealing?

Joan's pride was dangerously hurt. After all, Kat's triumph hadn't been down to background; she had none. It wasn't down to money either; she was poor. But somehow she had managed to capture the affections of the two men Joan had wanted. It wasn't fair, Joan thought petulantly, it wasn't fair. And she wasn't going to get away with it.

'Robin Wells's mistress.'

'What is the matter with you!' Gwen snapped. 'You should be celebrating. That blasted woman is ruined, out of your way, and now you have a clear run at Andrew. Apparently he's broken-hearted. Came back from Australia thinking they were going to get engaged – engaged, I ask you! – and she'd already moved on to Wells, who's only one step up from a gangster. I mean, Duncan Pitt damn nearly ruined himself when he did business with the man. Anyway, be that as it may, Kat Shaw has made her choice. Obviously richer pickings with Wells than with young Pitt.' Gwen paused, studying her daughter's sulky face. 'You have another chance, Joan. You could really nail Andrew this time.'

'I thought you didn't want anything to do with him?' Joan countered. 'You said the Pitts were disreputable since his father was involved in that property deal.'

'Well, that's the past . . .'

'Since when, Mother?' Joan replied. 'It was only last week that you were going on about Duncan Pitt and how he would never be accepted into society again.'

'He's dying.'

'*What?*'

'Duncan Pitt is dying,' Gwen repeated patiently. 'He's only got a little while to go. And after his demise, Andrew will inherit – and that unpleasant affair with Robin Wells will be forgotten.'

'Dead and buried, hey?'

Gwen's pencilled eyebrows rose. 'That's a tart remark. Perhaps you would have more luck with men if you kept a sweeter tongue in your head, Joan. Remember, you can catch more flies with honey than you can with vinegar.'

Annoyed, Joan looked away. Was it *really* possible that she could get back with Andrew? She had never got over him. Or rather, she had never got over losing him. And after all, he should have come back and tried again. She was a catch, everyone knew that. He couldn't just turn his back on her . . . Still, she soothed herself, things had changed. Andrew was alone now; he would want her again. She would *make* him want her again . . . Her eyes narrowed. It would be sweet to get him back. It would also prove how irresistible she was. Especially now that she had been bested over Robin Wells . . . Oh yes, it might take Andrew a while to get over his broken love affair, but Joan would wait. In the end she would get the only thing that had ever been denied her – Andrew Pitt.

And this time she wouldn't let the chance slip through her fingers.

THIRTY-FOUR

Cold and soaked from a prolonged downpour, Ivan coughed several times and then shifted his feet. He was sure that if he waited long enough, Kat would come along. If he was right, she was due a visit to the Albert Edward that night. After all, hadn't he been watching her for the past two weeks? Seeing her nocturnal comings and goings from the dock? And hadn't she been absent for two days? So tonight, she was overdue.

Hearing a noise, Ivan ducked back, then watched his half-brother move out from the line of warehouses.

'How do, Jim?'

Jim blinked, remote in his misery. 'Ivan? Yer working nights again?'

He studied his lanky half-brother with curiosity. Damn it, he thought. Ivan had been working the day shift for months. But now obviously he was on nights again – and that was bad news for Jim.

'I finish at three,' Ivan said, slapping his arms to warm them. 'Aren't yer cold?'

'I don't mind the wet,' Jim replied, walking on, surprised when Ivan dropped into step with him.

He had always disliked his half-brother, and had grown to dislike him more over the past few months. Despite all the Shaw family problems, Ivan had never been known to help out. Never put his hand in his pocket, or offered so much as the money for a pint. Silky, generous to a fault, was still trying to recover his health and business. While the rest of the family had floundered, Ivan had prospered alone.

'Strange how Micky upped and left, weren't it?'

Jim shrugged. He didn't understand much any more. And if his son had wanted to get out of Amber Street, who could blame him? Maybe he would make good in London.

'Mind yer, with Robin Wells being after him, it were the sensible thing to do. To run.'

'He only ran *after* he hit him.' Jim said, feeling his old protectiveness coming back. 'Micky attacked that bugger, marked his face good and proper. And there's not many who can say that.'

'Not many who would live to talk about it,' Ivan said wryly. 'And I should bloody know. That bastard put his mark on me all right . . . Anyway, Jim, it's a good thing Wells is on yer side.'

Jim nodded, not wanting to think too deeply about *why* Wells was on his side. Those thoughts only made him want to reach for the bottle and avoid the looks of judgement on other people's faces.

'Of course, yer have to know how to keep him on your side.'

'Oh aye?' Jim replied listlessly, burning for a pint.

'Him being such a bastard and having people on the lookout for him everywhere. Wells knows everything that's going on, yer know? Not a thing that happens in this town gets past him.'

Jim stopped walking and looked at his half-brother with suspicion. Was Ivan working for Wells now? Had Wells scared him, threatened another amateur tattoo? Either way, Jim was on his guard.

'If there's a point to this, get on with it.'

'Hey, there's no reason to talk to me like that!'

'There's every reason!' Jim hurled back, swinging round, the watchman's lamp darting arcs of light over the dockside.

'Yer never wanted to help us before, so I don't suppose yer want to help us now.'

'Yer one to talk!' Ivan replied, his long arms folded across his concave chest. 'Yer can't even stay bloody sober!'

'You were always the first to judge people, weren't yer?' Jim replied, stung, 'but what the hell have yer done with yer life? Everyone thinks yer a bleeding creep.'

'And everyone thinks you're a bloody drunk!' Ivan snapped back, towering over his half-brother. 'Yer've no right to judge me. Everyone knows yer've been found wanting as a husband and father.'

'What do you know about being either!' Jim replied, incensed, and overreacting. 'No one cares about yer, Ivan. No one would spit on yer if yer were on fire.'

'I'm not fighting with yer! I didn't come here to judge!'

'Yer can't *stop* judging people,' Jim replied wearily.

'I know yer drinking on duty.'

Jim stopped dead. Here it was – Ivan was about to tell him that he had to report him. It was only right, after all: Jim had been hired to do a job, and he wasn't doing it. 'Yer been watching me?'

Ivan nodded.

'So what are yer going to do?' Jim asked, feeling light-headed even without a top-up of booze.

He didn't really care any more. It seemed that his whole family was falling apart, and now the only thing he had any real feeling for was beer. Or whisky or brandy, if he was flush. Anything alcoholic. He thought longingly of the taste, the heat, and then the soft swamp of relaxation, followed by the giddy, feckless slump into drunkenness . . . But even that was denied him now. Poor Jim Shaw couldn't get drop-dead drunk any more. Couldn't pass out, couldn't forget, even when he most wanted to. In the end the booze had cheated him. He couldn't dodge anything any longer. He could drink all he wanted, but he stayed sober. Sober enough to hear the whispering about his daughter behind his back, and sober enough to wonder where the hell Micky really was.

'OK, Ivan, yer've got me,' he said belligerently. 'So, I'm drinking on the job – but I can still do my rounds.'

'Drinking's not allowed on the Albert Edward, yer know that.'

'So what *are* yer going to do?'

Ivan knew in that moment that he could ruin his brother. But he had lost his appetite for righteousness and wanted to change.

'Nothing,' he said quietly. 'I just wanted to warn yer, that's all. Yer mind yer step, Jim, yer hear?'

Confused, Jim stared at him. 'Yer not reporting me?'

'No.'

'Yer up to something!' he said, mistrust obvious in his voice. 'I know yer. Yer never do anything fer nothing.'

Without replying, Ivan walked off into the darkness. Jim watched him go. He didn't believe his half-brother and wondered if it was a ploy to make Ivan's victory all the sweeter. Let him think he was off the hook, then strike . . . Frowning, Jim stared into the darkness, hearing Ivan's footsteps fade away. A wind was blowing up, making the boat masts swing, their rigging creaking like the bones of old whales. Within another hour, Jim knew, the anchor lines would be pulling against the stops, the water shifting as though heated from below. He knew all the river sounds, the dock language, the night music of the Albert Edward, but found no peace in it. Instead he craved the end of his watch. Fighting a desire to return early to the hut – and the beer he had hidden there.

Only pausing when he reached one of the far warehouses, Ivan waited. He could just make out Jim's faint outline in the distance and then saw him backtrack, making for the hut. Bloody fool, Ivan thought, couldn't *anything* stop his half-brother drinking? Still, he had tried to help . . . The thought pleased him. Maybe it wasn't much, but it was something.

Then he thought of Mary Armitage. Thought she might approve – and felt himself pale. What was he thinking? She would never know. And anyway, how could he impress her? Or even talk to her? She was too young for him, and too pretty . . . Embarrassed, he found himself flustered, relieved that there was no one to witness his discomfort. But he couldn't fight his growing feelings. He had been musing for a while about the publican's niece, even dreaming about her lately. And hadn't he felt real pleasure when he had seen her push her boyfriend out of The Horse and Cart?

Buoyed up by Mary's example, he wanted to make peace with himself. Repair his actions of the previous years and turn himself into a worthy man. So he waited, watching Jim disappear into the hut, and then leaned against the side of the warehouse. He heard the wind pick up and shivered, hunkering down into his coat, his long, thin hands deep in his pockets. An old cargo boat, *The Ensima*, was bobbing on the water, the lights in some of the cabins making watery glow worms on the tide. He had never seen the Albert Edward as anything other than a place of work, but that night the hollow moon made a monochrome film set of the docks. A solitary figure of a sailor became some detective in a melodrama, and the sound of the pub in the distance turned into the set for *The Blue Angel*. At once, anything was possible for Ivan Lomax. He didn't have to be morose, the family Job; he could change.

On that tide, under the dark rib cage of the northern sky, he waited for his moment. His passage on the road to Damascus. His redemption.

Passing some food over to her brother, Kat watched Micky rummage through the bag excitedly. He had stopped shaving and had grown a short beard, and his hair was long, falling over his forehead. The lad she had hidden in the warehouse had, within a matter of weeks, turned into a man. Unable to exercise much, he had put on weight, his frame filling out, his cheeks losing their hollow gauntness. He was, Kat thought with surprise, a striking man. But although his appearance had changed, Micky had not.

How are you? he signalled eagerly. *I missed you.*

'I know,' Kat replied. 'I'm sorry I couldn't get here for a couple of days. It's difficult.'

She paused, watching her words. All her brother knew was that she was hiding him and afraid of being caught out; he did not know that she had become Wells's mistress to protect him. And he must never find that out, otherwise he would go after Wells again. What Kat had to do was find a way of getting her brother off the docks and into hiding somewhere far away. But that was proving to be far more difficult than she had first thought. The docks were manned at all times, even at night, and if anyone caught them it would be a disaster. There was another, more practical problem. Money. In order for Micky to be safe, Kat knew it would be better to get him away by boat. Train would be too dangerous; she would have to transport him across town, and that was out of the question. She didn't know if Wells was watching her, but she wasn't about to risk Micky's safety finding out. No, they would wait until she had got enough money together to pay for her brother's ferry fare to Ireland. And some extra cash. He would need that, to support himself and get himself on his feet. Normally Silky would have stumped up, but he had nothing left after the attack, and Ma Shaw's savings had been taken by Jim. The Shaw family – always pushed for money – were broke. As for Kat, she might be the mistress of a wealthy man, but she had no personal money. Wells paid for everything, but he ruled his own wallet. He never gave Kat any money for her own use. After all, money would mean independence, and he didn't want that.

Preoccupied, Kat sat thinking. Only she, Silky and Ma Shaw knew Micky was in hiding at the Albert Edward – everyone else thought he was in London. Including Robin

Wells. And Kat wanted him to *keep* thinking that. Keep thinking Micky was well out of his reach. But whilst her brother was in Preston, he was too close for comfort. Wells had only to doubt her and follow her, and Kat knew it would all be over . . . So for the moment Micky had to stay holed up in the deserted warehouse, waiting. Every day made her more nervous, more terrified of slipping up. Or of Micky making a noise, alerting someone. After all, how quiet could a man stay, day in, day out?

Gently she touched her brother's shoulder, then hugged him. He smelled surprisingly clean, even scrubbing his teeth with a piece of rag to keep up appearances. Because – as Kat told him on every visit – tomorrow he might have to move. And he wanted to look decent, didn't he? Deep in thought, Kat watched him eat the pie she had brought him, then drink the milk. He was hungry, having already nearly finished the previous supplies. Her gaze wandered over the platform. Micky had partitioned it into two sections: one a makeshift bedroom, with blankets and sacking; the other a small area where he worked. Under the narrow-side window he had put an old crate, and he sat there, on the floor, drawing. Curious, Kat walked over to the window and sat down, looking at the scene her brother watched day after day. In the distance she could see the masts of the boats, and in the far distance the high points of the town and the church spires. Craning her head, she then looked down on to the dockside, realising that she could see the comings and goings at the far end.

'Don't look out of the window at night when the lamp's lit, will you?'

He gave her a patient look, then signalled: *No one will see me. I'm careful.*

She nodded, and Micky passed her a stack of papers. Surprised, Kat looked through them, page after page of drawings of boats, sea birds, landscapes, and then one of their father, walking with his lamp in the darkness. She felt profoundly moved.

'Have you seen Dad?'

He nodded, then signed: *He still doesn't know I'm here?*

'No, I didn't want him to know, in case he slips up. You know, if he gets drunk.'

Nodding again, Micky picked up his paper and a pen. Then he began to draw her, quickly and easily, Kat laughing and turning her head away.

'I hate being drawn!'

You never used to.

There were so many things I never used to mind, she thought, avoiding Micky's gaze. A moment later he passed her the sketch. He had drawn her as only a person can who knows another very well. Her face and her expression, and something he had seen that others would have missed – her sadness.

She studied it carefully.

'You get better all the time,' she said, impressed. 'I swear one day you'll go to art school. You'll get your chance. No one has talent like this and wastes it. You just have to be patient for a while longer. This won't be for ever, Micky, I'll get you away from here.'

He was listening, but shook his head. *Don't worry. Just keep away from Wells.*

She felt an overwhelming desire to cry, but restrained herself. This wasn't the time. But suddenly she was aching with loneliness. Her life was a fraud. She was lying to the people she loved the most and she felt like an alien in her new, unwelcome role. Allied to that, her grief over Andrew had left her limp as a piece of string. To have lost him was bad enough, but for him to see her as Wells's mistress was unbearable.

The light on the platform was fading, their shadows huge on the warehouse ceiling above. Thinking back, Kat remembered her childhood, looking out for Micky, and Billy snoring as he slept, the sound travelling through the narrow bedroom wall. She thought of the times she had waited at the school gates for her little brother, and the anger she had felt when Ma Shaw tore up Micky's drawings, forcing him into the mill. She remembered Christine's birth, and Andrew telling her he would be back in two months' time. *What can happen in two months?*

Turning up the light, Micky watched his sister, making her laugh unexpectedly when she looked over and he stuck out his tongue. Together they sat on the edge of the platform, their legs dangling over the rim, talking in their own secret language. Around them the evening lengthened, the gathering wind making darts at the tide, Kat forgetting for a little while that she had to return to the flat on Avenham Park . . . But when she *did* remember, she felt hatred for Robin Wells. A loathing that was terrifying. He had threatened the people she loved and stamped on her chance of happiness. He had towered like a hobgoblin over their lives for years. And now he had won.

'I have to go,' she said suddenly, picking up her bag. 'Be patient a bit longer.'

He nodded, but didn't press her to stay. For the first time, he wanted her gone. Wanted her home, out of danger.

Come again soon.

'I will, you know I will.' She leaned towards him, hugging him. 'I've left you food and milk. Some newspapers and paper to draw on.' She paused, fighting panic. 'Don't go out, Micky, please. Don't let anyone find you.'

I won't. I promise.

'It won't be for ever . . .'

What is it?

She paused, tense. 'What d'you mean?'

There's something the matter. Not just this, something else.

'There's nothing,' she reassured him. 'It's fine, everything's fine, Micky. I promise you, everything's just fine.'

* * *

Making patterns on the tablecloth with the blade of his knife, Andrew stared blankly at the sheet of white linen. In his mind's eye he could see – for the thousandth time – Kat's face, and hear her words: *You don't want Robin Wells's whore* . . . The violence of the vocabulary had unnerved him. It was so unlike her, and then he realised that it was Kat's way of shocking him, of giving herself time to escape. Slowly he traced a serpentine pattern on the cloth. He should have made sure they married before he left for Australia. He should have insisted. But would that have protected her? If she had wanted to go with Wells, she would have done, married or otherwise. But why *would* she want to go with a man she hated? And had hated for many years?

The story going around Preston was that Micky had attacked Wells and then fled to London. But Andrew didn't believe it. Trouble was, he didn't know *what* to believe. Maybe Kat had chosen to go with Wells for what he could give her – but couldn't Andrew have given her as much? Then again, Andrew wasn't her landlord any more, was he? So was that the real reason she had gone with Robin Wells? Did he have some hold over her? Shaking his head, Andrew stared at the sterile whiteness of the tablecloth. Perhaps he was just trying to make excuses, make himself feel better. Make the rejection less painful . . . But the more he tried to put Kat out of his mind, the more she haunted him. She had been so young, so full of hope and love for him. They had planned a future together, both of them teasing each other about being outcasts. But in the end they had had little in common after all. Certainly not enough to hold them together.

But to end up with Robin Wells, the man who had inadvertently disgraced his father . . . It was too much to tolerate, Andrew thought, digging the knife through the tablecloth and into the wood beneath. That bastard . . .

'Andrew?' He looked up, nodding vaguely as he saw Joan. 'Oh, hello there.'

She slid into the seat opposite his, crushed by his lack of

enthusiasm but determined not to show it. In fact, she was all easy charm, just as she used to be when they had known each other before. 'I'm so glad to see you again.'

'I'm afraid I'm not good company at the moment,' he said, putting down his knife and looking at her.

Her hair was newly arranged, her perfume reminding him of some long-dead memory. Her fresh, pert prettiness was a surprise to him, her light-heartedness welcome.

'You're always good company, Andrew, in a good or bad mood,' she replied, smiling and laying her hand on the table inches from his. 'I'm sorry to hear about what happened.'

He winced. 'Seems like I'm not very lucky with women.'

'It's not you . . .'

'How d'you know that?' he replied, surprised. 'How can you sit there and tell me it's not me. *You* of all people . . .'

'Oh, you and I just had a misunderstanding,' Joan said, keeping her tone light. 'I was very thoughtless . . .'

'No,' he said simply, 'you were honest.'

Her smile didn't falter. Whatever he said, she wasn't going to lose her temper – or her chance. She was here to be sympathetic, a cheerful shoulder to lean on.

'Actually I was very silly. But then everyone knows Joan Fairchild can be silly. Spoiled and silly. Sometimes so spoiled she doesn't know what she really wants until she loses it.' She smiled again. 'We used to have good times, didn't we? Life's got so sombre these days.'

Sighing, Andrew picked up the menu. 'You want something to eat? I mean, we're in a restaurant, we should eat.'

'What are you having?'

Glancing at the dishes, he shrugged. 'I dunno. I'm not that hungry. I suppose an omelette would do.'

'I'll have the same,' she replied easily.

Gesturing for the waiter, Andrew ordered two omelettes and then leaned back in his seat. He was still tanned from his time in Australia and his distant demeanour made him all the more attractive to Joan.

'How was Australia?'

'Big.'

'You got all the business sorted?'

He nodded. 'Yes, all sorted.'

'I'm sorry about your father being so ill,' Joan said kindly.

He felt suddenly consoled, wanting to talk. 'You know something, Joan? Life doesn't always turn out the way you think . . .'

You can say that again, she thought.

'People surprise you. But *you* haven't changed,' he said, smiling faintly. 'I'm glad about that.'

Now this was more like it, Joan thought, encouraged, as she leaned toward him.

'I'll always be here for you, Andrew,' she said sweetly, without pressure, but offering comfort. Just as a good friend would. 'You don't have to feel as though you're on your own now you're back home. I know times – and situations – have changed, but I won't let you go into a decline. We have mutual friends and interests. I really *won't* let you feel abandoned.'

'As I said, I'm not good company at the moment—'

She cut him off immediately. 'Andrew, do stop worrying about that!' she replied, good-natured to a fault. 'I don't mind. I mean, we're friends, and friends understand ups and downs. Besides, I'll soon have you laughing again,' she teased him. 'Before long, you'll be your old self. I mean, I'm here to help you in any way I can. Otherwise what's the point of being a friend?'

THIRTY-FIVE

'Where have you been?'

Kat jumped at the sound of Wells's voice, turning as he closed the door behind her. Her mouth dried with tension. Had he been watching her? Did he know that she had hidden Micky and had been visiting him?

Trying to keep her voice even, she smiled at him. 'I went to see Mum.'

'You're soaking wet.'

'I walked back.'

Curious, he circled her. She was dressed in a dark wool coat, her shoulders marked with rain, her stockings splashed. Lately Wells had felt a shift in their relationship, Kat at times almost warm with him. He took it as a good sign. Then he realised that – whatever the circumstances – people sometimes couldn't help but revert to their true nature. She couldn't see him day in, day out without sometimes being her old self. Or was there more to it than that? Still circling her, Wells admired her composure. God, she was good-looking, carrying the expensive clothes well, as though she was born to them. And then he looked at the pearl necklace she was wearing – the pale opalescence pulsating slightly against the vein in her neck.

'You look worried, Katherine.'

'I'm fine,' she said simply, walking past him. 'D'you want something to drink?'

'Why don't we talk?'

'About what?'

Wells wasn't sure what was different, only that something was. Kat seemed almost friendly.

'I know what you're doing.'

Her heart slowed, terror seizing her. 'What am I doing?'

'Playing me.'

'*Playing you?*' Kat said, laughing. 'That's rich, coming from you.'

He laughed in return. 'I don't scare you, do I? I mean, not really.'

'What do you want me to say to that?' she replied, hiding her anxiety and wondering where the conversation was leading.

'I can't have you, can I? I mean *really* have you.' Wells paused, caught somewhere between anger and confusion. 'You'll never be mine. I can't buy you, Katherine. I don't have enough money. No one has.'

'You're in a strange mood tonight. I'll get you a drink,' Kat said, pouring a whisky and passing it to Wells.

She wasn't sure why he was being so confiding, but she mistrusted him instinctively. Wells was always at his most dangerous when he seemed ill at ease. Sitting down on the sofa, she tried to keep her discomfort hidden. Had he seen her at the dock? Did he know about Micky? Was he building up to a confrontation? Trying to trap her somehow by discussing personal matters?

'Talk to me, Katherine.'

She paused for an instant before replying. 'Have you seen the paper today?'

'I mean fucking talk!' Wells snapped, sitting down beside her and staring into her face. 'Why can't we talk?'

'Why d'you think?' she replied, her tone remote. 'I'm going for a bath.'

'No you're not! You're going to *talk* to me. Sit here and talk to me, like couples do.'

'We aren't a couple. Not the way normal people are. We can't *be* like normal people. Or act like them. We can't make conversation and relax like normal people – and we never will be able to.'

Moved, he leaned forward and cupped her face in his hands. 'I want you to know something. I wasn't always like this. I was a better man once, I was someone different. I wanted a good life, not all this violence, this . . . I screwed up my life, Katherine. No one else did it for me. No one else was to blame. I had the best of everything, and I fucked it all up.' His eyes stared into hers, his expression unreadable as he suddenly turned away. 'I've had too much to drink, Katherine, I'm talking too much. Being indiscreet, showing my vulnerability. I've only ever done that once before. To another woman I loved – but she left me . . . I couldn't bear it if you left. If you betrayed me.'

Her heart was pumping, her mouth dry.

'I wasn't always this man . . .' His voice dropped, almost embarrassed, 'You would have liked me once. You could have loved me. You *could* have, Katherine. You could have loved me once.' Then he kissed her. Only this time it was a gentle kiss, hardly more than a touch to her lips.

Later that night as Kat lay in bed next to him, she stared upwards into the darkness and realised just how much danger she was in. If Wells discovered she was betraying him, God only knew what he would do to her, and her family. But there was something else, something that made Kat cold to the bone.

She would always remember what Robin Wells had done to her. But she was afraid that she might – if only for an instant – forget to hate him.

Troubled, Mary watched her uncle Horace walking the floor. Ten steps one way, ten the other. She had been watching him for over an hour as he kept up his measured pacing, his head bowed, his expression bordering on panic. Unable to think of anything helpful to say, she had remained silent, waving away Trevor Blaggett when he came to the back door. He had only come to apologise anyway, Mary thought dismissively, and he knew what he could do with his apologies. She would never forgive him for what he had said about Kat.

'Where would we go?' Horace said, finally pausing in the middle of the pub floor. 'Where would we go?'

Taking a deep breath, Mary thought about the altercation that had occurred that afternoon. She had been shopping, getting some provisions from Gregory Unwin, and had returned to find the pub closed. Surprised, she had walked in at the back, putting the food on the kitchen table – and then becoming aware of raised voices in the pub beyond. Walking to the door, she had kept herself hidden, and listened, recognising Robin Wells's voice at once.

'I don't want you here.'

'But I've made a good job of this place, Mr Wells, yer have to give me another chance.'

'I don't have to give you *anything*,' Wells had replied scornfully. 'You knew your days were numbered long enough since. If you'd had any sense, you would have been looking for a place before I kicked you out.'

'I've made a profit.'

'Barely!' Wells had countered. 'I could make more in a week than you do in a month.'

'Yer can't throw me out!' Horace had cried, anguished. 'I've my niece to take care of.'

'If I listened to everybody's sob story I wouldn't be in business and I wouldn't ever make a profit.'

'Profit isn't everything! This place is my home.'

'Really?' Wells had replied, unfazed. 'Looks like you'll soon be moving, then.'

It had taken her uncle nearly an hour to calm down, and then he had fallen into this rhythmic, silent pacing, the distracted, mindless movements of a good man who felt himself cornered. The pub was still closed, someone trying the door handle and then walking away, the daylight fading slowly behind the etched windows. Hearing the clock strike, Mary walked over to her uncle, touching his shoulder.

'We should open up. It's time . . .'

'What's the point!' Horace said brokenly. 'If Wells has his way, I'll not be landlord much longer. He'll have one of his cronies in here – and then what will the place be like? A knocking shop!' He stopped, mortified, as he turned to his niece. 'Sorry, luv, I weren't minding what I said.'

'It's OK,' Mary replied, walking to the front door of the pub and pulling back the lock. 'But we should open, Uncle. Maybe Mr Wells will change his mind.'

'Never! Yer know that as well as I do. He's been threatening me fer months. I knew this day would come, I knew it!'

Gently, Mary tried to calm him. 'But we still have to open. We *have* to run the business.'

He shook his head, overwhelmed. 'There won't be a business fer long. I've been a publican all my life, a good one too. Run a clean house, no prostitutes, drunks, louts. I didn't even have gambling in the back.'

'I know, I know,' she soothed him.

'We'll be turned out on the street, Mary. I promised yer parents I would look after yer, and I've let them down. And worse, I'll have failed you.'

Opening the door of the pub, Mary let in the first customer, then guided her uncle into the back room. 'You have a bit of a rest now. You've not failed anyone. You've done your best for me, always. Don't worry. Things look bad now, but they can change.'

Horace shook his head despairingly. 'Not with Wells! Nothing will change that evil sod.'

'Don't be too sure,' Mary said simply, kissing the top of his head. 'Don't be too sure.'

* * *

Stretching out his right arm, Silky extended his fingers, wincing at the pain. Then he reached out his left arm and repeated the action. Slowly he turned his wrist one way, then the other. It was stronger, much stronger, and his writing was improving. Before too long he would be able to sign his name, and then he would start work again. His gaze moved back to his right hand. The flesh had healed, but was still vividly red and scarred from the boiling water, the fingers curled in towards the palm like a claw. Inventive as ever, Silky had made himself a rubber tube, which he had wedged into his crippled hand, forcing the fingers away from the palm. The pain when he used it made him sweat, but every day he felt the twisted, buckled muscles stretch. One day, he told himself, he would use his hand again; he wouldn't stay crippled, with a deformed arm; he would make it work. He was tough enough.

He made himself another promise too: that he would ruin Robin Wells. Silky knew that his enemy believed he had won. Believed he had cowed Silky and managed to get the whole Shaw family under his thumb. But Wells was wrong, and he would realise that in time. But not yet. Not until Silky was recovered. He would let Wells believe he was untouchable. Let time pass, let his confidence grow. And then . . . Slowly Silky stretched his hand out, wincing. The thought that Kat had become Wells's mistress crucified him. He knew why she had done it, knew she had had no choice. But when he heard people gossip about his niece he felt only shame. Not for her, but for himself. He should have been able to stop Wells. He should have been able to keep Kat safe.

For Silky, the fact that he had been beaten up, burned and hospitalised did not qualify as an excuse. The damage was done. There was no road back for Kat, no way she could restore her reputation. She was a mistress, a kept woman, the lover of a known villain. Who cared *why* she had done it?

Silky cared. He cared so much that every day he had plotted and planned. Every day he had forced his beaten body back to health. Every day he had seen the remains of his tattoo parlour being rebuilt, people stopping to watch the progress. Down had come the boards from the windows, the black rafters of the upper storey replaced. Maybe it had been hurried, Jerry-built – because Silky only had a little money left. It hadn't mattered to him that the repair work had been cheap. All that had mattered was that his shop had got back on its feet, just as he was doing. When he opened again, he would effectively be sending out a message to Robin Wells: *I'm alive, you shit. I'm back.*

Over the last painful weeks, Silky had lived for revenge – for himself and his niece. It had driven him on, pushed him, until all he lived for was to see Wells destroyed. And then he would bring Kat home. One day he would triumph over the man who had intimidated his family and reduced his niece to being his whore. One day he would bring Wells grovelling to his knees.

One day he would have the power of life and death over his rival – and only Silky knew what the outcome would finally be.

Things were going swimmingly for Joan. In fact she had already told her circle that it was just a matter of time before she and Andrew got engaged. He had had a terrible time with that trollop Kat Shaw, but now he was getting back on his feet – after all, he was in the right crowd again. Joan had also realised – as had her mother and Ivy Pitt – that Old Man Pitt's imminent death would help her cause enormously. His unsavoury business reputation would die with him, and before long Andrew would be restored to full respectability. It was all working out perfectly, Joan told her mother. Andrew was falling back in love with her. She knew it. After all, who could resist her at her best?

'Well I hope you're right, Joan.'

'Of course I'm right! He's lucky to get me, after that awful business with the Watchman's Daughter. He will soon see that our marriage will be good for his business. Anyway, why are you being so cautious? You want this wedding as much as I do.'

'Of course, darling,' Gwen agreed. 'But I think you should slow down a bit.'

'Honestly, stop worrying.'

Her mother didn't look convinced. 'Joanie, dear, be careful. I don't want you to make a fool of yourself.'

'*Me!*' Joan replied, stunned by the notion. 'Andrew was always the right man for me. He just had to realise it.'

'Again.'

'Yes,' Joan said pertly. '*Again*.'

Arriving for lunch at an important hotel in town, Joan paused at the ladies' powder room to examine her appearance. Pretty, certainly; charming, oh yes. In her smart suit she looked neat and yet pert. Appealing was the word. Just like she used to be when Andrew was in love with her before. Smiling, she walked over to their table, bending down and giving Andrew a peck on the cheek in greeting.

'Hello there,' he said, watching her sit down. 'You look good.'

Joan smiled winningly. 'Dressed up especially for you.'

'That's nice,' he replied. 'I've ordered some fish for us. Is that all right?'

'Fine. So how's work going, Andrew?'

'Expanding. We're busy.'

'And your mother, is she well?'

'She's fine.'

Joan faltered momentarily. Andrew seemed remote, preoccupied. Time to play the sympathy card.

'I'm so sorry about your father's condition getting worse.'

'News travels fast – especially bad news,' Andrew replied distantly.

'I've always liked your father.'

He looked up, surprised. 'I didn't know that.'

'Oh yes,' Joan went on hurriedly. 'I like your mother too.'

He snorted. 'I've just heard about our mothers meeting! My father, the poor sod, isn't dead yet and those harpies have descended.'

Joan felt her composure shift. 'Our mothers had a meeting? I didn't know.'

'Really?' Andrew replied, holding her gaze. 'It seemed odd to me at first. After all, they don't like each other much. Then I realised what they would have been talking about.'

'What?'

'The fact that the memory of my father's dodgy business dealings will die with him and then I'll be respectable again.' He paused. 'In case you hadn't heard, Joan, Katherine Shaw went off with Robin Wells. The same man my father did such dirty business with. Did you ever meet Mr Wells?'

Unnerved, Joan wondered what to reply. Should she admit she knew him rather well – or would that distance Andrew even further? Or should she deny ever having met him? Cautiously she turned the question back on Andrew. 'Do you know him?'

He glanced up. 'Only by reputation. But I aim to change that.'

'What d'you mean?'

'It's not important.'

Oh, but it was to Joan.

'Are you going to meet up with Robin Wells?'

Curious, Andrew frowned. 'Why would that matter to you?'

She flushed. 'I'm your friend.'

'But . . .'

'Why would you want to meet Robin Wells?'

'Isn't that a strange question?' Andrew replied, mystified. 'Naturally I would want to confront the man who seduced Kat.'

She reacted without thinking. '*He* seduced her? I thought . . .'

'You thought I already had?' he replied coldly, leaning back in his seat. 'Of course, how could Katherine Shaw be respectable? Coming from a poor family on Amber Street.'

Flustered, Joan tried to get her thoughts in order. She had to stop herself overreacting, but when she heard Andrew mention the Watchman's Daughter, her confidence had plummeted.

'I didn't want to imply . . .'

'Just what *did* you mean, Joan?' Andrew asked, his voice even, borderline cool.

'Let's not talk about other people,' she blundered, her smile dazzling as she tried to turn the conversation round to less dangerous topics. 'I thought we could go round to see the Gardeners later. They bought a house on Avenham Park, lovely place. They seem to be a perfect couple . . .'

'There are no perfect couples.'

She laughed lightly. 'You're a cynic. Anyway, you always liked them . . .'

'Joan, you've been a good friend to me over the last few weeks.' Andrew paused. 'But that's *all* we could ever be now.'

'Andrew . . .'

'We can't restart some old romance,' he explained, smiling gently. 'You didn't want me, remember? And then I fell in love with someone else.'

Shaken, Joan stared at him. 'Andrew, we . . .'

'There is no *we*,' he said sadly, then shook his head. 'Oh, I understand. There was another reason for our mothers meeting up. Let me see if I can guess what it was. Now I'm no longer involved with a woman who was considered unsuitable, you and I could renew our romance?'

Flushing, Joan laughed. 'Andrew, how would *I* know what people are saying?'

'Because isn't it what you *want* them to say?' he asked her, knowing only too well that she had been telling friends about a supposed reconciliation. 'That we're close again?'

At that moment the waiter came over to their table with the fish and laid it down in front of them. A couple on the next table were laughing loudly at some private joke. Picking at the food with her fork, Joan's thoughts were jumbled, wondering how to play the awkward conversation.

Andrew was the first to speak. 'Why are you telling everyone a lie, Joan?'

'*Is* it a lie?' she replied, smiling although her heart was beginning to speed up.

'I'm fond of you, but . . . I'm still in love with another woman.' If he had plunged his knife into her throat she couldn't have been more shocked. 'Time's moved on, a lot of time has gone by. We can't resurrect something that's dead.'

'But I love you!'

He was mortified, rigid with embarrassment. 'You don't love me, Joan, you just think you do. You're used to getting your own way; you just want me now because I love someone else.'

'I *do* love you!' she replied, close to tears, the couple on the next table now listening in. 'I really do! I was so stupid to send you off like that, but there's not been a day since that I haven't regretted it.' She looked at him, trying to elicit some feeling. 'I know you care for me.'

'I did, once,' he agreed, lowering his voice to a whisper. 'I don't want to be cruel, Joan, but it was a long time ago.'

'*You could love me again!*' she said desperately. 'I could make you love me!'

'It's not possible,' he said, tempted to take her hand, but resisting. 'That was in the past. You have to find someone else.'

'Because *you* have!' she retorted brokenly. 'But Katherine Shaw's gone, Andrew – you've been left. There's just the two of us now, and we should comfort each other.'

'I don't want comfort! I want Kat!'

Joan was getting more reckless by the second. Her charm

had deserted her; now all she could think of was how people would laugh at her. How cheated she had been.

'How *can* you still want that woman, when you could have me?' she hissed. 'Think about it, Andrew. We're from the same class, we both have money, status. We could make a good couple, everyone knows that.'

'I don't care about money or position,' he replied, trying to make her understand his point of view. 'It's not important to me, Joan, can't you see that? I love Kat because she is who she is. Whatever she has done, I can't stop loving her . . .'

'But she's gone, and I'm here,' Joan whimpered, reaching for his hand and grasping it. 'I want to make you happy, Andrew, that's all I dream of.'

He pulled his hand away, trying to be gentle. 'Joan, don't do this . . .'

'Don't do what? *Beg?*'

'I didn't say that.'

'As good as!'

'Joan, you're upset, and if you're not careful you're going to say something you'll regret. I'm not what you want. Don't make yourself look cheap—'

'Don't make myself look cheap?' Her eyes blazed. 'But you like cheap women, don't you, Andrew? You like whores.'

Immediately he rose to his feet and threw some money on the table, the couple on the next table watching with obvious astonishment.

'Andrew, I didn't mean it!' Joan begged him, close to tears. 'Please sit down. Stay.'

He shook his head, his tone cool. 'I can't, Joan. To be honest, I couldn't spend one more moment of my life anywhere near you.'

Hearing soft footsteps approach, Ivan looked ahead, towards the narrow alleyway between the warehouses. Kat was leaving, hurrying away. He could tell from her constant turning round that she was suspicious, terrified of being seen. As well she might be, he thought. If Wells found out that she had lied to him, she would be in real trouble. Possibly even danger . . . From the shadow of darkness, Ivan studied his niece She looked tired, her expression hunted, the shopping bag – now empty of its provisions – folded and tucked under her arm.

Waiting until she was almost level with him, Ivan coughed, making his niece jump. Recognising him, Kat pulled her coat around her tightly, hiding the empty bag.

'Ivan.'

'How are yer?' he asked. 'Can I walk with yer?'

Surprised, she stared at him, her thoughts running on anxiously. What was Ivan doing out here? He had been on the day shift for months; why the sudden change now? And more importantly – her chest tightened at the thought – had he seen her? Followed her? Watched her? Did he – of all people – know where Micky was hidden?

'I was coming to see Dad.'

'Yer going the wrong way.'

She struggled to find an explanation. 'I wanted to take a walk first. You know how much I always liked the docks.'

'But I saw yer over by the warehouses. Yer dad works the quayside first.'

'I was . . .' She fought panic, then calmed herself as an explanation came to mind. 'I was just thinking about Billy. I went to look at the place he died.'

'It's deserted now.'

'Yes.'

'No one goes there,' Ivan went on. 'People are superstitious about the place. Say it's haunted by Billy's ghost . . . Yer not afraid of ghosts then?'

'I was never afraid of my brother – dead or alive.'

'Well, sometimes the people above ground are more frightening than the ones below.'

Swallowing, she started to walk, Ivan falling into step with her.

'Can I see yer home?'
'Why?'
'Yer might like the company.'
Nodding reluctantly, she tried to hide her unease. 'I didn't expect to see you.'
'I'm working nights now.'
'I see that . . . What do you want, Ivan?'
Surprised, he stared at her. His niece had changed; she was no longer the open, friendly girl he had known before. Now she was guarded, on edge. He felt suddenly uncomfortable around her, embarrassed by her situation and acutely aware that she suspected him.
'I'm sorry . . .'
She said nothing, just stared at him.
'. . . fer the ways things turned out. Fer you and Micky.'
Wincing, she replied, 'He's OK, he's in London now.'
'But he's not, is he?'
Kat flinched. 'I don't know what you mean!'
'Listen,' Ivan said hurriedly, 'I'm a miserable sod, but I've reason enough to want to get my own back on Robin Wells.'
'You can't use me for that!'
'I want to help yer!' he replied, mortified. 'Christ, what d'yer take me fer? I'm a right Job, but not a bastard.' She looked unconvinced as he hurried on. 'All right, I admit I've never helped anyone – in the family or anywhere else. I know that, and I'm right sorry fer it. But I want to do something to help yer now. I know yer hiding Micky on the docks.'
'You're crazy!' Kat replied, hurrying on, Ivan running after her.
'I know he's in that warehouse, yer can't deny it. I've seen yer, Kat, going in and out of there.'
She stopped walking, her expression panicked.
'Don't worry, no one else has. But someone *might.*' His voice was low. 'Yer can trust me, Kat. I swear yer can.'
Pausing, she looked away. If Ivan was going to betray her, he would already have done so, she thought. But then again,

maybe her uncle was trying to catch her out. After all, she hadn't admitted anything, had she? Was it worth trusting Ivan if it meant risking Micky's safety in the process?

'I told you, I just came to see where Billy died . . .'

'That's not true.'

'I'm going for my bus,' Kat replied shortly. 'You don't need to come any further with me. If you're on your shift, you'll have work to do.'

All Ivan's good intentions had blown up in his face. The years of being miserable and judgemental had resulted in this – his own flesh and blood mistrusting him. For a moment he was tempted to walk away, to brood as he normally did. But then he thought of Mary Armitage and realised that he didn't want to be the curmudgeon people knew. He wanted, more than anything in life, to change.

'I know Micky's in that warehouse. I know yer visit him,' he persisted. 'But he can't stay there for ever, Kat. Someone will see him, or they'll see yer visiting. Something will give him away – or someone might give him away to the wrong person.'

The name Robin Wells came to both their minds in the same instant. Glancing back towards the deserted warehouse, Kat thought for a long moment, then looked back to her uncle. There was something in the way Ivan was talking that was different. He seemed genuine. And besides, she had no choice but to trust him. Not when he knew about Micky.

'All right . . . I know he can't stay there much longer.'

Relieved, Ivan continued. 'I've an idea.'

'What idea?'

'Yer might not like it, but it's a way out . . . Yer know we have deaths here?'

She nodded. The Albert Edward had had its fair share of accidents, drownings, suicides, even murders.

'Well, there were a body washed up an hour ago. I spotted it in the east side of the dock. I pulled it in, tied it up against the iron steps there . . .' He paused, unable to read Kat's expression. 'It's the body of a young man. The face is mashed up, been caught in the tide, smashed against something . . .'

Kat's eyes were wide open as she listened to him.

'Don't yer see what I'm getting at? *We could pass it off as Micky*. Say he was coming back home from London. That he didn't settle in there and came back by boat.'

'No,' she said practically. 'Why would he pick such a long-winded route? He'd come back by train.'

'OK, say he came back by train and then came to visit his dad at the docks. Say he missed his footing, fell into the water. Had an accident. He could have got caught in the anchor chain, or hit his head on the quayside. There's accidents all the time, Kat, people would accept it. Especially if I put Micky's clothes on the body and identified it myself. Which I could – if I found it on my watch.' Ivan paused, mortified that she still didn't trust him completely. 'It would stop people looking for him. If they thought he was dead, he could stay here for a while longer – until you could get him somewhere really safe.'

'It might work . . .'

'Yer'd not be looking over yer shoulder all the time,' Ivan went on. 'God, Kat, I want to help.'

'But why? Why now?'

'I saw what yer did fer yer family,' he admitted sheepishly. 'Yer made me ashamed. Made me feel selfish. An old bugger who never thought about anyone but himself.'

Touched, she looked away. 'I'm sorry I doubted you, Ivan.'

'Yer had every reason,' he replied, returning to his previous theme quickly. 'Look, Kat, let me help yer. I want to do something good. Something that'll make me feel proud of myself fer once. I've thought it all out, it would work. Think about it – if everyone believes Micky's dead, no one will look fer him any more. And that means Wells. Even *he* doesn't go after dead men.' Ivan touched his niece's shoulder briefly. 'I know it would be hard to let everyone think yer brother had died – but with no one looking fer Micky, we could arrange to get him away for good. Yer'd not be sneaking around like this – and not running the risk that Wells will find out yer lied to him.' Ivan thought of his own run-in with Wells and shivered. 'Yer can't take the risk any more, Kat, yer can't.'

Anxiously, she nodded. 'But this body – who is it?'

'I dunno.'

'But what if someone reports the dead man missing? He could be someone's son or husband . . .'

'*Micky* is someone's son,' Ivan replied, his tone even. 'And someone's brother, and someone's nephew . . . Let me sort it out, Kat. Get some of Micky's clothes fer me and I'll put them on the body. Then I'll blow the whistle, report the corpse. Yer dad will see it—'

She flinched. 'Oh God, it'll break his heart! He lost Billy here—'

Ivan interrupted her abruptly. 'And if Wells gets hold of Micky, he'll lose his other son. And maybe he'll lose you too.'

Alarmed, Kat stared at her uncle. 'I never thought about what he might do to me.'

'Well I *have*. I've thought about nothing else fer a bit . . . Yer still don't realise what yer dealing with, do yer, luv? Yer might be pleasing Wells now, but what do yer think will happen if he finds out yer betrayed him?' Ivan drew back his sleeve, the crude tattoo visible. 'If yer've any second thoughts, think about this. Think about Silky, what Wells did to him, the poor sod. Think about what he could do to Micky – and then think about what he could do to you.'

I remember my uncle's words that night, and the shattering effect they had on me. Perhaps because the warning came from Ivan – such an unexpected source – it had a far greater impact than if it had come from anyone else.

So concerned had I been for my brother, I hadn't fully considered the danger I was in. Stupidly, I had believed that being Wells's mistress protected me. Gave me an immunity. And I had also been lulled into a feeling of power because of the growing devotion on the part of Robin Wells. A devotion I despised, still longing as I did for Andrew. But although I loathed Wells, I could see that he was more fond of me than he would have liked. My youth and inexperience had been a novelty at first, but it was my remoteness that spiked some perverse streak in his nature. Whilst I didn't want him, or anything from him, I was in control. Asking nothing, I obtained his devotion.

His initial callousness had mutated into concern, his indifference into affection. I know it irked him to care about me, but he couldn't help himself . . . And it was only then that I realised why he hated Silky so much. Robin Wells could control everything and everyone – apart from his own heart. The woman who, long before, had rejected him in favour of my uncle, he had loved. *And so the injury had not been just to his pride, but to the very core of him. The inner part of Wells, which hadn't been corrupt. Which had still empathised with others. And which – when torn open – bled all the humanity out of him.*

And then – years later – when ruthlessness was his primary trait, he fell in love with me. A woman who needed his protection. A woman who was powerless, dependent on him . . . 'Never dance with the Devil,' they say. Well that's true, but sometimes we have to. We move in tune to his music and in time to his steps. We learn how to respond to him and we learn how to survive with him. And if we're lucky, we learn to outwit him.

Because if we don't, he destroys us.

THIRTY-SIX

Calling in at Amber Street an hour later, Kat had a few quick words with her mother and refused Ma Shaw's invitation to stay for supper. Shrugging, her grandmother murmured something about people keeping odd hours and then turned to Anna, who was doing a little light ironing.

'Yer see,' Ma Shaw said, 'I told yer how busy they kept Kat at that new shop.'

Folding a pillowcase, Anna smiled at her daughter. 'I was thinking, perhaps you would like to take Christine to see the shop?'

Out of the corner of her eye, Ma Shaw could see Kat wince and covered for her. 'Well that's a fine idea. But I suppose it'll be a while before they'll welcome visitors. I mean, seeing as how customers come first.'

Looking for a chance to go upstairs, Kat was uneasy, trying not to seem on edge.

'I'll take Christine when I can.'

'Little girls like dress shops,' Anna went on innocently. 'I know I did. Even though we've never had much money for clothes. I mean, I'm not criticising your father, Kat, just saying that other things come first.'

'I know you weren't criticising Dad—'

'Not that there isn't plenty to criticise,' Ma Shaw interrupted, taking the pressed items from her daughter-in-law and looking curiously at Kat. 'If yer not staying, what yer hanging around fer, luv?'

Kat seized her chance.

'Oh, I wanted to get something of mine from upstairs,' she said, hurrying out and taking the stairs two at a time.

Once on the first floor she listened, then crossed the cramped landing and crept into the partitioned room Ma Shaw and Micky had shared. Old memories of Billy came back to her, along with the times she had woken Micky to go with her to the docks. In the dim light from the landing, she moved over to the narrow portion where Micky had slept, opening the cupboard and taking out an old shirt.

'Yer sure yer'll not stay fer supper?' Ma Shaw called up the stairs. Kat took a breath and crammed the shirt into her bag.

'No, I'm fine. I have to get back.'

'Well hurry, or yer'll miss the tram. They don't run so regular when it's late,' her grandmother went on.

Kat waited until she heard Ma Shaw walk back into the kitchen and close the door. Then she hurriedly crammed a pair of Micky's trousers into her bag along with the shirt, and tugged the zip closed.

'Got what you wanted?' Anna asked her daughter as she walked back downstairs.

Nodding, Kat avoided her mother's gaze. Lying was becoming too regular, too commonplace – and she hated the fact. If Ivan's idea went according to plan, yet another lie would be put into place that very night. A lie so devastating that it would shatter her father. Because Kat knew they couldn't trust Jim not to get drunk and slip up. Her mother was another matter. Anna would *have* to be told the truth – and sworn to secrecy. It would be hard for her, but less difficult than believing she had lost two sons.

'I have to go now.'

'See yer soon,' Ma Shaw called out, watching as Kat opened the front door.

'Haven't you forgotten something?'

She turned at the sound of her mother's voice, tensing.

Then she walked back into the kitchen, bent down and kissed Anna on the cheek. 'I love you,' she said simply.

It took Kat an hour to return to the docks, the tram ride slow, the walk hurried as rain began to fall. She was shivering with cold when she reached the outside of the warehouse. Her hair plastered down with rain, she looked very young, and very frightened. Ivan ground out his cigarette as she approached.

'Yer all right?'

'Fine,' she said woodenly. 'Where's Dad?'

'Don't get angry with me . . .'

'Why should I?'

'I gave him some beer.'

'*You did what?*'

'We need him to be asleep,' Ivan said firmly. 'He's dozed off, won't come round fer a bit. Don't look at me like that! I had to make sure he didn't catch us, or it would have been over before it began.'

Reluctantly Kat nodded, wondering exactly what she had got herself involved in. Suddenly Ivan's plan seemed dangerous, frightening – then she thought of Wells and realised they had no option but to carry it out.

'Did yer get Micky's clothes?'

She nodded again. 'Do you want them?'

Looking round, Ivan huddled down into his coat, his voice apologetic. 'I'll need a hand, Kat.'

'You want me to help you? she asked, thunderstruck.

'No, never mind, I'll manage on me own,' Ivan replied, wondering how he would be able to pull a dead body out of the water and on to the quayside.

'No, it's OK,' Kat reassured him, her throat dry. 'I can help you.'

'Good . . . Are yer ready?'

'I'm ready.'

With that, he began to walk, keeping to the shadows, Kat following just behind him. The rain – which had been light –

had changed into a heavy downfall, droplets jumping off the surface of the water, the dockside suddenly slippery underfoot after weeks without rain. The half-moon gave them some light, but not enough to expose them, Kat glancing back repeatedly to check that she hadn't been followed. To be caught now would be too much, she thought. Not now . . .

Reaching the end of the deserted third quayside, Ivan paused, then beckoned for his niece to approach. Anxious, Kat did so, watching as her uncle bent down and grabbed hold of a rope. It was tied to the anchor post, the other end disappearing over the side of the dock. Grunting, Ivan began to pull, Kat watching, holding her breath. Slowly he drew up the rope, inch by inch, then finally the top of a head emerged – only to disappear again when Ivan lost his hold on the rope.

'God!'

'Sssh!' Ivan warned her. 'Can yer help me?'

Nervously she approached, Ivan jerking his head to indicate that she should grab the rope on the quayside. Grunting, he pulled again, this time Kat tugging with him. The rope felt slimy in her hands, her palms wet with rain, her fingers clenched around it, her skin burning against the rough hemp. With one last effort they hauled the body up over the quayside, landing it like a huge bloodied fish.

Horrified, Kat stepped back. 'God . . . Oh God . . .'

'Don't look at him,' Ivan told her, placing himself between his niece and the corpse to block her view. 'Now, give me Micky's clothes.'

Her hands shaking, she did so, a sudden noise in the distance making her jump. Ivan tensed too, both of them listening. But luck was with them, the moon slipping behind the night clouds and hiding them in darkness as Ivan hurriedly pulled the clothes off the corpse and replaced them with Micky's. It was more difficult than he'd imagined, and he was breathing heavily with the effort as he moved around the dead weight.

'Lucky he's about the same size as yer brother.'

Alert, Kat listened and watched the quayside, standing on guard for her uncle. She hadn't really believed that Ivan would have it in him to carry out such a plan. But apparently he was more like Silky than she had thought. Both hard men when they needed to be.

Turning round, about to say something to her uncle, she paused, stunned. The moon had come out again and now shone on the corpse's face. It was battered, badly beaten, unrecognisable, but his hands were smooth and small, the hands of a very young man.

'He was just a child,' she said, horror-struck, looking at her brother's clothes, Micky's clothes, on the dead body. 'He must belong to someone. He must *be* someone . . .'

'He's Micky Shaw,' Ivan replied emphatically. 'Your brother and my nephew.'

'But . . .'

'*He's Micky Shaw*,' Ivan repeated. 'Keep telling yerself that, Kat, until yer believe it, and until yer can convince everyone else it's true. Because yer have to be convincing or this won't work. Yer hear me?'

Slowly she dragged her gaze away from the body, her mind clearing. 'Yes, I hear you.'

'Only we know the truth – and that's the way it has to stay. I'll tell the boss and then identify the body as Micky's. When I wake Jim, I'll tell him what happened. Say Micky were too beat up fer him to see and that I've sorted it out.'

'We can't do it,' Kat said suddenly. 'It's so cruel. It will break my father's heart.'

'We *have* to do it to keep Micky safe. No going back on it now. Come on, Kat, yer tough enough; strong enough fer ten men. This lad will be buried as Micky Shaw . . . Micky's dead now.'

'Yes,' she replied, her tone calm, controlled. 'My brother is dead.'

Sighing, Ivan glanced across the dockside towards the warehouses. 'I'll go and see him. Tell him what we've done.'

'No!' Kat said hurriedly. 'I'll tell him.'

'Yer sure?'

'I'm sure. Micky will take it from me, know it's the right thing to do.' She turned to go, then turned back to her uncle, touching his hand briefly. 'Thank you.'

He was visibly moved. 'Like I said – I wanted to do something good.'

'And you have. You've probably saved Micky's life.'

'Yeah,' Ivan said ruefully. 'Funny bloody world, though – when a man lives longer dead than he would alive.'

THIRTY-SEVEN

It had been a chance remark from Ginny Arthur that had solidified Joan's hatred. Having been spending less and less time with her friend, Joan had bumped into Ginny by accident at a party. Flushed with booze and giddily flirtatious, Ginny had been hanging on the arm of some fleshy middle-aged suitor, her lipstick slightly smudged, her shingled hair dishevelled, a cigarette in her left hand.

'Oh my word,' she said tipsily, 'it's Joanie. How are you, darling?'

'I'm fine.'

Laughing, Ginny leaned towards her companion. 'Joan is the last surviving virgin in the north-west – isn't that so?'

Flushing, Joan retorted, 'Well, that's something no one could ever say about you, is it?'

'No, thank God!' Ginny replied, glancing at her companion again, her tone dropping to a whisper. 'Poor Joanie had two men stolen from her, you know. And both by the same woman.'

The man laughed, amused.

'That's a lie!' Joan replied, embarrassed, but Ginny carried on, enjoying her ex-friend's discomfort.

'You know Andrew Pitt?'

'The property Pitts? Old Man Pitt's son?'

She nodded. 'Well, my friend loved him – but he chose a woman from the back streets. The Watchman's Daughter . . .'

'Shut up!' Joan said, horrified. 'I told you that in confidence.'

'And then that lady – I use the term loosely,' Ginny went on, her companion laughing and listening avidly, 'dumped Andrew Pitt and went off with Robin Wells.'

'You don't say!' the man replied, gazing at Joan with open curiosity. 'I heard about Wells's mistress. Good-looking girl, they say.'

'How could you!' Joan snapped at Ginny.

The room was suddenly silent, everyone listening, wondering if there would be a catfight, or some other welcome diversion. Joan Fairchild, pretty, spoiled and pampered, had really lost face this time.

Her fury at the world was absolute. How could people be so mean to her? How could they? Laughing at her – it was unbearable. 'How could you break my confidence?'

'Oh, *what* confidence?' Ginny replied coldly. 'Everyone knows what happened. And you've only yourself to blame, mooning around after Andrew Pitt and then letting Wells slip through your fingers. I heard that the Watchman's Daughter has him eating out of her hand now.'

'I never wanted Robin Wells!'

'You mean he never wanted you.'

Around them people tittered, Joan floundering, her humiliation crushing.

'How dare you . . .'

'Well I *do* dare – and that's the difference between us,' Ginny hurled back. 'You're just a tease, darling. A spoiled, superficial brat. And where's it got you? Andrew Pitt doesn't want you, even now. And Katherine Shaw's got Wells.'

Trembling, Joan snatched up her bag and headed for the door. The music hadn't started up again, and in the quietness she could hear the animated whispering, followed by laughter. Nothing in her life had prepared her for this public humiliation. Almost crying with self-pity, she walked out on to the winter street. There she stood in the rain, letting it soak her clothes, the cold pummelling her. All her dreams had been usurped, stolen by one person – the Watchman's Daughter. And what was even harder to bear was that her rival had none of Joan's advantages: no background, money, education or dowry. And yet she had *still* beaten her.

In that instant, Joan Fairchild felt the full force of her own humiliation – and the deafening resonance of Katherine Shaw's success.

'I'm sorry about your brother. I know you don't believe me, but I am.'

Rolling on to her side, Kat stared at the wall, Robin Wells sitting beside her on the bed. She was afraid that if she looked at him, he would know she was lying, that his instinct for betrayal would tip him off.

'I said I'm sorry,' he repeated, touching her shoulder. 'Even after what he did to me.'

She nodded, but kept her face averted.

'I could help . . . Can your parents afford the funeral?'

Her eyes closed against the question. How *could* he ask that in all seriousness? The very man who would have killed Micky if he had found him. But then again, he could afford to be magnanimous, thinking he had won. It was Kat's only comfort to know that he had been outwitted. That Micky was safe, out of his grasp . . . For an instant she wanted to turn round, look him in the eye and laugh. But she couldn't give any of them away.

'Katherine,' he said quietly, 'let me take you off somewhere.'

'I don't want to go away.'

'Then let me buy you something.'

'I don't need anything.'

'Just tell me what you want, and it's yours. Go on, darling, to please me.' Suddenly realising that he was begging, he stood up, then bent down and kissed her cheek. 'I'm not an unfeeling bastard.'

'I know that.'

'And I know how much your brother meant to you.' Sighing, he straightened up and left the room.

Kat stayed staring at the wall, only moving when she was certain Wells had left the house. Then she walked into the bathroom and pulled away the bath panel, reaching for a bag tucked away at the back of the empty space. It wasn't much, not enough for Kat to get her family out of Amber Street and away from Wells. But it was close to being enough to get Micky to Ireland. Over the previous fortnight her lover had relaxed his grip on his wallet and had begun to give Kat money. Money she told him she had spent on hair treatments, in Manchester beauty salons. Always picking things he could never ask to see. Money he had given her thinking he was buying her, when what he was *really* buying was an escape. The means for Micky to get away for good . . . Kat liked the idea, was almost amused by the irony of Wells subsidising his attacker's flight. Before too much longer, she thought, she would have saved enough.

But for the present, Micky had to stay hidden at the Albert Edward. Her brother had to play dead a little longer.

Not sure if he was doing the right thing, Andrew walked up the street, pausing opposite the tattoo parlour. Winter had set in hard, Christmas coming, and he had never felt so empty. At home, his father was clinging on to the last inch of life, his mother enraged that her plans had been thwarted.

'What in God's name is the matter with you?' she had asked him angrily. 'Why don't you marry Joan Fairchild and sort your life out?'

'I don't love her.'

'Force yourself,' Ivy had replied. 'Women live with men

they don't like every day. Half the marriages in England have nothing to do with love.'

'Half the marriages in England are unhappy.'

'So why should yours be any different?' she had replied drily, walking over to him. 'Your father doesn't have long to live, Andrew. I want you to take over the business and run it decently. Joan Fairchild is a respectable girl; she would help you in that way.'

'It's not going to happen, Mother.'

'So when your father dies, then what?'

'I'll take over the business and we'll carry on living here.'

Ivy had clicked her tongue. 'You *will* marry, won't you?'

'One day.'

'I mean, I couldn't bear to see you turn into some lonely old bachelor.' She had tried to smile and failed. 'What a mess our lives have become. I blame that Robin Wells; everything went downhill from the day he came to this house.' She had paused then, remembering. 'He walked into this room and I felt uneasy straight away. I couldn't put my finger on it, it was just something about him. I know it doesn't pay to regret things in life, but I would have liked to know what he said to your father that day. What it was that made Duncan act so out of character.' She had sat down, rigid in her corsets, comically poignant. 'He stole my husband from me, you know. And he took your father from you. I would give a year of my life to know what he said, what possible hold he had.'

'We all have reason to hate Robin Wells,' Andrew had replied, looking at his mother sympathetically. 'People he's cheated, lives he's ruined. If I was Wells, I wouldn't sleep at night. He has enemies everywhere.'

And now Andrew was looking at one . . . Steadily he regarded the newly renovated shop front, the tattoo parlour lit from inside, a shadow limping around behind the frosted glass. Making up his mind, he crossed the street and knocked on the front door. A moment later, a voice came from inside.

'We're closed.'

'It's Andrew Pitt. I came to talk to you.'

Immediately the door opened.

Andrew would always remember the shock of seeing Silky for the first time since the fire, and the way he struggled to control his reaction. Nodding for him to enter, Silky relocked the door, his face lit cruelly by the bright overhead light. He was still handsome, albeit strained, but his neck was burned and scarred, his right hand red and claw-like. Shuffling over to a seat, he sat down, wincing with the pain from his hip and burned left leg. Then he picked up a rubber tube from the table and pushed it into his right hand, thrusting the claw open as he began rhythmically to squeeze and release.

'How are you?'

'Well, I've given up the ballroom dancing,' Silky replied, his charm as potent as ever. 'How are you?'

'Not good.'

'I can imagine.'

'You're not fit yet, are you?'

'I will be. Soon,' Silky replied, still exercising his hand.

'Wells did this to you, didn't he?'

'We both know the answer to that.'

'And he took Kat.'

'Yeah,' Silky agreed. 'I let her down.'

'You couldn't stop it.'

'Oh, but I *will* stop it,' Silky said firmly. 'When I'm ready. When I'm fit.'

'What are you going to do?'

'I don't know yet.'

'Let me help you.'

'Thanks, but you're no street fighter.'

'I'm no coward,' Andrew replied coldly.

'I didn't say you were.'

'So let me help you.'

'Maybe.'

Keeping his patience, Andrew took a deep breath. 'You're

not the only one who has a grudge against Robin Wells. He took the woman I loved. And I want her back.'

Silky smiled. 'I hoped you'd say that.'

'But Kat won't have anything to do with me. I've sent her letters, but she returns them. I've even been round to Amber Street, left a message with Mary Armitage.'

'No luck?'

'No, none.'

'She's ashamed,' Silky replied. 'She won't talk to me either.'

'But I could sort all this out! I want to marry her and then I could support her family. She doesn't have to stay with Wells.'

'But she thinks she does. That she's made her bed, so she has to lie in it. Like everyone's so busy saying behind her back,' Silky replied, wincing as he changed position on his seat. 'She thinks she's ruined now. That's you're too good for her.'

'I don't think that.'

'No, but she does.'

'I want her back.'

'You said that already,' Silky replied, his tone even. 'But you want something else, don't you? You want revenge on Wells . . . I do too. But you know what's strange? I've learned something from him.'

'From Wells? What could anyone learn from that bastard?'

'How to fake. How to play-act . . . He thinks he's beaten me. Well I *want* him to believe that. I want him to believe he's got the Shaws cowed. That he's managed to hold my niece to ransom, to secure her family's future. That he's got us all trussed up in the palm of his hand. I want to give him time to crow, to relax . . . and to let down his guard.'

'Then what?'

Silky smiled, his dark eyes fathomless. 'Wait and see, Mr Pitt. Wait and see.'

* * *

Even though there was little money in and around Amber Street, people who knew the Shaw family sent flowers or wreaths when they heard of Micky's death. That Anna and Jim should lose another son was unbearable, they said. The Albert Edward must seem like a graveyard to them . . . It had been difficult to talk to her mother, but Kat had told her the truth about Micky, impressing on Anna the necessity for them to lie. For everyone – including her father – to think that Micky was dead.

'People *have* to believe he's been killed,' she said softly, making sure that no one would overhear them in the house on Amber Street. 'We have to lie.'

'I can't pretend to have lost another son!'

'You *have* to, Mum,' Kat insisted. '*You have to*. It's the only chance we have. Otherwise Micky will be in real danger. And you have to lie to Dad as well.'

Anna flinched, her face drained of colour. 'Dear God, how can I?'

'I know you don't want to, Mum, but think about it. If Dad knew the truth, he might get drunk and give us away by accident. If he doesn't know Micky is alive, he can't slip up.' Kat paused, taking her mother's hand and holding it tightly. 'I know what I'm asking, and I know how impossible it must seem, but we can't tell him. When Micky's got away, *then* we can. But not before then. Promise me, Mum, promise me you'll keep the secret.'

Nodding, a shaken Anna agreed.

Even though she was stunned by news of her grandson's death, Ma Shaw reacted typically, and arranged the funeral and a wake at The Horse and Cart. She didn't cry, and argued about the costs and ordered Horace around, even though he was shaken and Mary was crying.

'He were home,' Horace said incredulously. 'The poor lad had come home and gone to see his father. God, what a stupid accident.'

'They happen,' Ma Shaw replied, holding in her own grief.

'It's damn near killed Jim. I suppose he won't have his head out of a bottle now for the rest of his life.'

Shaken, Mary looked at the old woman, then wiped her eyes as she saw a customer come in. Whilst Ma Shaw continued to make arrangements with Horace, Mary moved down the bar towards the man, recognising him almost at once.

'Oh, hello, aren't you Micky's uncle?'

Flushing, Ivan nodded. *She had remembered him* . . . All this time he had thought that Mary Armitage hadn't even seen him, but she had. And she knew who he was . . . The thought made Ivan light-headed, struggling to act naturally.

'That's right, I'm Ivan Lomax.'

Mary's voice rose, and her eyes welled up with tears. 'It's horrible. Poor Micky.'

Ivan longed to hold her, to tell her it was all right, that Micky wasn't dead after all. But instead he hovered uneasily around the bar. 'It were awful.'

'I can imagine, poor lad. And he was so young . . .' Mary replied brokenly. 'I'm sorry, I should be serving you – would you like a drink?'

'All drinks free for members of the Shaw family,' Horace said suddenly.

Mary's eyes widened. 'But what about Mr Wells? He'll go mad if he hears you've been giving away free drinks.'

Ivan leaned forward. 'What about Wells?'

'He wants my uncle out,' Mary replied, dropping her voice and relieved to see that Ma Shaw had monopolised Horace again. 'He's throwing us out of the pub. Says we haven't made enough money.'

'He can't do that!'

'Of course he can,' she retorted, leaning towards him. 'That man can do anything – and no one can stop him.' Stepping back, she drew a pint and passed it over the bar. Ivan looked at it thoughtfully.

'Let me pay fer this.'

Stunned, Ma Shaw swivelled round. Even in her grief, she was unable to resist teasing her son. 'Dear God, Ivan, what's got into yer? Offering to pay fer a free drink?'

Ivan was embarrassed in front of Mary and shuffled his feet. 'I don't want to—'

'Yer must be sick.'

'Maybe I'm not quite what yer take me fer!' Ivan responded. Mary, impressed, watched him standing up to the redoubtable Ma Shaw. 'Maybe no one knows what I'm *really* like.'

'I think I do,' Mary said suddenly, Ivan turning away from his mother to look at her, awestruck. 'I think you're very brave. Finding Micky like that can't have been easy. It must have been hard for you.'

His mouth opened, but he was too stunned to speak. She was being sympathetic. No woman had ever been kind to him before, and the novelty left him limp as a rag.

'I . . . I don't know what to say.'

'I do. Enjoy your pint, Mr Lomax,' Mary said, smiling warmly. 'I reckon you've earned it.'

Only yards away, in the Shaw house next door, Anna sat silently, staring into the fire in the grate. She was trying to remember what Micky had been like as a child, whether he had been a good baby or not. Certainly he hadn't cried, but the reason for that no one had understood for several months – and then the horror of finding out that he was dumb . . . She wondered then what Micky's voice would have sounded like, and wished she could have heard it, if only once. She continued staring into the fire, keeping her face averted from Kat, who was tending Christine. It seemed such a short while since there had been four children in the house – then Billy had died, Kat left, and Micky was in hiding, to all intents and purposes dead. She remembered the way she had had to lie to Jim, and his reaction to the terrible news, the dull look of a man long out of luck . . .

Slowly Anna turned her head, listening for her husband's

footsteps and knowing that he would come to the door, pause outside, and then walk on. He had been doing that ever since Micky's death. Tried to come home, but then moved on. Unable to look at his wife or his mother. Unable to come to terms with the slow and crucifying demise of his family. And drinking, always drinking . . . Anna didn't know how he was paying for the booze, or holding down his nightwatchman's job. She didn't care any more. All she knew for sure was that the man she had loved so much had left her as certainly as her children had. Not physically, but mentally; Jim was barely alive. In debt to his past. In hock to his fecklessness. Ransomed to his own weakness . . . So every night he would walk past the house, then come back later, when everyone was still in bed. When no one wanted to talk, Christine lying beside her exhausted mother, Ma Shaw snoring upstairs. And Kat away at the flat.

He would come in, bumping drunkenly into furniture and muttering under his breath. Sometimes Anna could hear him crying in the early hours; sometimes he laughed idiotically in the darkness. But she never spoke to him. The ghosts of their two dead children moved between them and kept them apart. To have to bury two sons, to have to attend the funerals of their own offspring was wrong, Anna thought helplessly. It was bizarre, frightening, unreal – especially as one of those funerals had been a charade. And she had to keep it all a secret, grieve for a child who was still alive. Pretend to kind neighbours and friends that she was heartbroken. And all the time lying, lying to protect her child.

They say that happiness is dying in the right order, Anna thought hopelessly – so where did that leave them now?

'I have to see you!' Andrew said, running after Kat as she hurried down the street, away from the flat. 'I heard about Micky. God, I'm so sorry.'

Her head lowered, she avoided the curious stares of her

neighbours and walked on. 'Thank you for that, Andrew. But I can't see you again. You mustn't come here.'

'Because Wells might see me? I don't care about that.'

'Well I do!' she snapped back, looking at him and fighting the desire to reach for him, to touch him, hold on to him. To beg him, to say: take me away now, take me away from this town, this flat, this man. Pretend I'm the girl you left, the one you thought about when you were in Australia. Tell me about the landscape there, the wide hot skies, the heat, the towns. Describe what you saw and how we'll go there one day. Take my hand, Andrew Pitt, and never let it go again. Never let *me* go again.

But she couldn't.

'Andrew, *please* don't come here again.'

'I'm not afraid of Wells.'

'You should be,' she replied. 'And you'll only make things harder for me if you pick a fight with him. What's done is done, we can't change it. We're not the people we were.'

'I am who I was. You are who you were . . .'

She laughed, the sound hollow. 'How can you say that? Don't you know how people talk about me?'

'What you did, you must have done for a good reason. And I don't care about people.'

'You should, Andrew,' she told him calmly. 'It's people who rule the world.'

'Not my world.'

'Oh yes,' she replied, 'everyone's world.' Hurriedly she moved on, Andrew falling into step with her.

'Kat, I can't stop loving you.'

'Yes you can, Andrew. You can do anything – I've found that out.'

'Don't talk like that! It's not you,' he said, taking her arm.

Angrily, Kat shook him off. They had no future. Her future was with Wells; the security of her family was with Wells. She had no place for romance, for the glossy sheen of hope.

'Come back to me, Kat, please. Explain why you went to Wells and I'll accept it. I'll understand. I know there's a reason why you did it. Just come back to me . . .'

'As what?' she countered. 'Think about it – what would your mother say? Your friends? Your business colleagues? Don't say anything for a minute, Andrew, just hear me out. Bless you for caring about me, but it's over now. I have my place in the world and you have yours. You can't have a wife like me and still be accepted as a successful businessman.'

'Then I would rather have you.'

'You say that now, but in time you wouldn't,' Kat replied. 'In time you would look at me and wonder. Think about Wells and ask yourself a lot of questions that would be unpleasant.'

'I know you can't have gone with him out of choice!' Andrew replied heatedly. 'I know he must have something on you. He must have forced your hand. He did it with my father, so I know he has some hold over you as well.'

And then she wanted to tell him, to explain everything. But she resisted. Perhaps a little while ago she might have done, but not now. Now Kat realised that she had broken the moral code and could never repair it. If she was tainted, so be it. But she wouldn't ruin the man she loved at the same time. Wouldn't risk Wells harming him. Wouldn't risk what had happened to Silky happening to Andrew Pitt.

It was the greatest gift she could offer him – the gift of letting go.

'Andrew, go home. Forget me, and make a new life. A good life.'

'I can't forget you!' he replied adamantly. 'I want to know what hold Wells has over you.'

And then Kat saw it. Her escape – and his release.

'I'm sorry,' she said, her tone unreadable. 'Robin Wells has *no* control over me, no hold. I went with him because he could give me an easy life.'

He reeled back as though she had hit him. 'I don't believe that! I could give you an easy life.'

'You were in Australia!' she retorted, knowing she had shaken him and pressing her advantage. Forcing him away from her – and into safety. 'I was left alone here. Struggling, wondering if you were coming back. If Andrew Pitt was *really* going to marry me – Kat Shaw, from Amber Street. No one believed the romance would work, so how can you blame me for doubting you? After all, if you had really wanted me, you would have married me before you went halfway across the world. *What can happen in two months?* you said when you left. Well now you know.'

THIRTY-EIGHT

Looking up at Robin Wells's offices off Friargate, Joan Fairchild studied the windows. The gold script was ornate, confident – ROBIN WELLS. Esq., IMPORT and EXPORT – but with no mention of what exactly was imported or exported. Of course, it was the ideal cover for a business in a port town. Preston dealt with countries as far away as the USA, Sweden and Russia, so on the surface it would appear legitimate. Even with the increasing unemployment and hardship, the Albert Edward was keeping active, so who would question a man who was in the shipping industry?

Only that morning Joan's father had mentioned something about Wells, and how he would never do business with the man. Dismissively, Gareth Fairchild had brushed aside his wife's warnings not to be too hasty, and gone into his study. Gwen had turned to her daughter and smiled.

'Honestly, men! They never listen to reason . . . I must say, you look wonderful today, Joan. Like your old self.'

Smugly, Joan had smiled back. 'I feel better.'

'So there *is* more to life than Andrew Pitt?'

Yes, Mother, she had wanted to reply. There is revenge. But most of all there is Katherine Shaw, the instigator of my blistering unhappiness.

'You have such a lot to offer, Joan. It's just that you haven't found the right man yet. When you do, the romance will fall into place without effort.' Gwen had paused, patting her smooth hair, her tone devoid of irony. 'I never wanted you to marry into the Pitt family anyway.'

Well, that's one wish that *will* be granted to you, Mother, Joan thought, gazing up at the office windows and then continuing down Friargate. The humiliating episode at the party had been the last straw, her self-importance and confidence blown apart. She had been so badly treated. It wasn't on, Joan thought. Oh no, someone was going to pay for this. For making her look a fool . . . Walking on, she tried to make some kind of sense of her bitterness, but failed. Instead, her whole energy was centred upon the trio who had deceived her: the Watchman's Daughter, Andrew Pitt and Robin Wells.

The thought of Wells made her cringe. Had it been so obvious to everyone else that she was being duped? Mortified, she walked on past the town hall and the library, then along the first row of familiar shops, pausing momentarily to look at an evening coat. Disgruntled, she continued, passing the furniture shop and the estate agent, and the news boy standing on the corner and calling out: 'RED UPRISING IN SPAIN! Read all about it!' What was the use of politics? Joan wondered. People were talking about the Depression, the fall of the pound; there was even talk of another war. She frowned at the thought: all the young men going off to fight again, all the eligible bachelors gone . . .

Suddenly someone caught her eye, and ducking back into a shop doorway, Joan watched the woman across the street. The Watchman's Daughter, Kat Shaw. Her rival . . . Narrowing her eyes, Joan studied her: the fascinating face and voluptuous body, which could have been stunning if Kat Shaw hadn't underplayed them. In fact it surprised Joan to see how little attention she courted, how she kept her face averted in a desire to go unnoticed. Hardly the crowing whore or worldly mistress she had been led to believe. In truth, Kat Shaw seemed more like a young wife or mother going about her day-to-day business in a northern town.

The momentary surprise at Kat's appearance didn't soften Joan's heart for long. This was her rival. Something about this woman made her the winner – but what, Joan didn't know. Curious, she watched Kat walk on, and then, without thinking, followed her. Moving quickly, Kat crossed the street and hurried past the town hall, retracing Joan's earlier steps. Only yards behind, Joan followed her, vaguely wondering why, but compelled to do so. She had never seen her rival out and about before, and now her quarry was in the open she had a hunter's desire to track. Kat moved on quickly, stopping briefly at the grocer's, Gregory Unwin's, Joan pausing outside the shop and eavesdropping on the conversation taking place indoors.

'I'm so sorry about your brother, Kat,' the effeminate Mr Unwin said mournfully. 'Your parents must be so upset.'

'I just wanted to tell you myself, in case you hadn't heard.'

Outside, Joan listened avidly. The death of Micky Shaw had been all over the papers. Some horrible accident at the Preston docks. She remembered the other news – that Micky had once hit Robin Wells. And now he was dead . . .

'I just wanted to call by and see you, Mr Unwin,' Kat continued. 'You've always been so kind to me and my family. How's business?'

'Quiet,' he admitted ruefully. 'I have to stock makes I wouldn't have had on the shelves before. Regulars used to rely on me to get them specials, little treats you could only buy in Manchester, or from me. But that's all changed now. Nothing's like it was.'

'Not like the old days, is it?' she asked, looking round at the familiar surroundings. 'I can remember when I first came to work here . . .'

'Everyone liked you.'

'Micky used to wait for me outside sometimes. Life was so simple then.'

He looked at her sympathetically. 'You're always welcome here, Kat. I hope you know that.'

'Oh, I do,' she replied, her tone warm. 'I've always known that.'

Moving away from the doorway, Joan just had time to get out of sight before Kat left the shop. She paused, waved at Mr Unwin, then moved on, continuing across town into the more miserable, poorer areas. Although uneasy with the changing surroundings, Joan kept up her scrutiny. She had the advantage – knowing what the Watchman's Daughter looked like – whereas Kat wasn't even aware of her existence. Stimulated by the chase, Joan found herself buoyed up for the first time in weeks, and kept following, only stopping when Kat stopped, and turning away if she looked round. Past the shops they went, each street becoming more impoverished, Joan hurrying to keep up as Kat walked into Amber Street.

So this was her home, was it? Joan thought. This was the place Duncan Pitt used to own, the place from which Andrew used to collect the rents. The place he had first met the Watchman's Daughter . . . Joan's gaze travelled down the dimly lit cobbled street, cautiously eyeing up The Horse and Cart on the opposite corner. Some front doors, long in need of painting, were boarded with planks, a few windows blinded with nets, others left broken, a pigeon flying in and out of the upper floor of number 56. God, Joan thought, it was grim. Had it always been this way? And then she remembered that Robin Wells now owned Amber Street.

Moving into a doorway, she watched a woman come out of a nearby house, accompanied by two others. The three of them were heavily made up, and cheaply dressed, walking with their arms linked. So that rumour was true, Joan thought, stunned: one of the houses *was* a brothel. She tried to imagine what it would be like to live in such a street. To see the familiar – if poor – surroundings become sordid, the little pockets of respectability picked off like meat from a carcass. Stories she had heard, but only half believed, now echoed in her head. The flop houses Wells had allowed; the cellars of some of the houses rented out to the Chinese on the cheap; four families crowded into two rooms.

Hearing another door open, Joan ducked further out of sight, seeing Kat walk out of her home and pause on the street. She seemed nervous, ill at ease, turning to look one way then another, before setting off again. Some sixth sense tipping her off, Joan began to follow her rival again. Only this time she was aware that Kat was uneasy, and kept her distance. Where was she going? Joan wondered. Not to the flat on Avenham Park, that was obvious; she was heading in an altogether different direction. But where? Amidst the unfamiliar surroundings, Joan wondered if she should stop her stalking and return home. But though tempted, she was too curious to turn back, and continued instead. Down along Williams Street, along Stafford Terrace Kat walked, turning often. What was she looking for? Joan wondered. Was she meeting someone and nervous she might be seen? Now wouldn't that be a turn-up, the mistress cheating on her lover? Joan relished the thought, suddenly determined not to let Kat out of her sight. How sweet her revenge would be if she could see the Watchman's Daughter betray Andrew Pitt *and* Robin Wells. What a very explosive piece of information she would have there.

And what pleasure she would take in passing that information on . . . She could imagine Andrew's face when she told him that the woman he was still so obsessed with was even worse than people believed. And as for Robin Wells . . . So, she was such an innocent, was she? Joan thought, her face flushing with the remembered insult. Well, she wouldn't be so innocent any more. She would show everyone how worldly she could be. Because *she* would be the one to inform Mr Wells that his mistress was cheating on him. Not bad for a naïve nobody. Not bad at all . . .

Quickening her steps, Kat suddenly hailed a tram and climbed aboard. Joan followed. Once inside, she sat by the doorway and paid her fare, keeping her eyes on Kat, who had taken a seat halfway down the vehicle. Every few moments Kat would turn round, or look out of the window, checking her watch repeatedly. My God, she *was* meeting someone! Joan thought with delight. This whim of hers was going to pay off handsomely . . . Slowly the tram moved on, leaving the tight knotting of streets and moving towards the outskirts of town. The minutes wore on relentlessly, Joan beginning to wonder if she was getting out of her depth as they left Preston and headed away from the town. Then gradually the tram began to empty of housewives and children, working men getting on board instead, Kat shrinking against the window to make more room.

Trying not to look obvious, Joan regarded the men curiously. From the way they were dressed, in donkey jackets and overalls, she presumed they were factory workers – but where was the factory so far out of town? And then she realised that they weren't going to an industrial works; they were heading for the Albert Edward. Surely Kat's clandestine meeting wasn't with a sailor, was it? Joan almost laughed out loud, imagining Wells's expression when he heard that he had been cuckolded by a sailor. That the most feared and most powerful man in Preston had been duped for a jack tar.

The tram ground on further, Joan snuggling into her coat, Kat glancing out of the window, deep in thought. Only momentarily did Joan worry about getting back home. She would manage somehow. And anyway, what was a little inconvenience compared with the uncovering of the Watchman's Daughter's secret? She would walk to Germany and back without shoes rather than miss this . . . Wincing as the man next to her started to smoke, Joan noticed that everyone on the tram had stood up and was preparing to leave. So they had come to the end of the line, had they? she thought, amused. Well, Kat Shaw certainly had.

Waiting until the vehicle had emptied and Kat had got off, Joan left too, keeping her distance. Dressed in a dark coat, she went unnoticed as she followed the men, Kat walking on her own, a little apart. The dockside came into view slowly, the ships' bellies underlit by the lights reflected on the water, the smell of ozone and steel marking the December air. Joan pulled her collar up around her neck and moved closer to a small group of women as she followed Kat – not wanting to be conspicuous and spotted so late in the game. But as the women talked in relaxed tones, Joan could see from Kat's rigid body movements that she was nervous. She hardly walked ten steps before gazing round, pausing often. Joan walked past her once so as to not give herself away, but when she had gone another few yards, she turned a dark corner and then looked back, allowing time for Kat to pass her again. Watching in the shadows, she saw Kat pause, rummaging in her bag and giving everyone off the tram time to walk on. Then, when she was sure she was alone, Kat took a carrier bag out from under her coat and turned suddenly, heading towards a bank of warehouses.

So she was going to meet her lover in a warehouse, was she? Joan thought gleefully. What a sordid place for an assignation. But then what did anyone expect from the Watchman's Daughter? Walking slowly to avoid making a sound in the yawning night, Joan followed, watching as Kat paused outside a deserted warehouse. On the side of the building was a sign – THIS PROPERTY IS UNSAFE. Kat walked to a side door and unlocked it. After a moment's pause, Joan followed her, but Kat had locked the door from the inside, forcing Joan to look for some other means of entry. Eager to catch her rival out, Joan moved around the perimeters of the warehouse, finally coming across a broken window. Pushing back the board that covered it, she hitched up her skirt and climbed inside, taking care not to make a noise. Once inside, the darkness hit her, the old engines and machines rearing up around her and dwarfing her as she felt her way along. Gradually her eyes adjusted to the dim light, and then, hearing a voice, she stopped in her tracks and listened.

It was the Watchman's Daughter, talking . . . Eagerly Joan moved forward, her gaze drawn upwards, towards the faint light of a lamp on the level above. Kat was up there with her lover, Joan thought, inching further outwards and seeing the shadow of a man and a woman thrown up on to the vaulted ceiling above. Transfixed, she watched, then moved closer, straining to hear the conversation.

'I'm so glad to see you,' the Watchman's Daughter said, her shadow hugging the man's shadow, Joan's eyes widening. 'I was thinking about you all day . . .'

I bet you were, Joan thought bitterly.

'I know how hard it is for you. But it won't be long now, I promise.'

Won't be long for what?

'You've been so patient.'

God, Joan thought, why didn't the man reply? Why wasn't he talking? She inched further forward. From her new vantage point she could see the underside of the platform, and watched as Kat moved towards the edge. Come out, Joan willed the man, come out and show yourself.

'We've fooled everyone. Pulled it off. You can relax now . . .' Kat went on, Joan's mind working frantically. 'I said it would be all right, didn't I? I promised. You'll be away from here soon.'

Her mouth dry, Joan listened, then ducked into the shadows as she heard the man move, waiting, transfixed, as he came into her view. Then she took a breath. Even with his beard she recognised the young man who had been in the papers. The young man who had met with such a tragic accident. The young man who had hit Robin Wells and had to run for his life. The young man who was supposedly dead.

Christ, Joan thought, keeping to the shadows. It was Micky Shaw . . . The Watchman's Daughter didn't have a secret lover; she was visiting her brother . . . Joan's mind ran on eagerly. A lover would have been a bombshell, but a dead brother was incredible. No wonder Kat had been so careful, so anxious not to be followed. Joan leaned against some old machinery, her heart banging. But how had she managed to pass off another man as her brother? Certainly she had had help. Joan remembered the article in the local paper, about how Ivan Lomax had found his nephew's body – only it wasn't Micky Shaw's body. It was some stranger's, and Lomax had lied when he had identified it. Just as Kat had lied. To the town, and to Robin Wells – the very man who had been after Micky.

Her heartbeat was so rapid, Joan was certain that they would overhear her before she could make her escape. Of course she knew what she *should* do – go to the police at once. After all, a crime had been committed. But she wasn't going to take the good citizen's role. There was someone else who would be far more interested in Micky's incredible escape from death. Someone who needed to know that he had been duped by his mistress. That he had been lied to, fooled . . . Joan could almost feel the sensation of triumph warming her skin. Who would have believed that Robin Wells had been so naïve? So unworldly? Right under his nose, Kat Shaw had tricked him. Now, Joan thought, seeing her revenge coming nicely to fruition, how would his reputation as a cunning, ruthless man stand up to that? Biting her lip to stop herself laughing, she moved back to the window and climbed out, replacing the board after her. Then as quickly as she could, she hurried away from the Albert Edward.

The ships' hooters called after her in the darkness. They sang out, cried from the water and the dark belly of the sky, their gloomy echoes trying uselessly to make her turn back.

THIRTY-NINE

New Year, 1934

Walking towards the back door of the tattoo parlour, Ivan hesitated. He was feeling out of place, aware that the last time he had been on the premises he had been tortured by Robin Wells – given a message with the end of a tattoo needle. Touching his arm, he shuddered at the memory, then knocked. Immediately Silky opened the door and ushered him in. All the evidence of the arson attack was gone; the place seemed revived, but curiously characterless, the touches that had made it so obviously Silky's no longer visible.

'Well you're a sight for sore eyes and no mistake . . .' Ivan shuffled his feet, embarrassed, as Silky continued. 'I would never have thought you had it in you, Ivan. But I'm impressed. You fooled everyone with that stunt on the docks. I'm only sorry I wasn't in on it.'

'You weren't up to it then.'

'I'm good now,' Silky said firmly. 'Back to myself.'

Ivan didn't like to say that his half-brother looked like he still had a way to go with his recovery, so he nodded instead. Certainly Silky had regained some of the weight he had lost, and his limp was less pronounced, but his right hand was still hideously deformed. One thing that was back to normal, though, was his demeanour. Silky's self-imposed exile was obviously over.

'I asked you round to have a talk,' he went on, gesturing

for Ivan to take a seat. 'You did really well, but we still have to get Micky away from Preston. And I've found exactly the place to send him.'

Ivan's eyebrows rose. 'Yer have?'

'Ireland.'

'Ireland?' Ivan echoed. 'Why there?'

Smiling, Silky leaned back in his seat. 'Kat and I have worked it all out. You remember Queenie, the lady Robin Wells and I fell out over?' Ivan flinched. 'Well, I've found out where she's living now. In Ireland – how lucky is that? She's married, got a couple of kids. So I wrote to her about Micky. She runs a boarding house near Dublin, and she said she'd be glad to take Micky on. He could do some work for her and help her run the place.'

'Sounds good,' Ivan replied, pleased to be taken into his glamorous half-brother's confidence. Obviously Silky thought of him as an equal now.

'The way it looks at the moment, we could move Micky at the end of next week. We've got enough money together and it's organised with Queenie, but I've been talking to Kat and she's nervous. She was saying something about wanting to bring it forward, that Wells was acting oddly and she wasn't sure he wasn't on to her.'

'Christ,' Ivan said, unnerved. 'What can we do?'

'Move Micky as quickly as we can. I'll need your help.' As Ivan nodded, Silky wondered once again just what had effected the momentous sea change in him. 'Look, I've got to ask you something, Ivan.'

'What?'

'All this hero stuff . . . I mean, I don't want to seem cruel, but it wasn't your way before.' Silky paused, studying his half-brother, then smiling faintly. 'My God, it's a *woman*, isn't it?'

Ivan's face paled. 'I never said . . .'

'She must be something,' Silky went on encouragingly. 'Who is it?'

'Yer won't tell anyone?'

'Nah.'

'I don't want to look stupid, yer know, have people laughing at me.'

'Who is she?'

'Mary Armitage.'

'Horace's niece?' Silky asked, his eyebrows rising. 'She's—'

'Too young fer me?'

'Well, she's—'

'Too pretty.'

'For God's sake, Ivan, let me finish! I was going to say she wasn't the type I thought you'd go for.'

'I don't go fer any type,' Ivan replied, discomforted and all too aware of his half-brother's impressive record with women. 'But Mary's special. I could look after her. She's got no one, no family – apart from her uncle – and she'll need a home soon. I could give her that.'

'Why will she need a home soon?' Silky asked, frowning.

'Wells want to turn them out of The Horse and Cart.'

A slow, unreadable expression passed over Silky's face. 'When?'

'They don't know fer sure. Soon.'

'Does Mary Armitage know how you feel about her?'

'Nah, but she knows who I am, and that's a start. She made me feel right welcome the other day. And she's not a soppy girl; she stood up fer Kat, did Mary. Might seem a bit dopey sometimes, but she's got spirit.'

'I wouldn't tell her that.'

'About her spirit?'

'Nah,' Silky said, fighting laughter. 'About being dopey. The expression is "fragile", or "delicate".'

'I like that,' Ivan replied wistfully. 'Yeah, I could call her delicate.'

'Have you asked her out?'

'Nah!'

'Don't you think you better? I mean, you can't jump from admiring her at a distance to looking after her for life without a few walks or cuddles in between.'

Paling even further, Ivan shifted around on his seat. '*Cuddles!* I don't . . . I can't . . .'

'Have you ever kissed a woman, Ivan?'

'Yeah, sure I have!' His voice faltered. 'Well, no . . . I mean . . . No.'

'What about flowers?'

'I don't kiss flowers!'

'No,' Silky said patiently. 'I mean – have you given Mary any flowers?'

'Should I?'

'It would be a start.'

'What kind?'

'Something pretty. So you can say you saw them and they reminded you of her.'

Nodding, Ivan was trying hard to take the information on board. 'Then what?'

'Ask her if she would like to take a walk in the park.'

'What if it's raining?'

'Ask her if she would like to go to the cinema.'

'I dunno,' Ivan replied, suddenly overawed by the intricacies of dating. 'What kind of film?'

Silky was enjoying himself enormously. To think that his half-brother was turning into a Romeo. The idea pleased him. It was good to think about something positive, something that wasn't to do with Robin Wells.

'A romantic film.'

'Nay!'

'Well you can't take her to a war film, can you?'

'But a romance . . .'

'All right, go and see a Charlie Chaplin film.'

That went down better with Ivan. 'Then what?'

'Walk her home afterwards,' Silky replied, leaning forward in his chair. 'And when you get to the front door of The

Horse and Cart, you kiss her on the cheek, say you had a lovely evening and that you'd like to see her again.'

'Film. Kiss on cheek. Lovely evening. Ask to see her again,' Ivan repeated, committing it all to memory. 'What if she says no?'

'She won't say no.'

'She might.'

'No woman refuses to go out with a hero,' Silky replied, watching Ivan's confidence blossom. 'Remember, you *are* someone now, Ivan. You believe that – and she will too.'

Lost in thought, Ivan stared at his feet, imagining his evening out with Mary Armitage. Silky's romantic advice had been useful, but calling Ivan a hero had propelled his half-brother into a world of untold possibilities. Suddenly Ivan Lomax was capable of anything. He could face anyone, stand up to anyone – *and be brave . . .*

A long minute passed, then Silky coughed and turned back to Ivan.

'We have to get Micky ready to move. We have to prepare him, get some things together, some clothes. He can catch the ferry boat from the Albert Edward over to Ireland, that'll be easy enough. But we'll have to scrimp up some more money.'

'I've got a bit.'

Silky nodded. 'Me too. And Kat said she wanted to pay for the ticket.'

'But it'll be dear!'

'She wants to do it,' Silky replied. 'It means a lot to her, Ivan. Let her do it. Let her get Micky safe; it'll make sense of everything she's done.'

'What about afterwards?'

'I want Kat away from Wells. When Micky's really out of his reach, she can leave him.'

'But he could still turn the family out of Amber Street.'

'Yeah, I know,' Silky agreed morosely. 'And I doubt Jim will have that job for much longer now. He's drunk more often than he's sober. Not that he's falling about the place;

he's just moving around like a ghoul. Even with Wells's protection, his days are numbered.'

Ivan shook his head. 'What the hell happened to Jim?'

'He was never very strong. He wanted to be a happy man – but life had other ideas for him.'

'Yer know,' Ivan said, finding generosity difficult, but easier as he practised, 'I've got a bit of savings. I could dip into them. I mean, if they're needed.'

'Thanks,' Silky replied, surprised, 'but you'll need those for your own life. And for your new wife – if you get a move on and nab Mary Armitage before some other lad does . . . I'll be honest with you, Ivan: I've had to call in some favours to get this place repaired. Had no choice, had to get the business up and running again. That bastard Wells damn near finished me off . . .' He paused, thinking about Kat. 'I want her away from Wells.'

'We all want that.'

'But first,' Silky went on, 'we have to get Micky away. When Micky's safe, we can relax. But not before then.'

Eyeing him carefully, Kat walked around the desk. Having just finished a long telephone conversation, Wells was relaxing, reading the afternoon edition of the paper, his post spread out in front of him on the desk. In the time they had been together, Kat had seldom come to the office, but today she had been compelled to call by. Ignoring the hostile look from Wells's secretary, she had entered her lover's office and been surprised by his obvious delight at seeing her.

'Hello, darling!' he had said, spinning round in his desk chair and walking over to her. 'Don't tell me, you've been shopping?'

Forcing herself to smile, Kat accepted his kiss on the cheek. She had taken extra care with her make-up and clothes, knowing how much he liked people to admire her. But the strain was telling on her and she was ill at ease.

'Are you OK?'

'Fine.'

'You look pale,' he said, bending over her and putting his hand on her forehead.

She wanted to brush it away, but resisted. 'I'm fine, a bit cold perhaps.'

'January – what d'you expect?' he said, pretending to shiver. 'I was just thinking, we should go away for a while. On a holiday, somewhere hot. Would you like that?'

I would rather die, Kat thought. Who would want to go away with him? To be stuck on some boat, some train, with everyone pointing them out and knowing she was his mistress . . . Her thoughts slid back without warning. To Andrew and to his promises of Australia, the high skies and heat. The finding of a new country with a new husband. Marriage to the man she loved, being with a man she respected, rather than feared. The intensity of loss hit her like a body blow.

'Are you sure you're OK?'

She nodded, feeling more trapped than ever. But she had to live with it. Perhaps one day there would be an escape, but for now all she could do was cope. Day in, day out, without thinking too much, or looking back. Without letting too much reality percolate. There was only one way she could survive – by using her position. By getting help for others. It was the only means of coping available to her. And it made her situation almost bearable.

'I never ask you for anything, do I?'

He sat down on the edge of the desk, his eyes unblinking. God, she thought, you *are* frightening. I know you love me, but today even I find you terrifying.

'What is it, Katherine?'

'I want to ask a favour.' She knew that she was breaking a private code. Having long since decided never to ask Wells for anything except protection for her family, she was now about to break her own promise. And in breaking it, she realised she was making herself vulnerable. Colluding in their relationship. Becoming more the mistress and less the reluctant hostage.

'What's the favour?'

'It's about The Horse and Cart . . .'

'That bloody dump!'

'Please don't turn the Armitages out.'

'It's business.'

'They're friends of mine,' she replied, her tone even. 'They need to keep their home.'

'They're losing money.'

'You don't need to take over that pub; you've got other places . . .'

'Yeah, because I made a good deal.'

Her curiosity was suddenly piqued. 'With Duncan Pitt?'

He eyed her carefully. 'The old man died last week. Did you know that?'

Shaken, Kat looked down. 'No, no, I didn't.'

'Fancied yourself part of the Pitt dynasty, didn't you? Well, whatever you thought, darling, you and Andrew Pitt would never have married. He was only playing with you.'

She felt such hatred for Robin Wells then that she could have knifed him on the spot. But what was the point in protesting, or even reacting? Better not to show her hand; let him think he had beaten her.

'I'm sorry to hear that Duncan Pitt's dead. But why did he do that business deal with you?'

'He was greedy.'

'Is that all?' Kat asked, her tone innocuous. 'I thought you might have had something on him.'

'Really?' he said, his tone unreadable. 'Why would you say that?'

'You usually have something on people. Isn't that how you get what you want?' Her voice was even, almost admiring. 'You know everything about everybody – that's what people always say about you. And it's true, isn't it? So what did you have on Duncan Pitt? You can tell me. The old man's dead; what harm will it do now?'

'Duncan Pitt had a secret . . .'

She nodded, encouraging him. 'I thought as much.'

'. . . that he would do anything to keep hidden.' Wells paused. 'Most people have secrets. Or something to protect.'

'So what was *his* secret?'

'You're being very curious, Katherine, and it's not like you.'

'Maybe I'm showing an interest in your business. You always complain that I'm not interested enough.'

He was enjoying the sparring, liked to see her spirit. And besides, she was right – what harm could it do to tell her now that the old man was dead?

'Duncan Pitt's fortune wasn't built on hard work and luck; it was built on a death. He cheated a man called Stanley Gorman, who then committed suicide.'

'God,' she said, shocked.

'I told Pitt that I would expose him if he didn't hand over the property to me. Of course he did.'

'But he never explained to his wife or his son,' Kat said, unable to look at the man in front of her.

'Probably being thought a dodgy businessman was better than being exposed as a fraud and responsible for driving a man to his death.'

'But it drove Duncan Pitt to his own death.'

'I wasn't responsible for that,' Wells answered her, unfazed.

'So the whole Pitt business is built on a crime?'

He nodded. 'And it won't be the first successful firm, or the last, that is.'

Taking a deep breath, Kat looked at him. 'Will you do me that favour? Will you let the Armitages stay in The Horse and Cart?'

'I don't like you interfering in the business,' he said, his tone freezing to indicate that the subject was closed. 'Let's go out for dinner later. Somewhere nice. Get yourself dressed up.'

'I don't want dinner. I want a favour. The only favour I've ever asked of you,' she persisted, pressing him. 'Mary is my closest friend; she has no home but the pub. And Horace runs a decent house.'

'I'm not interested in a decent house.'

'No, you're not, are you?' Kat replied, her expression one of disgust. 'I forgot. Decency has never been your strong suit.'

His good humour nosedived. 'You really should mind that temper of yours.'

'But it's *you* that has the temper, *you* that has the upper hand. *You* that holds all the cards.'

He caught her by the wrist and pulled her towards him. 'You're pushing your luck.'

'And God knows, you never do that, do you?'

Kat knew how far she was pressurising him, but she had been uneasy for days. Wells had changed in some way and she was wondering if he was on to her. Did he know about Micky? He had said nothing, but there had been a shift in their relationship. It was obvious that she had the upper hand now, because he was becoming so fond of her. But it was also becoming obvious that he resented it. Any betrayal from her would have a cataclysmic effect. Which was why Kat had to know where she stood. For her sake, and Micky's.

'You're hurting me.'

'You asked for it, Katherine,' he said, looking at her, excited and irritated in the same moment. 'You can't hide anything from me. You know that, don't you?'

Her mouth dried. 'I don't have anything to hide.'

'Good,' he said, his face only inches from hers, his tone softening. 'I'm very fond of you, Katherine. You know that. But don't rely on it. Don't take my affection – or me – for granted. Or . . .'

'Or what?' she countered, suddenly reckless. 'What will you do to me? Set fire to me? Pour boiling water over me?'

His expression darkened, his voice warning. 'Your uncle's a liar if he said it was me!'

'My uncle's never lied! And he never said it was you. I just *know* it was.'

Clasping her wrist even tighter, Wells stared into Kat's face. He was surprised by her attitude and wondered anxiously if she was thinking of leaving him. After all, now that her brother was dead, perhaps she was prepared to let the rest of her family fend for themselves.

Sobered by the thought, he found himself wavering. 'What is it?'

'What?

'The favour?'

'Let the Armitages stay in The Horse and Cart.'

'I'll lose money.'

The words were out of Kat's mouth before she had time to check them. 'Would you rather lose money, or me?'

Touching her cheek with the tips of his fingers, Robin Wells paused, then kissed her on the lips. The action was fleeting, his breath only lingering against her mouth for an instant before he pulled away. Rigid, Kat stood immobile, waiting for his answer and wondering why she had been so stupid, risking an argument at such a perilous time.

Slowly Wells traced the outline of her throat and shoulder, her hand coming to rest on her left breast. 'I can feel your heart beating . . .'

She said nothing.

'. . . bump, bump, bump, bump.' He leaned down, resting his head against her chest. 'It's beating very quickly, Katherine. Why is that? Are you excited, fired up? Or afraid? *Are you afraid of me?*' Slowly he straightened up, staring into her face, his eyes unblinking. 'You're not going to leave me. And you're not going to threaten me ever again. Do you understand?'

She remained silent, her heart thumping.

'The Armitages can stay in The Horse and Cart. As a

favour to you, Katherine. But you've angered me, and I want you to know that. You've relied on my feelings for you and said some hard things, things no one else would have got away with.' He let go of her wrist and moved back behind his desk, his expression cold. 'Don't *ever* push me again. Don't overstep the mark, Katherine. Or, by God, you'll regret it.'

FORTY

Standing by the back door of The Horse and Cart, Ivan was shaking. He tried, unsuccessfully, to tell himself that he was a hero and that heroes weren't afraid of anything, but it didn't work. The bunch of flowers he had bought was beginning to wilt in the cold air, the violets seeming a slight and miserly gift. Oh Jesus, he thought desperately, was he reverting to his old self? Not now, not now . . .

'Oh, Mr Lomax!' Mary said suddenly, coming up behind him and catching him unawares. 'What are you doing round the back?'

He went blank, all the tips from Silky getting jumbled up in his head. 'I got flowers for the cinema.'

'What?'

'Not war flowers . . . erm . . . would yer like a walk with flowers? . . . Kiss the flowers?'

Her expression was baffled. 'I don't know what you mean, Mr Lomax.'

'I was thinking . . .' Ivan went on, miserably inarticulate, 'would yer like . . . Yer can stay here.'

'What?'

Taking a deep breath, Ivan composed himself, suddenly remembering his hero's role. 'Yer and yer uncle can stay at The Horse and Cart. Kat told me to tell yer that Wells has changed his mind. Yer can both stay here.'

'Oh my Lord!' Mary replied, clapping her hands and

hugging Ivan without thinking. 'Oh my Lord, my Lord!'

Dropping the bunch of violets, Ivan took his chance and grabbed hold of her, swinging her high into the air and then twirling round and round with her. Laughing, she squealed with pleasure, jumping out of his arms and then stopping dead.

'What is it?'

'I've trodden on your lovely flowers,' she said, bending down and picking up the crushed violets. 'Were they for someone special?'

'They remind me of yer.'

'All crushed?' she said, smiling gently. 'Were they really for me?'

His mind cleared suddenly, his senses coming back to him as he made his play for her. 'I've been watching yer fer a while, Mary, and I wondered if yer would like to walk out with me. I'm not much to look at, but I'm honest and I've some feelings fer yer.'

'Oh,' she said simply. 'Fancy.'

'I think yer very . . . delicate.'

'*Delicate* . . .' she repeated, flattered.

Ivan persisted gamely: 'Fragile.'

'*Fragile*. Oh, fancy . . .' Mary said again, then slid her hand through his arm and smiled up at him. 'Fancy that.'

'Silky!'

He winced as he heard Kat's voice over the phone. 'What's up?'

'We have to get Micky out. Tonight.'

'Tonight!' Silky replied, shaken. 'It's all organised for the end of the week. Why so suddenly?'

'Wells is acting oddly. I think he might be on to me.'

'Are you sure?'

'No, I'm not sure, I'm just uneasy. Something's not right.' She paused, putting her fear into words. 'I'm scared.'

'Get out of that flat *now*, Kat.'

'I will, I will. I just have to get some things together for Micky. Can you organise something, Silky? Get him moved tonight? We have to hide him somewhere else.'

'Don't worry, I'll fix it.'

'I'll bring the money and Micky's ferry ticket,' she added, turning round hurriedly as she heard the front door open below. For a long moment she held her breath, then relaxed as she heard the footsteps move past her door.

'You have to get out of there.'

'I will. Sssh!' Kat said suddenly, listening.

The footsteps were coming back down the stairs, and had now paused outside her door.

Smugly confident, Joan Fairchild walked up the back steps to Robin Wells's office. Seeing a light on, she knocked, surprised to find the door opened by a narrow-faced man.

'Yeah?'

'Is Mr Wells here?'

He looked over his shoulder. 'Are yer in?'

'Depends who wants me,' Wells's voice came back, amused as he walked out from the back room and spotted Joan. 'Well how nice to see you after so long. Come in, Joanie, come on in.'

Jerking his head at the man to leave, Wells ushered Joan into his office, pouring her a sherry and sitting her down. He was curious, wondering why she was there. After all, no one had seen the Fairchild heiress for a while, Ginny Arthur having broken off their friendship. Wells sighed to himself. Ginny Arthur was a stupid woman. Good in bed, but indiscreet, couldn't keep a secret – but then what did you expect from a scrubber with a burgeoning drink problem? He could picture his ex-lover when she was forty, skinny, with dry skin and a bitter tongue, going the rounds of parties, looking for the sex that would become less and less available to her.

'Joanie?'

She looked at him, putting on her most winning smile, then crossed her legs, knowing that he was looking at her.

'How are you?'

He smiled his best paternal smile, nonplussed by the question. Did Gareth Fairchild need business help? It must be something like that. Joan wouldn't be here for personal reasons; there was no spark between them, and she wasn't mistress material. So it had to be business.

Relishing an entrée into the Fairchild concerns, Wells urged her to continue. 'Is there something I can do for you?'

'Well . . .'

'Or for your father? I heard he was having a little trouble with his European imports. I could look into it.'

Joan flinched. The last thing she wanted was for her father to know she was involved with Robin Wells. If he had even suspected she knew the man, he would be thunderstruck. God, she thought, becoming slightly nervous, maybe she should have taken her revenge at a distance.

'It's not about my father. Or his business . . . In fact, I would rather he didn't know I'd come to see you.'

She paused, Wells studying her. And then he remembered that Joan had been in love with Andrew Pitt. The same Andrew Pitt who had loved Katherine . . . It was getting more interesting by the minute, he thought, amused. How peoples' lives swam – like quick little fishes – in and out of each other's patch of water.

'I won't tell your father you've been here,' he promised. 'I don't have any dealings with him.'

'Good,' Joan replied, nodding. 'Could I have a glass of water?'

'Why don't I pour you a sherry?'

'I don't want anything alcoholic,' she replied, watching him fill a glass of water and hand it to her. She was playing for time and knew it. Her confidence had melted and now she was horribly aware of what she had come to do – and what it would mean. Her courage was sinking fast, her voice faltering. 'I think perhaps I shouldn't have come.'

Out of patience, Wells leaned back against the desk and folded his arms. He had been mildly interested before, but now he was fascinated. He had seen the same hesitancy before, in people who had something explosive on their minds. Something they had come to tell him, or sell him. And he knew, in that very instant, that this was when Joan would either confide or lose her nerve. And he was too curious to let her do the latter.

'Come on, tell me why you came to see me.'

She smiled again, only this time it didn't work. Get out of here, she told herself, you're out of your depth. 'I was just passing and thought I'd drop in.'

'At eight o'clock at night?' His eyes went cold. 'No one just passes this part of town at night unless they have a specific reason. Why don't you just tell me the reason, Joanie?'

'It's nothing,' she said, reaching for her coat. 'Nothing at all.'

'I think it is.'

'I have to go . . .'

'Oh, sit down again, Joanie, and tell me all about it. You want to really, you just need persuading.' He leaned over the desk. 'What's on your mind?'

'Honestly, it's nothing.'

'Fine,' he said, turning away. 'You can see yourself out.'

Embarrassed, Joan struggled to her feet, putting the glass down on his desk. Collecting her coat and bag, she paused, incensed that he had turned his back on her and dismissed her. Who the hell did he think he was? she thought, enraged. He was a crook, everyone knew that. He should count himself lucky that she even talked to him. Everyone knew what Robin Wells was, and he thought he could treat *her* like a rubbing rag. In that instant Joan's petulant temper turned into fury. She had had enough of people taking her for granted. It was time to settle the score, once and for all.

'It's about your mistress.'

Slowly he turned, Joan catching the look on his face and regretting that she had ever opened her mouth.

'What about Katherine?'

'It's nothing . . .'

'Spit it out!' he barked. 'You came here to tell me something, so fucking tell me. Don't piss about pretending you're finding it hard going; just tell me.'

Cowed, Joan found herself stepping back, almost as though she expected him to hit her.

'Her brother died . . .'

'I know that!' Wells snapped, his survival instincts aroused. There was something in the air that he could sense, something that was threatening to him. 'What else?'

Joan was shaking. 'He drowned at the Albert Edward . . .'

'Yes. So?'

She wanted to run, but couldn't. She was suddenly aware of Robin Wells as others saw him – someone terrifying and dangerous. Someone to avoid. And yet she had come to expose the Watchman's Daughter. To assuage her own bitterness by betraying Kat Shaw . . .

And suddenly she couldn't do it. 'I have to go . . .'

Wells was round the desk immediately, blocking her exit. 'You can go when you tell me why you came, Joanie. Tell me,' he said, his tone changing, suddenly soothing. 'We're old friends. And old friends share secrets. It *is* a secret, isn't it? Some secret you want me to know about?'

She nodded, dumbstruck.

'I like secrets, you know, always have,' he went on, eerily composed. 'I like having secrets, but I particularly like having other people's secrets. You can play with a secret, Joan, did you know that? It's not what people have, it's what they *hide* that matters.' He smiled, the expression false. 'So what is this secret you want to tell me about Katherine?'

'I was wrong, it was nothing,' Joan blundered, trying to smile. 'I was wrong . . .'

'Well you know something. I think you're having second thoughts. And that's OK,' he went on reasonably. 'Everyone has second thoughts at some time in their life. Even me. But the difference here is you're buggering me about and I don't like that.'

Backing further away, Joan began to stammer. 'I . . . I . . . wasn't . . .'

'What *is* it about Katherine?'

'Nothing . . . It's nothing . . .'

'Tell me!'

'Her brother isn't dead.'

For a long moment they looked at each other, Wells finally returning to his chair and sitting down. Waving his hand, he motioned for Joan to do likewise, and then leaned across his desk towards her.

'Micky Shaw isn't dead?'

'No.'

'But they found his body.'

'It wasn't him,' Joan replied, transfixed into talking, desperate to make a friend out of this frightening man. 'Micky Shaw is still alive.'

'How d'you know that?'

'He's hiding in one of the deserted warehouses down in the Albert Edward dock,' she went on, struggling to keep her voice steady. 'I don't know how long he's been there.'

'Who hid him?'

'I don't know.'

'*Who hid him!*'

Joan could hardly speak, she was so afraid. 'I don't know!'

'You do. You saw someone with him, didn't you?' Wells went on, his tone warning. 'You followed someone – that's how you found Micky Shaw hiding, isn't it? You were following someone.'

'I didn't follow anyone!'

'You are a bad liar,' he said quietly. 'A very bad liar, Joanie. *Who did you follow?*'

She was close to tears, guilt and fear making her almost incoherent. 'I didn't mean to . . .'

'I think you did. I think you meant to follow this person and it came as a bonus when you found out what else was going on.' He paused, looked at his hands and then sighed. 'You followed *Katherine*, didn't you? It was Katherine, wasn't it?'

Christ, Joan thought, what had she done? *What had she done?*

'I don't know who it was!'

'Yes you do.'

'I'm not sure.'

'You're sure,' he said, his tone ice. 'You have to tell me now exactly what you saw.'

'I . . . I . . .'

'Take your time, Joanie, relax. Just tell me.'

'I . . . I was following her from the town. I don't know why, I just wanted to catch her out. I thought she might have a lover.' Joan paused, aware of the terrible events she was setting in motion, and yet desperate to somehow turn his anger away from her, on to someone else. 'She went to the docks and I watched her, then I followed her into the warehouse . . .'

Wells kept silent, listening.

'Then I saw her. Only she wasn't meeting anyone. Not a lover, I mean. She was visiting her brother.'

'You're sure it was him?'

'I saw him, Micky Shaw! They sat on the platform in the warehouse. She was talking to him, telling him: *We've fooled everyone. Pulled it off . . .*'

Wells could feel a vein begin to pulse at his left temple. 'She said that? *We've fooled everyone?*'

Eagerly, Joan nodded. 'Yes, yes, she said just that. Then she said, *You can relax now. You'll be away from here soon.*'

The vein kept throbbing in Wells's temple, his vision going in and out of focus. He had been betrayed. By the woman he loved. And Jesus, she *knew* he loved her; he had told her. Had made himself vulnerable, and she had played on it. Played him for a fool. *We've fooled everyone* . . . Everyone: the town, the police, and him, Robin Wells. The hard man, her lover. The man everyone feared – except Katherine. She had outwitted him, outsmarted him . . . He should, Wells thought through the haze of his anger, be impressed. But he wasn't. He felt only a creeping sense of déjà vu. The woman he loved had betrayed him. And worse, she had lied to him. Lain in his arms, in his bed, and lied to him. Asked him for a favour! Jesus, *a favour!* Wells thought, his head hammering with pain. She had known that she owned him. Oh, he might have tried to disguise the hold she had over him, but they both knew how powerful it was. He would have died for her.

And what had she done with the knowledge? Cheated him, fooled him, done what no man had ever done – made him look small. Staggering to his feet, Wells leaned against the desk. He hated the Shaw family, hated every member of it. Hated the drunk father, the mewling mother, the dumb brother, the cripple-handed Silky – and above all, he now hated Katherine Shaw. He hated her with an intensity that made his blood thick; he hated her with the force of humiliation and rejected love. He hated her as only a man can hate a woman who has played him for a fool.

'Get out,' he said suddenly, turning to Joan. 'Get out of here!'

She flinched, seeing the intensity of his rage, and terrified of what she had done. 'I could—'

'Get out! You've done what you set out to do. Now get out of here,' he said, slumping back into his chair and then slowly glancing back to her, his expression bewildered. 'What was it for?'

'What . . . what d'you mean?'

'What did you do it for?' His voice rose. 'What did you get out of it, bitch?'

She stepped back again, closer to the door, anxious to escape. 'I don't know why I did it . . .'

'Oh, you know. People like us, we know why we do everything.'

'I'm not like you!'

He smiled mirthlessly. 'You weren't like me this morning. But now you are . . . You're rotten, Joanie, and you can't even begin to understand what you've done.'

Wincing, she stammered, 'I didn't mean it . . .'

'You *did* mean it!' he thundered, then let his voice drop, his tone sinister. 'Take some advice from an old friend about how the game is played. What you have to do now is enjoy it, Joanie. That's the pay-off for people like us. We get to watch the fallout we've created.' His voice followed her as she backed away. 'You can sit and watch what you did, Joanie. Take full responsibility. And remember – whatever happens now, it's because of you.'

FORTY-ONE

Hearing the frantic knocking, Ivy opened the front door. Surprised to see Joan Fairchild, she smiled, and then paused, realising that this was no social visit.

'I have to see Andrew!' Joan blurted out, hurrying past Ivy into the hallway. 'I have to see him!'

'He's not here,' Ivy replied, astonished. 'What on earth is the matter?'

Ignoring her, Joan paced the hall. 'I've done something terrible. Something terrible . . .'

'Perhaps Andrew can ring you when he gets in?'

Spinning round, Joan turned on her. 'I have to wait for him!' she replied, distracted.

'Does your mother know you're here?' Ivy asked suddenly, suspecting some kind of plot on the part of Gwen Fairchild.

'No, she doesn't! Why should she?' Joan replied, unnerved. 'No one knows. And you mustn't tell her. You mustn't tell my parents what I've done!'

'I don't know what you *have* done,' Ivy replied, relaxing as she heard the sound of Andrew's car drawing up outside. 'Ah, that's him now. You can explain it all to my son.'

Without allowing Ivy to utter a word, Joan caught hold of Andrew's arm as soon as he walked in the door. Surprised, he looked at her, still stung from their last meeting. And then he noticed the dishevelled hair and the scared expression in her eyes. The memory of their old friendship stirred inside him and made him concerned for her.

'Joan, are you all right? You look scared out of your wits.'

She had hoped for some tenderness from him for so long, and now here it was. An echo of the camaraderie they had once enjoyed. But it wouldn't last, Joan realised; when she told him what she had done, he would never look at her again with anything other than revulsion.

'I've done something terrible . . .'

Irritated, Ivy raised her eyebrows. 'I think you'd better take Joan into the study and calm her down.'

Guiding her into the other room, Andrew closed the door behind them, Joan walking up and down restlessly.

'What's happened?'

'I went to see Robin Wells.'

He flinched at the name. 'I didn't even realise you knew him. God, are you all right? Has he done anything?'

'No, no, it's not like that!' Joan reassured him, avoiding his gaze and then hurrying on. 'I've done something I'm ashamed of, Andrew, so ashamed . . . I was so jealous of you and Katherine Shaw. I wanted you to love me, Andrew. You know how I feel about you . . .'

He was experiencing the slow coldness of unease. 'What have you done?'

'I didn't mean to—'

'What is it, Joanie?' he asked, trying to sound calm. 'You have to tell me what you've done.'

'I went to see Wells a little while ago and he was beside himself. He was so angry, so frightening . . .'

'Why?' Andrew asked, trying to make sense of what she was saying. 'Why did you go and see him? Do you know him?'

'I've known him for a while.'

Surprised, Andrew shook his head. 'But why did you go and see him?'

'I wanted to get my own back.'

'On who?' Andrew asked, knowing instinctively and dreading Joan's reply.

'I was so jealous of her . . .'

'*Kat?* You told Wells something about Kat?' He moved towards her, trying not to lose control. 'Joan, what did you tell him?'

'That her brother isn't dead. He's alive,' she said, nodding, trying to get her point across. 'Micky Shaw is alive. They faked his death, Andrew, fooled everyone . . . I saw the Watchman's Daughter visit him. I followed her to a warehouse on the docks. Micky Shaw isn't dead; he was hiding all the time.'

'What?' Andrew asked, his tone even, fighting panic. 'You told Wells that Micky Shaw wasn't dead? You told him that you saw Kat visit him? *You told Robin Wells where the lad he wanted to kill was hiding?* That Kat had lied to him?' He caught hold of Joan's arms, shaking her. 'You bloody idiot! Do you realise what you've done? You could have killed them both!'

'I didn't think!' Joan screamed, terrified and ashamed. 'I didn't think he would be so angry.'

'What did you think he would do?' Andrew snapped. 'Reward you? Pat you on the head?'

'I just—'

'You're insane.'

'I didn't think—'

He cut her off. 'When did you see Wells?'

'Just now,' Joan said, her voice trembling. 'About an hour ago.'

Turning on his heel, Andrew made for the door, Joan running after him, Ivy coming down the stairs and watching, dumbfounded. Opening the front door, Andrew turned to his mother and then pointed at Joan.

'Keep her here.'

'*What!*'

'Keep her here. I don't want her tipping Robin Wells off.'

'I wouldn't do that!' Joan said helplessly. 'I wouldn't do that!'

'I don't know what you'd do any more,' Andrew replied coldly. 'I don't know *you* any more.'

Rhythmically squeezing the tube he had made for his right hand, Silky sat in the chair in the tattoo parlour, staring at the newly replastered walls. And waiting. After their brief phone conversation, Kat had called her uncle back a moment later and reassured him that she was all right. Wells *hadn't* come home, the footsteps hadn't been his.

'Thank God for that. Now get out of there,' Silky had told her.

'I will. I'm getting the money together and I'm going to the dock to see Micky. Can we move him tonight?'

Silky had nodded over the phone. 'I've got him on a boat. Not the ferry to Ireland, Kat, that's not going to leave until the morning. But I've got him hidden away on a Swedish ship. He can get on the ferry tomorrow.'

'Can you trust the captain?'

'I saved his skin once,' Silky had replied. 'I can trust him.'

'I'm going to make my way over to the Albert Edward as soon as I've got the money and some things together.'

'Kat, are you *sure* you're not just panicking? Rushing into this? You've no evidence. Why would Wells be on to you?'

'It's just a feeling. A hunch, Silky. He's been suspecting me for a while,' she had replied, walking into the bathroom and pulling off the side of the bath. 'He's suspicious . . . I don't know anything for sure, just that I'm frightened. For myself, and most of all for Micky.'

'That's good enough for me,' Silky had replied, alarmed. 'I'll meet you at the dock.'

'At nine,' Kat had said, keeping her voice calm. 'At nine o'clock. Be there.'

Silky kept staring at the wall. In another few minutes he would leave for the dock, but for a moment he just wanted to wait, be calm, shore up his energy. The old photographs had perished in the fire, but he had hung his blackboard up with the prices listed. By the end of the week – with a new apprentice starting work – Silky Shaw would be back in business. He sighed as he kept up his exercises. He had made some real progress; the doctors who had written off his hand were now surprised by the advances he had made. Oh, he couldn't use his right hand properly, but in time he would make it workable again . . . Sighing, he kept up the exercise, his mind going back to Queenie and the time they had first got together. So many years ago, when she had been Robin Wells's girlfriend, when Wells had been just a roughneck, not a ruthless bastard. When Silky had been cocky and full of himself . . . They had had a good time together, for eighteen months. Not that either of them thought it would last for ever. And Silky had been flattered, not triumphant over Robin Wells, just happy Queenie had chosen him. But Wells hadn't seen it that way, and the grudge he had borne Silky had festered, expanding year by year into the overwhelming feud that now threatened to consume them both.

One two, one two, Silky kept up his exercises, forcing his hand to move, to work. He was strong again now, strong enough to take on Wells. He squeezed the tube grimly, controlling his breathing and his fury. All they had to do was get Micky hidden away for the night and then put him on the ferry in the morning. Silky had already phoned Queenie, to let her know that his nephew would be arriving early. Tomorrow Micky would be safe.

Silky thought back to the time his nephew had first come to work at the tattoo parlour. He had been teased about his youth, his gangling looks and his handicap, ribbed about losing his virginity. It had been a slow process, but gradually Micky had adapted, his skill winning the hard men over . . . Silky thought of Kat then, of the way she always talked about her brother. Micky was going to be a painter, she said over and over again; one day he would be a respected painter. Well why not? Silky thought. When he was safe in

Ireland, he would have some time on his hands, opportunity to get back to his arty stuff. Queenie might have a bed and breakfast to run, but she was a soft enough touch, and easy to get along with. He suddenly imagined Micky drawing a sketch of his ex-girlfriend, and Queenie putting it up on view in the guesthouse. But most of all Silky relished the prospect of getting Micky away from Preston, out of the clutches of Wells. They had been lucky there – Ivan really coming up trumps. But luck, Silky knew only too well, didn't last indefinitely. And apparently it was running out fast.

Sighing again, he relaxed his right hand and looked at the clock, then heard a quick rapping on the window. Surprised, he glanced at the visitor, opening the door when he realised it was Andrew Pitt.

He knew at once that something was wrong. 'What is it?'

'Wells knows about Micky.'

'What!' Silky exclaimed. 'How?'

'That doesn't matter. All that matters is that he knows Micky is still alive, hiding at the Albert Edward – and that Kat deceived him.'

'Jesus,' Silky said, reaching for his coat. 'She was right.'

'What?'

'Kat – she suspected Wells was on to her.' Silky moved to the door.

Andrew followed, his voice reproachful. 'Why didn't you tell me about Micky? Why didn't you tell me he was still alive?'

'Why would I?' Silky asked, pulling the door closed and locking it hurriedly. 'The fewer people that knew, the safer my nephew was.'

'But he isn't safe *now*, is he? And neither is Kat if Wells finds her.' Quickly, Andrew pointed across the road. 'I've got the car, we can drive to the docks.'

Hurriedly they climbed in, Silky pulling his coat around him, Andrew grinding the gears as he pulled away from the kerb. 'Where is Micky hiding?'

'In the old warehouse that's been closed up for ages. The place where Billy died.'

Staring fixedly ahead as he drove, Andrew swore when it started to rain, turning on the windscreen wipers. 'Does Kat go there every night to see him?'

'No, not every night.'

There was sudden hope in Andrew's voice. 'So she might not be there tonight?'

'Oh, she'll be there,' Silky replied, fighting unease. 'Doesn't this car go any faster?'

'I'm going as fast as I can! Why are you so sure she will be there tonight?'

'Because I'm due to meet her there. Because we're bringing things forward. Micky was supposed to be moved at the end of the week, but Kat got spooked, so now we're hiding him on a Swedish boat overnight until he can get the ferry in the morning.'

Andrew's voice was uneasy. 'So she'll definitely be there?'

He nodded. 'She's taking him some money and a ferry ticket.'

'To the warehouse?'

'Where else?'

Andrew's voice faltered. 'And Wells knows about the warehouse.'

Impatiently, he pressed his foot down on the accelerator, urging the car to go faster as they left Preston town centre and headed for the outskirts and the dark reaches of the Albert Edward beyond.

Kat watched her brother eat, smiling when he looked up at her. She had explained everything to him in detail, preparing him, reassuring him that they could trust the Swedish captain and that he would be on the ferry the following day. Surprised, he had signed back, asking her why they had brought the timing forward, and she had told him that it was just to be safe. To be extra careful . . . He wasn't fooled for an instant. He was frightened, but damned if he was going to show it. Having made him repeat her instructions twice, Kat leaned back against the wall, looking round. For too long the warehouse had been her brother's hiding place; for too long she had sneaked in and out, praying no one would see her. Admittedly it had been easier after everyone believed Micky was dead; in fact Kat had even let her guard down a little, but soon it would all be over. Micky would be in Ireland and Kat could relax. No longer having to watch what she said, avoiding any word or intimation that could betray her to Wells . . . She shuddered at the prospect of being found out and then calmed herself. It was nearly over; before long her brother would be out of the country.

'Have you got your ticket and the money safe?' she asked.

Micky smiled and signed back to her: *You keep asking me that.*

'I just want everything to go perfectly,' Kat replied, glancing over to the cloth bag Micky had packed full of his possessions. 'You know which quay the Swedish boat is at?'

He nodded patiently.

'Don't attract attention. Pull the cap down over your forehead and don't make eye contact.' She paused, her hands shaking. 'Just hand the captain your ticket and do what he says. He'll hide you tonight and then get you over to the ferry in the morning. He's a friend of Silky's. You can trust him. When you get to Ireland, Queenie will meet you at the dockside. Get her to telephone me as soon as you can to let me know you're safe.'

I will. You keep telling me all this.

'You *will* get Queenie to phone me, won't you?' Kat asked him suddenly. 'And when you're safe in Ireland you can write to me. Don't go off and forget me, will you?'

He took her hands, feeling how cold they were, and rubbed them gently. *How could I forget you?*

'And keep drawing and painting, Micky. You'll make your fortune one day.'

Thank you.

'For what?'

For everything . . . I'm sorry, all this was my fault.

'It wasn't your fault, Micky,' she said hurriedly, trying to reassure him. 'You did what you thought was right. You were protecting me, I know that.'

Keep away from Wells, won't you?

She smiled, fighting emotion. 'I will.'

He's dangerous.

'I know,' she replied quietly. 'Micky, remember how much I love you. Remember you're my brother and remember all the good times we had together, before all this happened. Don't look back and judge Dad too harshly, or worry about the family. I can look after them. And don't worry about me either . . . I always get through. Remember that, Micky: I always survive.'

A sudden noise outside startled them both, Kat blowing out the lamp and listening. Footsteps sounded, then voices, then fists banging on the door, followed by silence. Scared, Micky clung on to her hand, Kat motioning for him to move to the back of the platform and hide behind the boxes whilst she slid to the edge and looked down. The warehouse was deserted below, but she could hear voices coming from outside and the sound of someone rattling the lock. Please God, she thought, let it be their father, drunk on one of his binges, or Ivan, come looking for her.

But she knew it wasn't. Knew it was no one benign. Knew that in these final hours – on the last day before Micky fled England – they were on the verge of being discovered.

And there was nothing she could do about it.

Behind me I could hear Micky's breathing, quick and shallow, and wondered if I should run out of the warehouse to try and draw their attention away from him. But I knew that would be a futile gesture. If they had found the warehouse, they had found us. No one had any reason to come to that place. Why would they, unless they had been tipped off? Unless they knew we were there.

I remember the sensation of panic, of despair, of frustration. We had been so careful for so long; to be found out then – just as we planned to move Micky – was unbearable. And then I wondered how anyone had *found out. To all intents and purposes Micky was dead. No one looks for a dead man. Unless they knew he was still alive – and who knew that? Only myself, Silky and Ivan.*

I regret to say now that for a moment I suspected my uncle, then immediately felt ashamed. No, Ivan wasn't the one who had betrayed us. Someone else had . . . Sitting on that platform, waiting, I stared down into the darkness and remembered Billy, and thought of my father, regretting the pain I had caused him by faking Micky's death . . . Then the banging started again. A slow, rhythmic sound like someone beating a war drum, with that incessant, deadly repetition. And I knew then that it was over. That we were no longer safe. That luck – capricious and vicious by turns – had deserted us.

Did I know who was outside? Of course I did. I knew it without hearing his voice, or seeing his face. I knew it because the atmosphere was thick with his bitterness; the night heavy with the sourness of a person without conscience or empathy. I knew it as a goat senses a mountain lion, or a moth the dark, clawed wings of a bat. I knew it in the way a vole knows a cat is near, or a fish seeks cover at the shadow of a hawk.

There were only inches between us, the thickness of a door. And I swear he was so close, I could feel the heat coming off his skin.

FORTY-TWO

Andrew stopped the car by the dock gates and got out. The rain was still falling. Silky moved over to him, both men staring into the pungent darkness. There were no sounds, no noises, only the rain beating on the water and the restless lapping of the late tide.

'You think Wells will come here?'

Silky nodded. 'Of course he will! I think he might already be here. He won't have waited, once he knew Kat had lied to him. He'd have to come after her. He'd want to find Micky and Kat together – and catch both of them out.'

Andrew felt the hairs stand up on the back of his neck. 'Would he hurt her?'

'What d'you think?'

'We have to get to her!'

'Wait,' Silky warned him. 'He won't come alone. The only chance we have is to surprise him.'

'He had a head start on us.'

'Only if he left straight away,' Silky replied, looking round cautiously. Beckoning for Andrew to follow him, he moved into the shadows, edging his way towards the far side of the dock and the lumbering hulks of the warehouses. In the distance there was a dim light coming from the hut, but otherwise the dockside was in darkness.

Urgently Silky tapped Andrew on the shoulder. 'Follow me and stay close.' Then he moved forward towards the gap between the quayside and the warehouses. He knew that if they were going to be seen, it would be in these few yards when they were exposed, without cover. Checking Andrew was behind him, he began to run, fast and silently, Andrew following, both of them making for the shadow of the warehouses.

Once there, Silky leaned against a wall. Andrew was breathing heavily. 'You're out of condition.'

'And you're fit,' Andrew replied, keeping his voice low. 'D'you know where we are?'

' 'Course I do. Micky's in the warehouse at the end of the final row. Must be three hundred yards from here.' He looked round, his eyes accustomed to the dim light. 'I can't see anyone. Not even a car.'

'There's a light over there.'

'That's the watchman's hut.'

A few moments passed, both men walking quietly towards the bank of warehouses. Suddenly Andrew tensed. 'Can you hear that?'

'What?'

'Over there,' Andrew went on. 'Jesus, look, in the distance. Isn't that a light?'

Far off there was a flicker of illumination, like torchlight, followed by the sound of banging. As if someone was thumping a wall, or the door of a building; a fretful, peevish child slamming their fists against the side of a cot. Only the sound wasn't petulant, it was threatening, the noise echoing around the still night. The rain still falling, Silky began to run again, Andrew following as they crisscrossed the webbing of warehouses, heading towards Micky's hiding place. Breathing heavily, Andrew watched Silky with surprise. He was agile, much more athletic than he looked, and very fast on his feet. Just managing to keep up, Andrew saw Silky suddenly put up his hand, both men keeping to the shadow of the warehouse, where they stopped.

'Can you see?'

'What?' Andrew replied, staring ahead.

'There's two men over there. By the warehouse door.'

'Yes, yes, I see them now.'

Feeling him tense, Silky caught hold of Andrew's sleeve. 'This is no time for playing the hero.'

'Kat's in there!'

'But *they* aren't. Not yet,' Silky replied, 'and they don't know we're here. We have to go round the other way.'

'And meanwhile, what if they break in?'

'Have you another suggestion? You're no fighter, Andrew. You mean well but you wouldn't stand a chance. The only advantage we have is to take them by surprise.' Silky paused, thinking ahead. 'You go round the back, I'll come from the right.'

'And then what?'

'Then we have a fight on our hands.' He paused. 'Are you up for this?'

'Would I be here if I wasn't?'

Satisfied, Silky motioned Andrew to move in one direction, and then began walking towards the warehouse.

Running as silently as he could, Andrew came up to the back of the building and paused. The warehouse was vast, banking on to one side of the quay, the water only a couple of yards away from him. Hidden by shadow, he could feel the vibration of the knocking, and could imagine only too easily the terror that Kat would be feeling, knowing she was trapped and that Wells was coming for her. As for Micky, he would be beside himself, waiting for the door to burst open.

Come on, Andrew thought, come on, Silky . . . Straining for the sound of his companion's voice, or for any command, Andrew listened. Then, exasperated, he edged around the corner of the building and looked ahead. He could see a man trying to break down the warehouse door, and Wells standing beside him, his face expressionless. And then Andrew noticed a figure walking towards the warehouse. Sauntering, unconcerned, as though it was the most natural thing in the world to be out at night on the Albert Edward Dock, moving towards two violent men.

Silky . . .

'Jesus,' Andrew said under his breath. What the hell was he doing?

Wells was thinking the same thing. Slowly he pushed himself away from the side of the warehouse where he had been leaning and stared at the approaching figure. He felt two conflicting emotions in that instant – rage and amusement. Rage at having never managed to beat his rival, and amusement at Silky's nerve.

'Fucking hell, if it isn't the cavalry.'

Smiling, Silky approached him. 'I think you should go home.'

'Shall I carry on?' the narrow-faced man asked Wells, the latter giving him a bleak look.

'Christ, don't listen to him, you moron! Break the bloody lock!'

'Don't,' Silky said simply.

Andrew ducked back around the edge of the warehouse and moved along the parallel side, his hands laid flat against the wall, the impact of the banging and wrenching of the lock vibrating through his fingers. Momentarily unable to make out what Silky was saying, he inched along, finally reaching the far end. From there he had a view of the man breaking in – Wells's back was turned to him, and the other man was putting his shoulder to the door and trying to force it open.

'I said, don't do that. Go home,' Silky repeated. 'You don't want a fight.'

'*A fight?* With you? You one-handed mutt,' Wells said, his tone dismissive. 'You want to get out while you can and stop interfering in business that has nothing to do with you.'

'This *is* my business.'

'Oh, piss off home, Shaw!'

From his vantage point, Andrew could hear the exchange and wondered what to do next. He was unarmed, had never been a fighter – but was more than willing to prove himself. If only he knew what Silky was going to do. If only he had tipped him off.

But Silky was busy baiting Wells. 'You can't beat me.'

'Beat you! Look at yourself: you've got a limp and a wrecked hand. You *are* beaten, Shaw,' Wells replied, exasperated. 'And what's more, I've had more than enough of you and your bloody family.'

'So why are you here?'

'You know why.'

'And you think I'm going to let you get away with it?'

Amused, Wells looked round. 'I don't see police. I don't see the bloody troops.'

Slowly Andrew continued to edge along the side of the warehouse, looking around. But there was nothing he could use as a weapon. If Silky was playing for time by causing a distraction, Andrew was woefully unprepared to start an attack.

'Look, Shaw,' Wells went on, his back still to Andrew, 'if you turn round now and walk away, I'll let you go. We've had our differences in the past, but that was between me and you; this is something else. Although by rights I *should* knock your bloody head off. You knew about Micky, didn't you?'

Silky nodded. 'Yeah, I knew.'

'And so did Kat,' Wells replied, shrugging. 'She lied to me.'

'I'm glad.'

'I cared about her!' Wells retorted, stung. 'I really cared about her.'

'You blackmailed her into being your mistress; you ruined her reputation.'

'I gave her a home!'

'You gave her a bad name!' Silky retorted. 'And you never gave anyone anything that didn't profit you somehow.' He turned to Wells's companion. 'Step back from that door.'

The narrow-faced man obeyed.

Wells was incensed. 'The hell you will! Get it open.'

'I said step back!'

And then the narrow-faced man turned suddenly, and caught sight of Andrew approaching him. Acting from instinct, the man ducked, Andrew throwing a punch and missing. In the same instant, Wells wrenched the warehouse door open, but before he could enter, Silky knocked him out of the way.

'Kat! Micky!' he shouted, hearing their footsteps coming down from the platform. 'Get out of here! Run!'

Being the bigger man, Andrew had overpowered Wells's accomplice and was just turning to see Kat emerge from the warehouse when Wells hit him with a heavy piece of timber. Pain exploded in Andrew's head, and he lost consciousness, plummeting forward, his vision blurring as he slid to his knees. Then he fell, a dead weight, on to the dockside.

Micky glanced over to his sister, watching as Kat lifted the piece of wood Wells had dropped and began to walk towards him. Her eyes were unreadable, without feeling, her lover watching her.

'What are you going to do now, Katherine?' he said, almost exasperated. 'Put the wood down.'

Unblinking, she kept walking towards him, Wells smiling and backing away, towards the edge of the quayside. He was laughing, amused.

'Put the wood down, Katherine.'

Ignoring him, Kat kept walking.

'Come on, girl, you didn't think I was going to hurt *you*, did you? I care about you. But you should have told me about your brother. You should have trusted me.'

'Would you have helped him?'

'Sure I would,' Wells lied, still backing up. 'But you have to see that any man would feel a bit angry to be lied to. Now give me that.' He lurched forward suddenly, grabbing Kat's arm and trying to pull the wood out of her hand. They struggled, but although Wells was much bigger and heavier, he lost his balance and tripped backwards, putting up his hands in mock submission. 'OK, OK, just put the fucking wood down. We can talk.'

Still holding the wood but backing up to keep some distance between them, Kat shook her head.

'We could never talk. You talked, I listened. You told me what to do. I did it. I had no choice in any of it, Wells, and you know that. You had me because we made a deal – my family's safety in return for being your mistress. It was a business deal, no more than that.'

He looked at her oddly, a brief exchange between them. In that instant Kat remembered their relationship, their lovemaking – and their one, tiny moment of connection.

'Katherine, you know as well as I do there was more to it than that.'

'Never!'

He shrugged, reverting to type, malice marking his face and voice.

'Whatever you say, Katherine. But you didn't trust me. You lied to me about your brother.'

'You would have let Micky go if you'd known he was still alive?'

'Sure.'

'No you wouldn't,' she said, her voice cold.

He sighed expansively, still not taking her seriously.

'Look, if you want to hit me, hit me. Just get it over with. You want to hit me, fine.'

'But I *don't* want to hit you,' Kat replied. 'I want to kill you.'

And then Silky made his move. He came from behind Kat and grabbed the wood out of her hands.

'No,' he said. 'Not on your conscience. On mine.'

Slowly, he advanced on Wells. Now afraid, Wells backed away from his old rival. He was in trouble and he knew it. His hands raised, he watched Silky's approach and continued to retreat, finally coming to the edge of the quayside and realising he had nowhere left to go. Panicked, he felt his heels go over the rim of the dock, and struggled to keep his footing. He could hear the water lapping below and smell the acrid ozone of the Ribble tide.

'Now,' Silky said coldly. 'Step back.'

'*What?*' Wells croaked.

'Step back.'

'Are you mad!' Wells turned to Kat, his voice imploring her. 'For God's sake, help me!'

'Step back . . .' Silky repeated.

'I can't swim! I'll drown!'

'God, I hope so.'

And then Wells lost his footing, his arms flailing as he fell backwards, his head striking the side of the stone quayside steps. Slowly he slid under the water, unconscious.

Kat ran over to the dockside and looked down. She could see bubbles rising and wanted to turn away, but couldn't. Mesmerised, she picked her way down the steps, not knowing if she was trying to save Wells or simply watch him die. For an instant she lost sight of him. And then, as she reached the bottom of the steps, she saw his face reappear under the water, his eyes open and staring as his weight dragged him down, under the depth of the unfeeling tide.

FORTY-THREE

Dabbing at the blood with a cloth, Kat sat beside Andrew, who was nursing a deep cut on the back of his head. Beside them, Silky was banking up the fire in the back room of the tattoo parlour. He was remote, silent. A few minutes later Micky walked in, clean-shaven, dressed in some of his uncle's clothes. Smiling, Kat looked up at him, but no one spoke, and Micky walked on out into the back yard to have a quiet smoke. The horror of the evening had made its mark on everyone. As for Andrew, he had put up a good fight, but when he came round Wells had gone, Silky standing at the edge of the dock, looking into the water. When Andrew asked Kat what had happened, Silky interrupted and said simply that Wells had drowned. Andrew knew better than to press him. He realised that what Kat had said so long ago was true – he was no street fighter. But Silky was.

It had taken Silky Shaw many years to get even with Robin Wells, but in the end he had had succeeded in the most conclusive way possible. The fact that Andrew didn't know exactly how Wells had died was oddly irrelevant. And nor did he really care. Wells was dead and Kat was safe. To his amazement, Andrew realised that that was all that really mattered to him.

Kat rinsed the cloth in a bowl of water. Transfixed, she watched the clear liquid turn to crimson, an image of Wells flashing into her mind. His narrow-faced accomplice had fled as soon as the fight started, Wells striking out at Andrew ferociously. She could hear the sound of the wood against his skull and winced, then remembered the burning heat that had flared up inside her. The hatred she had felt for Wells had intensified at that moment into blinding, unstoppable rage. And she knew – *knew for certain* – that she would have killed him if she had had the chance . . . Slowly she wrung out the bloodied cloth, her hands shaking. What had she become? she wondered, incredulous. Not just a mistress and a whore, but a killer? Was *that* what Robin Wells had done to her?

And in the same moment she realised something else about herself. That she had had no fear. That all she had cared about was protecting the man she loved. Yes, she would have swung the piece of wood. Yes, she would have heard the same sickening thud as it had struck Wells's head. And yes, she would have seen him dead, if, by killing one evil man, she could have saved a good one.

Slowly Kat looked up, glancing over to Silky. Thank you, she thought, her heart filling. Thank you for taking that weapon from me, for taking the responsibility of Wells's death. *Not on your conscience. On mine.* Because Kat knew that although she would have been able to live with her crime, it would have cost her dearly. She was tired of hiding her feelings and of lying. She had no wish to deceive Andrew. Duping Robin Wells was one thing, but not Andrew Pitt. Yet he would never know what had really happened at the Albert Edward. He would never know that between herself and her uncle, they had caused Robin Wells's death. Some knowledge cannot be shared, Kat thought, resigned. Even with the person you love the most dearly. *Because* you love them the most dearly.

Kat realised something else then – that she would never be free of her past. Even with the death of Robin Wells, she was locked into her reputation. The scandal of being the Watchman's Daughter. People would never forget that she had been Wells's mistress. That she had been involved with her uncles' plotting. Involved in hiding her brother, and passing off a corpse as her own flesh and blood. She had overstepped so many boundaries – and even though it had been for the best of reasons, she was now beyond normal society and life. There might be escape for Micky, and revenge for Silky, but she was trapped.

Aware of her introspection, Andrew had been watching her curiously. He could sense her relief, but also her sadness. But what had happened that night had changed him too. He had seen, for the first time in his life, real evil. Had experienced fear and felt an overwhelming compulsion to fight for the person he loved. It was true, he *was* no real hero, no back-street fighter, but when he had gone with Silky to that dock, he had discovered something in himself that he had never suspected before – an ability to stand up and be counted.

Wincing as Kat continued to clean his wound, Andrew said quietly, 'Not much of a fighter, am I?'

'I wouldn't say that,' she replied. 'You did well. You went for it, and that's the important thing. You didn't hold back.'

'I thought I was going to lose you. I thought something was going to happen to you.'

'Something *would* have happened to me if you and Silky hadn't come along.'

Overhearing her, Silky nodded. 'No one must find out that Wells drowned. We have to let people think he left town. I'll put the word out that he went back to London. No one will miss him. Or spend much time looking for him. He had no friends. And the property he took from your father will revert back to you in time, Andrew. There were no papers signed, were there? So it's still legally the property of the Pitt family.'

'I don't want it,' Andrew said simply, catching Kat's eye and frowning when he saw her expression. 'What is it?'

'Nothing.'

'*What is it?*'

'I know why your late father handed that property over to Wells.'

'I've been trying to find that out for years . . . Why did he do it?'

'You won't like it.'

'Come on, Kat, tell me,' he urged her.

'When he was just starting out, your father defrauded someone. A man who later committed suicide. He made his money by cheating a man called Stanley Gorman . . .'

'Stanley Gorman?' Silky echoed behind them.

Kat turned, surprised. 'You knew him?'

'I knew of him. He had a daughter. When he died, she was left on her own, to fend for herself. In fact you knew her indirectly, Kat.'

'I knew her?'

'Missie Shepherd,' Silky said sadly. 'You remember how your father used to talk about her? That poor kid who was on the game. She used to walk the docks. Her mother died very young. Bit of a rough bird, used to sleep around. In fact everyone believed that Missie was actually Robin Wells's daughter.'

'Oh God,' Kat said, stunned.

'Not that he ever recognised her, or helped her out. Remember how Missie worked the Albert Edward? Well, after Stanley Gorman killed himself she had to – she had no money, no family, no home. Wells never admitted she was his kid.'

Kat shook her head. 'They never found out who killed her, did they? Dad used to say that she was murdered by one of her customers. It was Dad who found her body.'

'So my father was responsible for two deaths,' Andrew said coldly. 'Stanley Gorman and indirectly Missie Shepherd . . .'

Suddenly hearing the doorbell ring in the tattoo parlour, Silky walked out, Andrew turning back to Kat.

'I don't want anything to do with the business any more! I don't want to touch it.'

'But . . .'

'I'm going to start again, Kat – but not here. I'm going back to Australia. I've got contacts there, I can build up a business. I won't have much money, but I'll build a life, a good life. Are you game? We'll marry here, then go there as a couple.'

She stared at him, hardly able to answer. He was inviting her to join him. Her dream was finally coming true. All the times she had longed for him, and now he was here. All the times she had dreamed of going to Australia, and now she had the chance. He was asking her to go with him. To join him. *He still loved her*.

'Are you *sure* you want me to go with you?'

'I want you to marry me, Kat.'

She stared at him, then shook her head. 'I can't. I want to, but I can't.'

'Yes you can! No one will know us there. No memories of the past. No one will give a damn where we came from, what we've done. No curiosity, no judgement. You can be who you want to be, wipe the slate clean. We can go there – you and me – as a couple of nobodies out to make their fortune.'

Flinging her arms around him, she clung to him. 'I want to be a nobody! I want to start again. I want to go with you. I only ever wanted to be with you. I never loved anyone but you. I never stopped thinking about you, even when I believed I'd never see you again. But . . .'

Andrew frowned. 'What is it?'

'Can you *really* forget?'

'Forget what?'

'What I did. Who I was. Who I was with,' Kat replied, her tone urgent. 'Can you look me in the eye and honestly tell me you can forget? That it won't come between us? That some time in the future you won't look at me and wonder? That one day, away from Preston and these streets, you won't think of the docks and Robin Wells, and then look at me and hate me?'

Firmly he took her hands. 'I'll be honest with you, Kat, I can't promise much. I can't promise I'll make a fortune, buy you everything you ever wanted, cars, jewellery, furs . . .'

'I don't want those things! They mean nothing to me.'

He smiled. 'I can't even promise I won't get fat, or bald. I can't put my hand on my heart and say that sometime in the future you won't look at me and wonder what happened to that young man you once knew . . . But I *can* promise one thing – on my honour, on my life: that whilst I think, I will treasure you. Whilst I breathe, I will want you. And whilst I live, I will love you.'

They nearly put out the flags on Amber Street, Hover Terrace and Ratcliffe Row. Robin Wells had left Preston! News went round fast, woman to woman, door to door, man to man. In mills, docks, pubs, everyone gossiped. Wells had left the town and suddenly a weight had lifted from the Preston streets. Families who had bowed under the yoke of his increased rents cheered when they heard the news, his brothels and flop shops turned out by their neighbours. The depression that was threatening the whole country was still crushing, but the added pressure of Wells's viciousness had gone. His stranglehold over the community was over, and Silky knew that before long he would be relegated back to being a creature of fable, a bogeyman.

Before anyone could really celebrate, Kat knew that they had to sort out the problem of Micky's resurrection. And the inevitable questions about just who was buried in his place. Uneasy, she stood outside the door of the Amber Street house, wondering what to say. How *did* you explain a faked death? How could she possibly prepare her father for such a shock? How did a person excuse what would seem to be such cruelty? The news of the death, the funeral, the grief?

No one had ever considered what would happen if Wells died. The eventuality had been so remote that Kat had never thought beyond getting her brother to safety. She knew then that the police would become involved, and dreaded the investigation. How it would become common knowledge that she had hidden Micky to save him from Robin Wells. Her little brother, her shy, withdrawn little brother would become infamous overnight.

Taking a deep breath, Kat realised that putting off the inevitable was pointless and went round the back of the house, calling for Ma Shaw.

Wiping her hands on her apron, the old woman walked out, looking hard into her granddaughter's face.

'I 'eard about Wells. The bugger's moved on then? No one will be asking after him and missing him.'

'Yes, he's gone. Back to London, bigger fish.'

Ma Shaw studied her granddaughter, dropping her voice. 'Did Silky fix him?'

Kat nodded. 'Never say a word, but yes. Silky fixed him once and for all.'

'Good. That's good. I always knew he would do fer him one day.' She paused, noticing a sudden movement by the outdoor privy. 'Oh God, Jesus, it's our Micky! He's home!' Flinging her arms out, she grabbed hold of her grandson and hugged him tightly, Micky looking horrified at Kat over her shoulder. 'I never thought I'd see yer again.' She paused, fighting emotion and glancing at Kat. 'What about yer father? He'll have to be told before someone sees Micky and blabs.'

'I know,' Kat agreed. 'I just don't know *how* to tell him.'

'They'll be plenty of questions asked too.'

'I know that.'

'About you and Wells.'

'I know,' Kat said softly.

'People will understand, luv.'

'But will Dad understand about Micky? How do you tell a father that the son he thought was dead is really alive?'

'You don't,' a soft voice said behind them, Anna walking out of the back door. 'You've done enough, Kat, *more* than enough. I've already told your father all about it, and he understands.' She moved further into the yard, her voice wavering as she saw her son by the back gate. 'Is it you, Micky?' She moved towards him, touching his arm. 'I thought I'd lost you. Thought I'd never see you again. That you'd be spirited off and that would be it. But you came back.'

'And he's not going away again,' Kat said softly. 'We're a family, Mum. We're all safe. Things can be like they used to be.'

Anna nodded, squeezing her daughter's hand. 'Your dad's took it bad, Kat. All the gossip – and there'll be more to follow.'

'Is he at the Albert Edward?'

Anna nodded. 'He spends a lot of time down there. At the pubs. He's changed, Kat. He's given up. I can't get through to him.'

Then she turned back to Micky, touching his hand, his arm. Touching a ghost made flesh. Reaching out for the child she had believed lost, and who had been returned to her.

For the second time, Ivan Lomax was in the newspaper, on the first page. Not bad, he thought, almost worth being investigated by the police, even though they had given him a hard time. Questions were asked over and over again. Why had he passed off another man's corpse as his nephew? Who had helped him? *Who was the stranger*? When Ivan couldn't tell them, the police talked about having the body exhumed, and searched the Missing notices for that period to see if they could find anyone of a similar description. But the unknown person had not been missed, or reported, and after giving the matter more consideration, it was decided that they would leave the corpse undisturbed, but change the headstone so that it no longer read MICKY SHAW.

The attention had made Ivan nervous at first, and he had

only built up his courage when Kat arrived and told the police that it had been *her* idea to pass off the unknown body as her brother. Of course Ivan couldn't let her take the blame, and insisted it had been *his* plan and that he had deliberately and wrongly identified the corpse. Then Silky arrived and told the police that it had been *his* idea. The only point on which they all agreed was that Robin Wells had been after Micky Shaw and that they had had to fake the boy's death to protect him. The police knew enough about Wells's reputation to realise they were telling the truth, and had heard about the Watchman's Daughter becoming his mistress. They had also heard about the stranglehold Wells had had over the whole Shaw family and accepted the explanation of the faked death.

Of course, they could have proceeded with the matter if they had wished, but the Depression was on and the police were glad to be rid of a mobster. A man who had even managed to exert some influence within their ranks. A few half-hearted attempts were made to trace Wells, and he was put on a Missing Persons list, but then word came that he was in London. A letter apparently from Wells himself. Closing the file, the police took Wells off the Missing list and breathed a sigh of relief that he had moved on.

But then there was still the question of the body that had been buried. And the headstone. And the mock funeral . . . They could, if the police had chosen to, have charged the Shaws. But although a crime had been committed, the Shaws were a local family, and no one had ever been an apologist for Wells. Besides, the police suspected that the long-running feud between Silky and Wells had come down to a fight – and that Silky had run Wells out of the county. So, excused if not absolved, Ivan, Silky and Kat appeared in the paper again, alongside a photograph of Micky Shaw. The *resurrected* Micky Shaw. The local hero.

Having been hidden away for so long, Micky was uncertain about the attention and hesitant about his notoriety, insisting that he was going to stay in Preston now and work for his uncle again at the tattoo parlour . . .

'You look grand,' Mary said suddenly, cutting into Ivan's thoughts. She was impressed by him and relieved to have her belief in Kat vindicated. You see! she told everyone. Kat only went with Robin Wells to protect Micky and her family . . . Smiling, Mary looked at the newspaper photograph again. If she was honest, she had to admit that Ivan wasn't handsome, but he *was* very brave. After all, how many men would do something so amazing? Wasn't he a hero, a real honest-to-God hero? *Her hero*. And it would be lovely to have her own home now that her uncle Horace was safe at The Horse and Cart.

'We should frame your photograph.'

Ivan flushed. 'I don't think . . .'

'Oh, but we should!' Mary went on, teasing him. 'All the girls will be after you now, Ivan.'

He was suddenly unnerved. 'I don't want all the girls! I only want one.'

'But you could have your pick of the town.'

He hugged her to him, uncharacteristically impulsive. 'I've *got* the pick of the town, Mary. And I want to keep yer . . .' He coughed nervously, then rushed on. 'Will yer marry me?'

'Oh, Ivan,' she said simply. 'When?'

Preoccupied with his own thoughts, Silky glanced through the door into the tattoo parlour beyond. He could see Micky leaning over a customer, preparing the inks for a tattoo. Only a week, Silky thought, and everything was back to normal. *Better* than normal, notoriety bringing in custom. The hard men liked to come and talk about Robin Wells, Micky's close escape, and the faked death, which had become a local legend. One or two – old acquaintances of Silky's – wondered why Wells had left so suddenly, but no one pursued it. No one dared. The feud between Silky Shaw and Robin Wells had been long and vicious, but it was now resolved. Silky was back to work in his restored shop, and Wells was apparently back in London. If they suspected that there had been foul play, they never voiced their thoughts – just developed an even healthier respect for Silky. The man some had written off had triumphed.

Silky smiled to himself, still thinking. It was strange, but no one asked the obvious question. No one wondered whether Robin Wells would return. It was just accepted, with relief, that he had moved on. A myth that was perpetuated by Silky's contacts. A month after the letter purporting to be from Wells in London came news that he was trying his luck in the USA, working in the gambling city of Las Vegas. Typical, people said, best bloody place for him.

But in reality Robin Wells was deep at the bottom of the River Ribble. Anchor chains and water currents had stripped him of his expensive clothes, his wallet falling into a silt pocket, the money soggy with mud. Naked and bloated, he rotted under the waves. Out of sight, out of mind. Not mourned, not missed. His eyes remained open, becoming milky, looking upwards to the dark north-western sky. And slowly, very slowly, the tide nudged his body out of the dock and gas filled up his stomach and intestines, making him buoyant.

Whilst everyone else in Preston got on with their lives, Robin Wells was chivvied and hustled along the river bed, travelling the length of the Albert Edward and heading towards the far end of the quay. And as his body decomposed, he began – slowly and inexorably – to rise.

FORTY-FOUR

It was very late when Kat entered the Albert Edward Dock, hoping that it would be the last time. The place she had visited so often as a child had been a witness to too much fear and loss, and she no longer felt at home there. Slowly she walked between the warehouses, passing Micky's deserted hiding place. She had no wish to ever go in there again. Let Billy's ghost rest in peace and Micky's drawings be food for the mice in winter. She thought of her last visit, of the hammering on the door, and then Andrew and Silky showing up. Andrew, the man she loved; and Silky, who loved her enough to kill for her.

It wasn't just Micky who had been saved that night; it was Kat too. The death of Wells had released her whole family. But not if Kat stayed in Preston. And so she was coming to say her goodbyes. Goodbye to the Albert Edward, the memories, the past. Goodbye to Billy, and goodbye to her father . . . Taking a deep breath, she thought of Andrew and let her imagination soar. Within weeks they would be married, and then they were moving to Australia, the other side of the world, away from anything that could harm them. A brand-new, pristine life, just ready to live. No more sordid flat by Avenham Park, no more Friargate, no more docks. She was leaving her family, Gregory Unwin, the Armitages, The Horse and Cart, Amber Street. Everything known and familiar to her she was leaving. And she couldn't wait.

Spotting the dim light in the distance, Kat walked towards it. She had taken off her scarf and was letting the river breeze ruffle her hair, the salt wind cool on her skin. In front of her fell her shadow, the moonlight overhead marking out her route as she approached the hut. She remembered the times she and Micky had looked out for their father, when his thirst had got the better of him. And now he was never really sober. Not wanting to be too drunk to function, but wanting desperately to be sozzled enough to stop caring. Kat knew only too well the impotence her father felt, and curiously held no anger for him. Jim Shaw wasn't a bad man, or a good man; he was just a man with a fault. The world had asked too much of him. Had he married another woman, had had another mother, had been less prone to recklessness, he would have had all the potential to be a happy man. But he had been weak, and weakness had been his downfall.

Suddenly Kat thought back to the night she and Micky had watched the three Shaw brothers play cards. So long ago. When their father had been a good-natured man, Silky had been perfectly handsome, and Ivan had been the family Job. They had played cards and the children had watched them and Kat had thought them glamorous, as only a child can see adults, before they learn to judge them. But every one of them had now changed beyond recognition . . . Walking to the edge of the dockside, Kat paused, looking into the deep water of the River Ribble. Her reflection gazed back up at her, motionless, before the wind stirred the tide again. She thought of Robin Wells, of his fall, and the way he had slid so slowly under the water. Then she turned away and walked up to the door of the hut. About to knock, she hesitated, then walked in. She was tense, automatically expecting to see her father asleep in the chair. But Jim wasn't there. And on the table was the ledger, opened, his handwriting having marked out the day's date at the top of the page. He was sober, she thought, thank God.

Walking out, she headed for the quayside. It had always

been her father's habit to work the dockside, then the warehouses, and tonight was no exception. Glancing left and right, she looked about her, hoping not to come across him drunk against a wall or lying under one of the boat tarpaulins. It no longer mattered if he kept his job. Micky was bringing in a good wage again, and the rent for Amber Street was going uncollected. In time – when Robin Wells didn't show up – the property would revert back to the Pitt estate and the old rents would come back into play. Or maybe Ivy would sell the Preston terraces . . . It didn't matter. Kat had enough money put by to cover emergencies, and she knew that her brother and her uncles would help out – if it became necessary – when she was gone. As Silky had told her, she had done her part; it was time to move on.

Deep in thought, Kat remembered Billy and the night he had died, so unexpectedly, a young life lost. That had been the beginning of her father's decline. That, and then Micky's apparent death . . . Too much for a simple man; too much for Jim Shaw.

'Dad?' she called out suddenly, seeing a moving light. 'Is that you?'

The light came closer, the watchman's lamp becoming clearly visible. And then suddenly Kat was transported back to being a child again. To sitting in the kitchen at Amber Street the night her father came home triumphant. He had just secured the job as nightwatchman and was showing them all the lamp, the heavy black iron lamp – the sign of his trade. He had polished it so proudly, Kat thought, a lump coming into her throat. And then he had demonstrated how to light it . . . The memory that followed was almost painful: her parents sitting on the back steps, the light from the watchman's lamp illuminating their faces. They had been in love then, her mother adoring Jim Shaw, seeing only good in him. Hopeful, forgiving, kind . . .

'Dad?' Kat called out again, moving towards the lamp.

And then she saw him, walking with a blank expression on

his face. Without animation or life. Without hope for a future, or memory of a past.

Unbearably moved, she ran towards him. 'Dad!' she said simply, putting her arms around him.

He blinked, like someone coming round from a long illness. Uneasy, he pulled back to look at her. 'Kat, what are yer doing here, luv?'

'I came to see you, Dad.'

'Yer haven't been here fer a long while,' he said, holding up the lamp and looking into his daughter's face. 'Micky came home.'

'I know, Dad,' she said, nodding.

'Are you coming home too?' he went on, obviously confused. 'I hear such things, Kat, I don't know quite what's true and what isn't. I think I remember you and yer brother filling in fer me here. Were that right, Kat, did yer do that?'

She nodded again. 'Yes, Dad.'

'There were other things yer did – things yer shouldn't have . . .' he said, tailing off. 'I weren't a good father. Weak, like my mother always said. No good to anyone.'

'You were the best you could be,' Kat said simply, 'and I loved you. I'll always love you.'

He straightened up suddenly, pulling himself to his full height. Pride, something Jim Shaw hadn't felt in a long while, swelled up inside him. 'I don't know why yer love me, Kat. I haven't done anything good enough to deserve it.'

'You've never done anything bad enough to prevent it.'

He swallowed, finding it hard to speak. 'Why yer here, luv?'

'Because I'm going to marry Andrew Pitt,' she told him, smiling. 'The bad times are over. I've got a good life coming, Dad. He loves me and we're going to Australia to start afresh. You'll be in charge of the family again.' She was urging him on, hoping she could reignite something in him, some purpose. 'Micky's back, and he needs you, Dad. He hasn't got

Billy any more; he needs someone he can look up to. And then there's Mum . . .'

'I'm not good enough fer her.'

'She doesn't see it that way,' Kat replied, taking the lamp from her father and holding it high. 'Look, Dad, can you see how far the light travels? Do you know how much it can illuminate? *You've* got to be that light now. You've got to keep the dark away. You're the nightwatchman, remember? And when I've gone, all the responsibility will fall on you. But you can carry it, Dad, I know you can.' She passed the light back to him. 'Take the lamp – it's your watch now.'

FORTY-FIVE

It was a Russian seaman who spotted the body, calling out to his shipboard colleagues and pointing to the water ahead. Under a heavy March downpour, a bloated, half-decomposed corpse bobbed on the tide, the rain darting against the decayed face and open eye sockets. On the horizon, grey smudges bled into white cloud, heralding more rain and a later storm.

'There, over there!' the man cried out again.

A couple of his comrades let down a lifeboat and clambered in. A few moments later they were alongside the body, hauling the remains into the boat and throwing a tarpaulin over it. Muttering a quick prayer, the Russian sailors took the lifeboat back to the main ship.

Later, at the Albert Edward Dock, irritated at being called out in the rain, Mr Fleetwood watched the seamen bring the corpse down the gangplank, and then jerked his head towards the storeroom at the head of the quayside.

'Put it in there,' he said sharply. 'Man or woman?'

One of the Russians, one with some knowledge of English, spoke up. 'It's a man, I think. Too big for a woman.'

'Well, it won't be the first body that's washed up around here. Or the last. They come from as far as Liverpool and even Ireland. They can fall overboard in the middle of the sea and still get pulled back to shore. Strange how the tide brings people in.' Impatiently, Fleetwood followed the sailors into the storeroom and then lifted the tarpaulin off the corpse, wincing. 'Oh God, not much left of him, is there?'

'He must belong to someone.'

'People go missing every day.'

'But he would be reported missing, wouldn't he?' the man asked.

'Only if someone noticed he'd gone. Or cared.'

The seaman seemed saddened by the thought. 'Will they find out who he is?'

Fleetwood shrugged. 'I've been working at the Albert Edward for over thirty years now, and some bodies never get claimed. Accidents, falls, suicides, I've seen them all. Whoever they were in life, whatever they did, however rich they were, they ended up here. Picked clean by the fish and buried without a marker.'

The following day a simple notice was put up on the entrance gates of the Albert Edward, in the local newspaper, and in the town hall. It reported the finding of a body at the docks. Cause of death unknown. The corpse was described as being that of a male, early middle age, about six feet tall. No distinguishing marks. Nothing to say who he had been in life, or what he had done.

A week after the rotted body of Robin Wells was dragged out of the sea, he was laid to rest. Having no relatives to claim him, mourn him, or pay for the funeral, he was accorded a pauper's grave. With unintended irony, he was buried in the plot next to Missie Shepherd. No one realised that father and daughter had finally been reunited, Robin Wells – laid to rest beside the daughter he had never recognised – and who he would now spend eternity with.

By the strangest coincidence, I read the notice in the paper on the very day Andrew and I left England. I saw the description of the body found at the Albert Edward and realised at once who it was. I didn't know until a while later where he had been laid to rest. It seemed that justice, in heaven and on earth, had at last been done.

What can I tell you about my life that followed? Andrew and I married and then headed for Australia. I remember only too well my amazement at the place. Having been born and raised in a small industrial town, I couldn't believe the size of the country, the space, the air, which was never full of smog or thick with northern rain. As he had promised, Andrew did *build up a business, and soon prospered, but it took me a long time to settle.*

My dreams were interrupted by memory. I would sometimes wake and think I was back in the flat at Avenham Park, or cowering in the warehouse the night Wells came after me. The early hours especially seemed populated by shadows. I would imagine Wells in my bed, Andrew gone. Or my father falling off the quayside into the water below. I would see him call to me, and when I bent to drag him out, he would turn into Wells and pull me under the water to drown with him.

But we learn to trust again – if we are lucky. And I was.

In the years that followed, we had three daughters, and

Andrew spoiled them all, proud of his four girls, as he calls us. Over the years, news came regularly from home. Ivan married Mary Armitage and they ran The Horse and Cart with Horace, helping him out when he got too old and fat to cope. My little sister, Christine, grew up and trained to become a nurse. She has visited Australia several times, and talks of settling here one day. As for Micky, he worked for Silky for a number of years part time, whilst he trained at the Manchester College of Art. His past, so colourful, worked in his favour and made a minor celebrity out of him even before his talent made his name. To date Micky hasn't married, but I think that's only a matter of time.

Joan Fairchild married a man from Yorkshire and moved to that county, after which we heard no more of her. To everyone's surprise, Ivy Pitt took over the business and made some good money. As we had hoped, the properties reverted back to the Pitt estate. After all, there had been nothing in writing to confirm the deal with Wells. My mother-in-law still knows nothing about Stanley Gorman.

And then there is Silky. My beloved uncle – my clever, brave, ruthless Silky. I miss him. I miss the fun we had at the tattoo parlour when I worked for him, and the way he was always a constant in my life. Whenever he phones – because Silky isn't the type to take time writing – he tells me about the new woman he is seeing. He tells me that his hand is getting stronger by the day. He tells me he misses me . . . Neither of us ever mentions the night Robin Wells died, but I know how much I owe him. When he said – 'not on your conscience, on mine' – he granted me something most people long for, and few achieve – a clear heart.

Of course there are my parents left – and what of them? My mother was never strong, but she carries on with the help of Ma Shaw, who will probably never die and still lives with them. And my father writes to me often. He was the one who told me that they had finally found the man who killed Missie Shepherd. The same man who attacked me that night at the docks – the night Micky saved me. It turned out that I knew him, indirectly. He was the narrow-faced cohort of Robin Wells, the man Micky tattooed with a bird, the man who had been Wells's mouthpiece. The same man who had killed Wells's daughter, without knowing who she was. I often think of that. Wonder what Wells would have done if he had known. Apparently they caught the killer when he was attacking another woman and in the end he was hanged. I imagine Missie Shepherd will rest easier knowing that.

Otherwise my father's letters don't say much. He just tells me about the Albert Edward, and often mentions Billy. If I believe what he says, then my brother's ghost walks the quayside with Missie Shepherd. And maybe he's right. The docks were always a strange, enchanted, dangerous world. There were always sirens of greed, loneliness, despair and evil calling from the river depths. And hope – the most fragile, priceless emotion known to any of us.

I hoped *my life would change, and it did. I* hoped *I would be with the man I loved, and in the end I was. I* hoped *that my father would pull himself out of despair, light his lamp and walk the docks again, on watch, with his head held high . . . And now when I dream, lying next to the man I love, I see my father holding the lamp, the light wide and clear. I know in my heart it will never dim, or go out. And I know it is bright enough to cross land and ocean to reach me wherever I am.*

Because whatever happened to me in the past, and whatever may follow, I was – and will always remain – the Watchman's Daughter.

Just for You

ALEXANDRA CONNOR

Find out . . .
All about Alexandra Connor

Meet . . .
The author

Picture . . .
Alexandra's kind of day

Revealed . . .
A snapshot of the thirties

Try . . .
Alexandra's favourite recipes

ALEXANDRA CONNOR

Born in Lancashire and educated in Yorkshire, Alexandra Connor has had a rich variety of careers, including photographic model, cinema manager and personal assistant to a world famous heart surgeon.

Yet, incredibly, it was only after being stalked and beaten up in London that she found her real forte.

During her convalescence, Alexandra discovered an ability to paint. A further relapse resulted in her writing her first novel.

Although traumatic, Alexandra believes that the beating up changed her – and gave her a life she could never have imagined before.

As well as writing over twenty acclaimed sagas she has also written thrillers and non-fiction books. When she isn't busy writing, Alexandra is a highly accomplished painter and presents programmes on television and BBC radio. She is also a Fellow of the Royal Society of Arts.

An interview with Alexandra Connor

What gave you the idea for THE WATCHMAN'S DAUGHTER?

I always want to set the books in different backgrounds, so that the reader has a change of scene, and doesn't get bored. So the docks seemed exciting. All those ships, gloomy shadows and sailors!

You're a renowned artist as well as a successful writer – do you ever feel torn between writing and painting?

Someone once asked me – if you had to choose between writing and painting, which would you choose? Well, that's like asking which leg I'd like to have broken! I need both. And when I write I picture my people and places as though I'm painting them.

What do you enjoy most about writing?

Lying and getting paid for it! Joking apart, it strikes me as a tremendous act of faith that a reader goes into a shop and puts down hard earned cash to buy my IMAGINATION! Getting letters from readers is wonderful too. I like to know if my books touched them, or made them think. I like to know about them.

What advice would you give to any aspiring authors?

Above everything, keep at it. Talent is all very well, but persistence is the magic formula. And if you really want to be a writer you will have no choice. The ideas keep coming, they wake you at night, they follow you in the car, they drum into your head like woodworm. A writer is compelled to write.

How did you start writing?

I had been ill and read a book. After I finished it, I thought – I wonder if I can do that? It wasn't arrogance, I just ploughed in. The first book was awful, but luckily someone spotted something worthwhile in it, and I was off.

How did you end up having such an eclectic range of occupations?

As you know, I was stalked and then beaten up by two men. After an operation, I had a choice to go under or get back out there. So I wanted to prove myself and I set about teaching myself to paint. I knew I could get a likeness, so I persisted with the technique: talked to scientists and read everything I could so that later on no one could look at my work and say – 'she doesn't know her stuff'. This preparation lead to commissions and exhibitions and now my work is collected in places as far apart as Japan and New York.

I started writing after a relapse, and again, pushed away at it. You see, I had something to prove – that those two creeps hadn't ruined my life. You could say that I live by the Italian motto – 'People of any breeding take their revenge cold.' And to that I will add my own motto – 'Strive and Thrive!'

What do you do in your spare time?

I love collecting antiques and getting bargains. Haggling is a life enhancing experience for me. I also own over two and a half thousand books, including some rare art books. Cinema comes high on the list too.

Hobbies:

Time is very limited, so hobbies don't play a big part in my life, although we have too many animals and I once rescued and hatched two abandoned eggs, which turned into Mallard ducks! Oh, and took in a one-legged duck called Sabine.

Future ambition:

My great passion for the future is Merisi. I intend to set up a summer school for artistically gifted children. A home environment where they can live for a month and soak themselves in paintings, literature, sculpture – and not feel like nerds. Which many kids do at school, when they don't fit in with the so called 'cool' kids. Merisi would be a safe, inspirational haven for them to mix with their like-minded peers.

You see, I love the technology of today, love the excitement of cities and the ever increasingly fast pace of life – but there should be a place of stillness. The arts stimulate the soul. If we forget that, we cheat our children of their heritage and the inspiration of some of Man's greatest achievements.

My Perfect Day

Well, what a question to ask! Are we being honest, or is this a make-believe day? Perhaps I should let my fantasies run riot . . .

As this is my day, I will presume that I am on my own, so here goes . . . I would have a full English breakfast on the Orient Express, on its way to Russia, followed by a private viewing in the Hermitage Museum (this is a fantasy, so time would be elastic). Then I would have lunch with Caravaggio, Oliver Cromwell and Andy Garcia, followed by a deep-sea dive in the sea off the Indonesian Islands, swimming with the sea snakes. Later that afternoon, I would jump off a very high cliff onto a million marshmallows! (I've always wondered what that would feel like . . .)

After that, I would continue into Rome and buy several Versace outfits and shoes, stopping off to see the Raphaels in the Vatican and to gawp at the Berninis whilst eating a large ice cream. Following this, I would have a private showing of *A Matter of Life or Death*, which is an incredibly old film, but as pertinent now as when it was made. Then go to Rio de Janeiro and get all the kids out of the gutters and over to Merisi.

Finally I would have dinner at the Cipriani in Venice with all my family and my father (who is dead, but you did say this was my perfect day) and then go to sleep in the four poster

bed with music playing and the skylight open to the stars.
(I bet you're sorry you asked . . .)

A snapshot of the world . . . the 1930s

24th May 1930 Amy Johnson became the first woman to fly solo from England to Australia

8th February 1931 James Dean born

25th December 1932 British Union of Fascists founded by Oswald Mosley

11th June 1933 Gene Wilder born

26th September 1934 The Scottish National Party founded

1st August 1935 *The 39 Steps*, directed by Hitchcock, released

18th July 1936 Spanish Civil war begins

12th May 1937 Coronation of George VI

September 1938 Britain, France and Italy agree to the dismemberment of Czechoslovakia by Germany

3rd September 1939 Britain declares war on Germany

Alexandra shares her favourite recipes

LANCASHIRE HOT POT

My mother, Ella Crossley's, recipe

(In the cold months, use pork chops. In summer, use lamb chops for this recipe.)

Slice potatoes and onions and put in a casserole dish, alternate these slices with bacon rashers. Then add another layer of potatoes, onions and bacon. On top of this place lean pork chops (from the top of the leg). Place a thin layer of potatoes on the top. Add a little water and seasoning, and if required, stock.

Cover with greaseproof paper or a casserole lid with hole in the top.

Place in electric oven at 180°C. If using a fan-assisted oven 160°C. Gas 4–6.

When the potatoes start to soften, take off the cover and turn the pork chops over. Then put the casserole back in oven until the pork is cooked and slightly browned.

Enjoy!

BREAD AND BUTTER PUDDING

(My sister, Diana Brierley-Jones's, recipe)

This will feed four people.

Slice half a currant loaf, then butter one side of each slice. Cut the slices into four triangles.

Place in buttered, oven-proof container.

Whisk 2 eggs, with approximately half a pint of milk, plus 2 teaspoonfuls of sugar and a quarter of a teaspoonful of ground nutmeg.

Whisk together.

Pour over bread. Scatter 2 teaspoons of sugar. Sprinkle the top with ground nutmeg.

Allow to stand for 15 minutes.

Place in pre-heated oven at 180°C, gas mark 5, for approximately half an hour.

Remove and serve when pudding has risen and the top is brown and crisp.

Serve with cream or ice cream!